PENGUIN BOOKS
SHORT CIRCUIT

Michael Mewshaw was born in Washington, D.C., received his B.A. from the University of Maryland, and earned a Ph.D. from the University of Virginia. The author of five critically acclaimed novels—*Land Without Shadow*, *Earthly Bread*, *The Toll*, *Waking Slow*, and *Man in Motion*—as well as an award-winning work of nonfiction, *Life for Death*, he has been awarded a Fulbright Fellowship, a grant from the National Endowment for the Arts, and a Guggenheim Fellowship. His articles and reviews have appeared in *The New York Times*, *The Nation*, *The New Statesman*, and many other newspapers and periodicals. Mr. Mewshaw lives in Rome with his wife and two sons.

MICHAEL
MEWSHAW

SHORT CIRCUIT

PENGUIN BOOKS

PENGUIN BOOKS

Viking Penguin Inc. 40 West 23rd Street,
New York, New York 10010, U.S.A.
Penguin Books Ltd, Harmondsworth,
Middlesex, England
Penguin Books Australia Ltd, Ringwood,
Victoria, Australia
Penguin Books Canada Limited, 2801 John Street,
Markham, Ontario, Canada L3R 1B4
Penguin Books (N.Z.) Ltd, 182–190 Wairau Road,
Auckland 10, New Zealand

First published in the United States of America by
Atheneum 1983
First published in Canada by
McClelland and Stewart Ltd. 1983
Published in Penguin Books 1984

LIBRARY OF CONGRESS CATALOGING IN PUBLICATION DATA
Mewshaw, Michael, 1943–
Short circuit.
Originally published: New York: Atheneum, 1983.
1. Tennis—Tournaments. 2. Sports—Corrupt practices.
I. Title.
[GV999.M37   1984]   796.342   83-25770
ISBN 0 14 00.7278 0

Printed in the United States of America by
R. R. Donnelley & Sons Company, Harrisonburg, Virginia
Set in Electra

To Marc and Paul Wiegand *on court*
To Fred Harrison and Alston Jennings *off court*

CONTENTS

SHORT CIRCUIT

GENOA

THE Colombia-Excelsior, like many old-fashioned luxury hotels, faces the train station. During the days of horses and buggies, parasols and bustles, the *piazza* out front must have been as serene as the hotel's façade. Back then, a guest might have been tempted to lean out and look downhill to the port, or uphill at the labyrinth of streets, some as narrow as footsteps, as dark as tunnels, as steep as stairways. But now the windows had to remain shuttered against the ceaseless traffic which sluiced through the *piazza* with all the shrill harmonics of a Formula One automobile race.

The day I arrived in late February there were indications of other disconcerting changes. Next door to the Colombia-Excelsior a sign advertised EVERY DAY SEXY MOVIES. This made the films sound less erotic than humdrum, and the posters on the marquee displayed the predictable tits and pistols, black stockings and whips.

Looking for livelier stimulation, I passed up the Every Day Sexy Movie and lugged my suitcases to the hotel entrance. No one rushed out to offer a hand. The bellboys were on strike. They had scribbled their demands on cardboard placards and taped them to the columns outside. They wanted more money, better working conditions, and dignity for all workers.

In the lobby it looked as though the *lumpen proletariat* had determined to take possession of the place until their demands were met. Sprawled on the green baize furniture, hunkered down on the ornate double stairway that curved away to the

mezzanine, loitering beneath an enormous chandelier and talking loudly enough to set its cut glass quivering, these scruffy,
animated young men in blue jeans and sneakers were not, however, an occupying army of disgruntled workers. They had every
reason to be pleased with the conditions of their employment.
Professional tennis players, they had gathered in Genoa for the
Bitti Bergaimo Memorial tournament, one of twenty-two events
on the World Championship Tennis circuit, which offers eight
million dollars in prize money.

The winner here would walk away with $100,000 for a week's
work—more loot than the Wimbledon or U.S. Open champion
carries off. Even losers wouldn't fare badly. If knocked out in
the first round, they'd receive $2,000 for their day's labor, and
if they cared to play doubles, they could pick up another $500
for being beaten.

World Championship Tennis had expected a tournament with
a $300,000 purse to attract the very best players. But the rankings
of the thirty-two men in Genoa ranged from the mid-teens to
the mid-500's. Only two stars from the top ten had bothered to
show up—Ivan Lendl, a hollow-cheeked, twenty-two-year-old
Czech dressed in designer jeans and a fleece-lined bombardier
jacket, and Vitas Gerulaitis. Unlike the other players in their
blue denim, Vitas wore what appeared to be a pair of white
flannel lounging pajamas with a purple stripe down the legs.

After I dropped my bags in my room, I repaired to the bar,
where the choral figures of tennis—agents, tournament directors, clothing and equipment reps, and journalists—lamented
that no amount of prize money was enough to attract the top
players.

"It's the Grand Pricks." One man spat out the competing
circuit's name as an obscenity. "They have tournaments this
week in Monterrey and Cairo."

"It's not just the Grand Prix," said another man. "These guys
don't need to play. They can afford to pick their spots and wait
for the right deal. Look at Borg."

For the next half-hour they "looked" at Bjorn Borg. Their
eyes narrowed and they seemed to peer down the Mediterranean

littoral, just over the Italian border, to Monte Carlo, where Borg was luxuriating in a five-month break from tennis.

"He could drive here in a couple of hours," a journalist said, "and win a hundred grand. But that's not enough for him. A hundred thousand bucks, two hundred, a million doesn't mean a damn thing. He's got contracts guaranteeing him over six million a year. So why should he bother?"

"It's his wife. She's sick," an Italian defended the Swede. "He wants to stay near her."

"Bullshit," said another Italian, a man who represents some of Borg's European interests. "Mariana isn't even in Monte Carlo. She's in Switzerland at a clinic."

"Well, I said it was because she was sick."

"No, it's not her kidney stones. It's the marriage that's sick. Bjorn wants to enjoy himself. He's done nothing but play tennis for ten years. Now he's found the fun of life."

"It's a shame," an agent said. "He was the perfect machine."

"The perfect tennis machine," a journalist agreed.

"The perfect money-making machine," the agent corrected him. "Mark McCormack saw to that. Say what you like about IMG [International Management Group], McCormack knows how to market. Look what he did with Arnold Palmer. Just watch what he does with the Pope."

"The Pope?" asked the incredulous Italians.

"Sure. McCormack is handling the Pope's trip to England. But look at Borg . . . ."

And again they "looked" at Borg. They gazed into the distance with such fixity, they spoke of the five-time Wimbledon champion with such intensity, the young Swede might have been there in the bar, as palpable as the bottles of Strega and Grappa. It was this way whenever tennis people gathered to exchange gossip. Eventually they began to discuss Bjorn Borg. Would he come back? Could he come back? Did Mariana have cancer? Was the marriage breaking up? Had Bjorn suffered a breakdown? Was he leaving his coach, Lennart Bergelin? Was it conceivable he would play the qualifying rounds of every Grand Prix tournament he entered after his comeback? Like the silences in certain musical compositions, like the lacunae in a Henry Moore sculpture, like the white spaces on a page of modern poetry, Bjorn Borg's absence had become more significant than other people's presence.

"You know what it is?" said the Italian who handled some of Borg's business interests. "Bjorn's having a mid-life crisis."

"For Crissake—" I spoke for the first time, appalled that that piece of psycho-babble had crossed the Atlantic and drifted down to this corner of Italy—"he's twenty-five years old."

"But in experience, in tennis, he's lived as much as a man of fifty. What's left for him to do? He's asking himself now what to do with the rest of his life."

It was a question with which I was personally well acquainted. Not caring to listen to agents, journalists, and clothing distributors hazard their weighty opinions, I left and caught a courtesy car to the Palazzo dello Sport.

The first match was one which the tragic chorus in the bar had disparaged as the exemplification of all that was wrong with tennis. "Would you pay to watch Birner play Elter?" one reporter demanded.

I said I would and I meant it. But I was getting in free. I had press credentials and would be stringing articles on the tournament to Associated Press.

Whatever my own interest in a first-round encounter between players ranked No. 64 and No. 73 on the Association of Tennis Professionals computer, it wasn't shared by the public. Except for me, the press section was empty, and thirty spectators were scattered throughout an arena which holds eight thousand. While Peter Elter of West Germany and Stanislav Birner of Czechoslovakia warmed up, workmen sauntered around, pasting up promotional strips for Fila, Braniff Airlines, Hyatt Hotels, Barclay/Visa credit cards. Since paying customers didn't cover the costs of the event, advertising was of crucial importance, as was television. The semifinals and finals of the Bitti Bergamo tournament would be broadcast live in Italy on an independent station, Canale 5, then transmitted by delayed tape to Mexico. Each week World Championship Tennis also packaged a program of highlights which had been pre-sold in two dozen countries.

As Elter and Birner continued to hit, I strained forward, squinting to follow the yellow blur of the ball which streaked back and forth like a berserk canary. Neither man had *that* much power, and I wondered whether I needed to change the prescription for my glasses. Then I realized the overhead lights were off. The sole source of illumination was the arena's translucent dome, which let in the milky winter light and the magnified shadows of roosting pigeons.

The heat wasn't working either, and the Palazzo dello Sport, situated like an immense oyster at the edge of a wharf, exuded a damp, penetrating chill from its poured-concrete walls. When the players complained, they learned that as an economy measure the mayor of Genoa had decreed that heat and light would be switched on in the arena only between four and ten p.m. That was fine for players scheduled for evening matches, but miserable for everybody else, including the spectators.

Suddenly the public-address system snapped on with a shriek, and a woman, breathless with enthusiasm, announced, "The Fila team is taking the court." Linesmen, ball boys and girls, and the umpire paraded out in formation and in uniforms supplied by Fila. The linesmen, none of whom looked older than fifteen, wore glossy red warm-up suits with white piping and peaked caps. Despite the chill, the ball boys and girls had on black shorts and skimpy tee shirts with white piping. Bringing up the rear, the umpire, a plump man, sported a tight white outfit with red piping and a peaked cap which gave him a moronic appearance. He smiled in embarrassment. He would have been more embarrassed had he realized a large cardboard tag full of laundry instructions dangled like a breechcloth over his fleshy buttocks.

When the match started, the players generated their own heat and electricity. Both Elter and Birner are small men. But while Elter has the muscular, compact physique of an athlete, Birner resembles a penguin who has been put through the spin cycle in a washing machine and hastily dried. Pudgy and rumpled, his hair perpetually awry, he walks with a flat-footed waddle, and his every movement seems mechanical, as if he had to memorize the strokes which came naturally to Elter. Still, he can compete on even terms with almost anyone in the world, and players who take him lightly are apt to suffer the same fate as Peter Elter, who lost the first set 6–2.

"*Scheisse!*" The German slammed his racquet to the carpeted court. Startled, the swarm of pigeons on the translucent roof wheeled away, then resettled.

Before the second set a workman dashed out with two trash barrels camouflaged as Coca-Cola cans. Yet Elter appeared to draw inspiration from them. He stopped trying to overpower Birner and started mixing his shots, hitting deep, then short, lofting topspin lobs, then hammering crosscourt drives. Birner had trouble adjusting to the change of pace and dropped the second set 6–1.

Faces flushed, chests heaving, the two tiny, ferociously combative men dug in for the final set. Following the standard tennis adage—don't stay with a losing game—Birner switched tactics and discovered a chink in Elter's armor. The German didn't like to come to the net. On short balls he'd rush in, whack a return, then scurry back to the baseline. So Birner sucked Elter to the net with dropshots, and passed him down the line. When Elter was serving to pull even at 6–6, Birner broke him and won the set and match. The German shouted "*Scheisse!*" then marched contritely to the net and shook Stanislav Birner's hand.

It was no rash claim to have said I would pay to watch Birner and Elter. I like tennis, whether it's McEnroe versus Borg, or two journeymen lunging at each other's jugular veins. Having come to the sport late—until ten years ago I had never seen a match—I harbored a convert's unqualified faith and attempted to make reparation for the failings of my past life with total devotion. I played three or four times a week. I latched onto good players, persuaded them to hit with me, and never passed up an opportunity to test myself against somebody much better, somebody who could teach me a lesson, be it on the backhand or in humility.

Once, after a blizzard, I abandoned my pregnant wife and drove over a snowy pass in the High Sierras to Reno, Nevada, where a friend had arranged for me to meet an Australian who had dropped off the professional tour, although he held victories over Adriano Panatta, Italy's former No. 1, and Yannick Noah, the current French champion. At nine a.m. on a frigid December morning the fellow agreed to play me on an outdoor court which had slick patches of ice at one end. He took the icy end and beat me 6–0/6–0. But I turned around and drove back across the Sierras exhilarated, convinced I had been the real winner.

That first day in Genoa I felt the same exhilaration watching Birner and Elter. Caught up in the match, I forgot the cold, I forgot myself. That was all I asked—to escape myself. It was three days after my thirty-ninth birthday and, staring down the gun barrel of forty and middle age, I was anxious for a change. I wouldn't say I was suffering a crisis, "mid-life" or otherwise, and, unlike Bjorn Borg, I wasn't wondering what I'd do with the rest of my life. I assumed I would go on writing. But I was bored, mostly with myself, a not uncommon emotion when I am marking time between books, and I didn't care to fall back into my familiar routine.

In part, I was prompted to change by the kinds of books I had produced in the last few years. After publishing a novel set against a drought and famine in Africa—reviews, pro and con, described it as mordant, bleak, and unrelievedly depressing—I had done a nonfiction account of a fifteen-year-old boy, a childhood friend of mine, who had been sentenced to life in prison for murdering his parents. When an editor called from New York and proposed that I write a book about the twenty-eight black children who had been killed in Atlanta, I recoiled, fearing I had been typecast as an apostle of gloom and cataclysm. Longing to write something lighthearted, uplifting, and funny, I decided to combine the twin passions of my life, tennis and travel, and follow the men's professional tour for a few months.

At the very least, I expected to see some exciting tennis. And, who knew, perhaps I could persuade a few players to hit with me. More than anything, though, I hoped that the beauty and symmetry, the mesmerizing geometry of the game would elevate me to that state of grace which men experience in the face of any action, athletic or artistic, that is infused with genius.

Although I had no desire to retreat to the childish myths that dominate most writing about sports, I expected to discover a less complex world than the one I inhabited. I imagined that a career in tennis, unlike a career in literature, involved little compromise, no ambiguity, no troubling shades of gray, just stark yet reassuring black and white. The ball was in or it was out. No game ended in a deadlock. You won or you lost. If you were better than somebody, you could prove it. You could play him and beat him, and afterward nobody could deny it, for the rating system wasn't based on subjective opinion or critical approval or slightly refined gossip. Reputations weren't bestowed by friends, connections, and tax-free endowments. They were forged in the heat of the head-on competition, and thanks to the miracle of transistors and microchips, the results were relayed around the world. What purer, more straightforward meritocracy could be imagined?

Between matches I went to a restaurant in the Palazzo dello Sport reserved for journalists and players. There I ate lunch with David Schneider, a gregarious South African. Although the professional tennis tour is said to be apolitical and people from disparate backgrounds mix on superficially polite terms, there are frequent controversies and personal tensions. A Grand Prix tournament had been scheduled in Copenhagen for the following week and many of the players in Genoa had planned to enter it. But when several South Africans attempted to sign up, the Danish government, in an anti-apartheid gesture, denied them visas. Since the Association of Tennis Professionals insisted the event be open to all players, the tournament was canceled.

An outsider on several scores, Schneider is Jewish, holds an Israeli passport as well as one from South Africa, and is a member of the Israeli Davis Cup team. "When my plane gets hijacked," he jokes, "I have twice as good a chance of getting killed."

A tall, lean fellow of twenty-seven, he has a crooked nose that can make him appear scowling and pugnacious. But then he smiles, or breaks into laughter at his own expense, and that first impression of pugnacity vanishes. Considering all the difficulties confronting him in his career, his sense of self-deprecating humor is his saving grace. He is ranked "somewhere in the 200's," and, as others might view it, his role in life is to be beaten. He isn't even listed in the 1982 *Guide to World Championship Tennis*. Unable to get straight into most tournaments, he must play the qualifying rounds, a murderous rite of passage held on the weekend preceding the main event.

"I thought of going to Cairo this week and playing the Egyptian Open," Schneider told me. "They have a weak draw and I probably could have gotten straight in. I'd like to see Cairo. And after the tournament I could have crossed the Sinai and gone to Tel Aviv. I've got to go there to work out for Davis Cup.

"But then I started thinking," he said, sprinkling Parmesan on his lasagne. "With my luck, I'd play great in Egypt. I'd get to the finals. The match would be televised throughout the Middle East. My moment of glory. Then some nut would get the bright idea that I was too good a target to pass up. I mean, a Jew with a South African passport, I'm a terrorist's dream. Okay, maybe it's only one chance in a thousand, in a million! But I decided it wasn't worth the risk. I'll go to Cairo someday as a tourist."

Instead, he had traveled to Genoa to play the "qualies," as they're called, and he had lost in the second round. Normally, that would have meant a wipe-out for the week—no tournament, no money, not even a chance to hang around and practice. But World Championship Tennis, now locked in competition with the Grand Prix, had started offering prize money for qualifiers. David Schneider had earned $600 for losing in the second round, and since he would play doubles in the main draw, he was sure of making $500 more. "At least the week won't cost me money," he said.

As a member of the ATP, Schneider received, in exchange for his $620 annual dues, the services of two road representatives and two trainers, a $25,000 life-insurance policy, $25,000 worth of medical insurance, a high-interest checking account, $2,500 worth of lost-property insurance, free Adidas clothing, free VS Gut racquet stringing, free luggage, and a subscription to *International Tennis Weekly*, the official ATP newspaper. But with travel expenses on top of his meals and hotels, he figured he still needed $1,000 a week to break even.

When I pointed out that there were cheaper places to stay than the Colombia-Excelsior, which charged players and journalists a reduced rate of $70 a night, Schneider said it wasn't worth changing hotels. For one thing, he didn't speak Italian. For another, he doubted the courtesy cars would pick him up anywhere except at the official hotel. Since he traveled back and forth to the Palazzo dello Sport several times a day, anything he saved on accommodations would be eaten up by taxi fares.

What Schneider didn't mention was the importance that players place on eating and living well on the circuit. Some of them express it in practical terms. Economizing at cheap pensiones and third-rate restaurants raises the risks of sleepless nights and gastro-intestinal ailments. But there are also the subtler matters of ego and morale. To beat a man, you have to believe you're as good as he is. And it's hard to keep believing that when he's going first-class and you're traveling steerage.

I asked Schneider what the difference was between winners and losers. Was it speed or coordination or strength or timing? Or some alchemic combination of these elements?

"It's a question of confidence," he claimed. "The difference between me and Jimmy Connors isn't mechanical. It isn't so much a matter of his shots being better than mine. Any pro can hit winners in practice. But Connors can pump himself up and go for winners during a match. He has the confidence that he can hit one from anywhere on the court."

Inevitably, the conversation turned to the consequences of the war between World Championship Tennis and the Volvo

Grand Prix. For four years the WCT had been part of the Grand Prix, a circuit within a circuit under the aegis of Texas billionaire Lamar Hunt. But from the beginning the partnership had been prickly, and Hunt finally got fed up with the irresponsibility of the top players, who often skipped his tournaments in favor of lucrative exhibitions, and with the fickleness of the Grand Prix, which sometimes scheduled events that conflicted with his own. In 1982 Hunt decided to reclaim his independence.

In what was viewed by many as a retaliatory move, the Men's International Professional Tennis Council (usually referred to as the Pro Council) changed its rules and obliged players to commit themselves to ten Grand Prix tournaments a year. Then it decreed that all WCT tournaments were special events, thus reducing the circuit to the level of a series of exhibition matches. This meant that men who played WCT events would receive no ATP points. Theoretically, a player who chose to make an exclusive commitment to WCT could win all twenty-two tournaments, earn over two million dollars, but wind up without a world ranking. It also meant that a man like Bjorn Borg, who refused to commit to ten Volvo Grand Prix tournaments a year, would have to qualify for any event he wished to enter, including the French Open, which he had won six times, and Wimbledon, which he had won five times.

"This situation is good for guys like me," David Schneider confessed, and for a moment we contemplated the astonishing figures. The competing circuits would offer $25 million, an $11 million increase over last year. There would be 22 WCT tournaments on top of the 87 Grand Prix tournaments. And that didn't include the 51 non-circuit events or the 100 satellite tournaments, or the countless exhibitions and non-sanctioned round-robins.

"You'll see guys dodging back and forth," Schneider said, "playing WCT to pick up the prize money, then playing the Grand Prix for ATP points. But it's bad for the game. The stars are already spread too thin. A lot of tournaments are going to fold unless the top players support them. But as for making Borg play qualies, that's ridiculous. He's one of the greatest champions of all time."

When I pointed out that the rule was the same for everybody and that an exception for Borg might destroy the ATP and wreck tournament tennis, Schneider said, "I admit Bjorn doesn't give much back to the game. He comes, he plays, he collects his money, and he leaves. But it's not a team sport. It's an individual sport, it's a selfish sport. Maybe Bjorn thinks he's doing his bit, making his contribution to the rest of us, just by showing up occasionally and putting people in the stands.

"I'll tell you this, though. If Bjorn does play the qualies, he'll find it's a different world. Everything's against a qualifier. The courts are bad, the conditions are bad, the officiating is bad. Take the qualies at Wimbledon. The courts are like cow pastures. It's always raining and cold there. And Bjorn could come up against some hard-serving Australian or American kid and get bounced out before he ever got his game grooved. Believe me, it could happen. Personally, I think he'll realize that and refuse to play the qualies."

In a swift role-reversal David Schneider swung the discussion away from tennis and asked me questions. Had I been to Israel? What did I think of it? How much did I know about South Africa? He asked the titles of my books. Had I read Alan Paton and Nadine Gordimer?

At the time, this didn't strike me as extraordinary. Schneider's interest in other subjects, his polite curiosity about a man with whom he had just eaten a meal seemed normal. But I was to learn how rare these qualities are in the self-referential world of the circuit.

That afternoon the sun slipped behind a bank of clouds, plunging the Palazzo dello Sport into gloom. Alone once more in the press section, I kept my topcoat buttoned and a scarf knotted around my neck. There were still fewer than a hundred souls rattling around in the cavernous arena, and when one of them dropped a soft-drink can, it detonated against the floor like a grenade, startling the players and scattering pigeons from the roof.

On court, Tony Giammalva hurled himself into every shot,

and at six feet three and 195 pounds, he had a lot of weight to put behind the ball. His opponent, Tim Wilkison, looked delicate by comparison, and as he lost the first set 6–3, it seemed he could do no more than stab at the blistering groundstrokes Giammalva blasted by him.

But then at four p.m. the heat roared on with the flapping sound of a crippled pelican, and stale air swirled through the building. The lights flickered on too, and I blinked as though emerging from a dim cave into full sunlight. Tim Wilkison blinked too, but more in wonderment than at the glare. At last he could see, he could read Giammalva's racquet, he could take the ball on the rise and rifle it back. Wasting no time, Wilkison won the second set 6–1 and the third 6–4.

Back at the hotel, I spoke with Wilkison, who allowed as how he had been relieved when the lights went on. But he, like David Schneider, felt confidence was the key to victory. He had played Tony Giammalva before and come from behind to win, and so, even after the disastrous first set, he believed he could do it again.

A soft-spoken fellow of twenty-two, Tim Wilkison has the boyish sweetness and sincerity of somebody who might have been a student vice-president at his hometown high school in Shelby, North Carolina. Although a winner of three Grand Prix titles in his brief career, all of them on grass in Australia and New Zealand, he had had to struggle against inconsistency. Once ranked as high as No. 31, he had plummeted to No. 131, then labored back up the ladder to his current rung, No. 65.

"The hardest thing on the tour," he told me, "is coping with losing. You're alone in a strange place and it's easy to get discouraged. With me, it always takes a string of good wins to get my confidence up, but just one bad loss to get me down. I guess that's the difference between the top players and the others."

It wasn't only losing that got Tim Wilkison down. Life on the road in Europe sent him into a funk. He missed home and said things were different here. Even buying a newspaper was hard. When I told him the kiosk in front of the hotel sold English-language papers, he felt that proved his point. He was used to having a paper delivered to his doorstep.

And he missed American music. True, many Italian radio stations played American rock, but they introduced the tunes in a foreign language and that ruined it for Wilkison.

"You order something to eat," he went on. "The waiter speaks maybe a few words of English. So at best you get something pretty close to what you want. Even when you order steak and they bring the right thing, it's not the same."

Now that the tournament in Copenhagen had been canceled, he faced the grim prospect of a free week. He would have flown back to the States, but he had committed himself to other European tournaments in following weeks and he didn't care to go through jet lag again. He guessed he'd fly to London and find an indoor practice court. He wasn't petulant, he didn't complain. He simply expressed his sincere, boyish unhappiness.

Although many might consider it a pleasant challenge to imagine how a man with an income of over $100,000 a year might amuse himself in London, Tim Wilkison wasn't looking forward to it. "It's going to be a long week, you know, with no matches to play."

During the evening program I left the press section and poked around behind the scenes. I was reminded of a television studio or a movie set where a combination of enormous financial resources and daunting technical expertise had managed to create no more than an impression of total impermanence and incalculable cheapness. Hidden by bleachers, half a dozen prefabricated modules of plastic and fiberboard had been set up to serve as a players' lounge, a press room, a transportation switchboard, and a bank. At the bank, which I could have broken into with my bare fists, I met Alan Maundrell.

A mild, shy-looking man with sandy hair and a slight stoop, the result perhaps of bending over accounting ledgers, Mr. Maundrell is an employee of the Barclay banking group in London. He has no particular interest in tennis, plays no sport, and has no hobby. "Not unless," he adds, "cooking might be considered a hobby. I'm a bachelor and I cook for myself." Because he's single and free to travel—"as long as there's someone to water the plants in my apartment"—he accepted the assignment of handling the money on the WCT European tour.

Among other things, he bears the responsibility for paying the players. In a country like Italy, with its baroque bureaucracy and confusing laws about currency exchange, that can be difficult. Thus, for the tournament in Genoa a Roman banker had been hired to expedite matters.

As Alan Maundrell explained it, after deducting twenty percent to cover Italian taxes, he had to be prepared to pay a man in any fashion he might desire. If a player asked for his prize money in cash or traveler's checks, Mr. Maundrell obliged him. If he wanted it telexed to his bank back home or to his numbered Swiss account, that was the individual's prerogative. It was also the individual's duty, not WCT's, to deal with the tax laws, currency regulations, and fiscal authorities of his own country.

In the case of Communist players, this raised tantalizing questions. Some of them were supposed to remit a percentage of their earnings to the national tennis federation. But if they accepted their winnings in dollars, or had the loot transferred to bastions of capitalism, it is hard to know how the commissars could keep track of the cash flow.

Since it was not just the revenue agents in one's native land who might chomp a bite out of a man's earnings, every player had good cause to ponder the consequences of entering tournaments in countries like Nigeria, which often took over six months to transfer prize money. Other countries were more efficient, but not always to a player's advantage. The United States, for example, was quick to tax its citizens and foreigners alike. Thus Bjorn Borg, who was having seventy percent of his income raked off by the IRS, drastically reduced his appearances in America. Since Borg is a resident of Monte Carlo, where there is no personal income tax, it was wiser for him to play tournaments that deducted little or nothing from his winnings. In England, for instance, tennis purses won by foreigners are, according to Alan Maundrell, not subject to U.K. taxation.

Players must also remain alert to currency fluctuations which may shrink their earnings. On the Grand Prix circuit the rules remind all participants that although prize money is always stated in American dollars, it "shall be converted into the local currency at the rate of exchange prevailing at the close of business in London on the following dates: the first Monday in August of the previous year for tournaments beginning on or before June 30th; the first Monday in February for tournaments beginning after June 30th. . . . Any loss or gain in exchange due to the fluctuation in the rate of exchange shall be borne by the players." In 1981 at Wimbledon, players lost thirty-five cents on each pound when sterling sagged against the dollar.

I left Alan Maundrell and his pre-fab bank feeling as I do after most financial discussions—dazed and much poorer. So I sought out the WCT trainer for what I expected to be an informative and upbeat conversation.

Informative it was, upbeat it wasn't. A wiry, wisecracking fellow no older than the players, Steve Parker first started attending to the physical needs of athletes when he was a student at Southern Methodist University in Dallas, Texas. Back then he worked with American football players. After graduating with an MA in psychology, he switched to soccer and served as a trainer for the Olympic team, then for a professional team, the Dallas Tornados.

Prepared to hear dithyrambic praise for his charges, I asked whether he was impressed with their condition and ability.

"Not particularly," said Parker, who has a lean, guileless face which remains calm even as he fidgets with his hands and feet.

Puzzled, I tried again. "How do they stack up against other athletes you've worked with?"

He said he couldn't compare them to football players. The sports were too dissimilar. Most tennis players simply didn't have the size and strength to compete in football. Basketball, also, demanded extraordinary size and the capacity to absorb punishment.

Still assuming Steve Parker agreed that tennis players were good athletes, I invited him to compare them to soccer players.

Again he surprised me. Soccer players, he said, were faster, fitter, stronger, more agile. He just didn't believe tennis was such a demanding game. It was unlike other sports in which the slightest physical shortcoming meant certain loss, maybe even the end of a career. Without mentioning names—"You've got eyes. Just watch the matches"—he said many world-class tennis players were slow, overweight, and grossly out of shape. He suggested I watch their footwork, watch their soft, thick midsections, and watch how quickly they soaked through their shirts, even in this cool arena.

Although he granted that some men trained hard—that is to say, they practiced long hours—Parker contended they went about it in an unstructured, non-analytical fashion with little regard for, and even less knowledge of, their bodies. In his opinion, too much emphasis was placed on hitting tennis balls, too little time was devoted to drills that improved stamina, speed, and coordination. After long breaks too many men tried to play themselves into shape, with the result that they suffered muscle tears and cramps. The Europeans, he said, tended to lack upper-body strength, but resisted pumping iron for fear of becoming musclebound. The Americans were inclined to be dedicated long-distance joggers, but that brought on shin splints, blood blisters, bruised feet, and bad knees.

He couldn't understand why men who depended on their bodies to make a living—and a very handsome living, too—didn't take care of themselves, didn't eat right, didn't cut down on drinking, didn't seek expert advice and medical attention, and didn't take logical measures to prolong their careers. "In team sports they'd have coaches and trainers and doctors on their asses all the time. But most tennis players are on their own. That's the problem. They're alone, and unless they hire a coach to travel with them, there's a tendency to let things slide—until they slide right out of the game."

Describing the services he attempted to render, Parker stressed that success in tennis depended as much on intangibles, on confidence and emotional equilibrium, as it did on physical conditioning. He wasn't a great believer in massages, but most Europeans swore by them, so there was a masseur on the WCT circuit. "We'd bring along a witch doctor or sorcerer if they wanted one and believed it helped. Belief is a big part of it," he said.

· · ·

At ten p.m. the heater clicked off and the building cooled. By the time Bill Scanlon trotted out to play Per Hjertquist, trumpets of frost formed at my lips when I breathed. In the umpire's chair sat a short, thick-set black man, an American who spoke with the assurance of someone who knew his job, knew his duty, and knew himself. He had no reluctance to caution a player for misconduct or to correct a linesman who had made a bad call. Wearing tortoiseshell glasses, a blue blazer and gray slacks instead of the white Fila warm-up that had left the other umpires looking like ice-cream vendors, this fellow had an unmistakable presence.

After the match I caught up with the man, whose name was Jason Smith, and asked him to tell me about his job. Since it was past midnight, he begged off until tomorrow, but he said he loved to umpire. "It's the best seat in the house," and although you couldn't make a living as an official, "things were getting better."

But for Jason Smith things were about to get worse, and he would find himself unthroned from the best seat in the house.

Returning to the hotel, I rode in a courtesy car with Bill Scanlon, an American who had just won his first-round match, and Christophe Roger-Vasselin of France and Russell Simpson of New Zealand, who had yet to play. They discussed court conditions in the manner of truck drivers huddling in a diner to talk about a rough patch of road.

Roger-Vasselin: "How are the lights on overheads?"

Scanlon: "Not bad. No problem picking up defensive lobs. Sometimes offensive lobs, especially ones going straight back, give you trouble."

Simpson: "My philosophy against short guys is not to lob so much. It just gives them practice."

Russell Simpson was due to fly to New Zealand next week for a Davis Cup match against Spain. I asked how long the flight was from Rome to Auckland.

"Three Valiums long," he said.

Someone cracked a joke about the Japanese Airlines pilot who had gone haywire in the cockpit and crashed his plane into Tokyo harbor.

"I never fly JAL," Simpson said, "because all the Japs smoke. I can't bear breathing cigarette fumes for thirty hours. But no matter what airline I take, I always stumble off the plane feeling like I need a chiropractor. There's never enough room. I've started going business-class to get more space. First-class would be better, but I can't afford it. If it was up to me, I wouldn't ever fly. But then I couldn't play tennis."

At the Colombia-Excelsior I stepped into an elevator with Vijay Amritraj, a tall, smiling Indian who was born in Madras and now lives in Marina del Rey, California. His hair is iridescent black, like the wings of a crow, and his skin is so dark, his teeth and the whites of his eyes appear startlingly bright and large. His gold neckchain and Rolex watch also seem larger and brighter than natural.

"See the matches tonight?" I asked.

Vijay went loose-limbed with laughter. "I never watch tennis. I hate watching tennis!"

The WCT guidebook characterizes Amritraj as "probably the most popular player among his peers on the pro tour . . . an articulate gentleman who is also a great ambassador for his sport and his country."

More than matching WCT's esteem for him, Vijay was the lone player to commit himself exclusively to the WCT tour. He explained that he had done this with the full understanding that he would have to qualify for any Grand Prix event he cared to enter. He simply preferred WCT tournaments; Wimbledon was the one non-WCT event he wanted to play.

Although Amritraj didn't mention it, he might have had other reasons for signing with WCT. Along with his brothers Anand and Ashok, he owns a film-production company in Hollywood which develops movies and television specials. Al G. Hill, Jr., President of World Championship Tennis, is listed as "general partner of Amritraj Productions." In May, Amritraj Productions would be awarded the rights to produce the 1981 WCT Highlights film.

When I asked what his reaction would be if Bjorn Borg were allowed to play Wimbledon without qualifying, Vijay said he would object strenuously. A rule was a rule and should apply to everybody, even to Borg. Oh, Borg was a great champion, but every man had "certain minimal responsibilities to the game and to the other players. Borg contributes to tennis by playing, but in no other way."

In his sunny, diplomatic manner Vijay expressed displeasure with players who violated the rules of their union and misbehaved on court. He thought fines were ineffective; miscreants should be suspended for six months to a year.

Since he was scheduled to meet John McEnroe in a Davis Cup match next week, I asked if he was ever tempted to retaliate and do something dramatic to curb what he considered to be the American's chronic misconduct. For an instant Vijay's smile vanished and he drew himself up to his full height of six feet three. "I'd never lower myself to that level."

Rules were rules, he repeated. They should apply to everybody. Too many exceptions were made; too often the top players received preferential treatment. For instance, Borg had a contract as touring pro with Caesar's Palace in Las Vegas and was obligated to play its annual tournament, the Alan King Classic. Since it was a Grand Prix event and since Borg had failed to sign up for ten tournaments, he would have to qualify. But on the weekend when the qualies would normally be held, Borg was committed to play exhibitions in Japan. Unwilling to skip these highly profitable performances, Borg had refused to play the qualies as scheduled. Caesar's Palace had then threatened to cancel the tournament.

In other sports the cliché holds that no player is bigger than the game. But in this case every priority had been reversed and the schedule had been revised to accommodate one man—Bjorn Borg. Vijay told me the qualies in Las Vegas had been shifted from the weekend to Monday and Tuesday, delaying the start of the tournament until Wednesday.

Smiling ruefully, shaking his head, Vijay Amritraj wondered about the inconvenience, the unfairness to everybody else. "It's ridiculous. Doesn't anybody have the courage to stand up and do the right thing?"

Tuesday morning snow flurries fell on Genoa and the palm trees in the *piazza* tossed their fronds in a howling wind. WCT officials were shocked at how cold it could be on the Italian Riviera and complained that bad weather might keep attendance low.

In the lobby I spotted Balazs Taroczy waiting for a courtesy car. Three weeks ago the ATP office in Paris had told me Taroczy would be playing the Egyptian Open.

"Thought you were in Cairo," I said.

"There's no money there this year. Nobody's in Cairo—only three players in the top hundred."

"The prize money's the same as last year," I said. "Seventy-five thousand dollars."

Taroczy shrugged. A Hungarian with a high, pale forehead and dark eyebrows, he looks more like a graduate student than a world-class athlete, the No. 15 player on the computer. He has a degree from the University of Economic Sciences in Budapest—which is fitting for a Communist who won $188,175 in 1981.

"Last year," he said, "they had extra money at the Egyptian Open. There was a good field. This year they don't have any money."

An Italian journalist standing nearby performed a classic gesture, the light friction of thumb against fingers. "He means under the table."

To be precise, Balazs Taroczy meant "appearance money" or a "guarantee." In a throwback to the time when tennis was supposed to be amateur but the stars received secret payments, top players now demand as much as $100,000 above and beyond any prize money they might win. In *World Tennis*, ATP President Harold Solomon referred to guarantees as a "cancer within tennis," "dirty and illegal money . . . no different from the graft a politician might take." Yet, by his estimate, "appearance money and other guarantees are paid to the top players about 75% of the weeks of Grand Prix tennis."

Others maintain that Solomon underestimates the gravity of the situation. They claim that only the French Open, Wimbledon, and the U.S. Open don't pay money under the table.

Unlike these three Grand Slam events which automatically attract the best players, most tournaments need to offer bribes or inducements if they hope to sign star players who will bring in sponsors, television contracts, and fans. Such inducements are strictly against the rules of the Pro Council and subject violators, both players and tournaments, to fines of up to $20,000 and suspensions of up to three years. But, according to Solomon, the rules are "feebly enforced" and "members of the Pro Council have been some of the very people who have violated the guarantee rule, which they created."

After raising potentially explosive questions—"Does this money show up on a player's income tax statement? Does it show up in tournament books as guarantees paid to players? Wouldn't the IRS have a field day with this one?"—Solomon concluded that "unless something is done quickly, tennis may surely follow the path to self-destruction already trod by pro wrestling. What happens to the credibility of the game if fans perceive—true or not—that a player has no incentive to win?"

Balazs Taroczy and I shared a car with Vijay Amritraj, who, even on this cold, bleak day, was bright with smiles.

"Hello, AP," Vijay said to me. "Don't ask me any questions. I just gave all my good quotes to UPI." Then, turning to Taroczy, "How is your lovely wife?"

"Fine. And yours?"

Vijay went limp with laughter. "I'm not married."

"But you will be?" Balazs inquired. "You are to be?"

"Yes, by the end of this year. We have a date. It's a matter of finding a girl."

"You have her?" Taroczy wanted to know.

"I think so. I went home to meet her. I think we found the

one. That is, my mother found her. A very nice girl. Things need to be arranged, though. We have a date. December 29. Now we just need the girl."

Because Vijay kept giggling and Balazs was grinning, I thought it was a joke. But no, it was true. This "articulate gentleman," this "great ambassador for his sport and his country," will have an arranged marriage, and his mother has spent years interviewing over two hundred girls, pursuing the perfect match. For while Vijay is an eligible bachelor, he is also an obedient Hindu. Much as he admires the scientific precision of his Ferrari 308 GTS, he recently flew home to have a leg injury treated by an herb specialist. Although a graduate in commerce and accounting from Madras University, he is incorrigibly superstitious, and when on a winning streak, he gets up on the same side of the bed every morning until he loses. Vijay Amritraj may sound like a mass of contradictions, but in that sense he is no different from most men on the circuit and no different from the sport/business of professional tennis, which is one of paradoxes and profound disjunctions.

On Tuesday, Adriano Panatta, Italy's leading crowd-pleaser, called from the ski resort of Cortina d'Ampezzo and said he had a fever and, on the advice of his physician, couldn't play in Genoa.

With this tournament already under way and Italy's Davis Cup match against England due to start next week, what was Panatta doing in the Dolomites?

"He is training in the snow," quipped one reporter.

Understandably, WCT officials were displeased. Although Panatta might be years beyond his prime, he had won the Italian Open and French Open in 1976 and he was still a star in his homeland. Handsome, impetuous, sulky, and unpredictable, capable of beating Borg or of swooning in front of an utter unknown, he was the sort of player who put paying customers in the stands.

Now the tournament's brightest local attraction was Corrado Barazzutti, who was difficult to market except to hard-core tennis fans who understood and admired his Byzantine strategies. To the uninitiated spectator it often appeared that Barazzutti was trying to anesthetize his opponent, to bore the other man and all onlookers into a coma. Sometimes, during Corrado's long, slow rallies, people in the stands started jeering or laughing. They threw paper airplanes, pieces of loose change, and beer cans. Still Barazzutti plodded on, living up to his nickname, "the Little Soldier."

Given Barazzutti's reputation for dogged patience, I was amazed to see him flail at the ball and rush the net against his first-round opponent, a lowly qualifier. He appeared in a hurry to complete the match, but he lacked the equipment to play that kind of forcing game and lost the first set 6–3.

There were a few hundred spectators on hand, and they whistled and hooted. To them it seemed that Barazzutti's mind was elsewhere, and they were right. His body might be in Genoa, but in his mind Corrado was already on the road toward the Adriatic coast. He had agreed to play two events this week—the WCT tournament on a hard court and the semifinals of the national club championship outdoors on a clay court in the town of Forlì, which was all the way on the other side of the country and didn't have an airport. So Barazzutti would have to drive four hundred kilometers over the Appennines, catch a night's sleep, play his match, then make the return trip to meet his next opponent in Genoa.

But first he had to dispatch this pesky qualifier, and for Corrado there was only one way to do that. He took his time and chloroformed the fellow with painstakingly placed shots. Night was falling when he finally won the third set 6–1 and raced to his car.

If Barazzutti continued winning in the WCT tournament, he faced a difficult decision. On Saturday, when the semifinals were slated for Genoa, he was scheduled to play in Turin for the finals of the Italian club championship. It was anybody's guess what Corrado would choose to do.

In a similar situation last summer Ilie Nastase had been playing a tournament and, simultaneously, a series of exhibitions. When he reached the finals of the tournament, he defaulted.

That same day he played an exhibition match. There is no more graphic example of where the money is and where the loyalties of many players lie.

That evening there were still fewer than five hundred people in the Palazzo dello Sport and all the Italian journalists had remained in the press room watching a televised soccer match between Italy and France. Their shouts and cheers echoed throughout the arena, far louder than those of the paltry clutch of spectators.

Reporters blamed the small crowd on the weather, on the televised soccer match, on Panatta's defection, and on WCT's ignorance. "There should never have been a tournament in Genoa," one man told me. "Genoa has no tennis tradition and it's a tight-fisted town. Calling an Italian a Genovese is like saying he's a cheapskate. These people hold onto their *lire* like it was their cock."

Then he said, "You hear what happened to that black umpire?"

"Jason Smith?"

"Yeah. He wouldn't wear a Fila warm-up suit and they fired him."

"Who fired him?"

"WCT. The other umpires were going to walk out with him. But the promoters convinced them to stay. It would have killed the tournament. They're already using all these kids as linesmen."

"Where's Jason?"

"Haven't seen him. Ask the WCT people."

I went looking for John McDonald, the International Director, and when I couldn't locate him at the Colombia-Excelsior, I scouted the lobby for anybody wearing a WCT badge. I finally spotted a young lady in a beige suit and horn-rimmed glasses who appeared to be all business. Short, dark, and intense, she wore gold laurel-leaf earrings, gold neckchains, and a gold bracelet. Her name was Robyn Lewis and she was the International Broadcast Coordinator for WCT. Actually, she explained, it was a bit more complicated than that; WCT had laid off its international TV rights on a Dutch company, Strengholt Televideo International. "Strengholt makes the sales. I make the product and deliver it."

"Are you based in Dallas?" I asked.

She arched her eyebrows. "Are you kidding? I live in Hollywood."

She had planned to go shopping, but agreed to drink a *cappuccino* and discuss her work.

With her experience in TV production and in promoting rock shows, she wanted to develop scripts and produce feature-length films. But "I was sick of Hollywood, sick of living with sharks and piranhas. So I thought I'd go with sports for a while. Look what I got."

What had she got? I asked, postponing questions about Jason Smith.

Well, it wasn't what she had expected. "I wasn't hot for this job," she said as we took a table in the bar, which was deserted except for us. Robyn lit a cigarette and chain-smoked while talking. "I told a friend I didn't want to spend months traveling around the world with a bunch of jocks. He said tennis players are all college graduates, they're smart. But that's nonsense. They're just not very bright. I never see one reading a book. They're not interested in anything except tennis. Maybe they're just too shy, too scared to go out of the hotel into the city. They don't even come on to the hostesses. These hostesses, they're all models and I'm sure when they were hired they expected a lot of action. I bet they're surprised.

"My friends keep asking, 'Are you partying and doing coke all the time?' I tell them it's a bore," Robyn said, tapping the ash from her cigarette. "But nobody believes me. Sometimes I get so fed up with this job, I say, 'Look, I just have to go shopping.' It drives me crazy not to get off into town and shop."

After apologizing for preventing her from shopping, I admitted I had learned things at this tournament that were different from what I had expected. I thought I knew tennis, but—

"This is entertainment," she corrected me. "Not tennis. Even the vocabulary is Hollywood. We're selling 'stars.' I joke about

it. I see the p
their costume

So she felt
preparation fo

She laughed
version of Holl
like visiting a
people and try t
know. I keep w
don't. Look, ten
tained. I persona
as important as v

Smart, sassy, a
WCT and the Gi
battle, could, if ha
"These political w
wise, what is there

At a WCT tournament in Mexic
stitute umpire and found a se
chair. "He was adorable. I
and put him to work in
more to the tour tha
There seemed
She confir
up. He fel
an ump
But

As she saw it, controversy wasn't killing tennis. Controversy was one of the few things that made it marketable. Yet tennis authorities were foolishly trying to suppress those aspects of the game that attracted customers. "Why shouldn't players argue with umpires and the linesmen?" she demanded. "Arguing is interesting. It wakes people up. Take Nastase." Everybody criticized the Rumanian; they claimed he was disgraceful, unsportsmanlike, obscene. Yet Robyn regarded him forthrightly as someone she could sell. "He's no longer a great player. But people come to see him whether he wins or not. The stars are the attraction, not the game."

I quietly demurred and attempted to explain my own interest in tennis. Robyn Lewis remained unmoved. She knew what TV stations, sponsors, and viewers bought. If enough people shared my feelings, "it wouldn't matter who played, we could market it. But we can't. People don't buy the sport. People buy stars."

When I asked what constituted a star—wasn't it enough for a man to be an exceptional player?—she said, "No. They've got to be entertainers if they want to keep getting the kind of money they're paid now."

Then she cited an example of someone who had "star quality."

City they had needed a sub-
enteen-year-old boy to sit in the
he had *it*. I would have hired him
very tournament. He could have added
a lot of players."
no better opportunity to ask about Jason Smith.
ed that he had refused to wear the Fila warm-
it made him look foolish and he believed it violated
ire's neutrality to become part of a promotional package.
WCT had a contractual deal which dictated that everybody
on court, except the players, had to wear Fila. As Robyn put
it, repeating a favorite theme, Jason's mistake was that "he thought
this is tennis. He's wrong. It's entertainment."

Weren't there crucial differences between tennis and entertainment? I asked.

She considered this a moment, toying with her cigarette lighter,
then observed, "Coming out of rock and roll, I find it interesting
that a lot of players don't have an entourage—you know, agents,
managers, PR men who travel with them to protect their interests. Just talking entertainment-business-wise, the ones who'll
make it are going to have an entourage."

Why? What did they need protection from?

In her opinion, if players were making millions, that meant
there must be a lot more for the people who controlled and
marketed the game. She couldn't believe how naïve the players
were, how little effort they expended to stay informed about
what was being done with their careers. "These people just don't
know," she said.

In the following days, as I tried to track down Jason Smith,
I found my attention wandering from the court. During one
match I stared up at the roof of the Palazzo dello Sport, where
several workmen were walking across the translucent dome, their
shadows enormous and distorted. It was as if I were gazing up
from the bottom of a swimming pool toward people who had
magically acquired the power to walk on water. The sight was

disconcerting and set me on edge. I expected the men to plunge through at any moment and fall with an ugly splat to the court.

It seemed to me I had started to see tennis in much the same fashion. Somehow I had slipped beneath its glittering surface and was peering up at it from a new perspective. This, too, set me on edge and I wondered what else might come plunging down around me.

Although he has won few major titles and in recent years has sometimes dropped out of the top ten, Vitas Gerulaitis has always been extremely popular, nowhere more so than in Italy, where he is marketed as a sex symbol. He used to endorse a racquet appropriately named the Wilson Stiff Model, and posters of him clutching this product can still be seen on billboards, even though he now has a contract with Snauwert.

Vitas' wavy blond cascades of hair and his reputation as a playboy have long sustained an image which has been successful to the extent that simple realities are ignored. For one thing, on close inspection he is hardly a handsome man. His long beak of a nose tends to be tanned a different color from the rest of his face, and his tiny eyes are as close-set as peas on either side of a knife blade.

For another thing, his tennis game is far less potent and dramatic than are those photographs of Vitas with various models, starlets, and café-society climbers. His own father, a teaching pro, refers to his son's second serve as "a baby serve." The key to Gerulaitis' game is speed. To win, he has to scramble and retrieve every ball, rush the net and volley. But to do that, he needs to stay in shape.

For much of 1981 he wasn't, and his ranking dipped into the low teens and his image suffered considerable damage when he was assessed over $5,000 in fines for misconduct at the U.S. Open. After a three-week suspension he traveled to Australia and became embroiled in another ugly incident. During a match in Melbourne, with the score tied at five games apiece in the third set, Vitas refused to play on after what he regarded as several bad calls against him. Tennis columnist Bud Collins, seldom known to be negative, called this default "the most unprofessional act of the year. He should be suspended for a year, or more, because that is cheating the public."

Because of the company he keeps off court, and his erratic performances on court, Gerulaitis' career has been plagued by rumors about drugs. Just last month, however, Gerulaitis had redeemed himself in the eyes of some critics by playing well in the Masters. In a dramatic final he forced Ivan Lendl to the limit of his formidable talent, taking the first two sets and holding a match point against the Czech in the third, before losing in five hard-fought sets.

When I tried to arrange an interview, Vitas was wary. "I've always been cooperative with the press, but last year they seemed to do stories just to put in their own opinions. They'd take one sentence I said or half a sentence and stick it with what they believed. Anything to make their point. I got so pissed off at Flushing Meadows I stopped talking to them until it was costing me so much money"—in Grand Prix events, players are fined $1,000 if they skip the post-match press conference—"I had to start talking again."

I assured him I was interested in *his* opinions, not my own, and as I waited for him to make up his mind whether to grant an interview, I asked why he always wrapped his racquet handle with adhesive gauze between change-overs.

"People think all that taping is bullshit. Superstition or something. But look!" Vitas opened his right hand. The palm was slick with sweat; perspiration purled along his lifeline. It was always like that, he said, even when he wasn't playing, and he found it impossible to get a firm grip on a racquet.

"I've done everything," he said. "I've tried hypnotism. I've gone to doctors. One doctor gave me these pills. Right, they dried me up everywhere—except my hand. I was dying. I had to drink a hundred Cokes a day. But my hand was still wet and the racquet kept slipping around. I don't think it's I'm so nervous. It's my metabolism. That's why I can't get to sleep at night. It takes me hours. I mean, unless it's six in the morning or something, it always takes me hours to get to sleep."

Although Vitas claimed otherwise, he did strike me as nervous, high-strung, bristling with excess energy. I told him I wanted to discuss his image.

"What about it?" His narrow gaze swept over me.

"I've heard people say you're Bob Kain's [Kain is his agent at IMG] greatest creation."

Vitas bridled. "Bob Kain couldn't create an image out of a bar of soap. I've had my image ever since I was a junior. You can ask the players that."

"It's something you're proud of, then?"

"Well, the playboy image probably got me bigger contracts before I deserved them. But it's been detrimental, too. Every time I lose, they say it's because I'm not in shape. It's funny. Last year at the French Open, I *wasn't* in shape and the French press jumped on me. But the year before, they loved me for living like them—for going out and having fun. I made it to the finals and they loved me. Next year, I lose in the first round and they really dump on me."

How badly out of shape had he been?

"I had gained about five pounds. That's a lot for me. I used to eat anything and always weigh one fifty-five. People started telling me I had lost a step. I had to work hard to get it back. I'm twenty-seven now. I figure I'll give the game two more years. I feel I can be not just one of the top players again, but maybe No. 1. I'm not saying I can stay there all year. My concentration won't last that long. But I can definitely win a major. I can win a Wimbledon, a U.S. Open. I know I can beat McEnroe. I can beat Lendl. Whenever I am in the States, I don't fool around New York City. I go to Florida and work out with Harry Hopman. If I had started working this hard on my serve at eighteen, I'd have a fucking good serve by now."

I said I'd like to discuss his serve and get an idea how he felt his image had worked to his detriment. After a lengthy debate about times and places, we made an appointment for that evening at the hotel.

When I went to his room, there was a note taped on the door. Gerulaitis was sorry. But he had decided to go out on the town.

•   •   •

Instead, I interviewed Bill Scanlon, a voluble Texan nicknamed Scaz. While Vitas Gerulaitis feels ambivalent about his playboy image, Scanlon believes his own image has been largely negative and he has spent years attempting to overcome a reputation as a quitter.

His career had started in 1977 on a thunderously high note. After capturing the National Collegiate Athletic Association title, Scanlon embarked on the circuit by beating Harold Solomon, Adriano Panatta, and Ilie Nastase twice in one month. He ended the year by earning over $96,000 in prize money, and he signed a contract with Fila for "a total package"—which is to say, he agreed to wear their line of clothes and use a racquet which they were supposed to design expressly for his game.

Then, abruptly, Bill Scanlon began to slide back into the anonymous throng ranked around No. 100. He lost his touch and blamed the Fila racquet. Like many pros who accept huge sums of money to switch racquets, Scanlon discovered that he didn't feel confident with the new one. He told Peter Bodo in *Inside Tennis*, "When I signed the contract, I understood that they'd try to make something like the Wilson Kramer, a flexible stick with a medium head. What they made is more like the Dunlop Maxply—a little stiffer in the body and lighter in the head. It just isn't my style."

Another man might have solved the problem with a common deception. He could have had his old racquet camouflaged to resemble a Fila. But Scaz kept using the Fila and continued losing.

He also admitted to Bodo, however, that his racquet wasn't the only thing that had gone light in the head. "I was accumulating vast amounts of money. *That* was the start of my decline." By the age of twenty-two he owned two cars, one of them a Mercedes, a Piaget watch, and two expensive guitars. Then he rented a couple of apartments—he always seemed to do things by twos—and "quit working as hard. I started spending all the money I made. . . . I was throwing it around. . . . I was spoiled, I guess."

Tennis ceased to be fun, and he found life on the tour lonely, deracinating, a blurred kaleidoscope of interchangeable hotel rooms, sports arenas, and courts. "I'm alone out there, and I can't handle it. There's just two of us, me and the other player, against each other and against the world. That's where a coach would help—knowing there's somebody there for you."

Before he found help, things got worse. As we ate pasta in the players' restaurant in Genoa, he looked back to the low point in 1978 when, in his words, he "turned into a basket case" and dropped off the tour. "I didn't retire. I became a degenerate. I would have started drinking before noon—if I ever got up before noon."

In retrospect the story sounded improbable even to Scanlon— washed up at twenty-two, still making good money from endorsement contracts, but lacking all desire and direction. And his comeback seemed as strange and sudden as his decline. Like any wealthy, drifting "degenerate," he decided to fly to Hawaii to visit friends. They urged him to enter a tournament in Maui and do them a favor by trying, for a change. Scanlon's ranking had sunk so low he had to play the qualies, but with his friends in the stands urging him on, he made it into the main draw, beat John McEnroe in the semifinals, and won the title.

Thereafter, he traveled with a friend, who not only serves as a coach, but as an all-round arranger, companion, and rooting section, someone Scanlon can be sure is always behind him. Like so many players on the tour, he feels the day is over when the top pros can go it alone.

Despite his recovery, Scanlon nurtured no illusions about the circuit and he disabused me of my benign notions about the ATP computer. "We're rated every week, and the rankings are publicized all around the world. Think what that means." His voice welling with emotion, his face lightly dusted with freckles, his thick hair tousled, he might have been an undergraduate pleading with a professor not to judge him by some bloodless standard. "You live and die by those numbers. For some people, your whole identity is your ranking. I once heard someone ask a player, 'How are you?' He answered, 'I'm No. 29 this week.' Not 'I'm happy' or 'I'm depressed' or 'I'm making it day to day.' Just 'I'm No. 29,' like that said it all.

"People outside tennis figure if you're winning, you must be happy. You have to be! If you're not happy, they tell you, 'You've got it made. Try working for a living and see how tough it is.' I've stopped trying to explain to them the way it is. Anybody asks about Genoa, I'll tell them what they want to hear. I'll say, 'Great!' I won't say it was snowing or the hotel was too expensive or the beds were so lumpy you couldn't sleep. After matches I always answer journalists the same way."

Suddenly Scanlon segued into an uncanny imitation of Bjorn Borg. " 'For sure I play good. He play good, too. But I think maybe I play the big points better.' That's what people want to hear from tennis players. You tell them the truth and they get upset, angry. One thing you're never supposed to do as an athlete in America is admit any weakness. Every time I lose, I know people will throw it up in my face and say I'm a quitter."

I could have assured him that wasn't true. He had come back. Now ranked No. 35, he had won over $197,000 last year. But then Bill Scanlon is that rare player who was no longer deceived by the facile consolation of numbers.

That night the top seed, Ivan Lendl, played the last Italian in the tournament, Corrado Barazzutti. While some matches are made of fire and ice, this one demonstrated different degrees of iciness. Both Lendl and Barazzutti are cold, remorseless base-liners, but when Barazzutti hit a snow flurry of groundstrokes, Lendl answered with an avalanche. Although Barazzutti retrieved ball after ball, seldom giving the Czech a cheap point, Lendl was as steady as the Italian and infinitely stronger, especially off his forehand, which he unfurls like a whip. Driving the ball deep from corner to corner, he ground the Little Soldier down like a glacier.

The other reporters had raced off to file their stories when somebody behind me leaned close and breathed, "I, too, am journalist."

As an opening gambit, it was a nonpareil conversation-stopper, sort of like having the gent standing next to you at a public urinal announce, "I, too, am man."

I concentrated very hard on the tournament program.

But the fellow didn't give up. When one of the glamorous hostesses glided past, he observed in thickly accented English, "Italian girls are all so stupid. They always want to be important. But then they tell men they have to be careful."

This time when I didn't respond, he settled into the seat beside me. He was young, in his mid-twenties, and wore a double-breasted gray suit, a pink shirt and blue tie. His breath was aromatic of *cappuccino*, and when he smiled, he displayed all thirty-two teeth and a broad, glistening expanse of gum. "I, too, am journalist," he repeated and presented his card. "Can I have yours?"

I didn't have a card, and this seemed to puzzle him. While he examined the press badge on my lapel, I stared again at the program.

"This is sad," he said, indicating the program's cover, which might have been designed by an untalented child. The black stick figure of a tennis player was lunging at a red ball with an unstrung racquet. Or perhaps it wasn't a racquet after all. It could have been one of those wire wands which children dip into soapy water, then blow bubbles.

"Very sad," he repeated.

Viewing his remark as an aesthetic judgment, I agreed.

"You see," he said, "this is because the tournament is a memorial."

"Pardon me?"

"Because this is a memorial event, they want sad cover. No happiness. No lots of colors."

"I see," I said, although I hadn't the vaguest idea what the man was talking about.

"Bitti Bergamo is the name of the tournament. And Bitti Bergamo is dead. He was Italian Davis Cup captain. He was deathed in a car crash."

"I'm sorry. An automobile accident—that's awful."

"No, a car crash." Then, with no transition, he asked, "You like Fila? I represent much better clothe-ess. Before we make only ski clothe-ess. Now tennis." He told me the players who wore his label. "I make PR for them. Not selling. Only PR with important players."

"Thought you were a journalist?"

"I am that, too. I am journalist, PR man, agent, clothe-ess representative, special-events organizer . . ." He needed all his fingers to keep count of his business activities. "Now I want to become tournament director. This tournament should be in my town, Naples. Tennis is much very much followed there. Genoa is no good tennis town. Too cheap. Plus, last year they have exhibition here. Ocleppo beats Lendl. Amritraj beats Panatta. People don't believe it's serious. This does not make such good propaganda for tennis in Genoa."

Smiling, he nudged my shoulder. "Next year you come and write about my tournament in Naples."

I said I didn't know where I'd be or what I'd be doing next year.

"You come. You'll like Naples. Anything I can do, you tell me."

As I considered things I might suggest he do, he asked, "How about my English?"

"How about it?"

"How's the grammatical?"

"Not bad."

"I want to get better. But I have no time for study. I'm too busy."

As I was to learn in the following months, many journalists, and not just Italians by any means, keep busy holding down half a dozen other jobs in tennis. Behind the Iron Curtain a press card might serve as cover for an intelligence agent, but on the circuit it provides an umbrella under which entrepreneurs reach out with octopoid tentacles to control as many corners of the sport/business as they can. With so much money at stake, there is no pretense, not even any lip-service, about journalistic objectivity. Snouts buried deep in the feed trough, reporters routinely turn out fulsome articles on tournaments, officials, and players with whom they have close financial relationships.

In any other business such practices would be regarded as

grave conflicts of interest. But in tennis they constitute standard operating procedure, and little effort is wasted on discretion, much less secrecy. The unctuous young gentleman I met in Genoa was a rank amateur compared to the large agencies whose wrap-around deals are blandly described in *International Tennis Weekly*, the official newspaper of the ATP.

For example, Pro Serv, a major agency in the sport, not only promotes individual Volvo Grand Prix tournaments, it represents all of Volvo's tennis interests, even at events where IMG, the other major agency, controls specific rights. What's more, Pro Serv employees and clients are frequent contributors to journals which cover these tournaments, and Donald Dell, the head of the agency, is often in the enviable position of acting as a TV commentator at tournaments which his firm manages, for a fee, and whose television rights he has marketed, for a fee, and whose players he represents, for a fee.

Small wonder that professional tennis likes to think of itself as one large, happy family.

I was still searching for Jason Smith, and I finally found him in the hotel bar, the spot where players, reporters, agents, and officials gathered every evening to review the events of the day. Tonight they were debating whether this had been a good tournament or a bad tournament.

The question had nothing to do with the quality of the tennis or with the attractions of the town. For them, a good tournament was one with pretty hostesses, plenty of practice courts, reliable transportation to those courts, and a first-class, reasonably priced hotel.

Marshaling these criteria with all the rigor of an English schoolmaster, Buster Mottram, Great Britain's No. 1 player, gave the Bitti Bergamo tournament a failing grade. While he held forth with his emphatic opinions, I sat beside Jason Smith and waited for a quiet moment to speak with the now unemployed umpire. The wait was a long one; Mottram had a lot to say. He didn't like this part of the world—Italy, France, Spain, the Wog-world where reservations were always in doubt, baggage was always in danger, and hotels were rip-offs, or "whip-offs," as Buster pronounced it.

Mottram was an altogether different breed of animal from the other players. He seemed not to give a fig about international harmony, public relations, or projecting a marketable image. Once a member of the National Front, a neo-fascist organization in England, he reminded me of a character who had stepped straight out of an Evelyn Waugh novel.

Tall and gangly, wearing a fluffy white sweater and sucking on a pipe, he had a wispy mustache, an impish face full of moles which might have passed for freckles, and the look of an honorable schoolboy on holiday. His appearance was so completely out of keeping with his crotchety, Blimpish view of the world, I couldn't help wondering whether he believed what he said or was playing his outrageous opinions for laughs. Maybe Mottram himself didn't know. "I'm not a Nazi. I'm a conservative. You know, like the Tories. Well, actually," he admitted, "I'm a bit to the right of the Tories."

As I waited to talk to Jason Smith, Buster lectured everybody on the dos and don'ts of Italian hotel life. "You never eat breakfast in the hotel. Ten dollars for coffee and rolls, it's a whip-off! And you never use room service; they put on all these surcharges. Here in the bar you sign for everything you drink. Insist on signing for everything in the restaurant, too. And, whatever you do, you never make a long-distance telephone call from the hotel."

Jason, who had been listening in a distracted fashion, lurched into sharp focus. "What about the telephone?"

"Don't use it. Ever!" Buster knocked the ashes from his pipe and began scraping the bowl.

"Why?" Jason asked.

"They'll tack on a service charge. It can double or triple the cost."

The stocky black umpire sagged back beside me.

"Mind you," Mottram went on, "you must vet every item on your bill. They'll charge for calls you never made, for meals you didn't eat. They'll stick you with incredible charges. Once in Florence I was billed for a bottle of champagne. I fully expect to have a half-hour's argument at the front desk when I check out of here. I'll probably be billed for caviar. That's how it always is in these countries."

As Buster paused to suck on his pipe, someone asked what he was doing up so late. It was nearly two a.m. and he had to play the first match in the afternoon.

"No," Mottram insisted, "I play the evening match. I can sleep as late as I want."

Several players attempted to persuade him otherwise, but Buster wouldn't budge. He knew when he was supposed to play. He knew it as surely as his own name. Or at least he asserted it as forcefully as every *pronunciamento* he uttered. It took the combined efforts of all the players, officials, a few reporters, and a photocopied schedule to change his mind.

Smiling sheepishly, he unfolded his long legs and drained his glass of beer as he got to his feet. "Well, then, I guess I'd better get to bed."

After Buster left, Jason Smith sighed. Ignorant of the service charge on long-distance calls, he had spent all day on the telephone trying to make arrangements for next week. He would have checked out of the Colombia-Excelsior, but they accepted his credit card, while a cheaper place might have demanded cash. With the tournament in Copenhagen canceled, he would have to go two weeks without a paycheck. What was worse, he had to fly to Copenhagen anyway. Otherwise he'd break the sequence of his airplane ticket and have to pay a supplement on each subsequent flight to tournaments in Brussels, Rotterdam, and Milan. Copenhagen was an expensive city, Jason pointed out, and it would be cold there and he would be alone.

I said I was sorry. Wasn't there a chance of a reconciliation with WCT?

He didn't believe so. He was willing to wear a Fila patch on his blazer, but anything more than that . . . Well, he just didn't feel it was right to involve an umpire in a promotional deal.

The whole situation, upsetting as it was, had an ironic twist which turned up the corners of his lips in a tight little smile. In the past Fila and other clothing manufacturers had offered to pay him personally to wear their products when he was umpiring. But he had refused. After all, you didn't see baseball umpires or soccer referees advertising clothes and equipment.

"What if I'm up in the chair promoting Fila," Jason asked, "and a player comes out wearing Wilson or Ellesse? Is he going to feel I'm prejudiced against him? Will he feel that I'll favor the players wearing Fila?"

From behind his tortoiseshell glasses he fixed me with eyes which looked very tired. "Where does this thing stop? Already WCT has the umpire there on court before matches, spinning a racquet to see who serves, passing out balls for the players to hit into the crowd. All this hoopla, where does it stop? They'll have us jumping through hoops next."

Jason didn't sound angry so much as disappointed and deeply hurt. "I'm upset. I took a stand that could cut me out of half the jobs on the tour. If I didn't wear that . . . that costume here, I won't wear it anywhere else, and that means they won't let me work on the WCT. I feel bad. I feel I'm indulging my love affair with tennis at the expense of my wife and kids. I wanted to get to the point where umpiring was a profession, where we were treated as professionals. I can't keep on working as a charitable gesture."

Now, at least on the WCT tour, he couldn't work at all.

I bought us both a nightcap, then insisted on signing the bill, just as Buster had advised. But the barman explained that there was no bill. This was no penny-ante operation. The billing was computerized.

The wind off the Mediterranean blew a gale that night, rattling windows, shutters, and drainpipes. Yet, noisy as it was outside, it couldn't match the clamor on my floor of the Colombia-Excelsior. Three doors down, Vitas Gerulaitis' room was open, and hard rock, at high volume, screeched from a cassette recorder. Vitas was playing crazy eights with a few friends while a cluster of sycophants, a German tournament promoter, and

Ivan Lendl's Russian bodyguard, Sascha, all beefy shoulders and Beatle-style hair, looked on. Because of the cacophonous music they had to talk at the top of their lungs, and I heard the German promoter entreat Vitas to play his tournaments.

At daybreak the gale abated, but by then the bustle of the hotel had begun. Maids and bellboys rumbled up and down the corridor, dropping plates and pushing vacuum cleaners. Toilets flushed with the force of tropical waterfalls. When a radio roared to life in the next room, I gave up all hope of sleep and went out for breakfast. I was starting to sympathize with the players who bitched about the constant travel, the awful hotels, the killing schedule.

A quarterfinal match between Vijay Amritraj and Bill Scanlon was witnessed by a few hundred paying customers and no Italian journalists. I watched the first desultory set and part of the second, then joined the other reporters in a nearby restaurant where Canale 5 had laid on a five-course lunch for no discernible purpose—unless it was to announce what every member of the press already knew: namely, that Canale 5 would broadcast the semifinals and finals.

After coffee and liqueurs we each received two ties emblazoned with the Canale 5 logo and a bottle of Givenchy *eau de cologne*. ("Why not Chanel No. 5?" some irrepressible wag couldn't resist shouting.) Then, stuffed with pasta and woozy with wine, we stumbled back and phoned in our stories describing a match none of us had watched.

The evening program figured to be more exciting, and this prompted several players to drop by the courts. It's not common for players to show much interest in matches, not even those involving their friends. But they will occasionally stop and browse. In that respect they reminded me of writers who drift into bookstores not to buy, just to test the weight of a new novel, to check the cover and the binding and the author's bio, and to riffle the pages, sampling a line of prose here and there. But finally the book goes back onto the shelf, and the writer sidles down the aisle and out the door.

So it is with tennis players, who are too close to the sport to be impressed by anything short of a spectacular performance, are too knowledgeable about the PR process to believe in their own image or anybody else's, and, after a few laps around the circuit, are too cynical to be surprised by what newspapers call upsets.

Then, too, they have practical reasons to keep their distance from their fellow pros. Although they live together, travel together, eat together, and party together, they are still competitors and have to be aware that anything good that befalls one man happens at another's expense. They cannot afford to invest emotional energy in anyone else's match since the fellow they cheer to victory today may be out to beat them tomorrow.

Early in their careers they are forced to weigh the advantages of friendship against their own obsessions and decide how badly they want to win. Almost always the price of victory is isolation. The players point out that Connors, Borg, Vilas, and Lendl share a common quality. They are loners who eat in their rooms and practice only with coaches or close friends. To someone outside the circuit all players seem single-minded and self-absorbed, as if racing through life wearing blinders. But the top stars manifest a more exaggerated case of tunnel-vision, the kind which makes Connors view every opponent as an enemy, convinces Borg to stash his wife on the living-room couch during Wimbledon, and induces Lendl to treat everyone except his entourage with all the charm of a Stormtrooper.

That night, on the way to the court for the quarterfinals, I rode with Mike Cahill and Buster Mottram, who are doubles partners. They appear to be friends and to know each other well. They smoke pipes, share a fondness for fine wines, and enjoy joking about their respective shortcomings. Cahill calls Mottram "a pusher"—a player who, in tight spots, tends to push at the ball instead of hitting through it. Mottram calls Cahill "a cripple" because he wears a brace on one knee and needs an operation.

Yet there are striking disparities between them. Cahill, an American from Memphis, Tennessee, graduated from the University of Alabama with a degree in history and religion. Cahill

openly informs strangers, "I'm a Christian," then explains how
his faith helped his wife and him pull through when they found
out two years ago that she suffers from multiple sclerosis. Later,
when I mentioned Mrs. Cahill's illness to Buster Mottram, he
was shocked. His doubles partner had never told him.

As we sped toward the Palazzo dello Sport, the sleazy bars
along the port gave Genoa the look of a Levantine town. But
the weather was arctic, and all the whores hugged their fake furs
and hopped from one spiked heel to the other as the cold air
whistled up their bare legs.

When he learned I had lived in Texas, Mike Cahill said he
had spent over a year in Houston.

"I like the area around River Oaks Country Club," Mottram
interrupted. "You know, that boulevard leading up to the tennis
courts, the one with all the big houses. But otherwise Houston
is too Latin for me."

"Latin?" Cahill repeated, puzzled.

"Too many Spanish-speaking people."

A moment later, when I mentioned I now live in Rome,
Mottram spoke up again. "A lovely city, but it's a desecration
what they've done to the monuments. All that graffiti! Italians
don't deserve the place! Rome doesn't belong to Italy!"

"Where do you think it should be?" I asked. "In London with
the Elgin Marbles?"

Ignoring me, Buster demanded, "What do contemporary Italians have in common with the grandeur of Rome? With the
great Caesars—Augustus, Hadrian, Marcus Aurelius?"

"Caligula?" Cahill taunted his partner.

"Yes." Buster laughed. "They have more in common with
Caligula. I shouldn't be surprised if they all killed their mothers.
Really, these Italians—"

"Our driver's Italian," Cahill said. "He speaks English."

"Oh, be honest. The Italians are terrible."

Like me, Cahill was growing uneasy. "Buster's just getting
warmed up for our next doubles match. But we're not playing
Italians, Buster. We're playing a Czech and a Frenchman. What
do you have against *them*?"

"I've never cared for the Frogs," Mottram said.

The Gerulaitis-Smid match was the best of the tournament thus far. Both men played well, especially Gerulaitis, who goes into a curious concatenation of nervous tics before serving. He bounces the ball, dips his left shoulder, and swivels his head as if darting a glance over his right shoulder. Depending upon how much pressure he feels, he may swivel his head three or four times per point, and with his gold cockscomb of hair and prominent nose, he resembles a rooster checking the henhouse for interlopers.

Tonight the interloper was Tomas Smid, a strong, rawboned Czech with a black mustache and a blistering topspin forehand. Pouncing on three straight second serves, he rushed the net and broke to a 4–3 lead in the first set. But Gerulaitis, quick and inventive, broke back, tossing up several well-disguised lobs for winners. Then he scored with a couple of crosscourt volleys that won the first set 7–5.

After that, Smid lost heart and began slapping at the ball as if at an annoying gnat, and with as much success. Gerulaitis bolted to a 5–1 advantage and hung on to take the set and match.

The next quarterfinal pitted Ivan Lendl against his friend and mentor, Wojtek Fibak. Lendl seemed to regard this as little more than a clinic in which he, the young and talented pupil, tore his coach to shreds as part of an advertising campaign to prove what a fine teacher the Pole had been. But the crowd, which had paid for competition, sounded displeased to get education as a second prize. When Lendl beat Fibak 6–3/6–0, there were boos and, in the press section, some grumbling.

"A coach shouldn't be allowed to play his pupil in a tournament," one journalist complained. "It doesn't look right."

I replied that Lendl was walloping everybody these days. He had just come back after having had a forty-four-match winning streak snapped and he seemed determined to take it out on his friend.

Still the journalist objected to the appearance of evil and ran through a list of possible abuses, of suspicions a spectator might carry away, of potential damage to the sport's integrity. After all, Lendl virtually lived with Fibak and his wife. How could they be friends and business partners all day, then true adversaries at night?

Saturday morning the weather turned balmy. A tour bus pulled up outside the Colombia-Excelsior and a group of officials and journalists climbed aboard for a trip to Portofino.

We were scheduled to be back for the semifinal between Buster Mottram and Vitas Gerulaitis. But when it took forty minutes to reach the mountainous outskirts of the city, I knew better than to expect to see any tennis before late afternoon. Russ Adams, the bald, roly-poly WCT Chief Photographer and Tour Public Relations man, was also quick to understand the situation, and this presented problems for him. Although he had been dispatched to record the PR junket for posterity, he was expected to return and take snapshots of the semifinals, too. In Portofino he herded us through the narrow streets to the dock, posed us in front of pastel buildings and fishnets, clicked a few shots, then urged us toward the bus.

But several men ducked into a swank boutique to buy sweaters; a few others visited the town church, then shopped for postcards and souvenirs. By the time they all straggled back, it was noon and they were hungry. When we were approaching the huge white wedding cake of the Grand Hotel Miramare, Russ Adams suggested we push on and eat lunch at the Palazzo dello Sport. No one, not even the driver, paid him any mind.

We filed up to the terrace and dutifully read a plaque commemorating Guglielmo Marconi, who on this spot, in 1933, "with a brilliant stroke of genius and perfection of technique transmitted for the first time by means of microwaves of 60 CM radio telegraphic and radio telephonic signals to a distance of 150 kilometers." Daunted by Marconi's accomplishment, we dashed into the hotel bar and drank up bowls of champagne punch that had been provided by the regional tennis federation. Then we staggered into the dining room and gobbled a meal whose courses, it seemed to me in my groggy state, served as a chart of some evolutionary chain showing the development of sea life from simple flaccid organisms to molluscs and bivalves and scuttling crustaceans and finally to finned creatures.

As we ate, dignitaries at the head table praised the wisdom of World Championship Tennis, the responsibility of the press, and the undeniable beauties of this coast. They also passed around a rather odd map of Europe which made it appear that Santa Margherita Ligure was centrally located, not tucked away in an obscure bend of a small bay. Lines radiated from the town to distant cities, suggesting that Tripoli, Bucharest, Warsaw, Istanbul, Moscow, and Sofia had airlines or rocket sleds that transported hordes of tourists to this hotel.

As the coffee arrived, the man to my left asked in accented English, "What are you doing here?"

He was short and sturdy, with a rich tan, deep crow's-feet at the corners of his eyes, and a dark tangle of hair. When I told him I was covering the tournament for AP he said he hadn't seen me before. He was an Italian umpire and knew most tennis journalists.

I admitted I was new to the tour and added that I wanted to learn about it and write a book.

Smiling, he assured me I'd never understand the game unless I learned what went on behind the scenes. Most reporters missed the point, he said. They watched matches, but ignored, or were ignorant of, the chief factors which influenced who won and lost.

And what were those factors? I asked.

If you wanted to know the game from the inside, he said, you had to start at the hotel, you had to look around, keep your ears open, and find out which players had paid their bills and checked out before their matches. Those players didn't intend to win. While spectators and reporters might speak of sub-par performances and upsets, this umpire spoke bluntly of players who tanked matches. In his opinion, several men this week had lost on purpose in singles, either because they wanted to rest for Davis Cup or because they had a chance to take a holiday now that the tournament in Copenhagen had been canceled.

How had he come to this conclusion?

He had officiated these matches, he said. More important, he had known who had checked out of the hotel.

Why would anyone throw a singles match, I asked, with so much prize money at stake?

He laughed at my innocence. Except for the winner's purse of $100,000, the prize money wasn't enough to sway most players. Unless a man felt sure he had a shot at the final—tennis players were realists; they all figured Lendl or Gerulaitis would win—then he had to make a hardheaded business decision. If, for example, he won his second-round match, a player was sure of getting $8,000. But if his agent had arranged an exhibition or an endorsement appearance later in the week for as little as $10,000, he could tank his second-round match, take the $4,000 that went to the loser, and come out ahead. Sometimes the question was that clear-cut. Should a man win a match and lose money? Or tank and fly elsewhere to make money?

In WCT tournaments, the umpire emphasized, there was one factor missing from the usual equation a player had to balance before he decided whether to tank or try his best. There were no ATP points. In Grand Prix events a man might stick around, hoping to improve his ranking. Even if it cost him a little money in the short run, he'd earn it back in the long run if he leapfrogged enough steps on the ladder. But on the WCT circuit there was only money. If he had a better deal or compelling personal reason to cut out early, it was strictly a financial decision, and some players were so well fixed they could afford to act in ways which seemed illogical to outsiders.

It would be difficult to judge whether I was more stunned by what the umpire said or by the casualness with which he said it. He made no effort to speak quietly, and, in fact, several people overheard us talking, joined the conversation, and added their agreement. They all thought that what the players did was wrong. But that was just the way things were. Or at least the way they believed things were. This itself seemed disturbing to me.

On the bus ride back to Genoa I sat alone, sunk deep in thought, profoundly troubled. Much of what I had learned that week reiterated a single theme. Life on the circuit was not what

I had expected, was not what it appeared to be. If Robyn Lewis was right, pro tennis was merely entertainment, and if the umpire could be believed, the entertainment often amounted to little more than burlesque.

By the time we returned to the Palazzo dello Sport, Buster Mottram had won the first set from Vitas Gerulaitis. But then, before we had a chance to recover from lunch and the heartburn-provoking bus ride, Gerulaitis roared back to take the next two sets—6–1/6–2—and advance to the final.

For Italian journalists this semifinal had a single thread of significance. How did Mottram figure to do against Italy next week in the Davis Cup? During the post-match press conference they asked Gerulaitis for a prediction. But the subject didn't engage his interest. Never lifting his eyes from the newspaper he was reading, he offered monosyllabic responses.

One reporter tried to capture Gerulaitis' attention by making his questions personal. "Will you play Davis Cup this year?"

"Arthur Ashe hasn't asked me to."

"If he asked you?"

"I've played before," said Vitas, flipping a page and letting his eyes rove down it. "I sort of like playing. But I told Arthur, 'Either ask me for the whole year or forget it. I mean I've got to make my schedule. Don't just come to me when you need me.' "

"But would you play if he needed you?"

"No. I'm not playing Davis Cup this year."

When there were no more questions, Gerulaitis dropped the newspaper to the floor as if it were a soiled Kleenex.

In the second semifinal that evening Vijay Amritraj managed to stay on even terms with Ivan Lendl by forcing him to rush his groundstrokes. On almost every point the tall, graceful Indian swooped to the net and volleyed. But Lendl broke Amritraj's service once in the first set and in the initial game of the second, and that was enough to cop the match 6–4/6–4.

Still Lendl bridled with dissatisfaction, as if he hated to lose a point, much less a game. Once, late in the second set, Vijay had hit a short shot, giving Lendl an easy put-away. As the Czech charged forward to murder it, Amritraj raised his arms in amiable submission, then was astonished when Lendl clobbered the ball wide.

The crowd laughed. So did Vijay. But the Czech saw nothing funny about it. He complained to the umpire that Amritraj's submissive gesture had distracted him. Ivan Lendl seemed to have everything a tennis champion needed except a sense of perspective and a sense of humor.

It was after one a.m. and Tony Giammalva and I sat in the lobby of the Colombia-Excelsior discussing hands. An outsider might assume it's enough for a tennis player to have fast, agile feet. But hands are important, too. John Newcombe, for instance, was never particularly swift or agile, yet he compensated with great hands, especially at the net, where touch is paramount. Among current players John McEnroe is reputed to have the best hands in the business, and he deploys them like shock absorbers, taking all the steam off the hardest passing shots as he flicks back low, angled volleys.

As I had already learned from Vitas Gerulaitis, some players have a critical problem with their hands. They perspire heavily and have a hard time holding on to the racquet.

Tony Giammalva had a different problem. Or, rather, a potential problem which he attended to periodically with a razor blade. From holding a racquet six or seven hours a day, his hand acquired a thick crust of calluses. Knobs of hard, dry skin covered his entire palm and each joint of his fingers. From time to time Giammalva had to shave down the layers of dead skin. Otherwise, blisters formed under the calluses. This had happened to Bjorn Borg at the 1978 U.S. Open, and he went into the final against Jimmy Connors with a hand so inflamed it felt as if he were squeezing a fistful of hot cinders. On several points the racquet came pinwheeling out of Borg's grasp, spiraling away along with his chances of winning the one title he still covets.

While Tony and I were talking, Buster Mottram and Mike Cahill, smoking their pipes and carrying two bottles of wine, took a table next to us. After losing the semifinals in singles, Mottram had teamed with Cahill to win in doubles, advancing to tomorrow's final. In a buoyant mood, they invited Tony and me to share the wine.

Only one thing diminished their delight—the disparity between the prize money for winners and losers. The first-place doubles team would receive $15,000, the runners-up $6,000. They complained that to earn any real money, they had to win. But they were pitted against a formidable team of Czechs, Tomas Smid and Pavel Slozil.

As usual, the players' minds were on fiscal matters, and for a few minutes the talk turned to tax shelters, investments, and the advantages of incorporation. One could understand their obsessions. These men were young and earning decent incomes, but tennis careers are short and few players, except those at the very top, can continue to market their names after retirement. And there was always the threat of injury. Mike Cahill's knee might force him to give up the game at age thirty.

Cahill asked Giammalva, "Are Lendl and Vitas splitting tomorrow?"

"I don't know," Tony said.

Cahill's question struck me as a non-sequitur. But I believed I knew the answer. I told him Gerulaitis was leaving Genoa Monday and driving to Milan with a few fellows. Lendl wasn't going with them.

The players laughed, then explained that Cahill wanted to know whether Gerulaitis and Lendl had agreed to split the prize money. In singles there was the same situation as in doubles. The great disparity between $100,000 for the winner and $32,000 for the loser invited secret pre-match deals to divide the pot. They doubted Lendl would do it. He was on a hot streak and thought he would win. But they mentioned WCT tournaments in which the finalists had split. This struck them as logical. Far better, they said, to go into a final knowing you'd come out with $66,000.

I asked if this was a common practice. They assured me it

was, although they added that it happened mostly in small tournaments, in special events and exhibitions, and on the WCT circuit, all of which tended to have huge prize-money differences.

Shortly after two a.m. Tony Giammalva left as two Australians, Ross Case and Rod Frawley, arrived. Frawley was with his new bride, whom he kissed and sent up to bed. The Aussies were also celebrating, but for a different reason than Mottram and Cahill. They had lost in doubles and were now out of the tournament and enjoying a little spree before moving on to the next town. Case had signed on to help coach the English Davis Cup team in Rome.

Since the Aussies had lost to Slozil and Smid, they offered tactical advice to Mottram and Cahill as we all killed off the wine. I returned to the subject of prize-money splitting, and they discussed in detail a "split" which had occurred in a tournament where ATP points were at stake. (They gave me the name of one of the players and I was later able to corroborate the entire incident with him.)

Frawley pointed out that the difference between winning and losing a final on the WCT wasn't just $68,000. The winner also received a $40,000 bonus for qualifying for the WCT finals in Dallas. Thus the disparity—and, in their view, the unfairness—was far greater.

They stressed, however, that splitting usually took place between players of comparable ability. "It's not going to happen between McEnroe and me," said Frawley, laughing.

His mention of McEnroe knocked the conversation off track. They all began discussing Frawley's strife-ridden, foul-humored semifinal with McEnroe at the 1981 Wimbledon. When asked what his reaction had been afterward in the locker room, Frawley blurted an obscenity. On court his mustachioed face tends to remain immobile. But he was considerably more animated as he offered his opinion of McEnroe.

"They say he's a perfectionist. That's why he's always complaining. They say he demands perfection from himself and expects it from the linesmen and umpire. But I have a tape of our match. I've been through it a few times. Know how many calls he questions? Seventeen! Know how many were even close enough for a second glance? Two! The other fifteen he was just bitching. Maybe he's doing it to fire himself up. Maybe it's to upset the other guy. But don't give me that stuff that he's doing it because he's a perfectionist. Like I say, on fifteen calls there wasn't anything to question."

In other sports, I said, players settled disputes among themselves when they felt the officials had fallen down on the job. Wasn't there an enforcer in professional tennis who was willing to confront guys like McEnroe and make sure he didn't step out of line again?

Although they all admitted they had been tempted to strike out at obnoxious players, they explained that there were heavy fines and suspensions for anyone who fought on court, in the locker room, or anywhere on the tournament premises.

Only Buster Mottram owned up to having hit a player. It had happened in Monte Carlo. While he was showering after losing a match, Hans Kary, an Austrian, had poured a Coca-Cola over his head and Buster had slugged him.

Conscientious about minute details, Mike Cahill explained a problem about prize-money splitting. If an American was involved, or if the tournament took place in the States, there were worrisome tax implications. One player could claim the winner's share on his IRS return and pay the lion's share of the taxes, while the other man claimed the lower amount. Then the two could work out the difference in yet another secret arrangement. But this was tax fraud, a serious criminal offense for foreigners and U.S. citizens alike.

The alternative was for a player to declare exactly what he had earned by splitting. But this left a record which could cause trouble if anyone ever decided to investigate.

This fear of an investigation was as close as any of them came to acknowledging that splitting itself might constitute fraud.

Abruptly, they all went back to talking about doubles and about players who had reputations as "headhunters" and "target volleyers"—guys who hit at you instead of into the open court. There were fellows who, as Frawley put it, liked to "leave the basic blue bruises on your chest." They recalled friends who had been felled like oaks by shots to the testicles. Then there was Lendl—he had decked Gerulaitis several times in the Masters, once smacking him flush on the forehead. "That one shot at the Masters," Gerulaitis says, "was really a legitimate shot. He hit me from the baseline. That was a cannon shot, one of the hardest shots I've ever seen. Fortunately, I have nothing in my head to really damage."

When Ron Andruff, the WCT European Marketing Manager, passed through the lobby carrying several bottles of white wine, they cadged one from him. Then they debated how to open it. It was after three a.m., the bar was closed, and the night clerk at the front desk didn't have a corkscrew. Finally, Cahill used his pipe tool to force the cork down into the bottle.

As they worked at the wine, I asked once more about splitting. Why wouldn't players prefer to go out and give their best and grab the winner's share?

They swore that when players agreed to split, they gave their best. In fact, as they saw it, once a man knew he'd come out of a final with a good piece of money, he could relax and put on a better performance.

Doubles was different. The players admitted they sometimes tanked, and they told stories, which they found amusing, about matches where both teams were trying to tank or, funnier yet, where one man didn't realize his partner was tanking.

"We shouldn't be talking about this in front of a journalist," Frawley suddenly said.

For an instant they all stared at me. But when I said nothing, they went on with their anecdotes about dumping matches.

At four a.m. two tall girls in mini-skirts, blond wigs, and cheap furs came tottering in spike heels down the central staircase.

"Do you think they're whores?" Mottram asked in a voice that carried through the lobby.

"Of course they're whores," Frawley shouted.

"I say, you speak Italian," Buster said to me. "Do talk to them. Get them to come over for some wine."

"I think they're through for the night."

"But do ask them," he urged me.

Frawley and Case were making loud lip-smacking sounds and calling out in English.

"Do translate," Mottram kept at me.

"I think they understand. They'll come over if they're in business."

"I do wish they'd come over," Buster said wistfully.

But the desk clerk unlocked the door and released the women into the night.

Later, reading Arthur Ashe's autobiography, *Off the Court*, I realized Mottram has good reason not to make his own approaches to creatures who catch his fancy. Several years ago in Richmond he brought a transvestite back to the hotel, a fact he remained in ignorance of until he reached his room. Moments later he careened down the hallway hollering, "It's a man, it's a man!"

"Don't worry, Buster," Case consoled Mottram. "You'll get laid in Rome. There are always whores around the hotel. We want you relaxed for the Davis Cup. During the day I'll train you by imitating Barazzutti." Hunching his shoulders, Case stood up and stalked around, giving a fair impersonation of the Italian player.

Mottram sipped his wine, then commented in a voice far dryer than this local vintage, "Barazzutti resembles a wingless fly."

Next day I woke at noon. Downstairs Russ Adams dogged Ivan Lendl's heels, snapping photos of the Czech as he left the hotel and headed for the Palazzo dello Sport for the final. Adams wanted a shot of Lendl lifting his suitcases into the trunk of a courtesy car. But Lendl refused. "I never touch." He shrugged his right shoulder. "My arm, you know." Lendl gestured for the bellboy to load his bags into the trunk.

I rode to the final with Ron Andruff and John McDonald, the WCT International Director and a former Australian Davis Cup player. They were discussing yesterday's local telecast of the semifinals.

"It was excellent," said McDonald, a short man with a high forehead and sad eyes. "The announcer was terrific. He gave a thorough background on WCT. The picture was clear. Top quality. The only problem was the shot from the court-level camera toward the umpire's chair. There was absolutely no one in the stands. But the promotional strips came across great."

"Yeah," said Andruff, a sturdy Canadian with a shock of wheat-colored hair. "When you're in the stands, the colors don't come across that strong. But on camera they jump right out at you."

"Especially the blue," McDonald agreed.

McDonald stared out beyond the port to the Mediterranean, which glinted like foil in the sunlight. "God, it's beautiful weather. Too bad we didn't have it all week. But then maybe that would have held down the crowds," he murmured, forgetting that there had been no crowds earlier in the week and everybody had blamed the low attendance on the bad weather. Now McDonald had a new worry: for him, there appeared to be a lead lining in every silver cloud. "This nice weather, it could cut into the crowd today. People like to be outside."

"I don't know. We've got a pretty attractive final," Andruff said. "A replay of the Masters."

A former professional hockey player, Ron Andruff was a rookie at tennis, but he had thrown himself into it, bulky shoulders first. He played whenever he could, and when there was no free court, he kept in shape by skipping rope in his room. It was a habit he had picked up during his hockey career. His team had arranged for all the players to take boxing lessons, and skipping rope was part of a boxer's training program.

Why boxing lessons? McDonald asked.

"To build up your confidence for when there are fights," Andruff said. "Most guys are afraid of getting hit in the face. They think it's really going to hurt. But it doesn't. Once you know and once you know a bit about boxing, it gives you confidence."

"But isn't it tough to get traction on the ice? A guy could just slip away from you."

"Well, what you do is, you grab the back of a man's jersey." Andruff extended a meaty hand, demonstrating. "Not the front.

The back. You see guys grabbing the front, but that's wrong. When you grab the back of a jersey, he can't move his head and you can pop him with your free hand."

At the Palazzo dello Sport thousands of spectators had gathered at the entrances, waiting to rush forward the instant the doors opened. To a foreign observer it appeared to be a convention of ham operators, for many people in the crowd carried radios. Not portable radios, but car radios which they had had the foresight to unbolt from their dashboards to prevent thieves from stealing them during the match.

Inside, the lights and the heat had been turned on now that they weren't needed. Behind three flag-bearers, the Fila Team—ball boys and girls, linesmen, and umpire—marched onto the court and stood in formation. When a scratchy recording of the Italian national anthem blared from the loudspeaker, the crowd came more or less to attention, and the red-green-and-white flag was dipped. Then the Czech anthem boomed forth and its flag was dipped. And finally there was "The Star-Spangled Banner" and the red-white-and-blue was dipped.

After these flourishes I feared that the final would degenerate into mere entertainment. But it proved to be tennis—pure, exhilarating tennis. Lendl started off hitting with the force of a cannon, threatening to reduce Gerulaitis to so much fodder. Vitas tried to chip to Lendl's backhand and rush the net, but the ball zoomed back at him at such velocity he couldn't control his volleys. Lendl quickly broke to a 5–1 lead.

Struggling to stay alive in the set, Gerulaitis put more work on his first serve. Twice he thought he had won the game with aces; twice Lendl scrabbled to deuce. It took twenty points to do it, but Vitas held to 5–2.

Along with the game, the Czech appeared to lose some of his composure. When he double-faulted to 5–3, Gerulaitis held to 5–4 and then broke to 5–5 by changing tactics. Usually he tried to break down Lendl's backhand, hitting to it a dozen times in a row. But now he slapped a ball wide to Lendl's forehand, sprinted in behind it, and knocked off a volley.

The set went to a tie-break, and once more Lendl leaped to a formidable lead, 3–0. But Gerulaitis kept clawing away, and when he broke to 4–3, the Czech exploded and smacked a ball into the translucent dome of the arena. Vitas ran off three more unanswered points to win the first set in just over an hour.

In the second set Lendl suffered an early service break, and it seemed that his volatile nature had betrayed him. Yet although he lost his temper, he never lost control. Anger appeared to sharpen his concentration and his groundstrokes. He broke Vitas' serve three times in succession to capture the second set 6–4.

Gerulaitis continued to scurry around the court, yoyoing from corner to corner, from baseline to net and back. But Lendl had lifted the level of his game, and Vitas couldn't stay with him. When Gerulaitis hit with pace, Lendl sent the ball screaming back at triple speed. When he went for angles, Lendl proved himself the superior geometrician, hitting wider and wider until he chased Vitas into the box seats. The tall Czech won five games straight and took the set 6–2.

Gerulaitis never recovered. His gold cockscomb of hair drooped into wet ringlets, and his pink shirt turned blood red in damp splotches. During change-overs he dutifully retaped his racquet handle, but his attention to this detail seemed less practical than poignantly ritualistic, as if, like those men in prison camps, he believed he could hold off some unfathomable calamity by the simple expedient of shaving every day and giving his shirttails a military tuck.

On the opposite side of the net his executioner went about business in a perfunctory manner. Lendl got a service break early and made it stand up to win the fourth and final set 6–3.

I didn't wait around to watch the awards ceremony during which Lendl received a $100,000 cardboard Barclay's check as big as a pantry door.

DAVIS CUP

NEXT week in Rome, I went to the Foro Italico, which bustled with preparations for the Davis Cup confrontation between Great Britain and Italy. There I met Vittorio Selmi, the European Tournament representative for the Association of Tennis Professionals. Although based in Italy, Selmi spends much of his time on the road following the Grand Prix circuit from city to city, attending to the players' problems. Owlish and professorial in horn-rimmed glasses, he's an unfailingly patient and helpful man who speaks excellent English.

As we talked first in general terms, Selmi expressed a common concern that the top players were often selfish and unfeeling toward lower-ranked men. Jimmy Connors, Guillermo Vilas, and Vitas Gerulaitis refused to join the ATP, and other stars who were members failed to abide by the spirit, and sometimes the letter, of the union's by-laws.

There were also too few men, he said, who had drawing power. McEnroe, Borg, Connors, Lendl, Gerulaitis, and Vilas—they had marketable images; fans would pay to watch them play. Eliot Teltscher, Peter McNamara, Sandy and Gene Mayer might be almost as good, but they didn't attract spectators or sponsors. For promoters, the temptation was to avoid the risk of a tournament and invest in exhibitions and special events where they could guarantee match-ups between bankable names. The problem was, once people had seen a special event involving Borg, McEnroe, Gerulaitis, and Connors, they wouldn't accept anything less in tournaments. And once players were spoiled by the immense pay-offs for exhibitions, they had less appetite for competitions in which they might be knocked out in an early round and earn only a few thousand dollars.

It was a curious paradox, Selmi conceded. Tournaments helped a player build his reputation. But the higher he climbed on the computer, the less dependent he was on tournaments and the more he could concentrate on exhibitions. It had reached the point where the public couldn't distinguish among events. Wimbledon, the French Open, and the U.S. Open remained important. But everything else had slipped into the same category, and fans and some sports reporters no longer seemed to care about the distinction between a legitimate tournament and a barnstorming tour that bore more resemblance to vaudeville than to tennis.

Even Davis Cup had declined in significance. Some of the best players—Connors, Borg, Orantes, Higueras, Clerc—often skipped this traditional competition, claiming injury, exhaustion, the press of family or professional obligations. But generally it came down to money.

It was true, Selmi told me, that Davis Cup continued to be important in some countries as a matter of national pride. But many players regarded it as just another marketing device, a means of keeping their endorsement fees high. While a man like Adriano Panatta might no longer have much impact on tennis worldwide, he could maintain his great popularity, not to mention his sizable income, in Italy by representing his country.

When I asked Vittorio Selmi if he thought that tournament tennis had been hurt by conflicts of interest, I expected him to insist that I explain what I meant. But he defined the situation for me, saying that of course it was a conflict when an agent promoted a tournament and also represented many of the players in it. He saw no harm, however, as long as players were accepted on the basis of their computerized ranking. If an agent restricted a tournament to his own clients, that would be wrong. Otherwise . . . Selmi shrugged. Agents might receive double, triple, or quadruple fees, they might achieve an unregulated influence far greater than that of the elected officials in the game, but that didn't seem to bother the ATP.

, As for appearance money and guarantees, he readily admitted these pay-offs were commonplace. He described a case in which a player had come to the ATP and accused a tournament of offering him an illegal inducement. But what could be done about it? "It's all black money," Selmi said. "It's under the table. How can you trace it? How can you prove it?"

The rule didn't strike me as so difficult to enforce, especially since the Pro Council Administrator was empowered to demand from players and tournament officials all records "relating in any way to such alleged guarantee[s]." With this information at its disposal and with so much loose talk on the tour, what was to prevent the Pro Council from eradicating what Harold Solomon had called "a cancer in the game"? Couldn't it start by capitalizing on the honesty of the player who charged that he had been offered a guarantee?

No, Selmi didn't think it was that simple. He repeated that it was all "black money" and nothing could be proved.

"What about 'splits'?" I asked, using the term players had used to describe prize-money sharing.

There was no pause, no effort at evasion, on Selmi's part. "It's the same," he said. "Of course it's going on. You hear the players talk about it. But it's a private arrangement. How could you police it?"

"Is there an ATP rule against splitting prize money?"

"We say how large the tournaments have to be, how many players, how much prize money. What private arrangements the players make among themselves . . ." His voice trailed off and he shrugged again,

"But you've heard about this?" I asked.

"Yes, it goes on. But it's between the players."

I returned to the Foro Italico on a cold, damp morning. Buster Mottram had complained that it was absurd to play outdoors on the first Friday in March and to schedule the opening match for 10:30 a.m. They should have played indoors, he said. But the Italians had no intention of doing that. Last year, on a fast indoor carpet in Brighton, Great Britain had upset Italy, and this year the Italians preferred to catch chilblains rather than make a concession to nature and risk another ignominious defeat.

Despite the home-court advantage, Italy's chances looked shaky. Corrado Barazzutti had come down with influenza after a week of dodging between the WCT tournament and the national club championships, and Adriano Panatta hadn't won a match since the previous October.

As he warmed up with Mottram, Panatta's handsome face was puffy, his haunches were heavy and slow. When he removed his jacket, there were snickers and rude comments from the bleachers. It wasn't just that Adriano had a paunch. He was wearing an undershirt whose shoulder straps were visible under the elegant turquoise tennis shirt which bore his name. The effect was laughable; it was as if he had worn sweat socks with a tuxedo.

But while Panatta had lost his waistline, he had not lost his touch. Disinclined to move himself, he made Mottram do all the running. Jerking his lanky opponent around with dropshots and deft lobs, he survived two set points and won the first set 7–5. In the second, with the crowd chanting his name, "Ad-ree-ano! Ad-ree-ano!" he saved three more set points, but Mottram ran down a dropshot to turn the tables on him, 7–5.

After that, Panatta had little left except a tragedian's sense of histrionic style. He gesticulated peevishly at the slippery court, at the perfidious ball which refused to do his bidding, and at the flags around the court which snapped in the wind. During a brief cloudburst Buster served out the third set 6–3, and after a ten-minute rest he returned to take a 4–1 lead in the fourth set.

By now the sky had turned dark and threatening, and so had the Italian crowd. Not content to cheer for their idol, they threw coins at Mottram and at the small clutch of English spectators who clustered around an old man in a top hat and a bright red John Bull costume. The old man waved the Union Jack and exhorted his followers, a group known as BATS, an acronym for the British Association of Tennis Supporters. Fortunately, they didn't appear to suffer any serious casualties, but everybody was relieved when Mottram served for the match in the fourth set.

The umpire tried to hush the crowd—"*Silenzio, per favore*"—and for an instant there was silence. Then, as Mottram tossed up the ball, someone screamed, "Keep quiet. He just broke his prick." Mottram caught the ball, recomposed himself, and killed the crowd's hopes, 6–4.

Adriano Panatta had showered before coming to the press conference, and his damp, pageboy-length hair framed the face of a *pariolino*, a boy from the wealthy Roman suburb of Parioli. To say someone is a *pariolino* is to accuse him of being spoiled and insolent. At this point in his career Panatta may be exactly that, but in the beginning his connection with Parioli was tenuous. His father was a custodian at the local tennis club, and like many European pros, Adriano entered the world of upperclass privilege through the back door. Now he had to contend with the unreasonable expectations of his fans and the fickleness of the Italian press.

"Are you surprised Mottram beat you?" a reporter asked.

"Surprised? No," Panatta said. "He played well. But I'm disappointed. You journalists all said I'd lose. I didn't think I would, but you did."

"Are you tired?"

"No."

"You haven't played much lately. You looked tired."

"I'm not tired," he insisted.

"You're wearing an undershirt," another reporter said. "You're playing now with a mid-size racquet. Is this because you're getting old?"

The pretty face glowered, but his voice was icily polite. "Many young players use big racquets. That means nothing. As for the undershirt, I wore it because I was cold. It's a cold day. Weren't you cold?"

"Will you play the doubles?" he was asked, as if he might be contemplating an abrupt retirement.

"Do I have a choice? Is there some way I can get out of it?"

The questioning continued with the cruel persistence of bear-baiting, particularly after Panatta revealed that he was leaving Rome right after the Davis Cup and flying to the Caribbean for two weeks of exhibitions. He didn't intend to play a real tournament until the end of March. At this rate, at the age of thirty-two, he'd never get back into shape, much less into championship form.

The Italians weren't interested in talking to Buster Mottram. They abandoned him to the British press, which asked for his opinion of the crowd.

"Terrible," Buster said. "They're animals."

During the second match a light drizzle fell and the pressureless Pirelli balls, slow and heavy under normal circumstances, became encrusted with clay and as spongy as lumps of mozzarella cheese. Corrado Barazzutti camped on the baseline, blunting the net charges of Richard Lewis, a blond lefthander who realized his lone hope was to finish every point quickly. After Lewis squandered his chance to serve out the first set, the match was reduced to a tedious war of attrition, with both men doing little more than shoveling the wet ball back and forth and praying for a lucky bounce or a netcord. With the score knotted at 8–8, still in the first set, play was postponed because of darkness.

By morning the sky had cleared, the court had dried, and Barazzutti quickly asserted his superiority. He finished the first set 11–9, then broke Lewis' service six times in a row to reel off the next two sets 6–1/6–1.

That afternoon Adriano Panatta joined Paolo Bertolucci against Jonathan Smith and Andrew Jarrett. Last year England had won the doubles, which was the key to their victory. Excited by the prospect of another upset, the British press arrived in force, and up in the stands the old man in the top hat and John Bull costume cheered on his legion of BATS.

On court the Italians didn't look much like a team. For one thing, they dressed differently. Panatta, as always, wore his personal line of sports apparel; Bertolucci was under contract to a clothing outfit called Schiopwatch. For another thing, while Panatta is a bit swollen around the midsection, Bertolucci is downright round. Nicknamed "the Pasta Kid," he has for years pursued a training program in which *fettuccine*, cigarettes, and lots of rest figure prominently. But somehow it works for him in doubles, where he doesn't need to run. Again and again against the English he kept the ball alive and cleverly set up shots which Panatta hit for winners. The Italians brushed aside Jarrett and Smith in straight sets.

On Sunday Mottram had to beat Barazzutti to keep England's hopes alive. His teammates, dressed as if for an assault on Mount Everest in red down-filled parkas provided by Coca-Cola, sat on the sidelines shouting encouragement. The section reserved for the Italian team was occupied by hangers-on, no players.

In a sloppy match marred by ludicrous mistakes and incessant service breaks, Buster got a set point at 5–4, but butchered a forehand volley while Barazzutti lay face down in the clay. Mottram wasted three more set points before he won 6–4.

After Mottram took the second set 6–3, the officiating turned as ragged as the play. Several times the umpire had to overrule the linesmen and points were replayed because of suspicious calls. When Barazzutti got a bad bounce, he slashed at the court with his racquet, gouging out a divot that had to be repaired by a man with a shovel. Looking close to tears or to some terrible act of self-abasement, the Little Soldier dropped serve yet again and Mottram ended his and everyone else's misery 7–5.

At the press conference a reporter asked Buster to repeat his opinion of the crowd's behavior.

"Terrible," he said.

Was it true, an Italian journalist inquired, that Mottram had called the Italians animals?

Buster adopted a detached, scientific attitude, "We're all animals, aren't we? Isn't that what Darwin wrote?"

"But did you say the Italian people are animals?"

"Who said I said it?"

"It was in yesterday's *Daily Mirror*," The reporter flourished a rolled newspaper. "It's right here."

Mottram acted surprised, then angry. He couldn't very well deny what he had said, but clearly he had not expected to be quoted. His scientific detachment evaporated. "If this line of questioning continues, the press conference is over. If you want to talk about tennis and today's match, I'll stay."

While they stayed to talk tennis, I went up to the dining room as the deciding singles match started between Panatta and Richard Lewis. The place had only a few scattered customers, but I had to beg a waiter to clear a table and serve me. He was anxious to return to the kitchen, where the cooks and other waiters were settling in to watch the match on a portable TV.

When the restaurant had emptied of everybody except me, a tall, gray-haired gentleman glided in. It was Cino Marchese, a ubiquitous figure on the professional tour. Before I set out on the circuit, I had been told that Marchese knew as much about the business machinations behind men's tennis as anyone in Europe, and in January I had interviewed him in his home, a sumptuous Roman apartment embedded in a crumbling palazzo. A garrulous man of great charm and aplomb, he had turned the interview into a dramatic performance.

Percolating with energy, he talked to me while pacing the floor, he talked to me while slouched on a sofa, and he continued talking to me even while he held a telephone to his ear and waited for a call to go through so that he could talk to somebody else. It was a portable telephone with an aerial, and Marchese carried it around the living room speaking in French, in Italian, and in flavorful English.

After one call he smiled and flourished his free hand. "That was my banker. I have no time to go to the bank, so my banker comes to me."

If Cino Marchese sometimes seems a bit taken with himself and the sound of his stentorian voice, he has good reason. His family had been in the jewelry business for five generations, as had so many of the people in his native village of Valenza Po, and he could easily have coasted along in guaranteed luxury for the rest of his life. But in middle age he grew bored and began looking for a new interest, a new channel for his talent.

"Tennis," he told me, "is often difficult and frustrating, but it's better than every year buying gold and going always to Tel Aviv to buy diamonds. I wanted to try a different business."

Not that he had forgotten the first principle of his family business. Selling jewelry, he said, was not all that different from selling tennis players, and he could call on years of retailing experience whenever he faced a problem. "There is no college for what I do. You prepare yourself by plunging in and doing. You go around and meet the peoples and get to be known. Then you either have the daring to do something or you don't."

Marchese had had the daring, the inventiveness, and the stereoscopic vision to get involved in virtually every aspect of what he calls "this business of tennis. Or should I say, this tennis business?"

Marchese was the Italian agent for Mark McCormack's International Management Group. In addition, he represented an ambitious new line of tennis apparel from Cerrutti 1881, which Jimmy Connors was under contract to wear—"Jimmy calls me 'the Spaghetti Man,' " Cino boasted—and in conjunction with several financial backers, he controlled the marketing and promotional rights to the Italian Open. He served as tournament director for Volvo Grand Prix events in Palermo, Bologna, and Venice, and for other tournaments in Bari and Perugia. At the same time, he organized exhibitions and special events, promoted clinics with John Newcombe and John Alexander, and represented "various informal interests." Finally, he was a journalist and churned out an occasional article on tournaments in which he had a direct or indirect interest. Unlike Connors, most people on the circuit call Cino Marchese "the Silver Fox," and not just because of his mop of gray hair.

That Sunday at the Davis Cup, Cino took a chair by my table, ordered a light lunch of cheese and fruit, and interrupted our conversation from time to time to check the portable TV and see how his client Adriano Panatta was doing. Although convinced Panatta would win, he wasn't altogether pleased with him. For one thing, he thought Panatta's upcoming Caribbean tour was a mistake. There wasn't enough money in it—just $40,000 for two weeks, Cino said—to make it worth the time away from tournament tennis. For another thing, Marchese couldn't forget what Panatta and his Davis Cup teammates had done to their former captain, Nicola Pietrangeli.

In Marchese's opinion, Pietrangeli had been the ideal captain. The greatest player in national history, he had won the Italian Open three times and the French Open twice. Just as important, he was a handsome man with enormous crowd appeal and the respect of tennis people throughout the world. Since a Davis Cup captain's job is less that of coach than of public-relations man, Pietrangeli had been perfect.

The problem was he was *too* perfect, too appealing, and the Italian players resented the attention he got. After a victory they felt Pietrangeli was too quick to take the limelight, casting them into the shadows, and after a loss they were enraged when he told the press that they needed to train harder. But in the end, as so often in professional tennis, their animosity had its foundation in finance. They objected that Pietrangeli was making too much money. Whenever he signed a clothing contract, endorsed a product, or made a promotional appearance, the players reacted as if every dollar that went to Pietrangeli came out of their pockets. Finally, they insisted that he be replaced by someone more malleable and less marketable.

As Cino explained it, "Italians are always wanting to murder somebody in the back. It was the same from the time of the Caesars."

Like a broker discussing the marketplace, he then brought me up to date on Bjorn Borg. The Swede was scheduled for a Grand Prix tournament in Monte Carlo in April, but there was no predicting whether he would consent to play the qualies. And if he played, Cino said, it was impossible to guess how he would perform.

As a Mark McCormack agent, Marchese worried that the company's most valuable tennis asset might stray. He expressed

the conviction—perhaps it was more in the nature of a hope—
that Bjorn would remain "loyable." But one could only guess
what Borg was doing and would do.

Cino believed that Bjorn was not just bored and fatigued. He
was deeply frustrated by his failure to win the U.S. Open, particularly in 1980, when the Swede thought that a few bad calls
had robbed him of victory. On court he hadn't complained, but
afterward, Cino said, he had seethed for months and had wondered whether being always a gentleman, always quiet, hadn't
deprived him of the final prize, the only prize that now interested
him.

As for McEnroe, Marchese had been in frequent contact with
his father, and he repeated what he had first told me at his
apartment in January. He was "negotiating" with Mr. McEnroe,
Sr., to persuade John to play the Italian Open. Cino was putting
together a deal between McEnroe and Lipton Tea, Italy. The
details were still being hammered out, but Cino was hopeful,
very hopeful.

Why, I asked, was there any necessity to "negotiate" with
players or their agents? The Italian Open was a prestigious title,
Rome was an attractive city, and the prize money had been
increased this year from $200,000 to $300,000.

Shaking his head, Cino combed his fingers through his silver
hair. I just didn't understand how hard it was to ensure the
appearance of star players. Look at last week's WCT tournament
in Genoa—a $300,000 purse, $100,000 for the winner, yet only
two top-ten players had entered. In Marchese's opinion, prize
money was a relatively insignificant factor for the best players.

"Here's how I break it down. For the top players, prize money
matters about fifteen percent. The place and the people they
know at a tournament may count about fifteen percent. ATP
points influence them thirty percent. But, most important, forty
percent of what influences them [to play a tournament] is what
they can get guaranteed, what they know they'll get just for
showing up."

What could they get? I asked.

"Anywhere from $50,000 to $100,000. But it's really only the top four or five players—McEnroe, Borg, Lendl, Connors, and maybe Vilas or Clerc if the tournament's in South America—who command that kind of money. These are the players who make a difference at the gate. Then there are men like Panatta who matter in a particular country. And although he's not so high in the rankings any more, Vitas Gerulaitis is important because of his image." (At about the same time, the *Washington Post* published an article containing similar allegations about appearance money and naming Borg, McEnroe, Lendl, Connors, and Gerulaitis and the sums they were said to be paid. The allegations were denied by representatives of the players.)

I said I had heard that whenever there was a great disparity between the winner's and loser's shares in a final, the players were apt to split. Cino agreed. It just went to prove his point: prize money mattered only about fifteen percent. The real jackpot was in guarantees and appearance money.

After Adriano Panatta served out the third set against Richard Lewis, icing a 3–2 win for Italy, hordes of spectators swarmed over the court. The flock of BATS fluttered down from their aerie, led by the doddering old man waving the Union Jack. Immediately he was engulfed by Italian kids, some of them on the mean edge of adolescence. They jostled him, they screamed obscenities, they knocked off his top hat, they tried to wrestle away his flag. Someone handed him an Italian flag and he waved that, too, in a display of good sportsmanship and international harmony. But the brats kept clawing at the leader of the BATS until he stumbled to his knees.

Afraid he had had a stroke or a heart attack, I bolted from the press section and fought my way to his side. Slipping an arm around the frail, beating birdcage of his ribs, I raised him to his feet.

"Are you all right?" I asked.

He nodded. His face was like antique parchment. He must have been eighty years old.

"Let's go before you get hurt," I said.

But he dug his heels into the clay. "Thank you. I'm fine now." Then he shoved aside my hand and scurried back into the maelstrom of kids and BATS.

I stood there watching him. He didn't want help; he felt no need to be rescued. Maybe I had over-reacted. Maybe I had been over-reacting ever since I set out on the circuit. Perhaps these tennis fanatics—fans and players, officials and agents— were a distinct tribe with mores that couldn't be judged, much less changed, by an outsider. They could only be observed and recorded. Like an anthropologist living among people who worshiped dirt or drank human blood or sacrificed their firstborn, I decided I would collect data, but leave it to others to determine what, if anything, should be done.

STRASBOURG

CATCHING an overnight train, I arrived in Strasbourg at daybreak and hiked to a taxi stand through a cold, pelting rain, dragging my luggage, which I had packed for a month on the road. The city, built on the banks of the Rhine across the river from Germany, was more Teutonic than French. Rows of half-timbered houses and shops with steep, gabled roofs loomed over brooding canals, and pollarded tree trunks, as stark as pieces of *avant-garde* sculpture, stood vigil in barren parks that looked as though they had been buffed clean.

The cab brought me to what appeared to be an enclave of America. The streets were broad, and grassy fields opened on either side. Each house had its own yard, surrounded by a superfluous fence. A Holiday Inn had been cloned to this corner of France and, behind it, a Hilton Hotel had been grafted onto a patch of sod that was still struggling to take root.

The Hilton was the official hotel of the WCT tournament in Strasbourg and provided rooms at half-price to players and journalists. The lobby, deserted at dawn, looked murderously efficient and new. A man plugged into a computer checked me in by punching out a program on a strip of aluminum foil, which he sheathed in cardboard. This was my room "key."

The room itself might have been designed by robots for robots. There was a glass coffee table on a trestle of tubular chrome. A lamp, also of tubular chrome, described a glittering parabola over the table and chairs. Muzak emanated from some mysterious source. Fiddling with a panel of buttons beside the bed, I managed to turn it down, but not off. Yet in my fiddling I flicked on the television, which broadcast an English version of Sergio Leone's spaghetti western *Nobody Is My Name*. Near the TV a refrigerated mini-bar offered everything from Coca-Cola to Moët et Chandon champagne.

Tempted as I was by the champagne, I went down to the coffee shop for breakfast. On the way I paused in the lobby at the deserted WCT hospitality desk, where the tournament draw and the results of first-round matches were posted on a bulletin board. John McEnroe, the top seed, had been scratched and his name replaced by Tom Cain, No. 668 on the ATP computer. Adriano Panatta and Andres Gomez of Ecuador had also pulled out; they were on the Caribbean exhibition junket. Third-seeded Johan Kriek of South Africa had been upset by the seesaw score of 1–6/7–6/6–0, by Trey Waltke, a man ranked more than a hundred rungs beneath him. These defections and upsets had depleted the top half of the draw and left Ivan Lendl as the lone gate attraction in the tournament.

Russ Adams, the WCT Chief Photographer and Tour Public Relations man, was in the coffee shop contemplating a basket of *croissants*. He looked up as I came in and welcomed me to his table. Normally cheerful, Adams seemed downcast this morning. He was awake early, he explained, to catch a flight to Miami for a United States Tennis Association meeting. Then he had to turn right around and fly back to Strasbourg for the finals on Sunday.

But it wasn't the prospect of this grueling transatlantic trip that had got him down. It was the tournament. McEnroe's withdrawal was the kind of catastrophe you couldn't predict and couldn't prevent, he said. Having twisted an ankle last week in Brussels, John looked as though he'd be out of action a month or more. It was a serious, legitimate injury. Yet the local tournament director, a rock-concert promoter called Harry Lapp, was furious and so was the French press, which charged that the announcement of McEnroe's withdrawal had been delayed to prevent damage to ticket sales. But Russ Adams insisted McEnroe had a right to wait until the last possible minute before making up his mind.

The last possible minute had been Monday at midnight, long after many first-round matches had finished. This meant the draw couldn't be redrafted to shift more balance into the top half. Now that Kriek had lost, most of the strong players were bunched in the bottom of the draw with Lendl. These men were almost as irate as Harry Lapp and the French press, for while they were knocking off each other, a mediocre player in the top half would have a cakewalk into the finals.

There had been still more trouble. Sandy Mayer, a real "locker-room lawyer," according to Russ Adams, had demanded a meeting with WCT officials to discuss the inequitable distribution of prize money in doubles.

When Zeno Pfau, the WCT Tour Supervisor and Referee, joined us, the litany of laments continued. Where Adams is a paunchy, bald, paternal figure, Pfau is a small, compact man with dark hair slicked down close to his skull. Since his job is to oversee the linesmen and umpires and to serve as final arbiter of the rules, a lot of complaints and problems land on his head. Just yesterday the linesmen had struck twice, and each time it had taken half an hour to coax them back to work. These linesmen were amateurs, Zeno told me, mostly town kids who were paid sandwiches and free tickets to the tournament. According to their interpreters, they had struck for full meals and more tickets. It may have been that the linesmen had previously been promised meals and more tickets; Zeno didn't speak French. Then again, he said, maybe they had smartened up and realized they had the leverage to make a few demands.

A waitress interrupted us. Russ Adams ordered cold cereal and fruit. Zeno Pfau asked for stewed prunes and scrambled eggs and bacon. "Make that bacon well done," he said. Then all talk swung inexorably back to the troubles.

Both men placed much of the blame on Philippe Chatrier. President of the French Tennis Federation and of the International Tennis Federation, Chatrier was a member of the Pro Council, which was intimately involved with "the other tour," the Volvo Grand Prix. WCT officials believed that Chatrier was responsible for the refusal of local tennis authorities to provide professional linesmen and the failure of any French players to compete in Strasbourg. Interestingly, the French players had chosen to participate in a minor Grand Prix event in Metz that offered only $75,000 in prize money.

Most distressing of all, however, there would be no live television coverage. Here they were offering more prize money than any regular tournament in French history, and they still couldn't get on TV. Pfau and Adams felt Philippe Chatrier must have exerted his considerable political influence to kill the possibility of a deal with any of the nationally controlled channels.

While the French press was covering the tournament, they seemed to regard it as some sort of traveling circus, and they had come down hard after Kriek's match, virtually accusing him of tanking. Well, Zeno said, Kriek had called him in the middle of the night and had asked for a doctor. That certainly suggested there was a medical reason for his feeble performance in the third set.

But even in complete health Kriek was an emotional player, explosive, easily flustered, capable of bolting to a big lead, then blowing it.

In Pfau's opinion, the whole question of tanking was something people tended to sensationalize. He wasn't claiming it never happened. But how could you be sure? How could you prove it when players had the talent to hit an inch or two from the line—in or out—with every stroke? Although it was his job to enforce the rule requiring "best effort," that was a difficult judgment call, just educated guesswork. "It can happen in any sport. How can you tell for sure? You can shave points in basketball. You can shank a field goal or drop a pass in football." One WCT official, who later requested anonymity, told me, "I don't care if people tank, as long as they put on a good show."

Wednesday morning I went to the court early to watch a first-round match between José Luis Damiani, the greatest player in the history of Uruguay, and Tom Cain, who had been substituted for McEnroe. Cain was a "lucky loser"—that is, the highest-ranked player to lose in the last round of the qualies. While critics had charged that WCT tournaments would be a bonanza for stars, they were turning out to be a gravy train for some low-ranked players.

The Rhenus Hall, where the tournament was held, resembled a huge garage. Normally it housed exhibits of industrial products, or hordes of screaming rock fans who thronged Harry Lapp's concerts. Now a blue carpet had been laid in one corner and surrounded by temporary stands. Empty stands. At this hour there wasn't a single paying customer.

Overhead hung a high-tech heaven of steel beams, air ducts, and fat pipes that interfered with lobs. Since the net was strung on an aluminum frame, let serves set off a racket like a marble rattling down a drainpipe. Damiani didn't much like this, and he liked it less when, leading 4–2 and 40–0 in the first set, he got what he believed was a bad call. Shouting "mother," "whore," and "shit"—he was speaking Spanish and so received no penalties—he began blasting balls yards beyond the baseline. After Cain came back to take the set in a tie-break, Damiani frittered away the second set 6–3, as if he cared nothing about the $4,000 riding on the match.

In his press conference Damiani announced he had no intention of playing any more indoor tournaments. He couldn't wait to get outdoors on clay. Confessing that he was not in shape, he confirmed the French press's doubts about this tournament by remarking, "It's a good chance to work on your game. With no ATP points, it's not as important."

Meanwhile, on court the Strasbourg tournament was fast losing its importance for Eddie Dibbs as well. A stumpy battler from Miami, Dibbs, the No. 6 seed, was struggling against Heinz Gunthardt, a supple Swiss who could rally from the baseline or rush the net and volley. Both men were bothered by the officiating and objected when the umpire kept calling the score wrong. Dibbs shouted at the Tour Supervisor, "Wanna fine the ump, Zeno? He made a mistake. Fine him! Oh, I see. It's only players who get fined for mistakes."

Dibbs sputtered and crashed 6–0 in the second set.

Back at the Hilton, several players sat in the lobby discussing John McEnroe's last-minute withdrawal. They claimed this must have been the result of a strategic agreement. By pulling out after the tournament had started, McEnroe could maintain—and WCT could support him—that he had "played" a WCT event and therefore, as the reigning Wimbledon and U.S. Open champ, he qualified for the WCT finals in Dallas.

But someone shot a hole in this theory by paraphrasing Rule 10, a kind of Catch 22 whereby WCT retained the right to change or violate its own rules—to do anything, in fact, which it considered to be in the best interests of its tour. If they wanted McEnroe in the finals, WCT could offer him a wild-card entry.

Trey Waltke, who had upset Johan Kriek, muttered, "I know what would happen to me if I signed to play here, then dropped out at the last minute. They'd fine me."

"That's the difference between you and . . . ." A journalist let his voice die, reluctant to emphasize the obvious. It was the difference between being No. 1 and No. 121.

That evening I rode to the Rhenus Hall with Sandy Mayer, an American who, like his younger brother Gene, is generally described as intelligent, articulate, and outspoken. Both graduated from Stanford University with degrees in political science, and both refer to themselves as staunch Christians. But there the similarities end. While Gene is round-faced and boyish in appearance, Sandy, four years older, has sharply chiseled features and a receding hairline.

When I told Mayer I was writing a book about the circuit, he said it had been done before and recited several titles that are essentially lyrical hymns in praise of the game.

I said I had something different in mind, an accurate account.

"Impossible," Sandy replied. "I just don't see how you could do it."

"What do you see as my biggest problem?"

"To do a book about the tour and show the way it really is, you'd have to be able to gain the complete confidence of the players. Then, to give a true picture, you'd have to be the kind of person who would violate that confidence."

I didn't intend to violate anyone's confidence, I told Mayer. I made it my practice to inform players at the start that I was gathering information for a book. If they didn't want to talk, I left them alone. But so far most people had shown little reluctance to discuss subjects which I would have thought were taboo. Admitting I had heard some troubling things, I added, "Life on the circuit is different from the way most outsiders imagine it."

Mayer spoke slowly, choosing his words with care. "I don't think tennis players are any different from other young, vital, physically talented people, whether they're rock stars, actors, members of royalty, anybody constantly in the spotlight." Then after a pause, "Anybody in the spotlight who has no responsibilities and feels he has no obligations to anyone except himself."

I was curious whether there wasn't one crucial difference between tennis players and the kinds of media creatures he had mentioned. "You guys have to stay in shape, don't you? I don't see you dying in your beds of drug overdoses."

We had reached the Rhenus Hall, and Sandy was taking his racquets from the trunk. "When I first came on the tour, there was only one drug that was regularly abused and that was alcohol. Some of the older guys overdid it and they're addicted. Now, of course, players are branching out into other drugs."

What drugs?

Sandy Mayer wouldn't specify.

As we entered the building, I asked to talk to him at length when he had the time.

"No, I don't want to do it," Mayer said. "I don't want to be a whistle-blower. I don't see that it would change anything."

It seemed to me, I said, if things were as seriously wrong with tennis as his tone implied, then someone should blow the whistle. If the game didn't reform itself, it risked having an outside authority imposed on it.

Mayer thought the intervention of an outside authority might be best for tennis.

"Maybe a book like mine could help," I suggested.

"I don't think so. You can't change human nature. I'll give you an example. For years everyone knew women's tennis was dominated by lesbians. But nobody wrote about it. Everybody pretended it was a personal matter, just a preference that had no effect on the sport. Then when the story broke and it was written up in one magazine or another about Billie Jean King and other women on the tour, writers still refused to draw any conclusions or make any judgments. They still maintained it was a private matter. The funny thing is, if you have some minor personal foible, journalists will jump all over it. But if it's something big, something serious, they back away."

In the press room a British journalist was interviewing a young American, Drew Gitlin, who had come up through the qualies to play singles and had just been knocked out of the doubles.

"What's Gurfein's Christian name?" the journalist asked Gitlin about his doubles partner.

Gitlin smiled. "Gurfein doesn't have a Christian name. He has a Jewish name."

The reporter's face went florid. "Sorry. What's his Jewish name?"

"Jimmy."

Once he had finished with Gitlin, the British journalist told me a rumor that was making the rounds. Several top tennis writers, just like top players, were said to be receiving appearance money. Fighting for media attention, tournaments were alleged to be inducing key members of the press to cover their events. While the rest of us had to pick up our own travel, hotel, and food bills, a select few had them paid by tournaments, with gifts and cash thrown in on the side. Such writers were reputed to have guaranteed access not just to the players, but to the hostesses as well.

Here in Strasbourg, however, there had been complaints about the hostesses. As a rock-concert promoter, Harry Lapp should have been hip. He certainly looked hip. Young and burly, he smoked fat cigars and wore blue jeans and a pink sweatshirt with THE HARRY LAPP ORGANIZATION stenciled in black across the chest. The members of his team were "roadies," more adept at unloading band equipment and setting up acoustical systems than in caring for tennis courts. The men all sported pony tails, earrings, mutton-chop sideburns, and Zapata mustaches.

But the women, the hostesses, looked like somebody's mother. Some of them *were* mothers, married women palpably bored by tennis and everybody involved with it. What the hell, people asked, had been on Harry Lapp's mind when he hired this crew?

The question troubled the press, the umpires, and tournament officials more than it did the players, some of whom had brought wives or girlfriends, others of whom appeared more interested in practicing or catching up on their sleep. It was this way at a lot of tournaments, I learned. Girls came to tournaments prowling for players, but often wound up with a linesman, an agent, a clothing rep, a reporter. One umpire who zigzagged between the WCT and Grand Prix tours led such a hectic social life he took to traveling with his own supply of penicillin.

That day there was only one piece of hard news. International Director John McDonald acknowledged his keen disappointment with Strasbourg and announced to Alan Page of Associated Press that World Championship Tennis would cut back from twenty-two to sixteen tournaments next year. By morning the story would go out around the world. By evening Al G. Hill, Jr., President of WCT, would be on an airplane from Dallas, rushing to Strasbourg.

Witnessed by about three hundred spectators, the Vijay Amritraj–Terry Moor match offered an enjoyable contrast of styles. Tall and graceful, the Indian glided to the net, ending points as quickly as he could. Moor, a chunky lefthander from Memphis, Tennessee, was content to stay back, wind up off his forehand, and lash topspin drives. While the American radiated power, Vijay seemed to demonstrate some arcane Eastern principle of negative force, of effortless fluidity which turned the other man's strength against him. He seldom wasted a step, seldom appeared to be expending any energy.

Some contended this was because Vijay didn't *have* much energy. There was a roll of loose flesh around his waist, and by the middle of the first set he had begun to perspire. Soon he was wet from his hips to his armpits and had been upset 6–4/6–4.

Now, at the end of the second round, three seeded players remained in the tournament, only one in the top half of the draw.

Back at the hotel, I took a table with Robyn Lewis, the producer of WCT's television package, and her assistant, Amanda Hackney, an attractive Texan with blond, frizzed hair. They had just flown in from Amsterdam, where they went each Monday to edit the film of the previous week's tournament. This commute was starting to wear on them, especially on Robyn, a self-described "classic Gemini" who half the time wished she lived on a farm and could pass her days making patchwork quilts and, the other half, wished she were in Paris or London and could spend her days making deals.

Vijay Amritraj wandered by, no less good-humored for having been beaten by Terry Moor. He joined us and, toying with the amulet on his gold neckchain, warned us the hotel sauna was co-ed. That afternoon he had been lolling naked in the Jacuzzi when two women, also nude, climbed in with him.

"What did you do?" I asked.

Vijay giggled. "Got out right away. I was embarrassed."

Nick Saviano, a swarthy, square-jawed American, came over and the talk turned to cars. Robyn Lewis mused that a DeLorean would be a good investment. Now that the company was threatening to go out of business, their cars might become collectors' items in a couple of years. Vijay, who had recently purchased a Ferrari 308 GTS, said when you played the tournament in Milan, you could arrange an excellent deal on a high-performance Italian automobile. And if you played in Stuttgart, you got an enormous discount on a Mercedes.

"Yeah," said Saviano sardonically, "they stand there beside the ATP computer and give you a discount according to your ranking."

Saviano, who has had trouble staying in the top hundred, had more urgent matters to discuss than luxury cars he couldn't afford. "We gotta talk about tomorrow," he told Vijay, and gestured that they should move to another table.

"We can talk in front of these good people." Vijay smiled at us.

Saviano seemed unconvinced. Still, he sat down. "What about the doubles tomorrow?" He and Vijay were slated to meet a team of South Americans.

Vijay turned thumbs down and blew a Bronx cheer.

Saviano blew a raspberry back at his doubles partner. "I got a plane out of here at three-thirty. If I'm not on it, I won't be able to play the qualifying this weekend in Milan."

Vijay went rubbery-limbed with laughter. "We'll let them serve," Vijay said. "We'll start right off letting them ace us every time."

"Hey," said Amanda Hackney, "I thought you guys went out to win."

"Yes, this is terrible, isn't it?" Vijay asked, smiling.

Robyn Lewis' face soured in disgust. "I thought this was going to be the thrill of victory, the agony of defeat, all that good stuff. No way!"

Next day I arrived early at the Rhenus Hall to watch the doubles. In the aisle leading from the players' dressing room to the court, I encountered Amritraj and Saviano, who paused to tell me they had been joking last night.

"Hope you didn't take us seriously," Vijay said.

"I don't care if I get into that tournament in Milan," Saviano swore. "I can always go to London for the week. I've got an apartment I can use there. I'm going to play to win."

Perhaps they did play to win. Perhaps the combined forces of José Luis Damiani of Uruguay and Ricardo Ycaza of Ecuador, two clay-court specialists, were simply too much for them that morning.

Damiani served first. Ace! Vijay barely moved except to swivel his head and watch the ball sail by. But the linesman made a late call, "Out!" Vijay's return of Damiani's second serve plunked into the net. Saviano's return hit approximately the same spot. Then Vijay was aced, Saviano slapped the ball long, and the Indian and American slipped behind 0–1.

A moment later it was 0–2 as Saviano delivered two double faults. When it came Vijay's turn to serve, he spun the ball into play, putting no weight behind it. There were a lot of loud groans, a lot of head-shaking at missed opportunities, at drop-shots that didn't quite clear the net and lobs that floated long. But Amritraj and Saviano never managed to break back and they lost the first set 6–3.

They could reasonably have claimed to be victims of lousy conditions. The Rhenus Hall was cold and members of the Harry Lapp Organization were tacking up promotional strips with sta-ple guns that sounded like machine guns. The crowd, if one could call it that, consisted of a passel of school kids who ambled in carrying plastic flags that advertised a soft drink. All during the match the kids clambered up and down the bleachers, mer-rily waving their pennants and ignoring the headmistress, who finally snatched up a microphone from Zeno Pfau's desk and shouted for them to shut up and sit down.

Then there was a dapper Frenchman, smoking a pungent Gauloise, who prowled around the perimeter of the court, dis-tracting the players. Perhaps he hoped somebody would mistake *him* for a player. He was wearing squeaky new Adidas tennis shoes, black shorts, a warm-up sweater, and, *la pièce de résist-ance*, a fulvous yellow scarf wrapped around his neck.

Saviano dropped his serve in the first game of the second set, double-faulting twice. On his serve Vijay flailed away as if bent on a comeback. But he whacked ball after ball straight into the net, and they fell behind the South Americans 0–3. When Saviano lost his service again to 0–5, I moved toward an exit. Amritraj noticed me leaving, waved, and smiled.

Minutes later, after losing 6–0, Vijay bumped into me outside the press room. Still smiling, he said, "I'm so pissed off. I've got such a temper. I'm so pissed off to lose."

·   ·   ·

In explanation, if not in defense, of what often goes on in doubles, professional tennis has a year-round calendar with more than a hundred tournaments on five continents. For players who make a handsome living off singles, the temptation is to treat doubles, which pays far less, as an opportunity for comic relief. If it doesn't interfere with their schedules, they'll give their half-hearted best. But if a doubles match causes the slightest incon- venience, they'll dump it. In simple economic terms—the only terms operative in tennis—why should they stick around for doubles which might earn them a few hundred dollars when, as the umpire in Genoa had pointed out, they can fly to the next tournament or exhibition and make thousands?

For a man like Nick Saviano, struggling to survive on the circuit, the economic imperatives are more brutal. Why should he stay in Strasbourg for the doubles when that would prevent him from playing the qualies in Milan? As it turned out, Saviano flew to Milan, made it through the qualifying rounds, and earned $3,150 for losing in the first round of the main draw. If he had advanced to the next round of doubles with Amritraj, he would have won $250.

However, it isn't always greed for a bigger jackpot somewhere else which leads players to tank in doubles and sometimes in singles. If they hope to preserve any personal life, they feel they are forced to cut corners. A cursory glance at Vijay Amritraj's itinerary for the first five months of 1982 reveals the pressures players put on themselves.

Starting on January 2, Vijay flew from Los Angeles to his fam- ily's home in Madras. Then he backtracked to Birmingham, Eng- land, for a WCT event, returned to Los Angeles, left almost immediately for a tournament in Delray Beach, near Miami, and swung back to his base in Los Angeles. The next tournament took him across the continent to Richmond, Virginia, after which he once more traveled to Madras, via New York City. From India he traveled to the tournament in Genoa, where I first met him, and during the two intervening weeks he had gone back to Los Angeles, had crossed the Atlantic again to Frankfurt, then to Munich for a WCT tournament, and here to Strasbourg.

Now that he had lost in doubles, he would fly to London and

on to Colombo, Sri Lanka, on "personal business"—which everybody interpreted as meaning he was going to visit the fiancée his mother had found for him. After five days in Sri Lanka he would be airborne for twenty-two hours enroute to a tournament in Zurich. Then he would touch home base in Los Angeles, leave for Houston and play a tournament, zip up to Dallas for the WCT finals, duck back to Los Angeles, leap-frog the Pacific, play an exhibition in Tokyo, and move on to Madras.

When I expressed incredulity at such a demanding—such a demented—schedule, Vijay assured me there was nothing extraordinary about it. Compared to years past, he had become a homebody. In 1976, for instance, he had taken 227 flights and stayed in 187 different hotels. "I traveled more than Henry Kissinger."

Tennis authorities acknowledge that players sometimes throw doubles matches. They decry this, but do little or nothing to stop it, thus creating an impression that doubles doesn't matter and that the rule requiring "best effort" can be tacitly suspended. Speaking for the record, these same authorities insist that singles matches are never, or at least very rarely, tanked. Off the record, everybody on the circuit concedes that tanking happens in singles, too. Generally they add that these thrown matches were "meaningless," an interesting assertion since money is always at stake.

In recent years some demonstrably meaningful matches have been widely reported as tanked. In 1981, in the Volvo Masters, an eight-man round-robin which annually determines the Grand Prix champion, Ivan Lendl lost to Jimmy Connors. Lendl and Connors were already assured of semifinal berths, but the Czech's strategic collapse forced Connors to meet Bjorn Borg in the next round, while Lendl got to play a much easier opponent, Gene Mayer.

Predictably, Borg beat Connors and Lendl dispatched Mayer, thus setting up a Borg-Lendl final. While Borg whipped Lendl for the title, the fact remains that after folding in front of Connors the Czech wound up winning more prize money—$50,000— and receiving valuable TV exposure. And, of course, he also got a shot at the title and its $100,000 jackpot. Far from tanking a "meaningless" match, he appears to have studied all the angles and done exactly what he had to do to fatten his paycheck. In any other professional sport this would have provoked a public outcry and swift discipline. But in tennis, tanking prompts little more than yawns of indifference.

That evening I interviewed Wojtek Fibak, who for months had been besieged by questions that had nothing to do with tennis. After the imposition of martial law in Poland, he had been asked repeatedly for his opinion of the military regime, of Solidarity, and of what posture the West should adopt. Treated by the media as a sort of Solzhenitsyn-in-jockstrap, Fibak had delivered pronouncements such as "I'm a fresh thinker and philosopher" and "Eastern Europeans are always wanting to talk philosophy, art, culture . . ." And "To me . . . the problem is that America is too free, too much democracy. There isn't enough discipline."

Not content to remain a political pundit and cultural critic, he regarded all knowledge as his province and wanted "to know everything about stocks, about art, about tax shelters, the price of gold, real estate in Beverly Hills."

When I turned to more mundane matters and asked if he had heard from his parents in Poznan, he said he had just spoken to them by telephone for the first time since December. He had planned to visit them, but they thought that was pointless and preferred to see him in Paris.

He said he was surprised to learn that the results of his matches hadn't been suppressed by the regime. After all, he had been quite critical of the coup. "But no more. Nothing I can say will make any difference or do any good. It's very frustrating."

As we talked, we sat in the stands watching Ivan Lendl lash a hapless opponent to ribbons. When not being interviewed about Poland, Fibak is often asked about Lendl. I, too, was interested in their relationship.

"This interview isn't about Ivan, is it? He doesn't like the press, and I don't want always to be speaking for him."

I asked whether Fibak felt their relationship had hurt his own game.

"My parents point out that what I've given Ivan, I've taken out of myself. I try not to worry about that."

"Will you go on coaching him?"

"I'm not a *coach*." Fibak reacted as if the word were a racial epithet. "We're good friends. I'm his helper. His mentor."

"It's a personal relationship, then, not professional?"

"Yes, it's personal. I help him with his investments and financial advice."

That sounded professional to me. I pointed out that Lendl and he were rumored to be involved in various business deals together.

Without bothering to deny or confirm this, he remarked, "I don't want Ivan to repeat certain mistakes I made."

Coming from a country like Poland, he explained, where there is no tennis tradition, he had had to be self-taught for the most part and he had gotten a late start. He had never touched a racquet until he was thirteen, and it had taken him years to persuade the Polish government to let him play as a professional. Then in 1976, when he climbed into the top ten, he felt he had failed to capitalize. Lacking experience or guidance, he had let too many opportunities slip away.

"I didn't choose the right tournaments," he told me. "You have to think about ATP points and playing on all surfaces and getting experience and playing where you have friends." It was this sort of advice he was giving Lendl.

I asked whether he would agree with Cino Marchese that as players signed for tournaments, they placed a lot of importance on ATP points, but even more on appearance money. Fibak confirmed that that was true.

For a European, however, he said it was also urgent to establish a base in the States. "What kills the Italians on the tour is they simply don't know and like America. I should have established a family situation in America in 1976. Ivan quickly established a place. He stays with me and he owns an apartment in Boca West in Florida."

Fibak is no less well established now than Lendl. He owns a baronial manor house in Greenwich, Connecticut, and an apartment in Paris. He has accumulated the world's largest collection of Polish painting, and he keeps a Mercedes in Connecticut and a Porsche and a turbo-charged Volkswagen in France.

"Tennis gave me everything," he admitted. "It opened the whole world for me." Still, he wouldn't encourage his children to follow his profession. "Too much tension, too much pressure." And the players on the tour seemed to have changed for the worse. When he first started, there had been brighter, book-reading men. Now the younger ones were ill-educated, limited, and rude, especially the Americans. "The educational system in the States is so bad."

After he retires, he said, he intends to maintain a base in the United States, but he wants his children raised in Europe—in Paris, not Poland. Like most players from the Communist bloc, he expressed no desire to defect, yet also no intention of returning to live in the East. And why should he when he could continue to skate back and forth?

While we were talking, a tournament official interrupted. He had called Paris, as Fibak had instructed him to, but had failed to obtain any information on the Concorde flight from New York. Fibak's wife and daughters were flying over to join him for a few weeks and he wanted to know whether they had landed yet. He told the man to go back and telephone Air France.

Minutes later the fellow returned, looking harried and hang-dog, and confessed he had failed again. He just couldn't get any information on the Concorde.

Exasperated, Fibak cut the interview short and said he would telephone Paris himself. He acted as if he had been forced to scrub the shower-room floor.

Late that night at the hotel I spoke to Corrado Barazzutti after he had dropped a three-set match to Fibak. I had been warned by Italian journalists that Barazzutti was a difficult man. But I always found him disarmingly honest and more likely to make things difficult on himself than on others. For instance, there was his manner of preparing for hard-court tournaments. "I practice on clay," he said. "Then I play here. It's just a question of mentality. I adjust my mentality to the fast surface. But I don't practice on it."

In truth, Barazzutti seldom seemed to adjust his mentality or his methodical style. Similarly, he didn't alter his wardrobe, which all that winter consisted of a filthy blue ski parka and faded jeans. The one thing that had changed was his standing on the ATP computer. Once in the top ten, a semifinalist at the French Open and U.S. Open, he had now fallen into the 60's. I asked him why.

"Problems in my life," he said, scraping a fingernail over his chapped lower lip like Jean Paul Belmondo in *Breathless*. "When you have a son, things become different."

"Oh, you have a little boy?"

"No, I have a daughter."

"How did she change your life?"

Corrado grimaced. "Before, my wife was always with me. But when the baby is born, she stops to come. She stay at home. I get lonely. I'm all alone playing, and all I want to do is go home. When I'm on the court, I just want to be home. For nine months I play very bad. Some players, they bring the babies with us in the hotel. But that's no good. I want my daughter at home. At a hotel she eats bad. Then she cries at night and doesn't sleep. Then I don't sleep. No, it's better for her to be home."

"What about now?"

"The baby is walking, she is starting to talk. There are less complications. I hope to do better again."

"Are you coming to America for the clay-court tournaments this summer?"

"No more. I no wanna play in America. It's too far and I'm tired. When I am young, it is all right," Barazzutti said, as if he were fifty-nine instead of twenty-nine. "I been on the circuit ten years, and my wife can't come with me, and I don't like to fly."

"You feel uncomfortable in an airplane?"

"I feel terrible. I feel *terrified*. Especially in America. They fly any weather there. I don't mind to fly one hour, maybe two, but not seven or nine hours. So I play small tournaments in

Italy this summer." He shrugged, scraping the fingernail along the fleshy curve of his lip. "Why go to America?"

Of Balazs Taroczy it has been written that he would be a household word if anyone outside Hungary could pronounce his name. Winner of the Dutch Open for five of the last six years and doubles champion at tournaments in Monte Carlo, France, Holland, Switzerland, and Japan, he is a master of consistency, someone who rarely loses to lower-ranked players.

But in the quarterfinals at Strasbourg he had a tough time reading Tim Mayotte's serve and could not put in enough of his own first serves to prevent the rangy, twenty-one-year-old American from taking the net. Never really in the match, Taroczy lost 6–3/6–4, leaving the top half of the draw without a seeded player.

At the press conference the French journalists were in a feisty mood. One man declared that Taroczy had been playing badly all week and was lucky to have squeezed through yesterday.

Balazs laughed. "I am always lucky. I'm lucky whenever I win. I'm lucky a lot." But now his luck had temporarily run out.

Did he care about losing today? How seriously did he take these WCT tournaments?

"There are no ATP points, but there's a lot of money," he said. "I take it seriously. $8,000 here is the same as $8,000 on the Grand Prix."

Tim Mayotte politely disagreed. "Balazs is already established. But for me the ATP points are more important."

One reporter complained that after almost three months of 1982 the top players still hadn't met in tournament competition. Why not? he demanded.

Mayotte suggested this might be best for the game. A bright, reasonable young man with a degree from Stanford University (at times it seems that all the Americans on the tour put in a few semesters at Palo Alto), he took pains to explain himself, pointing out that if the same stars collided week after week, their matches would lose intensity, not to mention crowd appeal. He believed it was wiser for players to build toward major events like the U.S. Open and Wimbledon.

Every time Tim Mayotte spoke, he seemed to confirm his reputation as a kid who was too nice to flourish on the circuit. Even he had expressed doubts whether he possessed, or cared to acquire, the toughness needed to win tournaments.

Balazs Taroczy was much blunter. "Maybe the tournaments cannot afford to have all the big players in the same event."

"Did I hear you right?" I asked.

Taroczy laughed. "Yes."

Now everybody laughed, and all the foolish pretense fell away as we faced the truth. Appearance money was the hard reality that controlled which stars played where.

In the next quarterfinal that afternoon it looked as though another seeded player would fall. In a hotly contested match Heinz Gunthardt had captured the first set from Sandy Mayer and was serving to stay even in the second when John McDonald, the WCT International Director, climbed up into the stands and sat beside me. Several days earlier I had asked to interview him and he suggested we talk now, right here, watching Gunthardt and Mayer.

Pale, drawn, and deeply fatigued, McDonald had been on the road for weeks. Indoor tournaments are always rough—on organizers, players, officials, even the press. Since there is usually only one court, matches start early in the morning and continue until long past midnight. But Strasbourg had presented its own peculiar problems, and McDonald had been under heavy fire. First there had been the difficult press conference after McEnroe's last-minute withdrawal. Then there had been Johan Kriek's calamitous defeat. Then McDonald had announced that WCT would reduce its tournaments by twenty-five percent next year. Now Al G. Hill, Jr., President of WCT, had called a major press conference for Sunday, right before the finals. So I was surprised when McDonald sought me out to talk.

I asked what the toughest part of his job was.

"Player withdrawals. There are too many tournaments and too few players who pull in fans."

Was appearance money part of the problem? I asked.

He assured me WCT didn't give guarantees or appearance money. Lamar Hunt was a man of high moral principle who insisted his tour live up to unbending ethical standards. "We have very strict rules," he said. "You'll never see players at WCT tournaments gambling or splitting prize money."

Naturally, at his mention of prize-money splits, I wondered whether someone had put out the word that I was asking awkward questions. With no way now of working up to the subject gradually, I bluntly told him I had heard otherwise. I had heard players were splitting at WCT events.

McDonald said he was astonished and swore he had never known anything about it. "These guys are too selfish to buy each other a drink."

It wasn't like that in his day, he rambled on. Back then the guys were all in it together. They were closer, less cutthroat. Why, he remembered one time on the Caribbean circuit, it must have been about 1962, when Lou Gerrard, the No. 1 player from New Zealand, lost his wallet and $1,700. This was in Venezuela and they were only making about $75 or $100 a week and Gerrard was desperate. So the other players held "a whip-around"; they passed the hat and collected enough to replace Gerrard's wallet and his cash. "I don't see the chance of anything like that happening with players today," said McDonald.

As he spoke, he kept his eyes on the court, where Gunthardt had dropped the second set and was scrambling against Mayer in the third. "It's important for Heinz to do well," McDonald muttered. "It'll really help us in Zurich if he has a big tournament here."

Trying to retrieve his attention, I said I had spoken to Vittorio Selmi of the ATP, who corroborated that prize-money splitting was going on. McDonald maintained that Selmi must have misunderstood my question. After I assured him that this wasn't the case, McDonald acknowledged that prize-money splitting would be a serious ethical and legal matter. But he just couldn't believe it was happening—which is, perhaps, why he didn't ask who had told me or which players were involved.

While his eyes remained fastened on the court, mine were fixed on him. Frozen in that attitude, peering intently in different directions, we must have looked like carved figures from separate friezes. Only when I swung back to the subject of appearance money did I manage to capture McDonald's interest. Although reiterating that WCT didn't give them, he agreed that "guarantees are a sickness in the game. There's a lot of creative bookkeeping going on. Jimmy Connors wanted a $100,000-a-week guarantee to play WCT. I told him, 'You can win $100,000 a week.' But he wanted a hundred more."

Then there was Donald Dell, the agent-entrepreneur-promoter-TV commentator. According to John McDonald, Dell had offered a number of his players to WCT, but demanded they be regarded as a package deal. To get the good ones, WCT had to accept them all. When WCT declined, Dell was said to have encouraged his clients to skip or to cut back on WCT events.

"Dell's always pressed for more jobs for more players. Then he does something like this." McDonald shook his head. It seemed to hurt him personally that there was so much opposition to WCT. Every week he sent telegrams to Grand Prix tournament directors, wishing them good luck. What did they, what did Donald Dell, have against WCT? "If it was a flock of exhibitions, if it was bad for the players or the game, I could understand. But we're putting on above-board, big-prize-money, open tournaments. We even pay prize money to qualifiers. I know what Dell wanted. He wanted guarantees for his players. Donald is insatiable."

Then McDonald excused himself. The match was over; Sandy Mayer had beaten Gunthardt to reach the semifinals. McDonald moved onto the court and helped put up some new promotional strips. Now, in addition to advertisements for Barclay's Bank, Hyatt Hotels, Braniff Airlines, and Fila, there were signs with the Martini & Rossi logo.

When the job was finished to his satisfaction, he seemed to

have an afterthought about the interview. As he climbed into the bleachers, I knew what was coming. It was just a question of which statement he intended to retract.

John McDonald stood in front of me, a small man in a blue blazer, his pallid smile not touching his damp, sad eyes. "Don't quote me on Connors," he said.

That evening I missed the quarterfinal match between Wojtek Fibak and Ivan Lendl, and met Frew McMillan in the Hilton bar. A slender South African whose trademarks are a white golf cap and two-handed strokes off both wings, McMillan is going on forty, but remains one of the premier doubles players in the world, having won seventy-four Grand Prix titles, including three at Wimbledon.

To his regret, people tended to forget that he was once an accomplished singles competitor and had been ranked as high as No. 20. He didn't feel his unorthodox style had prevented him from achieving his full potential. That is, he didn't think it had put him at a physical or technical disadvantage. But, looking back, he realized he had always played under a psychological handicap because so many coaches had warned him he would never beat the best players with his game. Now that Gene Mayer had made it into the top ten, slugging his groundstrokes with both hands, McMillan felt vindicated, felt like a trailblazer who had opened new possibilities for the next generation.

Wasn't it true, though, I asked, that Gene Mayer's style had brought on repeated injuries which just this past year had knocked him out of Wimbledon, the French Open, and the U.S. Open?

McMillan claimed that hitting with two hands was actually less likely to cause injury. Of course, you had to run more and stretch farther. That was Gene Mayer's real problem. He had such great touch and extraordinary shot-making ability, he had a tendency to neglect training and fall back on his natural gifts. Like a lot of players, he was often out of shape and the result was cramps, muscle strains, and tendinitis—disaster for a man who had Mayer's low tolerance for pain.

"This is my twenty-first year on the tour, and I've only once withdrawn from a tournament with an injury," McMillan said. "It's one of the things that distresses me most about players today—the lack of total commitment."

Predictably, he was also distressed by the paltry prize money in doubles. WCT should have showcased its doubles matches, he insisted, and helped change the public's perception of these events.

Playing devil's advocate, I asked how he could expect WCT, the Grand Prix, or the public to take doubles seriously when so many matches were tanked.

McMillan maintained "the abuses come from the small prize money. You can't blame players for treating doubles with contempt. They don't tank in big, prestigious events. The only tanking is when there's no financial inducement."

Ironically, while convinced that doubles had been undermined by too little money, he thought singles was being ruined by too much. After a few good years the top men were set for life and had no incentive to play tournaments. Big money, McMillan said, was turning off fans and shortening careers. It gave "players delusions of grandeur at an age when they were too young to handle it." Many of them complained they were under intense pressures and couldn't possibly play more than a dozen tournaments a year. But that was nonsense, McMillan declared. In his prime he had played forty-five weeks a year. Even now he played thirty weeks a year. The sad truth was that the men today didn't care whether anything was left of tennis after they retired.

Bjorn Borg was an excellent example of that. He acted as if he owed nothing to the game and didn't believe he should be subject to the rules. "If Borg doesn't realize fair's fair," McMillan said, "it shows he's become a creature of the system. There have never been any rules enforced in the past, so he probably feels 'Why should the rules apply to me now?' Just for once it would be refreshing to have someone of Borg's caliber have to abide by the rules."

By now the bar was crowded with people returning from the

Rhenus Hall, where Lendl had walloped Wojtek Fibak 6–0/6–4. Several players were clamorously drunk, badgering the waiters and making wisecracks to the pianist in the lounge. One well-known American reeled through the lobby and into the bar, bumping into tables and tripping over steps. He thumped John McDonald on the shoulder. Smiling, McDonald said, "How are you doing?" The player responded with another whack to McDonald's back, then stumbled away. "He's a great guy," McDonald said, and he seemed to mean it.

After Frew McMillan went up to bed, McDonald invited me to join him at a table with Alan Page of Associated Press and Bernard Dolet from L'Equipe, the French sports journal of record.

Although glassy-eyed with fatigue, McDonald was in an exuberant mood. Now that Lendl had roared past Fibak into the semifinals, he felt a crushing weight had rolled off his chest and he wanted to share a story with Page, Dolet, and me. Maybe then we'd understand what he had been up against all week.

After McEnroe pulled out and Kriek cratered in the first round, Harry Lapp, the local promoter, had demanded a meeting with McDonald. Enraged, he charged that his tournament was being sabotaged and he wasn't going to stand for it. Lapp said he was no fool, he knew what would fall out next. He had heard rumors that Lendl would let Fibak beat him. Since the Czech had won several WCT events and already qualified for the finals in Dallas, the gossip was that he wanted to make sure his friend qualified. If that happened, Lapp threatened to spill his guts to the press and call in the police.

McDonald had talked with Lapp until six in the morning, trying to convince him of the tournament's integrity and, at the same time, attempting to explain that upsets are always possible. "What if Fibak did beat Lendl?" McDonald asked us. "I was terrified at the prospect. Harry would never have believed me after that." But now, at last, the WCT International Director could relax.

Bernard Dolet of L'Equipe added a postscript to the story. Earlier this week Lapp had assured him there would be no more upsets, no more unexpected results, because he, Harry Lapp, had confronted McDonald and insisted that the matches go according to form for the rest of the tournament.

McDonald sighed. This was what came of doing business with rookies. "I've been in tennis twenty-five years. Here's a guy who's been in tennis five minutes and thinks he knows everything, thinks he can control who wins and who loses so that he gets the final he wants. We just can't convince some people that this isn't the Harlem Globetrotters or *Holiday on Ice.*"

Immediately I remembered the Italian journalist in Genoa who had objected that the close personal and professional relationship between Fibak and Lendl would inevitably lead people to be suspicious of their matches, regardless of which player won. Although I hadn't heard the rumors which Harry Lapp claimed to have heard, and while I had not discussed the matter with either Fibak or Lendl, I had talked with half a dozen players who participated in Genoa and in Strasbourg and who, speaking only for themselves, confessed that if they had already qualified for the WCT finals, they would let a friend beat them if that would let the other fellow qualify for the bonus pool and the finals as well.

To my mind, there can be no better example of why it is wrong—and more than wrong, dangerous—for tennis authorities to take a lax attitude toward tanking, be it in doubles or in "meaningless" singles matches. Once players are allowed to get away with tanking with the excuse of tight plane schedules, exhaustion, or whatever, it raises the unsavory suspicion that they might tank for other reasons—to do a friend a favor, to win a bet, or to satisfy some obligation incurred by an earlier secret arrangement.

Saturday afternoon the best match of the tournament took place in an all but empty arena. Terry Moor pitted his topspin passing shots against Tim Mayotte's serve and volley and won the first set 6–4. But in the second Mayotte overcame an early service break, then broke Moor to 7–5.

By the third set Moor's groundstrokes had lost their sting and he had no choice except to take the net before Mayotte did. Unfortunately, he has a big wind-up on his strokes and a loose-wristed follow-through which ruins his net game.

After losing, Moor explained, "I'm just not confident with my volleys. I know what I'm supposed to do—punch the ball with a short stroke. But I can't visualize it in my own mind."

Asked how he would prepare for the first final in his professional career, Mayotte, who is six feet three, weighs 180 pounds, and sometimes seems as ungainly as a yearling, said, "By the time you're on the tour, you have to assume you've got the strokes. Any world-class player can hit a winner if he can reach the ball. The problem is getting to it. The best players are the fastest. So I'm always working on my speed and movement."

That evening, before the second semifinal, I met the harried official whom Wojtek Fibak had sent scurrying around for information about the Concorde. A plump young German with disheveled hair, he had the title of Deputy Tournament Director. His name was Pascal Zimmer—"like room," he said—and he worked for STP, an abbreviation for Ski and Tennis Promotion, based in Stuttgart. Actually, he remarked, it would be more accurate to say he worked for Marcel Avram, the head of Mama Concerts in Munich. Avram, one of the most successful rock-concert impresarios in Europe, had recently agreed to promote five WCT tournaments. Some of them he and Pascal handled on their own. Others, like this one in Strasbourg, had been laid off on local promoters in a profit/risk-sharing arrangement which Zimmer declined to discuss.

He did, however, describe the rough contours of their deal with WCT. "On the Volvo Grand Prix the promoter takes all the risk. He has to come up with the prize money, the sponsors, everything. But if you have TV, you can get sponsors, and that's where you make money. With WCT, they keep the television and sponsor rights. We deliver a clean court and get to keep what comes from the spectators. There's less money, but less risk, too."

Since there hadn't been ten thousand paying customers at the

Rhenus Hall this week, I expressed doubts that there had been any profits at the gate. I had heard from one WCT official that the tournament would lose $70,000—although whether this would come out of Lamar Hunt's silver-lined pocket or the local promoter's wasn't clear.

Pascal Zimmer would only say that there was "too much tennis and not enough interest. The sponsors are the ones being cheated. They pay a lot of money. Then they don't get on TV."

It struck me as curious that rock promoters like Marcel Avram and Harry Lapp were plunging into another hit-or-flop enterprise. But it didn't seem strange to Pascal, who saw strong parallels between rock stars and tennis players, particularly Vitas Gerulaitis, Peter Rennert, and John McEnroe, who, Pascal said, "are on the fast line."

On the fast line?

Yes, Pascal repeated, and set the phrase to a rock beat so that I gathered he meant they were living life "in the fast lane."

"The players know they'll have fun at our tournaments," Pascal said. "We try to make them feel happy. In Munich, Earth, Wind and Fire was in town and we took all the players, even the qualifiers. And last year during Wimbledon, Pink Floyd was in London and we took Vitas and McEnroe backstage."

When I asked about specific similarities between rock stars and tennis players, he said they both had to put out one hundred percent every night.

"What about dope?"

As Pascal pulled a blank face and was, I thought, about to profess complete ignorance, I remarked that in America it would be rare to meet many students between the ages of eighteen and twenty-five who had never experimented with drugs.

"Players are about the same as students in the U.S.A." He would say no more than that.

"What exactly is your job during a tournament?" I asked.

"Everything. A lot of little things." He translated interviews, he made travel arrangements, he tried to keep players happy. "Like Ivan and Wojtek travel together a lot. So they always ask me to make sure they have a room close to each other. With a concert, it's usually one rock group a night and they all get along. But with a tournament, it's maybe fifty players with different personalities. Vitas doesn't like Wojtek so much, and Connors hates Lendl, so you have to be alert. It's difficult."

A large part of the difficulty, he said, was that he had to concentrate on only three or four stars, giving them treatment which the other players didn't receive and often resented. "And of course the stars are getting appearance money, which the other players aren't."

But Pascal felt he had excellent rapport with most players. He was an agent, as well as a Deputy Tournament Director, and he would soon be appointed the European representative of Pro Man, WCT's Dallas-based player-management group. He readily acknowledged this was a conflict of interest and explained how easy it was for agents, who were also tournament directors, to maneuver their players into signing for events they promoted. "They tell a player they have a big promotion deal, but only if he plays the tournament. Maybe they won't be as direct as that. But they'll convince a player that it's a good deal and in his interest to do the promotion and, of course, play the tournament."

When I asked about appearance money, Pascal said it sometimes came in cash. Or it could be concealed as an endorsement contract. In Stuttgart the top players got a Mercedes.

"I'm in the wrong business. They never offer journalists appearance money," I said, having heard rumors to the contrary.

Pascal Zimmer regarded me closely. "You want a car?"

"Nobody's going to give a Mercedes to a writer."

"Not give, maybe. But a big reduction. Ten or fifteen percent, depending on the model you want."

Before the semifinal I climbed into the television booth with Amanda Hackney and Robyn Lewis. Seeing the bleachers less than half full, Robyn said, "I'd have given away five thousand tickets to a charitable organization to fill up these seats." But since the match wasn't going out live, they could always crop the film to eliminate the empty seats from the WCT highlights. Presumably, the linesmen's strike which delayed the match was also deleted.

As Lendl stalked onto the court wearing his Czech Davis Cup jacket, Amanda asked, "What's that?"

"I don't know," said Robyn. "Cut it."

Both players appeared tense, and neither could control his first serve. Still, Lendl broke to a 2–0 lead, and after surviving two break points, he smiled, a sight as rare as a toucan in Antarctica.

"Get that!" Robyn exclaimed.

A few games later Mayer volleyed behind Lendl, wrong-footing him. The Czech swung at the ball behind his back, but the shot sailed long. "Dammit!" Robyn said. "It's an exciting shot and we missed it."

When the American lost the first set, he switched tactics, stopped hitting flat serves, and started putting spin on the ball, varying the pace to prevent Lendl from grooving his swing. He coaxed a few errors from the Czech, but could not cope with Lendl's power. Broken twice in a row, Sandy Mayer lost the second set and the match 6–4/6–3.

Since neither Robyn nor Amanda knew much about tennis and they confessed they didn't enjoy watching it, I asked whether this presented problems as they packaged the highlights. Not at all, they said. Very little depended on them. There was a format, a kind of shooting chart such as a movie director might consult, and it remained the same for every match. It didn't much matter what happened on court. At the studio in Amsterdam they simply edited their footage to correspond to the format. The emphasis seemed to be on exciting points, fluke shots, and crowd-pleasing antics. Regardless of the actual quality of the match, there was never a dull program.

"The WCT trademark is visual excitement," Robyn Lewis said. "That's the beauty of video tape."

As a rule, press conferences are of interest only to journalists and even they often skip them. Few tournament officials bother to show up. But Ivan Lendl attracted an all-star cast of inter-lopers. John McDonald and Al G. Hill, Jr., of WCT, Pascal Ziminer of STP, Marcel Avram of Mama Concerts, Wojtek Fibak, and a tall, regal, mink-clad woman who was with Hill crowded into the trembling modular structure which served as a press room.

Scowling, "the Ostrava Ghost," as Bud Collins calls Lendl, dropped his bony shanks onto a folding chair and glared at reporters as if he smelled something evil.

Hill shouted, "Good match!" and began clapping, but nobody took up the applause, and Lendl didn't look his way.

A German writer, a middle-aged woman, labored to express herself in English. "Were you surprised that your partner—"

"I don't have a partner," Lendl snapped.

Shaken, she attempted to rephrase the question. "Tonight when your partner rushed the net, were you—"

"I don't have a partner!"

The room fell quiet, and the woman flushed.

Lendl, palpably bored and contemptuous, sat waiting for the poor woman to try again.

"When McEnroe is your partner and he rushes the net—"

"McEnroe is *never* my partner," Lendl snarled.

Finally, Fibak took mercy and explained to Ivan what was already obvious. The woman meant "opponent," not "partner."

"It doesn't matter what I say," Lendl muttered. "They'll change it around anyway."

Fibak spoke again. I didn't catch the remark, but Lendl did and let the slightest trace of a smile soften the sharp edges of his face. "Only questions from the press. Marcel, please kick out everyone without a press card."

A British reporter asked the twenty-two-year-old millionaire to imagine he was a journalist. What would *he* like to ask Ivan Lendl?

Fibak piped up again. "When can I leave?"

Lendl laughed. "Do I have to do this again tomorrow?"

It would be too much to claim that the ice melted after that, but there was a definite thaw in the permafrost, and I thought perhaps the boy wasn't the churlish punk he appeared to be.

Maybe his surliness with reporters was simply a result of his schizophrenic political position.

The prime mover of Czechoslovakia's 1980 Davis Cup championship team, Lendl is regarded as a national hero and an exemplar of the superior Communist system. Yet, like so many players from the Eastern bloc, he is a resolute capitalist who endorses Adidas clothes and Kneissl racquets, Superga shoes, Linea Zeta grips and luggage, VS Gut, Ben Gay, and Orange Crush. The deal with Adidas for a distinctive new line of clothes with an argyle pattern on the shirt is said to guarantee him two million dollars against a five-percent royalty over the next three years. His tournament winnings for 1982 already approached a million dollars and it was safe to assume he earned as much from exhibitions.

But there is one thing Ivan Lendl cannot afford. He cannot afford to be conspicuous about his wealth. Apparently reluctant to let his countrymen learn how much money he makes, how luxuriously he lives, and how much of his income is invested in the West—all week he and Fibak attempted to kill stories about his real estate in Connecticut—he is hostile to any questions, no matter how innocuous, about his personal life, and he isn't a good deal more receptive to inquiries about his matches.

Predictably, when asked whether he thought Bjorn Borg should have to qualify for Grand Prix tournaments, Lendl responded in a fashion that would have made Lamar Hunt and his deceased rightwing daddy proud. Sounding like a Texas oil wildcatter impatient with petty governmental restrictions, he said, "I think each player is self-employed. We're not employed by the Pro Council. If, like Borg, you don't like their decision, then you just tell them what you've decided to do."

As for his own schedule, he declared that he had not decided yet whether to play Wimbledon. His goal was to win the French Open, and he wouldn't commit himself beyond that.

When there was another question about Wimbledon, Marcel Avram groaned.

"You just woke up?" Lendl asked. "Good morning."

His entourage laughed uproariously, ending the press conference.

. . .

On Sunday the WCT called a press conference of its own and invited journalists to prepare questions for Al G. Hill, Jr. Beforehand, I happened to pick up yesterday's edition of the local newspaper, *Dernières Nouvelles d'Alsace*, which ran a description of the Lendl-Fibak quarterfinal.

LENDL LOSES HIS BET AS THE PUBLIC BOOS, read the headline. According to Claude J. Eckert, it had been a mere "parody of a match" as Fibak fell behind 3–0 and "began doing jut anything, even serving underhand and putting up only a semblance of resistance." After losing the first set 6–0, the Pole had dropped three more games straight. Then, with the score 5–1, he suddenly put up a struggle, scrambled to 4–5, but lost 6–4.

Afterward Fibak had explained to reporters. "With Ivan, it's always the same scenario when we meet. We know each other so well he feels obliged each time to play against me better than against any other opponent. That discourages me totally. I have another philosophy of the game. . . . Before the match he threw me a challenge, betting a hundred dollars that I wouldn't win a game. It's true that at 6–0/3–0 I had only started to play. I won the bet. That will permit me to pay my telephone bill."

Recalling John McDonald's claim that WCT had strict rules against gambling, I wondered what would happen to Wojtek Fibak. At breakfast I met Alan Page, the AP stringer, and asked if Fibak had indeed admitted betting on the match. Page assured me he had, but explained that the *Dernières Nouvelles d'Alsace* had gotten the details wrong. Fibak's bet had been with a friend, not Lendl, and the wager was that the Pole wouldn't win three games.

As we were speaking, Fibak crossed the lobby and came over to us. He wanted to know if we were heading for Paris after the tournament. He had just taken delivery on a turbo-charged VW and needed someone to drop it at his apartment. He and Lendl were driving there in a Porsche.

Neither Page nor I could help him. But before he left, I asked about his bet. He acknowledged that he had made one, and yes, it was for $100 with a friend who doubted Fibak would win three games. He had won four.

· · ·

In the press room John McDonald sat at a table flanked by Al G. Hill, Jr., on his right and Harry Lapp on his left. Before they opened the conference for questions, each man made a statement. Actually, Harry Lapp's was more on the order of an oration. Having abandoned his blue jeans and pink sweatshirt for a dark three-piece suit, he resembled a well-fed diplomat as he delivered his ponderous assessment of the tournament. Although it hadn't been a financial success, he considered it "a moral triumph," and he said he was pleased to have brought big-time tennis to the Alsace region.

Apparently, in addition to its moral edification, this past week had been an educational experience for the French rock promoter. Far from being turned off by his debut in professional tennis, he had told an umpire he would probably try again next year. But he wouldn't bother with a tournament. He was thinking of staging a series of exhibition matches. That way, he would get the players and match-ups he wanted, not to mention more sponsors and far more spectators.

In contrast to Harry Lapp and his ornate rhetoric, Al G. Hill, Jr., sounded down-home, direct, and friendly. He didn't look it, but he sounded it. Three days and a continent away from Dallas, he still displayed that peculiar gift possessed by many wealthy Texans who seem most menacing when they smile and intimidating when they lower their voices. Everything about the man suggested contradictions. He wore a conservative blue business suit, but also a wealth of ostentatious gold jewelry. With crimped brown hair receding from a tan forehead, he had a fleshy face, but there didn't appear to be anything soft about him.

After a few preliminary pleasantries, he said he would entertain questions.

Directing my comments to John McDonald, I reminded him of his statement that WCT had very strict rules to protect the integrity of the game and to ensure that spectators understood its tournaments were honest matches, not exhibitions. There was, for example, the rule against gambling. I then showed McDonald and Hill the headline in the local paper and summarized what the article said and what I had learned that morning from Wojtek Fibak about his bet.

"Do you know what the stake was?" McDonald broke in.

"One hundred dollars," I said.

"Really?" McDonald chuckled, and he and Hill grinned at each other.

"What's the rule," I asked, "and what's your reaction to this headline?"

While the translator caught up with the conversation, interpreting for the French press, Al G. Hill, Jr., leaned over and whispered to McDonald, "The bet had nothing to do with the outcome of the match." Then a moment later, still whispering, "If Lendl had bet on the outcome of the match, that would be one thing."

When the translator was finished, McDonald declared, "I don't think we can be responsible for the amusing little comments made between players. I think we have more serious things at stake, and since it made no difference to the match . . ." Without completing that sentence or supplying a transition, he trundled on, "But what we're concerned about in all our contractual agreements with tournaments is that there is to be no gambling on the site. Some years ago Wimbledon allowed gambling, and it gave those in the game great concern because players were, in fact, able to bet on themselves. At *Wimbledon!*" he repeated. "And this is something you just cannot have in professional tennis."

"John," I said, "I want to understand you correctly. You're saying if there's a private bet between players, then that's not part of that rule?"

"Off court." McDonald embarked on a series of stream-of-consciousness fragments. "And if it's for an amusing. If it's for a dinner or whatever else. I mean, no way. You can."

Since the bet in question had not been between players, but rather between Fibak and a friend, was McDonald suggesting that this was less serious?

"It also had nothing to do with the possible outcome of the match," Hill interjected, a non-sequitur that seemed to be of the utmost importance to him.

"It had something to do with the score," I pointed out.

"Yeah, well, the bet, I think, was really between the two of them," Hill insisted. "As you know, probably, they're very close personally."

"No, it wasn't between the two of them."

"Well, even between Fibak and a friend, it was probably pretty much of a joke," Hill said. "If you understand the history at all of Fibak and Lendl, Mr. Lendl tries to make sure Mr. Fibak doesn't win *one* game. Ever! Because of their personal relationship. Now, if Mr. Lendl, for instance, were betting on the outcome of his match today, which he can control, I would think that would be the thing that we are aiming our interest in gambling at. It's to keep players from throwing a match in order to make money."

"What if the bet were for $100,000 instead of $100?" I pressed Hill.

"On four games?" he asked.

"Yes."

"Between some friends of Fibak and Fibak himself? I don't think that we can really do a whole lot about that. If it were to affect the outcome of a match, or if it were to affect either organized gambling, bookmaking, et cetera, then we would certainly very quickly step in to remedy that."

It seemed not to occur to McDonald or Hill that it was possible to bet on anything except the outcome of a match, or that a player could make money without throwing a match. Hypothetically, if Fibak had bet $100,000 that he would win four games from Lendl, he could have offered Lendl a healthy cut to let him take a couple of games in each set. The Czech would still have won, but by a narrower margin. This is the kind of dodge that has put college basketball players behind bars for point-shaving and has resulted in long suspensions or permanent banishment for international soccer stars who agreed to keep games closer than the odds-makers predicted.

But quite apart from any hypothetical case, the fact remained that Fibak bet on a match and, all of McDonald and Hill's demurrers notwithstanding, the Grand Prix Code of Conduct, upon which WCT's rules are based, says "no player shall wager anything of value in connection with any tennis event." (Despite my repeated pleas, nobody in Strasbourg or at the WCT office in London would provide me with the WCT rule book.) No exception is made for small bets or amusing bets or bets between friends or bets away from the tournament site. The rule is simply and categorically against gambling. Especially in view of the rumors that had so upset Harry Lapp—that Lendl was going to let Fibak win—I was surprised to have John McDonald dismiss the incident as a matter of no consequence.

But WCT was giving no ground today. They wouldn't say whether they would hold a tournament in Strasbourg next year, and when asked whether he was worried about the future of tennis and WCT, Al G. Hill, Jr., swore, "I'm not worried about the future of WCT. We've been in business for fifteen years this year. As far as tennis in general, I believe it'll continue to grow, even though it's in the midst of much confusion for the public."

The confusion, however, was not limited to the public. The press, too, had a hard time making sense of what had happened this week in Strasbourg. Several French reporters asked who would pay the hostesses who had gone on strike this morning, claiming they had not received the money due them. Would WCT cover Harry Lapp's losses and obligations? Or would local people have to bear the brunt of this failed tournament?

Fed up with this line of questioning, Hill asked about Bernard Dolet of *L'Equipe*, "Who's this guy, the business editor?"

Then Alan Page apologized for returning to a previous subject, but he didn't understand Al G. Hill's confidence about the future of WCT. "You set out a circuit for this year and you are now cutting back. I mean, after a small segment of the first year you're cutting back next year. Now, this must be worrying."

"There's been no official [announcement] whatsoever," Hill insisted, "about our 1983 and 1984 plans. We will make that announcement in the next two months as to what our plans are. But let me add one more thing. WCT is interested in quality in professional tennis and not merely quantity of events, being a multitude of events, or having as many players as possibly can show up. So should we make any changes, it'll be in the interests of the quality of professional tennis."

Page, who had sent out the story about the reduction in WCT's tournaments, sounded upset. "Does this mean the statement Mr. McDonald made to me—officially, I presumed—that there would be a twenty-five-percent cutback is not an official statement at all?"

"It is not. We are considering a number of alternatives." Any decision, Hill emphasized, would be delayed until the WCT finals in May. Not content to let it go at that, he rubbed salt in Page's wounds. "Conversations that may take place between one or two individuals are not official statements on policy of the company."

"Even if it is noted that these will be published?" Page asked.

"People seem to publish a lot of things," Hill drawled, "that aren't a hundred-percent accurate, that are taken out of the context of conversations."

My sympathy was with Alan Page, but after one glance at John McDonald's sad, weary face, I couldn't help feeling sorry for him as well. Before the spring was over, he would no longer be working for WCT.

Finally, however, regardless of where my sympathy lay, I kept Al G. Hill's last remark foremost in mind. Eager not to fall into any inaccuracies or contextual errors, I made certain I got a tape recording of the press conference.

In fact, WCT cut its 1983 schedule by more than 66 percent and announced it would hold only three events in 1984. It also filed suit against the International Tennis Federation, the Pro Council, and the ATP, accusing them of attempting to monopolize professional tennis.

The final between Tim Mayotte and Ivan Lendl provided no more than a tepid interlude between interviews. With the exception of a few shaky minutes in the second set when the Czech looked bored and lost his concentration, Mayotte was never in the match. As soon as Lendl dispatched him 6–0/7–5/6–1, we all returned to the press room.

Inevitably, someone asked why Lendl hadn't committed himself to play Wimbledon. He said grass wasn't his favorite surface.

But he intended to master it eventually. "Out of the question is not for me some years going to Australia."

Then he barked at the translator, "You talk ten minutes. I talk ten seconds. Just say what I say. They can't write all this anyway. They don't get so much space."

Richard Evans, an Englishman who regularly covers the circuit for the *Guardian* and *Tennis Week*, asked, "What was the difference between the first set and the second set?"

"I won 6–0 the first set and 7–5 the second set."

"What was the difference?"

"Put it this way," Lendl said, "I won six games in the first set and seven in the second."

"Try harder," said Evans, grinning by now.

"Well, he won no games in the first set and five in the second."

"Come on, Ivan, I want your analysis."

"Put it this way. He won more games in the second set than in the first."

I had the eerie sense that I was living a scene from Samuel Beckett, that I had blundered on stage during an absurdist drama and had been trapped there.

Mustering my remaining strength, I pried myself out of the chair. Out of the question was not for me immediately going to Milan.

MILAN

WITHIN minutes of arriving in Milan, I had a ferocious argument with the hotel desk clerk, then was invited by an aged lady to make love to her. I cannot say which was more distressing.

It was after midnight when I checked into the Excelsior Hotel Gallia and discovered that the discount rate for this Grand Prix tournament was $20 higher than I had been told when I telephoned for reservations. Perhaps as punishment for my protests, the management gave me a room the same size and cheeriness as a crypt. There was only one coat hanger, and it had been twisted into an antenna for an ancient television set. Furious, I flopped onto the bed—the mattress felt like a burlap sack stuffed with bowling balls—and dialed the front desk. No answer. I let it ring for five minutes and when no one responded, I charged downstairs to complain.

As I passed through the lobby, a lady waved to me. Blind with rage and further misled by my myopia, I mistook her for a journalist I had met in Genoa. Only as I approached the sofa where she sat did I realize this woman, despite her mane of blond hair, must have been close to seventy-five.

"Would you do a favor for an old lady?" she asked in French.

Assuming she, too, had had trouble with the hotel management, I said I would.

She patted a suede cushion on the couch. "Sit down, please." I did.

"Would you like to make love to me?"

Always insecure about my French, I murmured, "*Comment?*"

"Would you make love to me?"

"I'm married," came my unimaginative answer.

"So am I. What does that matter?"

"I'm happily married."

"I'm not," she said. "But that doesn't concern us. We're alone. With each other." Her hand, bright with jewels and blue veins, fell on my knee.

"I'm a Puritan," I said in faltering French.

Smiling, she looked even older. "I can change that. We'll have fun."

"Try the bar. There's a tennis tournament in town. The players are always looking for fun."

I pried her fingers from my leg and hurried up to my room. It wasn't until I stood under the fluorescent bulb in the bathroom, staring at my haggard mug in the mirror, that it occurred to me she might be a prostitute. The world's oldest working hooker, a refugee from stiffer competition in France, had she taken one glance at my white hair and wan face and figured I was just her kind of trick?

As I sank onto my bed of bowling balls, I clung to a single consolation. At least my room looked out onto a courtyard, not onto the cacophonous street.

At dawn I abandoned that consolation and all hope of sleep. Down in the courtyard a workman set off a reverberating din by banging a shovel against a cement mixer. I tried to call for room service, but when I couldn't rouse anyone's attention, I dressed, wobbled downstairs, and bumped into Buster Mottram, who launched into a venomous diatribe against Italy, Italians, their hotels, his room, the dreadful service, the extortionate prices.

I nodded in agreement. I would have added my own invective if Buster had allowed me the opportunity, but he blustered on without pausing for breath. Had I heard the racket in the courtyard? Did I realize the Gallia didn't accept American Express? Was I aware that a Continental breakfast cost seven dollars?

"Come on," he said. "This place is a whip-off. We can eat cheaper around the corner."

We covered the distance in a dog trot, Buster, with his ribbed white sweater, looking like a character from *Chariots of Fire*, I, with my ribbed red eyelids, resembling the alcoholic from *The Lost Weekend*. In a café where the waiters knew Mottram and had all memorized the words to "Bette Davis Eyes," which played incessantly on the jukebox, Buster drained two tall glasses of freshly squeezed orange juice and bolted down a couple of ham sandwiches while I disconsolately stirred my coffee.

Then, as we were jogging back to the hotel, Buster griped about his first-round match against Brian Teacher, an American ranked No. 12. He had just played and beaten Teacher in three close sets last week in Rotterdam. Now he had to do it again. It was a lousy draw and Buster didn't delude himself about his prospects. At the Gallia he stopped at the Volvo Grand Prix reception desk and asked the hostess to confirm his reservation on an afternoon flight to London. Then he dashed off to a nearby club to practice.

I rode to the arena with Peter Fleming. Best known as John McEnroe's doubles partner, Fleming is a tall, blond fellow who used to look preppy, but now affects a punk image, with a three-day growth of beard and hair that appears to have been cut by a committee. Hacked short on top, it stands up in spikes; on the sides and in back it dribbles in long, greasy strands down to his shirt collar.

I tried to strike up a conversation. My first remarks were met by monosyllables. The next few prompted no reply whatsoever. Just when I had begun to think this was a bit like driving through Milan beside a rack of frozen meat, Fleming spoke—and in Italian, no less. "What kind of car is this?"

"A Jaguar VJ6," said the driver.

Fleming pulled a knit cap over his head, coughed once, and remained mute for the rest of the trip.

The Palazzo dello Sport in Milan is huge and modern and looks like a flying saucer that has crash-landed on a parking lot. Unlike the Rhenus Hall in Strasbourg, this arena was well lit and had a color scheme that soothed the eye and made it easy to follow a tennis ball.

Easy for me, that is. Buster Mottram had considerably more

difficulty tracking the ball as it caromed off Brian Teacher's racquet. A fierce server, emphatic with his volleys and over-heads, Teacher was at home on the fast carpet. Although Buster made it a battle, Teacher dispatched him 7–6/6–4, in time for Mottram to catch the afternoon flight to London.

As usual, this early in a tournament the press box was empty except for me. Most journalists huddled in the press room spec-ulating about which players had pulled out, which ones might scratch at the last minute, and which ones were apt to be in shape if they did show up. The Volvo Grand Prix seemed to be suffering the same epidemic of defections as the WCT. McEnroe and Kriek had already dropped out with injuries. Eliot Teltscher and Raul Ramirez had withdrawn, and Ilie Nastase, Adriano Panatta, and Andres Gomez were somewhere in the Caribbean completing their exhibition tour.

While Panatta and Nastase had been given late starts, Gomez, the No. 8 seed, was scheduled to meet Mats Wilander, a seventeen-year-old Swedish qualifier, this afternoon. When Gomez didn't show up, a lucky loser from the qualies should have been substituted for him. In this case the lucky loser was another teenage Swede, Joachim Nystrom, who would have wel-comed the chance to earn ATP points and prize money in the main draw. But he never got that opportunity. Instead, the tour-nament director abruptly rescheduled the Gomez-Wilander match.

No explanation was offered, but the reason struck most people as self-evident. If the director defaulted Gomez, he might have to do the same to Nastase and Panatta, who also hadn't arrived. Obviously, he was reluctant to run that risk. Nastase and Panatta were big box office in Italy. Jimmy Connors and Guillermo Vilas were also playing in Milan, but since the prize money had been raised to $350,000—the largest purse in tennis, except for Grand Slam events—the tournament needed all the name play-ers it could get.

Meanwhile there was an unexpected attraction in the person of Chip Hooper, an immense, muscular black man who, after less than three months on the circuit, had catapulted from No. 235 to No. 35. As he loped onto the court to play Bruce Manson, reporters filed into the press box and stared, dumbstruck. At six feet six, Hooper was ten inches taller than Manson. His weight was listed as 210 pounds, but this appeared to be a gross underestimate. The blood-engorged veins on his biceps looked to be as large as Manson's arms. It was as if a tight end from the National Football League had been stuffed into a pair of tennis shorts.

Manson was a lefthander with a deceptively powerful serve. But he could never slip out from under the weight of Hooper's serve and he seemed surprised by the big man's mobility and the steadiness of his groundstrokes. When Hooper won in straight sets, Italian journalists wondered whether he was an aberration or a harbinger of the future. Did he herald the imminent arrival of dozens of giant, agile blacks who would revolutionize tennis as they had basketball and football?

At Hooper's press conference the interpreter, a pretty girl wearing just slightly less make-up than a *kabuki* dancer, told him, "I'll translate if you speak slowly."

"I can speak Spanish," said Hooper, who is a handsome fellow with high cheekbones and a *café au lait* complexion.

"Just speak English slowly."

"Where have you been?" one journalist asked. "Why haven't we heard of you before?"

"I been in school," Hooper said. "You know, studying."

"How long at the university?"

"Five years."

"You must have learned a lot."

Hooper shrugged. The gesture had seismic repercussions across the width of his shoulders.

"What is your degree?"

"Don't have a degree."

"No degree?" The Italians were confused. "After five years?"

"Well, I was hurt a lot. I broke my foot and I had two eye operations."

"So that kept you from graduating?"

"That, and I took off to play tennis."

"What did you study?"

"Business." Hooper smiled slyly. "And girls."

When the interpreter translated this as economics, the Italians were impressed. "You really should finish your degree," said one matronly reporter. *"Economica è molto importante."*

Finally somebody asked about tennis. How had Hooper made such rapid progress?

Chip had trouble understanding it himself. "It's weird. I started the year thinking it'd be great just to qualify for tournaments. Then I thought it'd be great to get into the top hundred. Now I think that's bullshit, being in the top hundred. I'm aiming for No. 15 by the end of the year."

"What's changed? Your physical ability? Or something psychological?"

"Both. You start winning, and then you know you can beat guys, and you see them choking . . ." He grabbed his thick throat and made a strangled sound. "It's weird."

"As a young player, who were your models?"

"Always liked tall players. You know, Stan Smith, Brian Teacher. Now I'm beating those guys."

"Other tall models?" the reporter persisted, transparent, it seemed to me, in his desire to hear Hooper acknowledge Arthur Ashe as his model.

But Chip said, "Cheryl Tiegs. She's a tall model and she plays tennis, too." He chuckled. "But I'm better."

The Italians were flummoxed. They asked me to write out Cheryl Tiegs' name and explain who she was.

"What's Chip in Italian?" one man wanted to know.

"You tell me."

"But what does it mean?"

"Doesn't mean anything. It's just a nickname."

"What's your real name?"

"Lawrence Barnett Hooper the Third." He intoned each syllable as if calling a roll of honor. "L.B.H., One Two Three."

"What's your father do? Was he a tennis player?"

"Nope. He's a doctor."

"Did you play American football?"

"Nope." Hooper was again smiling wickedly. "I was never big enough."

Then, as though on cue, he peeled off his damp shirt, exposing a massive high-relief of sculptured muscle. For a moment the room was silent. Then someone asked if he had lifted weights. Hooper said he had pumped a little iron. Between his eighteenth birthday and his twentieth he had shot up from six feet one to six feet six, and working with weights had filled out his huge frame.

"Has it helped your tennis?"

"Yeah, it makes you more aware of your body."

He didn't have to add that it also made others aware of it.

"Will you come back to Italy to play? The people here will like you."

"Good." He pulled on a dry shirt. "Maybe I'll get a clothing contract. Maggia gave me some stuff to wear. But I'd like to get some money, too."

That evening, in the showcase match, Corrado Barazzutti battled John Sadri in front of four hundred spectators. If there was any difference between the WCT tournaments I had seen in Genoa and Strasbourg and this Volvo Grand Prix event, it wasn't attendance. Not once during the week would the Palazzo dello Sport be filled to capacity. Promoters blamed this on the absence of McEnroe and Borg.

Others believed the tournament had made a mistake in allowing extensive local television coverage. But still others felt that television was the one thing which kept the tournament solvent. It excited public interest and convinced local and multinational corporations to pay to have their promotional strips pasted up around the court. Spectators, they said, were simply part of the set-dressing, like extras in a movie. And the beauty was, they didn't need to be paid. They bought their tickets, giving the tournament a little gravy to pour over the revenues from TV and advertising.

Whatever the explanation for the sparse crowd, it was a pity more people didn't watch Barazzutti go up against Sadri, a tall, ramrod-straight American who has the chiseled features and close-cropped hair of a highway patrolman. Like Chip Hooper, Sadri works out with weights and is an intimidating fellow as likely to lean on an umpire as on an opponent. His favorite ploy after a bad call is to stand close to the umpire's chair, stare at his racquet, and mutter loud enough for the official alone to hear, "I ought to break your face." If the umpire threatens to penalize him, Sadri innocently explains that he's just angry at his racquet.

When Barazzutti won the first set 6–3, Sadri was less subtle in his attempt to intimidate the little Italian. As they crossed over between games, Sadri bumped him with his shoulder, then muttered, "Get the fuck out of the way."

"Are you going to let him do that?" Barazzutti asked the umpire.

The official gave Sadri a warning for verbal abuse—he later explained it was impossible to tell who had bumped whom—and penalized him a point. That appeared to deflate the American, who went down 6–2 in the second set.

But the fireworks weren't over. When the Italian press asked to interview Corrado Barazzutti, he sent back word from the locker room that he felt like vomiting. Not that he was sick, just that he felt like throwing up. It was an impulse Barazzutti had often experienced since his Davis Cup loss to Buster Mottram. Convinced he had suffered unfair criticism, he didn't care to speak to Italian journalists. But they insisted, and he came and asked, "What do you pricks want?"

"Why are you so angry, Corrado?"

Why was he angry! Didn't they remember what they had written about him and the Italian Davis Cup team? "We beat England. Last year when we lost to them, oh, it was *terrible*. You said they were a team of shit, but they beat us because we're old and out of shape and no better than shit. You said we're not even a team. We're finished! Now this year when we win, you write it doesn't matter because we beat a team of shit. We're in the Davis Cup quarterfinals against New Zealand. But it'll be the same. If we lose, we're shit. If we win, we're still shit because we beat a team of shit. That's the way you journalists always are. That's why I feel like vomiting."

In the next day's newspapers Barazzutti's fiery obscenities were reduced to a thin, cold porridge of platitudes.

Players often claim to have been misquoted, to have been

burned by journalists. From time to time this may be true. But more often than not they are misquoted in a way which makes them look good, for the press generally feels compelled to protect players. Sometimes this entails eliminating obscenities or grammatical barbarities. At other times garbled sentences are edited into coherent statements. Sour grapes, inflammatory accusations, or simple callousness are judiciously deleted. Most important, all references to rule infractions and ethical misconduct are ignored. Players take it for granted that journalists are part of the tournament's promotional machinery and will print only what is flattering. With rare exceptions, the press goes along with the game, sweeping awkward truths down the memory hole.

At the hotel I met Mel Purcell, a friendly, tow-headed, gap-toothed boy from Murray, Kentucky, who had leaped into the top twenty and had been named ATP "Rookie of the Year" in 1980. With a flair for showmanship, he didn't wear a headband. Instead, he tied back his hair with what appeared to be a strip torn from a bath towel. He was fast and tenacious, and other players called him "Cell."

In the bar he ordered a beer and we took a table next to two middle-aged ladies who were drinking a split of champagne. They didn't strike me as Purcell's type, but he didn't seem put off by the fact that they were wearing mink coats while he was in jeans and tennis shoes.

"Hey, how you doing over there?" he called, and he wasn't discouraged one bit when they ignored him. He kept ogling them as he answered my questions.

He said he hated coming to Europe. He had been planning to play in Amsterdam later this year, but he had about changed his mind. "They don't like Americans. I saw in the papers where they burned the American flag there the other day. I try not to play places like that."

As for Milan, he couldn't help but have negative feelings about the town after losing his first-round match in a third-set tie-break. "This'll be my last time in Italy. I'm hyper, you see,

and hyper people aren't very patient, and if there's one thing you have to be in this country, it's patient."

The worst problem he had had to confront after his breakthrough in 1980 was the constant travel. It ground you down, he said, physically and emotionally. He had a bad cold now. He'd had it for weeks and it sure wasn't helping his game, and he knew it wouldn't clear up until he took a few weeks off. "Living on the road sounds great. People think you're out partying all the time, drinking and chasing pussy. What they don't know is mostly you're just in your room alone."

It might be better to travel with a girl, but it was hard enough on the road without assuming responsibility for somebody else's happiness. "A lot of marriages break up that way."

He told me about Brian Teacher, who had been playing in Australia in 1980 when he received a phone call from his wife in the States, informing him she was about to divorce him. Shocked and distraught, Teacher had been tempted to fly home. But he stayed and won the tournament, the Australian Open, a Grand Slam event.

"That's gotta be one of the most amazing wins on record," Purcell said. "I mean, under those circuinstances." Then to the ladies in mink, "How's that wine you're drinking?"

They still weren't interested.

"Here I am bitching about the travel," said Purcell, "and I've only been at it two years. I was talking to Mottram today. He's been at it ten years. And there's Australian guys like Phil Dent and John Alexander, they've been at it forever."

Not that there weren't compensations. "McEnroe'll never have to work another day in his life," Purcell said. "Me, I'm just going to go for it, I'm going to hustle my butt off. I figure if I make $100,000 to $200,000 a year for the next five years, I'll be set for life."

Brian Teacher strolled into the bar wearing designer jeans and an aviator's jacket. "Hey, wanna go to the disco?"

Like most tournaments, the one in Milan had arranged for players to get in free at a local night spot.

"Might as well," said Purcell. "I'm out of here tomorrow.

I've got about three weeks off. Maybe I'll stop in New York and call Mac and ask how his ankle is. Might take in a hockey game. Then I'll go home and get rid of this cold before I head out to play L.A. and Vegas."

Mel Purcell finished his beer, said he'd see me in Paris at the French Open, bid the oblivious ladies good night, and although it was one a.m. and he had a morning flight, he set off for a disco appropriately named Nepenthe.

After discussing it with several journalists, I gathered that gambling had long been a part of the tennis circuit, and during the days of "shamateurism," players sometimes depended on wagering to supplement their under-the-table income. In 1939 Bobby Riggs, that consummate American hustler, came to Wimbledon, quickly repaired to a betting parlor, and placed £100 on himself to take the singles at three-to-one odds. When he won, he plunked the jackpot down on himself in the men's doubles at six to one, then he let all his winnings ride on his success in mixed doubles. Clinching the hat trick at twelve-to-one odds, Riggs collected £20,000—over $80,000 at the prewar exchange rate.

As John McDonald had said, as recently as 1976 Wimbledon permitted a bookmaker to operate on the grounds of the All England Lawn Tennis and Croquet Club, and there was nothing to prevent players—all professionals by then—from betting on themselves, or against themselves. Although the ATP grumbled a bit about the impropriety, the betting shop was not shut for that reason. Apparently it just wasn't profitable. Wimbledon demanded a £20,000 fee from the bookmaker, and the players, showing considerable expertise and insider information, nearly broke the bank by betting on matches with attractive odds.

Today it is still possible for a player to stop at a betting shop in London and wager on matches at Wimbledon. He can do the same at American tournaments, either through Las Vegas or through any of the thousands of illegal bookies. Of course, such bets break the Volvo Grand Prix rules. But how, asked every journalist I spoke to, could the Pro Council police this

rule when it couldn't, or wouldn't, enforce the rule against appearance money?

Eager for an official response, I reasoned that the ATP or Volvo Grand Prix would have no choice but to act if a man admitted publicly that he had wagered on a match. Coming from America, where Paul Hornung and Alex Karras had been suspended by the National Football League for a year for betting $1,000 on their own teams to win, I naturally expected there would be an inquiry into Wojtek Fibak's case.

I made an appointment to interview Keith Johnson, a Volvo Grand Prix Supervisor in Milan. Then I telephoned Paris and talked to Paul Svehlik, the ATP Director of European Operations. As I described the incident in Strasbourg, Svehlik's reaction was the same as Al G. Hill, Jr., and John McDonald's: Fibak's bet hadn't affected the outcome of his match with Lendl.

That was correct, I said. But it could have affected the final score. Even if it hadn't, the Code of Conduct was unequivocal. "No player shall wager *any*thing of value in connection with *any* tennis event." Presumably, the stringency of the rule was to guard against the mere suggestion of impropriety and the slightest chance that the integrity of the game might be impugned.

Svehlik conceded there were troubling implications to Fibak's bet, and he said that if it had been made at a Grand Prix tournament and admitted at a press conference, then the Supervisor on the site would have looked into the matter "to see if it was something the player said in jest. Of course, it isn't a good thing to say even in jest."

Assuming the player hadn't spoken "in jest," would he be fined and/or suspended? I asked.

Svehlik hesitated to speculate. That depended on whether the Supervisor believed the bet had been "serious"—not whether it had taken place, but whether it had been "serious."

Unclear about this distinction, I moved from the hypothetical to the specific and asked what would be done about Fibak.

Although Svehlik spoke at some length, the essence of his answer was that neither the ATP nor Pro Council would do anything. In fact, the ATP wielded little influence on the disciplinary process. That was the Pro Council's bailiwick, and the ATP had only three members on the Council. Then, too, he explained, since World Championship Tennis had broken away from the Grand Prix, the Pro Council had no power to enforce its Code of Conduct.

Was there, I asked, any ethical standard a player might violate during an exhibition or a WCT tournament—I mentioned tanking, betting, match-fixing—which would prompt the Pro Council to take disciplinary action?

"Unfortunately, there isn't," Svehlik said. "We just don't have any standing outside the Grand Prix. What players do in their personal lives is not something we can control."

"And you consider a special event or a WCT tournament part of a player's personal life?"

"Yes. As I said, we would have no jurisdiction to call witnesses, or ask for an accounting, or apply penalties."

I had returned to the press box and was watching Andres Gomez of Ecuador sleepwalk through two sets with Mats Wilander when Keith Johnson joined me. A tall, slim, sun-tanned man with a crew cut and a Southern accent, the Supervisor corroborated Svehlik's opinion. The Grand Prix rules didn't apply to exhibition or WCT events. But he promised if there was betting at a Grand Prix tournament, "I'd feel compelled to look into the matter."

I expressed surprise that the Pro Council didn't concern itself with what players did in events that might bring them and tennis into disrepute.

Leafing through his ATP Media Guide, Johnson believed there was a rule which covered all eventualities. It was on the same page as the rule against wagers. Under the heading "Player Major Offenses; Conduct Contrary to the Integrity of the Game," it declared that players convicted of crimes punishable by imprisonment of more than one year might be deemed "to have engaged in conduct contrary to the integrity of the game of tennis. In addition, if a player has at any time behaved in a manner severely damaging to the reputation of the sport, he may be deemed by virtue of such behavior to have engaged in conduct contrary to the integrity of the game." The penalty was a fine of up to $20,000 and/or a suspension from the Grand Prix for up to three years.

As for whether this rule applied to Fibak, Keith Johnson couldn't hazard a guess. That would require a decision at a higher level. He could only file a report. "We're not out turning over rocks looking for these offenses," he said, "but if we hear of one, we feel we have to report it."

That evening the showcase match featured Adriano Panatta against Kevin Curren, a South African now based in Austin, Texas. As the linesmen and ball boys took the court, introduced by the public-address announcer as *"Il Team Panatta,"* Curren could have been forgiven if he had concluded he was fighting an army as well as a national idol. Everywhere he glanced, with the exception of the umpire's chair, there was a man with his opponent's name embossed on his chest. Panatta's clothing company had paid a promotional fee for the privilege of outfitting the ball boys and linesmen.

The way he looked warming up, Adriano needed all the support he could muster. Although tan from two weeks of sun, he seemed lethargic and soft. When I remarked that Panatta must be exhausted after his fourteen-hour flight that day from Panama, an Italian journalist said, "He is always sleepy—except sometimes very late at night."

A step slow and a split second late with his groundstrokes, he stumbled around, struggling to regain his form. Both men had trouble keeping their feet under them. The court was curiously slick, and several times Panatta fell with a splat, like a spoonful of pudding. Curren, slim and bony, came down like a crane that had had its legs shot from under it. But he stayed upright often enough to run out the set 6–3.

Then, with the crowd chanting his name, Panatta played a set that reminded everybody of what he can do when he's determined. He served and volleyed with the old authority, and mixed in an occasional dropshot that put Curren flat on the carpet again. But after taking the set 6–3, he had little left, and the South African started teeing off on his forehand, sometimes switching to a two-handed stroke which he smacked for wide, flat winners. Defeated in the deciding set 6–1, Panatta skipped the press conference, willing to pay a $1,000 fine to escape the Italian journalists and get to bed.

In the last match of the night—it commenced at eleven o'clock—few gave Ilie Nastase much chance against Brian Gott-fried. Going on thirty-seven, the Rumanian was the oldest man on the Caribbean tour and the only one who had to contend with a seeded player in the first round in Milan. Although Gottfried had fallen from the top ten, he was still ranked more than sixty rungs ahead of Nastase, and with his aggressive serve-and-volley style he figured to dominate the net.

At the start Nastase appeared in a hurry. He dropped serve and stalked to the other end of the court without sitting down. Perhaps he didn't want to cool off. Or maybe he was just eager to get this over with. He fumbled away the first set 6–1 and didn't use his chair until he had held serve to open the second set.

In retrospect, Gottfried should have seen that as a danger signal. But the curly-haired, hawk-nosed American is stolid and straightforward and not at all equal to interpreting Nastase's mercurial moods. Even writers favorably disposed to Brian are hard put to say something about him which doesn't sound comic or condescending. *Tennis Magazine*, for instance, revealed that "the Gottfrieds' biggest experiment recently was Brian's idea. He decided that he and his wife should try chewing tobacco. They did, but the habit didn't stick."

No magazine has had the audacity to speculate what Nastase's most recent experiment might have been, but it's safe to assume it involved something more exotic than chewing tobacco. This evening he had arrived at the court with a beautiful black girl who spoke only French and a 250-pound bodyguard named Bambino, who spoke only Italian and just two sentences that I ever heard—"Journalists are shit" and "I kiss all the pretty girls." While his traveling companions might suggest Nastase is a man of great tolerance, he has been known to call his opponents "niggers" and "kikes," and once in Hong Kong, when a diminutive Latin American came out to play him, he announced to the crowd, "I quit. I no play no midget."

For all his foibles, and despite the rococo curlicues of his psyche, Nastase once had as much talent as any man who ever played tennis. He demonstrated a measure of it tonight, jerking Gottfried around with touch volleys and taking the second set 6–1.

In the third set, which started at 12:30, Gottfried was badly let down by his backhand volley. It must also have been demoralizing for him to realize everybody in the crowd was cheering for Nastase. Even the umpire seemed benignly disposed and laughed along with the spectators when the Rumanian made as if to flip him a phallic salute, but stiffened three fingers instead of one. Gottfried scrabbled his way to a match point when Nastase was serving at 5–6. But then the American suffered a knee-burning fall, and Nasty squeaked into a tie-break. Again Gottfried fell, yielding a crucial point which was enough to give Nastase the match.

Since it was after one a.m., Ilie Nastase preferred to entertain reporters in his changing room instead of the press room. Drying his stringy black hair, Nasty sat in his jockstrap, confessing he had been lucky. You had to be lucky to win any tie-break. He also claimed the Caribbean tour had been good for him; he had lost a lot of weight working out in the equatorial heat. Now a few empty folds of tan flesh puddled around his waist.

When asked how long he would continue on the tour, he bristled as if he had been accused of growing old. He declared he would keep playing tennis as long as he was enjoying himself.

Meanwhile Bambino stood guard, enjoying himself in his own idiosyncratic fashion. The perfect caricature of a *mafioso* enforcer, he had a harsh, menacing voice, clawlike hands, and an immense belly which dangled over his belt like a Parma ham in a string bag. But there was a perpetual grin on his babyish face, and he seemed friendly even as he kept muttering that we journalists were all shit.

·   ·   ·

I had set out on the circuit with many misconceptions, none more ludicrous, I soon realized, than my assumption that since I loved traveling as much as I loved tennis, the experience would be doubly pleasurable. But if the tennis had turned out to be radically different than I expected, then the travel proved to be even less to my liking. True, I took trains, buses, boats, and planes, but the journey didn't lead to a place. It led to a condition, a kind of claustrophobic fugue state that distinguishes the psyche of a tennis pro.

At first I wondered why players didn't show more interest in the towns they traveled through. Why didn't they take advantage of the opportunity to meet people, to visit museums and landmarks, to sample the local cuisine? Yet I was forced eventually to curb much of my own enthusiasm for touring cathedrals, lounging in cafés, and strolling from art gallery to antique shop to restaurant. These self-indulgences had nothing to do with life on the circuit, and if I hoped to comprehend these men and their manias, I had to try to approximate their schedules. I can't pretend I entirely succeeded. For one thing, I wasn't playing and practicing tennis six or seven hours a day. But I stayed where they stayed, ate where they ate, and remained at the courts just as they did, killing time, talking, and staring blankly into space between matches.

Fatigue, boredom, nagging illness, homesickness, sophomoric humor, abrupt mood-swings, a feeling during the indoor season of living in a time capsule shut off from the sun, fresh air, and all outside influences—these are the hallmarks of the professional tennis tour and they leave little opportunity or inclination for cultural excursions. If a camera is the symbol for a tourist, then a Walkman headset is the symbol of the circuit. Whereas a traveler is eager to record what he sees outside himself, a tennis player is interested almost exclusively in his own space, in creating through acoustical cologne a placid inner environment.

The situation in Milan was worse than in most cities. Since the hotel was a long way from the Palazzo dello Sport, one had to waste hours every day commuting, and since the tournament provided free meals to journalists and players at the arena, there was one less reason to break out of the numbing rhythms, the narcotizing orbit of a closed circuit.

The dialogue in the dining room was like a dose of Librium; it had the flat inevitability of a dead man's electroencephalograph.

"My backhand's falling apart," an Australian complained. "I can't come over the ball with the Prince Woodie, I can't hit with topspin. Besides, Prince isn't paying me enough. I'm moving to a mid-size racquet."

"They make a lot of money, Prince does. Everybody's using one," said a South American. "But they don't pay."

"They pay me," the Australian said. "But not enough."

"Same with Slazenger," a Czech put in. "After they signed Vilas, they didn't have anything left for the rest of us."

"McEnroe, Connors, Lendl, Vilas, and Borg"—the South American spat out the names—"they get all the endorsement money."

"Of course, you can always sign with Kennex," the Czech said. "They pay a lot. But then you never win another match in your life."

In the first round Guillermo Vilas beat Steve Denton, a stocky Texan who until this year had fought a losing battle with his waistline. Now slimmer and more agile, he stayed close to Vilas, but went down 6–4/6–4. Tonight Vilas had to contend with Denton's doubles partner, Kevin Curren.

Just as he had against Panatta, Curren changed to a two-fisted forehand whenever he got a short ball. But Vilas began to exploit the weakness of this unorthodox stroke. Since Curren slides his right hand up to the racquet on his two-fisted forehand, it is difficult for him to switch quickly to the backhand, which he hits with one hand. Feeding him high, looping balls, Vilas coaxed Curren into going for his two-fisted winner. Then he slapped the ball to Curren's backhand and caught him shifting his grip.

At 3–3 in the first set, a bank of overhead lights blinked off and Vilas refused to continue until they were fixed. Jimmy

Connors, scheduled for the next match, came on court flourishing a cigarette lighter. "Play on," Connors joked with Vilas. "I don't want to wait around all night."

When the action resumed, the Argentinian ran off three straight games to 6–3. He had a harder time in the second set, but held on to win in a tie-break.

At his press conference Vilas peremptorily dismissed the interpreter. "I can answer in any language."

Having beaten Connors last week for the title in Rotterdam, he was as confident of his tennis as he was of his polyglot powers. When asked whether his recent success was due to his new midsize Slazenger, Vilas said, "The racquet is good, but it doesn't play by itself. I've worked a lot. That's the explanation."

He looked like he had worked a lot. Powerfully built, thick through the chest and shoulders, he appears to be a miniature replica of his burly Rumanian coach, Ion Tiriac. But Vilas has the soulful, azure eyes of a poet—which is what he aspires to be. At least, it's one thing he aspires to be. He would also like to be the No. 1 tennis player in the world. Although to an outsider his eyes might seem his best feature, they aren't the eyes of a killer and are therefore a cause of constant worry to his coach. In 1979, after Vilas had played his guts out for five hours, yet lost the finals of the Italian Open, Tiriac shook his head in disgust and told me, "My man just wasn't tough enough."

The effort to make himself tougher had taken its toll on Vilas. Now nearly thirty, he has kept his muscles firm and flexible, but his face shows signs of premature aging. The skin is rough, a web of prominent veins pulses at his temples, and deep crow's-feet gouge the corners of his eyes. In Milan he solemnly said, "There's one thing we can't escape. We get older every day."

Out on the court Corrado Barazzutti and Jimmy Connors were bumbling their way through a set which had already seen four service breaks. For all his grunting and growling, Connors has never frightened anybody with his serve. He just spins the ball into play, then falls back on his piercing groundstrokes.

But after losing the first set, Barazzutti began to adjust to the pace of Connors' shots and sent the ball floating back to settle like a dust curl on the blue carpet. Connors, as usual, made no adjustments. Or, as he would put it, he made no compromises. He kept slamming away at every stroke, allowing little margin for error. Ninety percent of the time he can win this way. But against the best players it was no longer enough for him to play his hard, deep baseline style. His game desperately needed another dimension, which he had been too stubborn to develop.

The fact was, since his last major title at the 1978 U.S. Open, Jimmy Connors had come to identify so closely with his mistakes that it now appeared he would never again realize his full potential. He seemed to prefer to lose, as long as he could lose his own way—belting the ball flat and hard, even when he knew that was the wrong tactic against players like Borg, Vilas, and McEnroe.

Some said his trouble had started as early as 1975 when Arthur Ashe snatched away Connors' Wimbledon crown with a lot of off-speed junk that exploited Jimmy's aggressiveness and his forehand, which was suspect on short balls. Connors couldn't be bothered to switch his grip and hit with topspin, he wouldn't work on his serve, which most experts thought could raise the level of his game by twenty percent, and he never developed a consistent net game to take advantage of his potent groundstrokes. He also remained devotedly wedded to a steel racquet, the Wilson T-2000, which no other pro would touch. Whenever anyone suggested he try a mid-size or large racquet, he replied that they were "for women, old guys, and sissies."

In the most insightful piece ever written about Connors, Frank Deford of *Sports Illustrated* pointed out that "Borg has worked on his game and it has matured. Borg, the machine . . . the robot . . . not the exciting, bombastic Connors, has put variety and spice into his game." It was as if he refused to change for fear he would lose his karma, or its contemporary equivalent, his image.

Ironically, in view of his macho swagger, he has admitted he fears a still greater loss, his mother's approval. "It isn't me if I don't play the game my mom taught me. . . . My mom gave me my game, and she taught me one way—that lines were made to be hit."

So, against Barazzutti, Jimbo went for the lines when it might have been wiser to throw up an occasional lob or to rush the net and volley. It cost him the second set. But he was playing *his* game. He stayed on court long past midnight, winning on his own terms, making no compromises and making no sense.

Since so few reporters had remained at the arena, we were once again allowed to visit the locker rooms rather than wait for the players to come to us. Only one Italian journalist and I were interested in Barazzutti, who had collapsed in a chair, naked except for a gold neckchain from which dangled a gold ingot. Even in a state of extreme exhaustion Barazzutti was tense as a whippet, his sinews twitching under the taut skin. Although disappointed, he was too much a realist, a fatalist, to yield to anger. Several years ago, before a semifinal against Borg at the French Open, Barazzutti had flabbergasted the international press corps by asserting that he had no chance. "The only way I can win is if they let me bring a gun on court."

Tonight he felt he had been "a little unlucky. Every week this winter I have been unlucky." It wasn't an excuse, just a statement of fact. In each tournament he had had a tough draw and had been beaten by Lendl, Smid, Fibak, and now Connors, not a shameful loss in the lot.

At Connors' changing room, reporters had been forced to wait outside along with Jimmy's entourage, which included his brother Johnny and a French-speaking black woman in a flamboyant blond wig. For all his on-court vulgarity, and despite the fact that he's married to a woman who bared the full panoply of her nether parts in *Playboy*, Jimbo is known for his obsessive modesty and never walks around the locker room without a towel tied primly around his waist.

Tonight he didn't appear until he had showered and pulled on a pair of warm-up pants and a black satin jacket with COM-MODORES WORLD TOUR embroidered on the back. His brown hair was fluffed up and shiny from the blow dryer. Like Barazzutti, he wore a gold neckchain. His had pendants that spelled TIG, short for tiger. Over the months I saw so many players with gold watches, rings, bracelets, earrings, and neckchains I concluded that, like Bedouin tribeswomen, they proclaimed their wealth and status by their jewelry. Stuck in short pants and tennis sneakers most of the day, they had few other opportunities for conspicuous display.

I asked Connors if there was any special satisfaction in winning a match in Milan against Barazzutti.

"Shit, no! I shoulda been outa here in two sets. I was running his butt off. But he hung in there."

Jimbo, however, showed no inclination to hang in here. Swept along by the tidal wave of his entourage, he hurried down the hall, tossing a few last words over his shoulder. "It's never over until you lose it, and you never win until the last point."

We journalists stood there chewing on this wad of bubble-gum wisdom. Then simultaneously we all realized what he meant. He and his entourage had gained a head start in the race for courtesy cars.

Any number of players in Milan had contracts to wear Ellesse clothes, but none was nearly as important to the company as Guillermo Vilas. Several representatives from Ellesse's headquarters in Perugia always hovered around the Argentinian.

One evening, while Vilas and Ion Tiriac were upstairs taking a nap before a television appearance, I met Gabriele Brustenghi in the hotel bar. With his long nose, mottled complexion, and wild wind-blown hair, he bears a bizarre resemblance to Tom Hayden, the '60s radical and Jane Fonda's husband. But Brustenghi is a member of the board at Ellesse.

A few years ago, when Vilas jumped from Fila to Ellesse, rumor had it that a million-dollar contract had persuaded him to switch. Brustenghi would neither deny nor confirm this figure, but he declared that whatever Vilas was paid—and it was substantial—he was worth it. By signing Vilas, Ellesse felt it had acquired a man whose image complemented that of Chris Evert-Lloyd, also an Ellesse client. While Evert-Lloyd was the key to the vast American market, Vilas had the rugged Latin looks which in Europe and South America sold not only sports apparel but other items of leisure wear which were just as profitable to the company. His handsome face had been on the cover of high-fashion magazines, and he had made cameo appearances in movies.

"Magazine advertising is very expensive," Brustenghi explained. "A single page can cost tens of thousands of dollars. But with Vilas and Evert we get the front page for our product—and you can't buy the front page at any price."

Then there was television exposure. "Chrissie was on TV twenty-two hours last year. You can't buy a minute of TV time for less than $90,000. But we have her on screen for hours."

It didn't take a gifted mathematician to compute the advantage to Ellesse. At $90,000 a minute, an hour of TV time cost $5,400,000—yet Ellesse was getting dozens of hours free. Or, that is, it was getting them for whatever it paid Evert-Lloyd, Vilas, and other players.

"It means a lot to have a champion wear your product," Brustenghi said. "Kids notice things like that, and children are very important to sales."

Signing and merchandising Chris Evert-Lloyd and Guillermo Vilas, who were already champions, was infinitely easier than taking a flyer in the volatile futures market. He cited the famous case of Thierry Tulasne, a French junior who had erupted on the scene at the age of sixteen in the 1980 Italian Open, where he beat Sandy Mayer, then stunned Vitas Gerulaitis, the defending champion.

Convinced that a new Borg had been born, clothing and equipment firms began a bidding war for Tulasne. Ellesse weighed in with an initial offer of $80,000 a year. Although Brustenghi admitted this was high for a player who had never won a professional tournament, he justified it on the grounds that Ellesse had been eager to crack the French market, which was essentially the Parisian market and which, according to him, had always been ambivalent toward the country's top player, Yannick Noah, who is black.

The war ended with Lacoste keeping Tulasne in French clothes at an annual cost of $200,000. Sergio Tacchini had tried to top

Lacoste with $230,000, but the contract had already been signed and, Brustenghi said, the market had been permanently bent out of shape. Now every teenager who caught a star on a bad day or upset an aging champion demanded $200,000.

A lot of clothing companies were losing money. But, in Brustenghi's opinion, the damage to young players was as devastating as it had been to business. Lucrative long-term contracts left many of them lazy and unmotivated. After his impressive start Thierry Tulasne had finished his first full year on the tour as No. 52. Now he had fallen to No. 85 and was forced to qualify for tournaments and, except for his preposterous clothing contract, he was indistinguishable from droves of other juniors who pursued a dream that they, too, could become millionaires, if not champions.

As Brustenghi and I talked, Ion Tiriac ambled over and flopped into a chair at our table. After his nap he looked rumpled and grumpy as a bear prematurely routed out of hibernation. John McPhee once wrote of Tiriac, "His body is encased in a rug of hair. Off court, he wears cargo-net shirts. His head is covered with Medusan wires. Above his mouth is a moustache that somehow suggests that this man has been to places most people do not imagine exist."

This is a good description, graphic and colorful, and I suspect Tiriac read it and has, ever since, been amused by the results he gets by playing on the impression it created. He seems to relish his evil appearance. Perhaps he believes it protects him against his better nature. Although he must grow weary of discussing his relationship with Vilas, he is usually accommodating to those who brave his forbidding stares and ask questions.

Tiriac no longer favors cargo-net shirts. Like Vilas, he dresses in clothes by Ellesse. On one hairy wrist he wears a thin gold chain and a gold Rolex watch. "I got it from Fila," he told me. "It was the only thing they ever gave me."

When the waiter came to take his order, I expected Tiriac to demand absinthe or a boilermaker or a triple shot of whiskey. Instead, he asked for a Pimm's Cup, the preferred drink of those genteel dowagers who show up every day at Wimbledon to gush about the hydrangeas.

Tiriac explained that he had begun coaching long before he met Guillermo. Back then he had struggled to inject some of his steely combativeness and strategic sense into the bubbles of mercury that fizzed through Ilie Nastase's veins. "You can't expect results in a few weeks or even a season," he said. "You have to commit yourself for years. And it's not a question of simply raising your man's ranking. It's a question of keeping it there."

That, he stressed, required constant vigilance. "Believe me, it is not the dream of my life to get up and hit tennis balls at five in the morning with Guillermo. But it is my job. He must work. If he takes off three weeks, it takes him six to get back in shape. I mean, mentally and physically. We've tried everything. Work is all that works."

Vilas entered the room, a sawed-off *gaucho* striding in off the *pampas*, wearing blue jeans, a belted leather jacket, and high-heeled boots.

At the bar he paused to chat with Peter McNamara, the Australian ace whose prognathous jaw and prominent nose are softened by a perpetual grin. Since both figured to play Jimmy Connors this week, they wound up comparing notes and complaining about Jimbo's delaying tactics.

"He takes a minute, sometimes more, between points," McNamara said. "When you're serving, he's always wandering around, looking at the crowd. Even when you think he's ready and toss up the ball, you suddenly realize he's turned away or he's picking at his strings."

Tiriac signaled for the bill, and although he had been there only long enough to drain his Pimm's Cup, he paid for everybody. Then he and Guillermo and half a dozen people from Ellesse set out for their television interview.

It was a moment to treasure. During my months on the circuit, surrounded by millionaires, this was the single time I didn't get stuck with the check.

In the quarterfinals Vince Van Patten played Peter McNamara one morning in front of a hundred spectators and over ten thousand empty seats. For Van Patten, a buoyant Californian with a mop of blond hair, this must have been reminiscent of rehearsing on an abandoned soundstage. Son of television star Dick Van Patten, Vince had performed in front of cameras from the age of nine, as the Bionic Boy in the popular TV show "The Six Million Dollar Man" and in a number of feature films.

Now he was a full-time, full-fledged tennis professional, No. 43 in the world. Just last year he had won a $300,000 tournament in Tokyo, dispatching José Luis Clerc, Gerulaitis, and McEnroe. But the Italian public and the tournament promoters seemed unimpressed. Not once that week had he played a showcase match.

A Volvo Grand Prix official informed me Van Patten received different treatment in the States, where his television popularity carried over onto the court. After his triumph in Tokyo he was also much in demand in Japan; next month he would participate in the Suntory Cup, a four-man special event in which he would get equal billing with McEnroe, Borg, and Vilas.

Van Patten's problem in Europe, the Grand Prix official explained, was his image. His flashy red bandanna and fresh-faced good looks might appeal to an audience in Malibu, but not in Milan, Paris, or Madrid. If he hoped to seize the public's imagination on the Continent, he had to capture a major title.

He appeared capable of doing that. He had already beaten Nastase and Tim Mayotte, last week's finalist in Strasbourg, and today, after recovering from a disastrous first set, which he dropped 6–1, he took the second 6–3. Then he parried with Peter McNamara throughout the third.

Once known primarily as a doubles player, the Australian had switched to a Prince racquet and crashed the top ten. Canny and resourceful, he provided the kind of challenge by which Van Patten could measure his progress. Judging by that yardstick, the American fell a few centimeters short of greatness—if, that is, one believed the linesman.

With match point against him, Van Patten poked a volley close to the baseline. It looked like a winner. Van Patten certainly believed it was. Even McNamara appeared ready to be convinced. But the linesman signaled long, and after a brief, futile appeal to the umpire for an overrule, Van Patten shook McNamara's hand and smiled like a trooper.

Later, at a press conference, McNamara conceded he thought the ball had landed on the line, but the day was long past when he would give away match points. They were all professionals, and the rule was that you played the official's call. In this case it had gone in his favor, and he took it.

Despite the disappointing loss, Vince Van Patten agreed to talk, and we met at his hotel room. Hobbling on bare feet, he opened the door and led me inside. Although in pain, he grinned and told me he had put the match behind him. What he couldn't put behind him were the blood blisters on the balls of his feet. It was the same problem some guys had with their hands. Calluses built up on the soles of his feet, and if he wasn't careful to shave them down, blood blisters formed under the hardened skin.

There was a girl in his bed. She looked slim and tall, but that's a guess. She never stood up. Van Patten climbed onto the bed beside her and sat with his back against the headboard. I could see the raw flesh on the bottom of his feet.

He introduced her as Arlene. No last name. Where Vince wore warm-up pants and a tee shirt, Arlene had on designer jeans, a black Ellesse tee shirt, and lots of eye-liner. As we talked, the two of them darted their eyes to a color TV, which had been turned on without sound to a cartoon program.

It struck me that Van Patten's career embodied a curious paradox. In America it is common for a star athlete to use his celebrity in sports as a springboard to the movies or television. But Van Patten had done just the opposite and he saw nothing odd about it.

"It's the same," he said. "You perform." Whether the game was tennis or acting, you needed stage presence and you had to concentrate.

Take the Borg-McEnroe rivalry, he said. "It's a show. Their

matches have a style. Tennis players are definitely entertainers. The game brings out true personalities."

With his background in show business, he could keep tennis in perspective, he claimed. When the pressure was on or he suffered a bad loss, he tried to laugh, as he had done today after that botched call on match point. "I'm not obsessed. I have a great drive to be the best. But that doesn't mean you have to cut out the rest of your life. You have to take time to smell the roses along the way."

He admired a guy like Vitas Gerulaitis. "He works harder than anybody. He parties hard, too, but he does it at the right times."

Did tennis players take drugs more or less than entertainers in other branches of show biz?

"I don't know anybody on the circuit who uses drugs," Vince said. "These guys are athletes."

Had his income declined since he left acting?

No, he was doing well. Last year he had won more than $97,000 in prize money and had earned "about $225,000" on endorsements, clinics, and special events. He conceded that his income was probably higher because of his TV celebrity.

Arlene piped up that she was a fashion model and understood his life. She assured me—or was she assuring Van Patten?—that she suffered from the same tight schedules, constant travel, and taxing physical demands.

Van Patten insisted tennis was "more satisfying than acting. If you beat a great player, it's on the computer and nobody can take it away from you. You can be a great actor and not get a role. You can make a good movie and have it fail and no one sees it. But if you win matches, they've got to recognize it. It's not subjective."

Then he seemed to remember his match today and admitted things were never altogether objective. He knew what it was to be treated as a star, and that's why he preferred to play in the States or Japan, where they made him feel welcome. They sent a limo to pick him up at the airport. They reserved a suite at the hotel and filled it with flowers and baskets of fruit. They showcased his matches; they didn't put him on court in the morning in an empty arena. Here in Milan, he said, it was clear that no one cared whether he won or lost, and this had practical consequences.

"If you're not important to a tournament, you don't feel good about yourself, and when you don't feel good about yourself, you don't play your best. And let's face it, you know when there are close calls, the top players are always going to get the benefit of the doubt."

For Van Patten, there was only one way to handle this. Forget about complaining. Forget about reforming the system. "You've just got to get there first. You've got to break through, get on top, and stay there. Once you're on top, it's easier staying there than getting there. People help you more than they did when you needed it."

Meanwhile he was resigned to the fact that the rules didn't apply equally to all players. Not only did the stars get the close calls, they were allowed to misbehave and violate the Code of Conduct. "Until people are interested in seeing tennis, good tennis, not just stars, you know they're never going to default a guy like McEnroe. Because if they do, then they don't have a tournament. It's not like football or some other team sport where even if you kick out a star player, people still want to watch."

In spite of Van Patten's sunny, equable voice, this sounded a bit like sour grapes, reminding me of the timeless gripe in all games—the stars get all the breaks!—and I was inclined to ignore it, until that night when Jimmy Connors met Tomas Smid in another quarterfinal.

From the start Connors played sloppily and seemed more interested in shocking the crowd and humiliating the umpire than in defeating Smid. After blowing the first set 6–4, he opened the second by shooting the umpire the *cornuto* sign, his index and little fingers extended, accusing the official of wearing the horns of a cuckold. In Italy men have been known to kill for such insults. The crowd whistled and hissed at Connors. But neither the umpire nor the supervisor imposed a penalty or a fine.

So Connors carried his obscene charade a step further. He slipped and fell on his backside and seemed to blame the umpire. Spreading his legs wide, he gestured to his crotch, inviting the man to have a go at him. Still there was no warning, no point penalty, nor was there one later when, objecting to a call, he banged the umpire's chair with his metal racquet, then shook the chair as if to topple the man from his perch.

In the press box Italian reporters were enraged by this behavior and objected that it had upset Smid, who lost his concentration and the match. They complained that the umpire was too gutless to control Connors and, what's more, that the tournament director had instructed officials not to enforce the Code of Conduct against the top players.

At the press conference a journalist told Connors, "You're lucky the umpire didn't fine you."

"He's lucky I didn't pull him out of his chair."

"Why?"

"You figure it out," Connors shot back. "You look like a smart guy."

"After the first set," said another man, attempting to defuse a tense situation, "were you afraid you might lose to Smid?"

"I'm not afraid of anything. Especially of losing."

"Why do you always touch your nuts during a match?" This reporter was every bit as belligerent as Connors. "Is it for good luck?"

The interpreter, a young girl, blushed and translated this as "Why do you touch a certain part of your body?"

"Turn your head," Connors told her. He stood up, shoved a hand into his shorts, and rooted around. "I'm just straightening out my jockstrap. Besides, it feels good to touch yourself." He taunted us with a cocky smile. "Haven't you ever touched yourself?"

Cino Marchese, the ubiquitous Silver Fox, the Spaghetti Man to Connors, cut an imposing figure in Milan as he moved smoothly from role to role, identity to identity, always deep in discussion with some agent, official, or player. On Saturday, March 27, he shed his press credentials, picked up a champagne glass, and proposed a toast. In the press room, before the first semifinal, he laid on several bottles of bubbly and plates of *petits fours* and hosted a reception to announce the consummation of the deal whose difficult negotiations he had described to me in January, then again in February and early March. John McEnroe had just agreed to endorse the Lipton Tea product Topspin. And, incidentally, he would also play the Italian Open. Smiling and shaking his silver locks, Cino Marchese cheerfully denied that the Topspin contract had anything to do with McEnroe's decision to enter the tournament for the first time in his career.

The semifinal was no livelier, and just slightly longer, than Cino's reception. After Guillermo Vilas brushed aside Sandy Mayer 6–3/6–2, the press trooped off to a conference which Mayer and Vilas attended together.

Sandy said he hadn't served well enough to win. He wasn't as steady as Guillermo from the baseline, and every time he rushed the net, Vilas passed him.

Had they been disappointed that no more than five hundred spectators had paid to watch their match?

"That's not my problem," Vilas said blithely. "It's the tournament's problem."

"There are just five or six players people want to see," Mayer said. Although he had been in the top ten before and had edged into those exalted heights again, Sandy Mayer admitted he had never really been a superstar. "More top-ten players are going to have to enter important events if we want them to be successful."

But Vilas maintained that it was impossible for the superstars to meet all the demands on them. He complained about the lack of privacy, the demented schedules, the dizzying flights through different time zones. He could sympathize with Borg and easily understand why he had dropped off the tour.

Mayer, too, commiserated with Borg. But then he qualified his sympathy. "When you look at Borg's schedule, what you don't see is the greed. You see the tournaments, but not the exhibitions, the clinics, the public appearances that make him millions of dollars." Perhaps if he cut back on them instead of tournaments, it would be better for him and everybody in the game.

Vilas didn't care for this line of discussion. "Players are individuals," he asserted. "They play where they want. If they burn out and need to rest, that's their business." With that, he ended the press conference.

If the quarterfinals suggested that officials were reluctant to apply the Code of Conduct to Connors, the semifinals raised questions about just which rules they were willing to enforce. Against Peter McNamara, Connors once more started sloppily, playing up to his ability only in patches. Meanwhile McNamara was playing over his head, hitting powerful crosscourt drives which Connors watched in disbelief.

In the press box, crowded tonight with tournament officials, people seemed to regard the match more with a sense of foreboding than disbelief. This ominous atmosphere was deepened when a black cat came bounding down the steeply banked tiers of seats. It sprang over my shoulder, its fur crackling with static electricity, then leaped to the next level, startling everyone. Yet the cat was scarcely less surprising than the score of the first set—6–1 in McNamara's favor.

Stung, Connors fought back, swept the second set 6–2, and kept the pressure on in the third. But just when he was poised to take the deciding set, McNamara held serve to 3–5.

Still Connors appeared to have things well in hand, and on his own serve he reached triple match point. The tournament officials in front of me relaxed for the first time that night. Now that it looked like they'd get the final they wanted—Vilas versus Connors—they joked about how nervous they had been. One man mopped his brow, then did a pantomime of wringing the sweat from his handkerchief.

But McNamara wasn't finished. He saved one match ball. Then another. When he saved the third and brought the game to deuce, the man with the handkerchief mopped his brow in earnest. More bullets of sweat popped out of his forehead as McNamara broke Connors' serve to 4–5.

Struggling to hold his own serve, the Australian clawed his way to 30–30 and watched Connors swat a ball well out. The linesman, however, called it good. McNamara appealed to the umpire for an overrule. The ball was so clearly wide he hadn't even swung at it. The umpire hadn't seen it that way. Connors had his fourth match point.

When, remarkably, McNamara saved it and evened the set 5–5, one tournament official in front of me shouted, "Prick!" And two games later, when the Australian overcame a fifth match point, there was a chorus of obscenities. They didn't know whom to blame more, McNamara or Connors or that damn black cat that had queered the first set.

In the tie-break Connors hit a netcord and crept to a 4–2 lead. But the tournament directors knew better now than to take anything for granted. Groaning and cursing, they looked on warily as McNamara won three points in a row—5–4 and the Australian was serving. If he held twice, he was into the final against Vilas, and the directors dreaded the prospect of more empty seats. They needed Connors if they hoped to compensate for a week of miserable attendance.

McNamara moved to a 6–4 lead. Two match points in his favor. Serving into the deuce court, he went for an ace and missed—just barely. He took something off his second serve, hitting it with twist. It landed close to the line. Connors smacked a deep return. McNamara reached it and rifled it back, but just before Connors struck the ball, the umpire shouted, "The serve was out. Point to Connors."

McNamara exploded. After refusing to overrule earlier, why had the ump spoken up now? Connors hadn't complained about the serve. And why hadn't he called it immediately? Why had he let them play two more strokes?

Unmoved by McNamara's objections, the umpire ordered him to play on. It was still match ball, but Connors was serving, and the Australian appeared to have lost heart along with his temper. He didn't win another point. He had survived five match balls, but didn't have it in him to do much more than slap at the sixth. As Peter McNamara trudged off court, I wondered whether he remembered yesterday's dubious call on match point against Vince Van Patten. Was it as simple as Van Patten had made it sound? Did the close calls always go to the higher-ranked player?

That night I had a hard time sleeping and found it impossible to remain in the role I had adopted after the Davis Cup, that of a detached anthropologist recording what he saw and heard, refusing to pass judgment. I felt angry and sick. It was fine to claim, as some did, that the ATP computer was objective and that if you were good, you could prove it. But what if you weren't allowed to prove it? What if you weren't in the top ten or weren't a marketable commodity and had to go on court knowing nobody wanted you to win and, what's worse, suspecting that the rules that applied to you wouldn't be imposed with the same strictness on your opponent? What if you had reason to suspect that star players were protected and umpires had their instructions?

Next day I spoke to Peter McNamara in the dining room at the Palazzo dello Sport. After his singles match he had had to play doubles and hadn't finished until three a.m. He had gone to bed at five a.m., but was up at noon to practice. With his auburn hair and high coloring, he looked bright and healthy after a workout and a warm shower. He was in the doubles final and couldn't let fatigue or frustration over the Connors match ruin his chances.

He wasn't brooding or bitter about what had happened. He could live with it, he said. To stay on the tour, you had to learn to live with a lot of things. But that didn't mean he liked them, and he wasn't reluctant to tell me why. He didn't object to the call itself. The serve had felt like it might have been a bit long. But the umpire was supposed to overrule only on obvious errors and he was supposed to do so at once. What irritated the Australian most, however, was that the call had come after the ump had refused to overrule earlier, when it would have helped McNamara.

With his jutting, crooked jaw he appeared to grin even when he was angry. But it was a knowing, sardonic smile from a fellow who believed he could be surprised now by very little. "When you're in a match like that," he said, "you know nobody wants you to win. Oh, maybe a few fans are rooting for the underdog. But you know the tournament director and most people want the final they figured on. They like a three-set semifinal decided by a tie-break—as long as the star wins. If Connors had lost the match on an overrule, just try to imagine his reaction—everybody's reaction."

He paused as if contemplating that inconceivable event, then he shook his head. "No, it wouldn't happen. Connors would threaten not to come back. The umpire would never work here again."

McNamara's wife, Kay, came into the dining room carrying a little boy. She plunked him on Peter's lap, picked up a tray, and went through the self-service lunch line. The little boy was named Justin, and he was a year old. He wore what looked to be a Walkman headset, but the earphones were part of an elaborate hearing aid. Justin had been born with tiny nubs of flesh where his ears should have been. The condition couldn't be corrected surgically until he was five.

As McNamara dandled Justin on his knee, Heinz Gunthardt, Switzerland's leading player, and Sherwood Stewart, an American, wandered over. Perhaps mindful of Peter's rough match last night, they began reminiscing about their early, difficult days on the circuit. For Stewart, who hails from Goose Creek, Texas, and has a receding hairline and a beard which makes him look like an Elder of Zion, this required a prodigious feat of recall. The memories and wounds were fresher in Gunthardt's mind. He had started his career by playing satellite tournaments in Austria, where, he said, the draw was always rigged to protect local players.

Neither man could top McNamara, who had labored in obscurity for years before breaking into the big time. He had played tiny tournaments in France where the winner was paid in bottles of wine. Then there had been the Italian satellite circuit; McNamara had won the championship in Sicily, enraging a partisan crowd, and had had to leave the court escorted by armed guards. But nothing could compare with the old Istanbul-Beirut-Cairo-Khartoum circuit. Players spoke of surviving, not winning, and they regarded their fiercest opponents as friends compared to the truculent border guards, virulent amoebae, inedible food, and debilitating ailments which decided who won and lost most matches.

The three men were laughing, but they didn't claim that those had been better days. They each earned over $200,000 a year and were millionaires, or well on their way to becoming ones. Yet, as they saw it, every circuit had its problems. As you climbed the rungs of the ATP ladder, you traded one set of troubles for another. On the satellite circuits you caught malaria, hepatitis, and cholera; in Super Series events you had to struggle against stars who were protected and tournament directors who were indifferent, or worse.

In a ceremony before the final, two ball boys marched onto the court carrying furled flags. As a recording of the Argentine anthem played, the national flag was unfurled. Then "The Star-Spangled Banner" boomed through the arena and the American flag was unfurled. It dangled upside down from its pole.

Connors should have regarded that as an omen and abandoned the match. Nothing went right for the American. Afterward he said, "The balls were heavy. The harder you hit, the more they floated." But his shots weren't floating long. They were sailing straight into the net. His forehand, in particular, let him down, and once Vilas saw how poor Jimbo's timing was, he served up a lot of screwballs and off-speed shots and won easily 6–3/6–3.

Considering Connors' feistiness at press conferences after victories, I was surprised how placid he seemed now. It was as if the loss had served as a release or acted as a tranquilizer. When a reporter pointed out that he had been defeated at three tournaments in a row, twice by Vilas on a hard surface, Connors said, "That's all right. The year is still young."

But how young did he feel? someone asked. He had looked lethargic. Had the McNamara match drained him?

He had been up late last night, he admitted. He had gone out to eat and hadn't gotten to bed until four a.m. But he refused to offer any excuses. "I should be able to come back after a late match and still play in the afternoon."

Had he enjoyed Milan? What did he like best about the city?

"I liked the Cerrutti store—" naturally, he's under contract to Cerrutti—"and that big church downtown," by which he meant the Duomo. "I had a good time here."

I asked how he coped with the losses. After all, I said, he had started his career with a reputation as a poor sport, and there had been articles that accused him of being the personification of blind American ambition. Some claimed he would quit rather than accept being second or third best. Yet here he was still playing, while Borg, his old nemesis and paragon of cool stability, had gone into temporary retirement immediately after yielding his No. 1 spot to John McEnroe.

"I handle pressure differently than Borg. I'd rather go berserk on court for thirty seconds than let it build up for years. If you keep it all inside, you're going to crack. I'd rather let it out. Look at Arthur Ashe. He kept it all inside for twenty-five years. Then, *boom!*—he has a heart attack. Like I say, I handle it differently."

"Do you think Borg has some way of releasing pressure off court?"

"I don't know, maybe he goes back to his room and tears it apart. But I let it off on court. I think that's healthier."

Then he repeated that the year was still young, and he cautioned the press not to count him out.

With a train to catch early the next morning, I spent another night at the Excelsior Hotel Gallia and, passing through the lobby after dinner, I noticed the old lady who had propositioned me last Sunday. It was, I realized, the best offer I'd had all week, and if an invitation from a whore can be considered as such, it was the first personal question directed toward me since I had talked to David Schneider a month ago in Genoa.

The woman motioned for me to sit down, but I remained on my feet.

"Still married?" she asked.

"Yes."

"You don't want me?" she said in a small, hurt voice, doing her futile best to sound coy.

"I told you, I'm a Puritan. Did you see the tennis this week?"

"You say you're a Puritan, but I wonder. What's all this about tennis players? Are you a *pédé*? Do you like boys?"

"I like tennis. At least, I used to."

"Where are you off to now?"

"Nice, then Monte Carlo."

"More tennis, more young boys." She gave me a dismissive wave of her fingers. "I have no time for games."

"It's a business," I said. "Not a game."

I had been referring to professional tennis, but she took me wrong and lifted her head sharply. "Yes, it's a business. I have mine, you have yours, whatever that might be. Good night, *monsieur*. If you don't want me, I don't want you."

NICE

NESTLED in the Parc Imperial, the Nice Lawn Tennis Club was surrounded by hills that provided examples of every architectural style that had been popular since the city became a resort. There were turreted castles with gray slate roofs, the glistening spires and onion domes of the Russian Orthodox cathedral, cubistic pastel villas, Moroccan façades with crenellated towers and keyhole arches, Art Deco houses, their sleek lines reiterated by iron railings, and immense slablike condominiums, each crowding the other, casting its neighbor into shadow and blocking its view of the Mediterranean.

Drugged by sunlight, dizzied by the scent of flowers, the nearby sea, and Gauloises Bleues, I remembered a quote from Ivan Lendl, who, for once, had spoken from the heart instead of from the cold, sullen computer center that controlled his tennis. Although he was winning $100,000 a week on the WCT circuit, he told me he couldn't wait to get outdoors "where you have some sun on your face and feel like a human, not a mole. Where you can sleep at night like normal, not play one day in the morning, next day at midnight, and next day in the afternoon."

A long-term victim of sensory deprivation, I drank in the fresh air, the dazzling colors, the delirious first taste of spring. After weeks in empty arenas I was also delighted to be surrounded by people. With a total of only $75,000 in prize money, the Championnats Internationaux de Nice hadn't attracted any of the game's superstars, not a single player from the top ten. Yet from the first day the Lawn Tennis Club was crowded with spectators who flocked to the beautiful red clay courts.

There seemed to me something instructive about this, an object lesson for Lamar Hunt and his competitors on the Grand Prix who counted on big money, hype, and inflated reputations to put paying customers in the stands. In contrast, the people in Nice appeared to have showed up for the sheer pleasure of watching fine tennis. The tournament, an annual affair since 1895, had tradition and continuity, and—unlike so many fly-by-night events confected for TV, packaged by agents, played by men going stolidly through the motions, and forgotten afterward by everybody except the local promoters who had taken a bath in red ink—it involved a sizable chunk of the community. Over a thousand women, children, veterans, and other amateurs played on courts beside the pros and attracted their own supporters.

True, the tournament smacked slightly of the small-time. When players wanted to practice balls, they had to shell out a twenty-*franc* deposit, and at the end of each day used balls were sold to the public. The linesmen were little children, no older than the ball boys, and they chirped their calls like a high-pitched chorus of tree frogs. There was even a pastry stand with homemade fare that reminded me of church bake sales. But I found all this charming, and so did the players. While no top names had entered, nobody dropped out either. In all my months on the tour Nice would remain the one tournament that hadn't suffered last-minute defections.

I also found it pleasant to contemplate the peculiarly French character of the event. Vendors sold *croissants*, *pan bagnat*, and *crème caramel*. The refrigerator in the press room contained no soft drinks. Instead, there were cool bottles of Vichy water, beer, and champagne. While other tournaments emphasize "internationalism" and display flags from the homelands of all the players, the center court in Nice was surrounded by sixteen French flags waving from poles that also bore the nation's tri-colored shield.

Although English is the *lingua franca* of the circuit and scores are usually called in it, then in the local language, the umpire here insisted on speaking only the language of Voltaire and Racine. This created confusion, but no more than the French refusal to employ tennis terminology which is common throughout the world. Rather than refer to the Grand Slam, for example, they allude to something called Le Grand Chelem, which sounds like a mysterious Middle East sheikdom. Last year at the French Open, Mark Edmondson, a burly, combative Australian, became irate at an umpire. "I know you speak English," Edmondson shouted. "Just tell me whether it's my advantage or his." The umpire feigned total incomprehension until Edmondson called him "an arrogant pig"—at which point the man proved himself bilingual by penalizing the Australian for verbal abuse.

Gallic idiosyncrasies weren't the only ones on display. With so many Spaniards, Italians, and South Americans competing, I had an opportunity to observe the Latin temperament in all its unsubtle extremes. There were winces, grimaces, frowns, sulks, groans, whines, fierce oaths, occult obscenities, imprecations, highly imaginative maledictions and invocations of the deity. My favorite artist of invective was José Luis Damiani, the explosive Uruguayan, who indulged in a love-hate relationship with tennis balls. When they did his bidding, he caressed them and, before serving, rubbed them against his ample belly. But when they misbehaved, he called them "my little whores" and cuffed them about as though they were unfaithful trollops who needed discipline from their Sugar Daddy.

There was, also, a good deal of excellent tennis to be seen. Undaunted by the aura of absent stars, other players demonstrated an impressive array of skills. This shouldn't have been surprising. It's a rare achievement for a man to be ranked among the top hundred in the world in any field. If the thing could be computed, it might be revealing to consider what such a ranking might mean in another sport. In America the hundredth-best football, baseball, or basketball player would be well known, well respected, and well paid. In soccer the hundredth-best player would probably be a national hero. But in tennis, for some reason, No. 100 on the ATP computer is dismissed as an utter mediocrity, a pathetic journeyman who plays boring tennis and can't draw crowds.

The tournament in Nice proved otherwise, and I wasn't alone in my admiration for Claudio Panatta, who advanced to the semifinals and, at last, escaped the broad shadow of his famous older brother, Adriano. And there was Angel Gimenez, a spunky little Spaniard who wears a golfer's cap and who at five feet four gave away more than a foot and fifty pounds to Andres Gomez. The giant Ecuadorian blew Gimenez off the court in the first set, but the Spaniard chased down every ball in the second, squeaked through a tie-break, and rebounded from a 1–4 deficit to win the match.

Then Ramesh Krishnan, a pudgy Indian boy, was pitted against Jimmy Arias, a seventeen-year-old American whose body appears to be built of doorknobs and coiled springs. The tighter the match, the more Arias hurled himself into each stroke, always hitting for the lines. Krishnan seemed fascinated by the symmetry of his own feather-soft shots and was content to keep the ball in play. By the third set Arias was hobbling with cramps, and Krishnan, supple as a yogi, paralyzed him with returns that had no more punch than a powder puff.

Balazs Taroczy whipped the Uruguayan Davis Cup team single-handed, surviving a match point against Diego Perez in the first round and another against Damiani during a cloudburst in the quarterfinals. Then, after defeating Claudio Panatta in the semifinals, he played a marathon match against the French No. 1 and great local favorite, Yannick Noah.

With the score knotted at a set each and 5–5 in the third set, Taroczy fell behind on his serve 15–40, but saved both break points and sent Noah belly-flopping onto the clay. Thereafter the Frenchman, a black immigrant from Cameroon, wore a chocolate bib of grime on his Coq Sportif shirt.

Again at 7–7, Taroczy had trouble with his serve, and when he slipped to 0–30, he looked finished. The French word for dropshot is *amorti*—literally, "dead ball." Taroczy executed two marvelous dead balls to bring himself back to life. He held serve and continued to hold, taking a 12–11 lead and, at last, breaking Noah to win the title 6–2/3–6/13–11.

The French journalist beside me was exasperated with Noah. "He looked tired, out of shape," the man said. "You know, he smokes."

Yes, I had seen Yannick yesterday strolling through the clubhouse with a cigarette dangling from his lips. But my attention had been taken more by the curious way he wore his tennis shoes. He had broken down the backs of the shoes and slid his feet into them as if they were a pair of those comfortable slippers that North Africans call *babouches*.

"I don't mean cigarettes," the journalist said. "I mean hashish. He admitted it in an interview. He mentioned other players taking cocaine and amphetamines. He named names. It caused a big stink here. Then suddenly everything was quiet and it was as if nothing had happened."

When was this? What magazine?

"September 1980," he said. "*Rock & Folk Magazine.* The interview shows why French players aren't *sérieux*. They always do well as juniors. But once they get their first good results, every door opens for them. They don't have to work anymore. Why should they travel the world chasing ATP points when they're already rich? Read *Rock & Folk* and you'll see what I'm saying."

With mixed feelings I made a note of the interview. All week, and especially during the final, I had experienced something approaching my old love for tennis. Now it seemed I had blundered into the shadows again, and it had happened as suddenly as the season along this coast can go from spring back to winter with the appearance of a single black cloud. It wasn't just what the man had told me about Yannick Noah that ruined my enjoyment. I could no longer avoid the primary reason for coming to Nice. Later that day I had an appointment with an umpire who had agreed to talk.

We met in Antibes at the Old Port—a misnomer now that the marina has been modernized—and from where we stood I could look up to the balcony of Graham Greene's apartment.

During an interview Greene had once complained to me about the noise from the port. I was reminded of him on this warm, bright Sunday evening both because of the racket of the marina and because the man in front of me bore all the stigmata of a character from Greene-land.

Tense, jumpy, hardly the sort for heroics, judging by his appearance, he was nevertheless determined to do the right thing. But he stressed that he wouldn't talk unless I guaranteed him anonymity. He demanded the same assurance of secrecy a penitent received in the confessional.

When I swore I wouldn't divulge his name, he said that wasn't enough. I had to promise not to mention his nationality or to describe him in any way that might reveal his identity. He did agree, however, to let me summarize his experience in professional tennis.

The Umpire had been a player himself, but never world-class. To stay in the sport he loved, he had become an official and had served as an umpire at events he could never have hoped to enter as a player. For over twenty years he had worked in Europe and in America, on the WCT as well as the Grand Prix circuit. He had worked at Wimbledon and at the Masters. He had worked special events and exhibition matches. There were few facets of the game he didn't know firsthand.

I explained what I had heard from a number of players, then I described the matches in Milan. I allowed that, in and of themselves, they proved nothing. Close, controversial calls were part of tennis. But it seemed important that so many players believed there was a double standard and, in some cases, actual collusion between tournament directors and umpires.

"Did the players tell you how umpires are hired and assigned to matches?" he asked.

"No."

"They've probably never given it much thought themselves," the Umpire said.

I told him I had always assumed they were assigned to tournaments on a rotating basis and—

"Assigned by whom?" he asked, impatient with my ignorance.

"By some independent agency."

"There's no agency, there's no independence. Oh, sure, there are national associations and federations of umpires, and supposedly they train and certify officials. But, finally, umpires are hired on an individual basis by tournament directors. You understand what I'm saying? They're personally chosen by the tournament director and they work at his pleasure. If he doesn't like a man, he won't hire him. And if he didn't approve of the way an umpire performed last year, he won't ask him back. I don't know all the details of the tournament in Milan. But I know what goes on at other tournaments."

"What?"

"You can figure it out for yourself. It all comes down to the fact that a director has a serious financial stake in a tournament. The last thing he wants is to hire an umpire who might default a star player, a player he's probably paid a $100,000 guarantee and who he's depending on to carry the tournament. These guarantees, this appearance money, they're what has turned the screws tighter on everybody. If you pay that kind of money, you can't afford to have a star lose early. Remember, the director has financial backers. He's not in it alone, and he's accountable to them. So he's got to protect himself every way he can. Naturally, he's going to hire umps with whom he has a close and cooperative relationship."

"Does he instruct them what to do?"

"He doesn't have to. I've heard other umps complain that they've gotten instructions, but with me it's always been implied. A tournament director will just remind you that a certain top player has a reputation for acting up. But if you're patient and handle him properly, everything will be all right. What he means is give the guy leeway, don't enforce the code. Let the man blow off a little steam."

"How much steam?"

"You tell me. When's the last time you saw a star defaulted? You had Gerulaitis defaulted last year in Australia. But he sat in his chair and refused to play. He defaulted himself. Other than that, just give me an example. No, I'll give you an example.

Frank Hammond defaulted Nastase against McEnroe in the 1979 U.S. Open. Did the Supervisor stand behind him? Not on your life! They put a new man up in the chair and let Nastase finish the match."

"Have you ever defaulted anybody?"

"Never! There've been times when I should have, but I didn't dare. I didn't believe the tournament director would back me up. Everybody would claim I had cheated them out of seeing a great player. Maybe if I explained things to the press, they'd write it up and I'd be a hero for twenty-four hours. At last someone stood up to Connors or McEnroe or whoever, they'd say. But I'd never work again, not in that tournament. Probably not anywhere."

When I told him about Jason Smith, who had been fired by the WCT for refusing to wear a Fila warm-up, the Umpire said he sympathized with Jason's desire to preserve his neutrality. But the Fila contract wasn't very compromising by comparison to what other officials did, or allowed to be done for them.

There were umpires, he said, who held positions as equipment and clothing representatives. How could they be neutral when they were in the chair and a player under contract to them was on court? Or, worse yet, what about when they officiated at matches where there was a player who had refused to use their product? Would he suspect the umpire was prejudiced against him? Could the ump be completely objective? The point, he said, was that umpires shouldn't get into positions that put them in a serious conflict of interest, undercut their integrity, and created a devastating appearance of evil.

He also believed there should be closer scrutiny of the business dealings between umpires and tournament directors. Why were umpires discouraged from fraternizing with players, yet permitted to maintain potentially compromising relationships with tournament directors? He told me of umps who routinely accepted lavish gifts and entertainment, and who let tournament directors set them up with women. "This is a business, a multimillion-dollar international business. People don't give things away free. I don't care if it's a new graphite racquet or a three-star dinner or a piece of ass, the guy that gives it expects something in return.

"Consciously or unconsciously," he said, "too many umpires become co-opted. Pretty soon their first allegiance isn't to enforce the rules. It's to the tournament directors. They want to keep working and keep enjoying themselves on the tour. It's a seductive way of life. But to continue living it, they have to please one man, the tournament director. You don't do that by defaulting stars."

"What about the other rules?" I asked. "What about close calls?"

"It's the same. Some umps get so friendly with the tournament directors, maybe they're not even aware of what they're doing. But the way it turns out, the top players get the close calls. Maybe it's unconscious. Maybe it's just that they sense how much the directors want the stars to win. But it looks bad, it looks like collusion. For all I know, it could *be* collusion because umpires have so many side deals going. Some of them are buying cars—Volvos, Mercedes, BMW's, expensive automobiles—at terrific discounts through tournament directors. I'm talking about umps getting $5,000 to $10,000 off the list price. You can buy some people for less. After that, how can they be independent? How can they go out and hope to do an honest job?

"Imagine how Americans would react if they discovered the New York Yankees had arranged for an umpire to buy a luxury car on easy terms and then fixed it so that that man worked their games. Or take European soccer. A lot of teams are sponsored by big corporations. What if one of them offered a referee a special discount on its products? There'd be a scandal, an uproar. Everybody would assume the worst. It puts the game in a terrible light. It destroys the confidence that the public and players have to have in us."

Was there any solution? I asked.

"Yes, a professionally trained, decently paid, and autonomous cadre of umpires. Look, I had a lot of friends, a lot of contacts in tennis, and I work more than most people. So the present system is to my advantage. But it shouldn't be that way. You just can't give tournament directors a free hand to select their own officials. That's one conflict of interest that's absolutely wrong."

Since the Umpire was so outspoken on this subject, I wondered where he stood on other questionable practices in the sport.

"What about splits?" I asked.

"Yeah, well, that's mostly in exhibition matches."

"I heard it's also happening on the WCT tour and in some tournaments with ATP points. Whenever there's a big disparity between the first-place prize and second-place, the players agree to shares45the money."

"I thought you were talking about splitting sets, not money."

"You mean they split sets, too?"

"Sure, in exhibitions they do."

"Why?"

"The promoter wants a longer match, more excitement, and if it's on TV, he has a time slot to fill. He'll ask the players to split the first two sets and play an honest third set."

"You know this for a fact?"

Indeed he did, and he cited an example from direct experience. Several years ago he had been scheduled to officiate at the final of an eight-man round-robin. Beforehand, in the locker room, he said he had listened, dumbfounded, as John McEnroe and Bjorn Borg discussed how they would orchestrate the match. McEnroe would win the first set, Borg would take the second, then they'd play an honest third set.

The final had followed this scenario down to the last detail. "I sat up in the chair," said the Umpire, "feeling sick."

"Weren't you tempted to say something?"

"What could I say? I just happened to overhear what I shouldn't have heard. Thank God it was only an exhibition."

This was one of those distinctions which tennis people always insist upon, but which eludes me. Exhibitions are frequently televised and reported in the newspapers as if they were legitimate matches. What's more, they are often hyped as Challenge Cups, Shoot-Outs, Grudge Duels, Tie-Breaks, decisive encounters between players determined to prove they're No. 1. Most important, they are watched by fans who pay good money, expecting to see honest competition. Yet over and over I was instructed that I should regard special events as altogether different from tournament tennis, and not subject to any code of ethics whatever.

I let the Umpire have it his way, but asked, "What if you had heard players agreeing to split sets at a Grand Prix tournament?"

He paused, dredged in the briny air of the marina, then sighed. "I don't know. Who could I tell? What good would it do?"

"You mean nobody would believe you?"

"No, I mean I couldn't be sure anybody would step in and do something. I'm just sure of one thing. If I went to a tournament promoter and told him his two top players had agreed to split sets—probably at his suggestion—I'd never work anywhere again."

The Umpire went on to reiterate that tournaments lived or died with their top players, and would do anything to protect them and keep them contented. "*Anything!*" he emphasized. "Promise them unlimited practice time. Wild-card their friends into the tournament. Pick up the food and hotel bills for their entourage. Get them girls. Drugs. Anything! I've seen tournaments thrown into a panic because the director couldn't come up with the drug the top seed demanded."

While the Umpire contended that drug abuse was probably no more prevalent among players than among others of their age and income, he admitted he had heard they were using cocaine and even heroin.

"I hear things," he said. "I see things. But I turn the other way. In this game that's everybody's attitude. Nobody wants to know the truth, nobody wants to consider the worst possibilities."

What were the worst possibilities?

It all came back to the vast sums paid in guarantees and appearance money. As he had already emphasized, once a tournament director invested $100,000 in a player, he naturally took steps to protect his investment, and this meant compromising umpires. But what about the agents and players who accepted those huge, illegal payments? Weren't they compromised, too? asked the Umpire. Wasn't it possible that a player who could be bribed into breaking one rule might be bought in other ways?

In his opinion, secret deals involving such large amounts of money invited other, more serious abuses. At the very least, they generated grave suspicions which might undermine the whole game.

"For example," he said, "I worked a tournament where a star was getting a guarantee. He lost in the first round. It looked to everybody like he tanked. The tournament director was furious. He went around telling people, 'Now he owes me one.' But what is it the player owes him? Does it mean he'll play next year's tournament for nothing? Or is it something worse than that?"

"Such as?"

"You name it. Maybe split sets to make a more exciting match."

"If we were talking about organized crime," I said, "a player might tank a match so that the people he 'owed one' to could make a killing on bets."

"You name it." The Umpire repeated, "I'm not saying it happens. But it *could* happen. Anything could happen, because pro tennis won't clean its own house. It's like a corrupt police department that investigates itself and always awards itself a medal for integrity."

MONTE CARLO

FOR decades tennis has served as a cornerstone of the spring social season in Monte Carlo, and with the finals scheduled for Easter Sunday, the tournament has always started on the preceding Monday. At least as far as the public was concerned, it started Monday. Although there were always qualifying rounds, these prompted little or no interest. But this year was different. This year Bjorn Borg was making a comeback, and because he had refused to play ten Grand Prix events, he had to qualify.

Borg had to qualify! To many people in and out of tennis, the idea sounded absurd. After a five-month lay-off he was still ranked No. 4 in the world. To force him to qualify . . . why, it was like making Muhammad Ali fight in the Golden Gloves, like putting Pélé back on a vacant lot in Brazil with a ball fashioned out of old rags, like shunting Nikki Lauda into the slow lane, like expecting Joe Namath to employ a dating service.

It was all the fault of tennis politics, newspapers complained, all part of the war between WCT and the Grand Prix. If you were a member of the Pro Council, you could attempt to explain that the ten-tournament rule was reasonable, that without it the top players would concentrate on exhibitions and let the tournament system that supported the rest of the players wither and die. You could, like Sandy Mayer, point out "the greed" in Borg's schedule. You could accuse the Swede of limiting himself to "shopping expeditions" at Grand Slam events. But, finally, you were wasting your breath. For most people, Bjorn Borg was a great champion and a fine gentleman, and it was ridiculous to force him to qualify.

Ridiculous it may have been, but it was also a box-office bonanza. The tournament in Monte Carlo was quick to realize this, and it announced that the event would officially begin on April 1. The qualies attracted two hundred journalists and several dozen photographers. General admission was $5 for the first three days and $10 for the finals on Sunday—the finals of the qualies, that is.

That week several mass-circulation magazines carried features on Bjorn and Mariana Borg. *Paris Match* ran a cover photo of the young couple embracing, and a cloying article praised their love match. The Borgs were said to be planning a family— presumably long-range planning, since Mariana and Borg hadn't been living together lately. Still, Mariana held out the fervent hope that children would arrive within a few years.

My own family had arrived more promptly from Rome. A friend had loaned us his apartment outside of Cannes, and I became a commuter. Each morning my wife drove me down to the tiny station in La Bocca, where I boarded a train for Monte Carlo, thirty miles up the coast. On one side of the track the Mediterranean spread like a cerulean platter toward a horizon lost in haze. On the other side the purple hills of Provence, flecked with yellow mimosa and dark green cypresses, rose toward the Maritime Alps, whose peaks were still snow-capped.

Most of the passengers appeared to be tourists and day-trippers. But there was also a colorful contingent of blacks who hustled fake ivory carvings, glass beads, fly whisks, snakeskin wallets, and leather bush hats. I imagined a vast factory in Marseilles mass-producing African *kitsch* and sending out these poor souls to sell it. I never saw anybody buy a thing.

The train passed through Cannes, then curved along the beach at Golfe Juan, cut through Juan les Pins and came to Antibes, where the nights were no longer so tender as in Scott and Zelda Fitzgerald's time, but where the mornings retained a lambent glow. Then it was on to Nice and the breath-catching bay at Villefranche and the tiny town of Beaulieu, which, viewed through a fringe of palm fronds, lived up to its name, "Beautiful Place."

And finally, just before Monaco, there was the modest village of Cap d'Ail, the garlic cape, home of those humble workers who swept the streets, serviced the condos, and drove the limos of the tax-free enclave next door.

It should have been a pleasant trip. But I had just had an umpire tell me enough about professional tennis to fill me with despair. I wasn't on my way to the Monte Carlo Country Club to watch Bjorn Borg make his comeback. I was on my way there to try to find out whether he had rigged a match with John McEnroe.

Like everybody on the circuit that winter, I had talked and thought incessantly about Bjorn Borg. Despite all that had been said and written about him, I decided that nobody had taken a comprehensive look at the man and attempted to piece together the incongruent shards of his character. This, of course, presumed that he had a character, that he wasn't simply a billboard, a blank page on which advertisers could scrawl their messages.

Borg seemed to me to have struck a Faustian bargain at some point in his young life and agreed to transform himself into an automaton in return for being made into the best tennis player in the world. Now a model of lobotomized decorum on court and off, he was praised as much for his tunnel-vision and his remorseless one-dimensionality as for his metronomical groundstrokes. With the tacit approval of the public and the cooperation of the press, he had suppressed every other aspect of his personality and ordered his existence to a single limited purpose. Each known fact about his life reinforced the notion that he was a sort of extraterrestrial being, alien, yet friendly and a fine example for kids.

He was said to have a pulse rate of thirty-five beats a minute, half that of the average human. He was said to sleep twelve hours a day. He was said to read Donald Duck comics and watch television during his spare time. A high-school drop-out at the age of fourteen, he was said to be quite bright. A multimillionaire, he was said to have sound basic values. A tax exile in Monte Carlo, he was said to be a homebody.

Regardless of what he later became—in image, if not in reality—he didn't start off as a poker-faced, exemplary little boy.

According to Peter Bodo's *Inside Tennis*, he "was an only child, and Saturday was designated as his day with his father, Rune. All Borg wanted to do was play competitive games . . . but when he lost, he would cry and carry on until he was sent up to bed. Many Saturdays ended in an early appointment with the sand-man, until little Bjorn calmed down a bit and learned to suppress his frustration. Inside, he remained furious."

As an adolescent he was still volatile, a screamer of obscenities, an enraged racquet-thrower. When the Swedish tennis federa-tion suspended him for six months, his conduct improved, but even after he set out on the international tour, he could be foul-tempered, headstrong, and obstreperous. During a practice ses-sion he and his coach, Lennart Bergelin, once got into a shouting match and nearly came to blows. When Bergelin smacked him on the head with a box of balls, Borg called his parents and threatened to quit tennis.

Although he never gave up the game altogether, he got a reputation for giving up in important matches. When the calls or the crowd were against him, he sometimes stalked off court and refused to return. Other times, when an opponent got the best of him, he stayed on court, but acted as if he didn't care whether he won or lost, and whenever questioned about his moody, unprofessional behavior, he refused to speak to reporters.

During this early period there was another spicy component to his image. With his long blond locks and lean Nordic face, he was portrayed as a heartbreaker pursued everywhere by group-ies. One British newspaper went so far as to print a photograph—a palpable fake—of Borg unbuckling his belt for a tryst in Hyde Park.

Then, miraculously, within the space of a year or two, all this was forgotten and Borg underwent a sea change so dramatic that nobody dared remind people of his previous incarnation. By the time he won his first Wimbledon title at the age of twenty, he had shucked his reputation as a quitter and a playboy and acquired the image that has stayed with him—unflappable, in-defatigable, impervious to pressure, impassive in victory or de-feat, the Ice Man, the robot, the perfect machine.

Not until the emergence of John McEnroe did Borg begin to

reveal his first serious cracks and fissures. To be beaten by a player whose moods were so transparent, whose emotions spilled forth like a spendthrift's money, and whose demeanor was so offensive must have been truly shattering to the Swede. How else explain his behavior during his last full year of competition?

In a match against McEnroe at the 1981 Volvo Masters, he objected to a call and refused to play on. Confronting the umpire, Mike Lugg, he kept mumbling, "Ask the linesman, ask the linesman." He spoke as if in a trance and never once during the incident blinked his eyes, not even when he was given a warning, then a point penalty. Desperate not to default him, Mike Lugg had to summon the Supervisor to convince Borg to continue the match.

Then at the 1981 U.S. Open, having already lost his Wimbledon crown and having just been crushed by McEnroe, he regressed to childhood. Live, on international television, he walked off before the prize-giving ceremony. Newsmen and TV commentators, anxious to preserve the image they had helped create, claimed Borg wasn't a poor sport, he wasn't like Connors, who had been accused of acting like a churl when he did the same thing at the 1977 U.S. Open after a defeat by Guillermo Vilas. Due to a death threat, they said, Borg had been placed under police protection and whisked away from Louis Armstrong Stadium.

In fact, there *had* been a death threat. But Borg knew nothing about it when he left McEnroe, the tournament promoters, and television announcers stranded at the net. "I was just very, very disappointed," he later admitted. "I couldn't face the idea of making a nice speech in front of all those people. I suppose I was a bad boy."

It struck me as the first entirely spontaneous thing Borg had done in years. Trapped for so long like a carcass in ice, he had warmed to his own emotions and awakened. A prisoner of an untenable image, at last he had understood what McEnroe meant when he said, "It's not humanly possible to be Borg." Or, as Connors had told me in Milan, a man had to let off pressure somehow. Better to yield to temptation and stomp off the court than keep all feeling volcanically festering inside.

As the train rocked along the tracks to Monte Carlo, it intrigued me to consider the possibility that the robot had rebelled, the computer had willfully shut down, the automaton had determined to reclaim its humanity. Was there in Borg's long layoff and in his reluctance to commit himself again full-time to the tour a parable of redemption? Had he made up his mind to become his own man?

I hoped so. And I hoped he would tell me he had never agreed to split sets with McEnroe. But I had learned enough on the circuit to know I had to hold myself in readiness for a countervailing possibility—that the machine had just been in the shop for repairs and would soon be back out on the street, as murderously efficient as ever, even if sporting still another image.

The Monte Carlo Country Club, site of the tournament, isn't in Monte Carlo. It clings to a craggy cliff just over the border in France. When I asked whether the tax-free privilege extended to the club, I was answered with the same stares of mute disbelief which met any question about homosexuality on the men's tour. In Monaco, money may be an all-pervasive obsession, but it is a passion that dares not speak its name—at least not to the press.

A series of terraces, like steps designed for a giant, descend from the Moyenne Corniche to the sea, with practice courts on top, then the sprawling clubhouse, then a patio with chairs and tables, then the show court, then a parking lot. The clay courts, the tablecloths, and the clubhouse are all much the same salmon-pink color. Beyond a stand of cypresses which serve as a windscreen at the far end of the show court, the blue of the Mediterranean meets the paler blue of the sky.

The press box, situated just below the lunch tables on the patio, offers an excellent view of everything except tennis. Gazing down at the court through a grillwork of green railings, I could, if I sat up straight, see both players, but not the net. If I slumped in my seat, I could see the net, but not the near baseline.

Set off at a discreet distance from the court, photographers knelt on a carpet, keeping a vigil for Borg. They hadn't been there for the previous match and they wouldn't wait around for the next. Similarly, most spectators—and there were more than a thousand, a decent crowd at any tournament—wouldn't stay to watch the other qualifiers.

The ball boys and linesmen marched to their posts wearing beautiful powder-blue outfits provided by Ellesse. The promotional strips around the court showed a bias toward high fashion—Céline, Piaget, Jacomo, and Benetton. Yet Borg came on looking like the kind of character Monte Carlo's omnipresent police would regard with rabid suspicion. Unshaven, his long hair lank and dirty, he wore a rumpled gray velour Fila warm-up.

Generally, the principality has no patience with the young, the long-haired, and the unwashed. The *New York Times* once called the place a "capitalist pustule" and said it had "a Mississippi-in-the-mid-50s mentality." But under the correct circumstances it can be as up-to-date as a newly minted dollar. It welcomed Borg, as well as Vilas, Clerc, and several lower-ranked players, just as it had welcomed a host of Grand Prix race-car drivers. It didn't much care whether these men actually lived here. Why shouldn't Borg, a tax exile from Sweden, become a residential exile from Monte Carlo and buy a villa on Cap Ferrat in France? Prince Rainier remained more than willing to provide a refuge from various revenue agents so long as the tennis players participated in the annual tournament and the racers entered the Grand Prix every May.

While Borg was stony-faced and serious, his opponent, Paolo Bertolucci, Italy's "Pasta Kid," was utterly relaxed. The ATP Media Guide listed Bertolucci at 170 pounds, which is probably a twenty-pound underestimate. But why quibble? Paolo soon figured to be fatter.

"Thanks to Borg, I'll stuff myself," he told reporters. "I had a bet with some friends that I'd wind up playing Borg in the qualifying. Each one owes me ten dinners.

"It's a strange business," Bertolucci said. "I've had some good results in my career. I've won tournaments in Hamburg, Florence, Berlin, and Barcelona. But now that I'm twenty-eight and playing the qualies, I'm a star overnight. I've never given so many interviews, I've never been followed by photographers before today. I've never taken a set from Borg, but I'm happy to play him. At least I won't lose to some unknown guy."

Lose he did. Bertolucci held a service break and seemed in control of the first set, but Borg managed to pull even, then broke to win 7–5. The second set was a mere formality, 6–0.

The consensus was that Borg looked rusty, indecisive, and vulnerable. At a press conference Bertolucci confirmed that anybody in the top thirty could have beaten Borg today. Although the Swede didn't respond to that, he admitted there had been moments when he felt "deconcentrated." For the next week he would make himself sound like frozen orange juice—concentrated one minute, deconcentrated the next.

When a journalist suggested that, much as he might not like playing the qualies, he needed them to regain his timing and match-toughness, Borg didn't see it that way. It was stupid, he said, to force him to qualify. The Pro Council had made a mistake with its ten-tournament rule and he demanded they change it. Unless they did, he might not defend his French Open title. He might skip Wimbledon as well. These weren't idle threats, he declared. He had no intention of compromising. The Pro Council had made the mistake, not him, and he wasn't going to help them save face.

Borg left the room before I could reach him. When I tried to arrange an interview through one of the tournament press officers, he gave me the same glazed look I had got when I inquired about the Country Club's tax status. Everyone wanted to speak personally to Bjorn, the press officer said, and he didn't want to talk to anybody, not even to *Sports Illustrated* or the London *Sunday Times*. I'd just have to ask my questions at the daily press conference.

I explained that mine weren't the kinds of questions that could be asked in public. To which the man replied, those were precisely the kinds of questions Borg detested. I could write him a letter or try to pass a message through his coach, Lennart Bergelin, or his agents at IMG. But, frankly, the press officer thought I was wasting my time.

· · · ·

Over the weekend and on Monday, while Bjorn Borg reduced two more qualifiers to smoky rubble, then started play in the main draw, I continued my attempts to reach him, and as I did so, I became better acquainted with Monte Carlo and its Country Club. I even bumped into the Grimaldis—quite literally bumped into them at the buffet lunch which journalists got to eat for a mere $15 while the public had to pay $22. Princess Grace wore large sunglasses and a floppy straw hat that hid her pale, plump face. With her were Princess Stephanie, looking like a street *gamine* in tight jeans, a tee shirt, and gobs of make-up, and Prince Albert, also in jeans and tee shirt, but looking like a young banker who had gone slumming.

Perhaps I should have asked Prince Albert to help me reach Borg. With his Walkman headset, its antenna quivering, the Prince appeared to be maintaining communications with sources throughout the hemisphere. Surely he could contact the reclusive Swede.

But it was one bump to a customer. Quickly the cops moved between me and the royal family. Everybody claimed there was no crime in Monte Carlo, yet they were everywhere, these cops, keeping a high, wide profile, packing Smith and Wesson revolvers personally selected by Prince Rainier. As a wealthy resident once told the *New York Times*, "It's a police state, sure, but they're our police."

One day after lunch, when a chill breeze combed in off the sea, kicking dust up from the court, the beautiful people on the patio grabbed their purses—the men and women both—and made an early exit. As the crowd dispersed, I spotted Butch Buchholz, Executive Director of the ATP, and decided that if I couldn't contact Borg, I could at any rate obtain an official reaction to what I had found out. For privacy, we moved to the indoor dining room and talked over a table littered with wineglasses and bread crumbs.

For a few minutes Paul Svehlik, the ATP Director of European Operations, joined us. I introduced myself, but he didn't appear to remember our recent telephone conversation about the betting incident in Strasbourg, and I didn't remind him. After Svehlik left, Buchholz ran on about the Borg dilemma and the ten-tournament rule and the Pro Council's desire to find a compromise.

Unprompted by questions from me, he then announced that the ATP was anxious to put more teeth in the Code of Conduct; they wanted to get involved in the disciplinary process. In fact, the Pro Council, of which he was a member, was meeting this week to consider the matter. Umpires, he said, had to get tougher, especially on obscenity. "Players want this. We want to put the pressure back in the locker room, with players exerting more influence on each other to behave."

A former champion, once ranked as high as fifth in the world, Buchholz is a big man with a fleshy face and a shock of dark hair flecked here and there with gray. He had been in the sun and had removed his suit coat, but kept on his tie. His cheeks were burned the same dull pink as his shirt. Genial and outgoing, he gave the appearance of complete earnestness and leaned forward for emphasis as he spoke. Then he cocked his head to one side and listened to me.

How reasonable was it, I asked, to expect players to discipline each other? Was that really a job for the ATP?

Buchholz believed it was and assured me the players were "absolutely willing to impose standards."

I told him what I had heard from the Umpire in Antibes and asked how an official whose first obligation was to a tournament director could possibly crack down on conduct violators. They'd naturally protect themselves and their employers, even if that meant letting players make fools of them and a mockery of the rules.

Buchholz didn't believe that there were improper relationships between umpires and tournament directors. If they knew the players wanted them to be tougher, then officials, he was sure, would crack down. It started with the players, he stressed. Besides, there were always supervisors on the site to oversee incompetent umpires.

I said, from what I had heard, it wasn't a question of incompetent umps, but rather of ones whose financial dealings or personal friendships undercut their objectivity and, in some cases, prevented them from reporting unethical practices. I told him the Umpire in Antibes had overheard two top players—I didn't specify Borg and McEnroe—arrange to split sets in an exhibition match.

"I find that hard to believe," Buchholz responded. "If this were going on, I definitely would have heard of it." He warned me to remember "This is a rumor business, and a lot of umps like a little attention, too."

The Umpire hadn't wanted any attention; he had demanded total anonymity. But Buchholz didn't buy his story about set-splitting.

When I mentioned appearance money, he admitted guarantees were a problem. As he saw it, however, the problem was one of definition. "It hasn't really been defined what constitutes an inducement. There are a lot of gray areas." How could you prove a player had accepted a guarantee, he asked, when you couldn't say what one was?

It seemed to me a simple matter for the Pro Council to interpret and implement a rule which, at least on paper, sounded clear. But I let this pass and inquired whether Buchholz had received a report about the betting incident in Strasbourg. I assumed Keith Johnson or Paul Svehlik had alerted him.

No, he hadn't received such a report, and he reminded me that Strasbourg was a WCT tournament, not bound by Grand Prix rules. When I brought up Supervisor Keith Johnson's point— perhaps betting, wherever it occurred, constituted behavior "contrary to the integrity of the game"—Buchholz said he doubted that the Pro Council could pass judgment on a player for his conduct in a WCT event. It did demonstrate one thing, though, he said, smirking. The other circuit sounded casual about betting. If there were ever gambling on the Grand Prix tour, he assured me, it would be halted.

"What about splits?" I asked.

He shook his head, baffled. He had no idea what I meant. As I explained, he seemed horrified. He swore he had never heard of prize-money splitting. But he was instantly aware of its implications. "This goes to the heart of the integrity of our game."

I told him that although I had learned about it on the WCT circuit, I had spoken to a player who had admitted splitting in a tournament that offered ATP points. Also an ATP official had said that prize-money splitting was going on, and he had not made any distinction between WCT and Grand Prix events.

What ATP official? Buchholz demanded.

His vehemence made me hesitate, both because I feared hurting Vittorio Selmi and because I felt I shouldn't tip every card in my hand. If the matter was as serious as Buchholz made it sound, I wanted to see how hard he would work to get the truth.

"I played under contract with Jack Kramer," he told me, his voice edged with distress and anger. "We fought our hearts out to win during those early years of pro tennis. But people kept thinking it was fixed, it was just an exhibition. It would break my heart to go back to that."

Ron Bookman, a smiling, bespectacled fellow, stopped by our table. Buchholz introduced him as the Director of Communications; among other things, he handled public relations for the ATP. When Buchholz told him that I believed players were splitting prize money, Bookman, too, was upset and said I should reveal the identity of the ATP official who claimed this was common practice. He scribbled a list and promised that if the man's name wasn't on it, then he didn't work for the ATP.

"He's on there," I said. If they were so eager to learn who had told me, I suggested they ask their officials themselves. And wasn't this a question they should raise with all the players in their union?

There was to be a meeting of the Association of Tennis Professionals later this month in Las Vegas, and they swore they would do just what I had suggested. Buchholz would return to Europe for the French Open in late May, so we arranged to meet then and review the situation.

Meanwhile I had a final question. Did the ATP intend to urge umpires to get stricter about tanking?

Once more Buchholz perceived this as primarily a problem

of definition. People talked all the time about tanking. But what did they mean?

"They mean losing matches on purpose," I said.

For Bookman and Buchholz, it wasn't that simple. They couldn't accept that any player ever went "out with his mind made up to lose." But, as Buchholz acknowledged, there were cases when a man "maybe loses his concentration or his temper or his mind. He just gets fed up and gives up. I've seen players get fed up and tank the finals at Wimbledon." This was quite different, he insisted, than starting off with the intention of losing.

From what I heard, there were indeed players who set out to lose. But even by Buchholz and Bookman's definition, tanking seemed wrong. Since we were Americans, I put it in terms of baseball. What if a player went into a game with every intention of winning, but then, at some point, for some unfathomable reason, lost interest and started dropping balls and striking out on purpose?

"The manager would yank him out of the game," Buchholz said.

"Is that all?" I asked.

"He'd probably be out for good."

Was the ATP willing to do the same and ban players who tanked?

Ron Bookman spoke up briskly. "I've seen qualifying matches stopped. We have a rule; players have to give their best effort. I've seen umps in qualifying matches say, 'This is not up to pro standards' and stop the match."

"And there was Nastase up in Canada," Buchholz said. "He got fined for not giving his best effort in a final."

I was familiar with that incident, and it didn't strike me as a convincing example of strict enforcement of the "best effort" rule. Initially penalized $8,000, equivalent to his purse for second place, Nastase had had the fine reduced to $6,000, which he and his lawyer defined—everybody in pro tennis appears to be a semanticist—as a contribution to the Canadian junior program.

Still, Buchholz contended, nobody went out to lose. "There are too many ATP points at stake."

Why didn't that dissuade players from giving up halfway through a match? If what Buchholz said was true, even the most distracted and disheartened player would realize he was about to blow a bundle of ATP points and pull himself together.

Buchholz repeated that he just didn't believe anybody set out to lose.

"Except in doubles," I suggested.

Even on this he waffled. He supposed it happened occasionally when a player had to catch a plane. But it wasn't often.

Tanking in doubles is so rampant I could only conclude that Buchholz, for all his apparent earnestness, either wasn't entirely candid or wasn't as close to the players as he liked to think. Reminding him of our meeting at Roland Garros in Paris, I took my leave of the two ATP officials and went back to searching for Bjorn Borg.

There was however a great deal to distract me. As I watched several early-round matches, I wondered whether any other sport was played under such drastically varied conditions. This past Sunday, Ivan Lendl and Peter McNamara had met in the finals of a tournament on a fast indoor carpet under artificial lights in Frankfurt. Now, two days later, they were outdoors on clay, contending with the sun and wind of the Côte d'Azur and having trouble with lowly opponents.

Indoors, outdoors, daytime, nighttime, carpeted courts, cement courts, composition courts, European clay, American clay, English grass, Australian grass—each new condition demanded an adjustment from a player. Blessed with more raw talent than McNamara, Lendl had less trouble regearing his game. After saving one set point, he rolled past a Chilean, Pedro Rebolledo, 7–5/6–2. But McNamara never found his rhythm and fell to the pint-size German Peter Elter, 6–3/6–2.

There were also serious psychological adjustments exacted by professional tennis. For Chris Lewis, a gifted player from New

Zealand, the price of coming so far in his career has been constant fear and he has never shown any reluctance to admit it. Lewis is terrified of flying. Yet if he wants to go on playing, he knows he has to spend hundreds of hours in airplanes, and still more hours on the ground dreading the next flight. With a pharmacopoeia of tranquilizers—Mogadon, Tranxine, Equanil, Valium—he copes as best he can and arranges his schedule to restrict his time in the air. He also keeps cars on three continents—Australia, Europe, and America—and drives to tournaments whenever possible.

Still, for all his planning, there are frequent complications. He had just flown from Australia to Germany, where he was supposed to pick up a new Mercedes and motor down to Monte Carlo. But when the Mercedes wasn't ready, he had had to rent a car and hadn't arrived here until Sunday night. The thirty-hour flight from Australia, then the long drive from Frankfurt, plus the fact that "I was loaded up with pills," resulted in the inevitable. Facing Guillermo Vilas in the first round, he played like "a piece of garbage" and lost 6–1/6–1.

Next day I came close to Bjorn Borg, but there was no chance to talk to him. He swept into the press lounge for what politicians call "a photo opportunity." Nicola Pietrangeli and Ilie Nastase were with him. Pietrangeli stroked Nastase's Adidas sweater. "That's nice," he said. "Do they make them for men, too?"

Nastase and Borg, the journalists, assorted sycophants, and hangers-on guffawed. Only Bambino, Nastase's bodyguard, was unamused. Or, rather, he was amusing himself in a different manner. He had cornered one of the hostesses, pressing his Falstaffian belly against her slender frame, and was delivering his alternate line of dialogue, "I kiss all the pretty girls."

When the photographers had finished, people swarmed over Borg and indulged in a feverish laying on of hands. Pietrangeli hugged him, Nastase squeezed his shoulder. Reporters patted him on the back. Tournament officials caressed him. Women kissed him. Finally, Bambino hugged and kissed him, too.

Far from icy or aloof, Borg appeared giddy with pleasure. He giggled and kept mumbling in answer to all questions, "Beautiful. Everything is beautiful. Just beautiful."

Before they left, I asked Bambino whether it was true, as I had read in a newspaper, that Nastase had given him a $9,000 ring he had won in a raffle.

Bambino laughed and replied with his version of "no comment": "Journalists are shit."

The following day, in a fashion familiar to commuters the world over, things fell apart. I arrived at the station to discover that the 10:24 train had been canceled. Since the next train wasn't due until 11:23, I bought a newspaper and read it over a second cup of coffee that set my pulse racing and my mind jumping about. The 11:23 turned out to be two filthy cars, already crowded to overflowing. I stood up as far as Antibes, where most passengers got off and I sat down. The relief was short-lived, however. A conductor announced there was trouble on the tracks ahead and everybody had to switch to a bus to Nice.

A minor inconvenience, I decided. I might be a few minutes late for the start of the Bjorn Borg-Adriano Panatta match. But there were worse things than riding in a clean, comfortable bus along the Mediterranean coast. The next train to Monte Carlo was scheduled to leave Nice at noon and I assumed we would arrive in time to catch it. Even if we were a few minutes late, I assumed it would wait for connecting passengers.

I assumed wrong on both counts. We reached the station just as the train was pulling out; the next one wasn't due for an hour. Since I had already wasted almost two hours covering twenty miles, the idea of another delay was insupportable.

"Why didn't the train wait for us?" I asked a lady at the information desk.

"I don't know."

"Who does know?"

"I don't know."

"Who should know?"

"I don't know."

"This is the information bureau, isn't it?"

She shrugged, monumentally bored by my questions.

"I'd like to speak to the person in charge here," I said.

She waved vaguely. "He's gone."

"When will he be back?"

"I don't know." The woman must have employed Ivan Lendl as a dialogue coach.

"Who does know?"

"I don't know."

"What's your name?" I asked, lowering my voice malevolently like a man who might have some influence with the Railroad Commissioner.

She remained unimpressed. "I don't have to tell you that."

"Why? Don't you know your name?"

"I don't have to tell you anything," she snapped.

"You *haven't* told me anything." My voice rose and ignominiously cracked.

"I told you the hour of the next train. It comes at one o'clock. Pleasant journey, *monsieur*." She bit off each word with a mouth that resembled a parrot's beak.

I barged out of the station and, with an hour to kill, went to eat lunch. Next door was a fast-food outlet called Flunch. Flunch for lunch! I should have known better. But it looked harmless enough—looked, in fact, like a simulacrum of McDonald's, right down to the menu, which offered *frites*, milkshakes, and a choice of Burger Simple, Burger Fromage, or Burger Big.

"Big Burger, *s'il vous plaît*," I said to the girl at the counter.

"You want what?"

"Big Burger," I repeated.

"*Ça n'existe pas*," she said. "That doesn't exist." Not that they were out of it or no longer sold it. No, it simply didn't exist.

I pointed to the menu.

"*Alors*," she said, smiling. "You mean *Burger Big*. I didn't understand. You see, in French the adjective comes after the noun. You should learn our language."

"It's *my* language!" I bellowed. " 'Burger' and 'big' are English."

"As you wish," she muttered.

"That's what I wish. A Big Burger!"

But I was lying. What I wished was to lay waste all of France. Where else in the world would one have to endure a lecture on grammar from a fast-food cashier?

Of course the one-o'clock train was late. Of course I arrived at the Country Club quivering with rage, nervous exhaustion, and nausea—the Burger Big had lodged somewhere in my esophagus. But I figured the worst had to be behind me as I settled down to watch the rest of the Borg-Adriano Panatta match, which was knotted at a set apiece and three games all in the third set.

Other members of the press were in no better mood than I. The day was overcast and chilly, yet they had come dressed to work on their tans. Fortunately, I had had the foresight to wear a ski parka.

Journalists were also annoyed at the Pro Council, which had called an hour-long press conference to discuss a major development. The Pro Council announced that no resolution had been reached on the ten-tournament rule or on the question of whether Borg would have to qualify for Wimbledon. The major development was that the ATP had voted to apply its conduct code to amateur events. Butch Buchholz believed if boys began playing under uniform rules from the age of twelve, there would be fewer problems when they turned pro. One French reporter wisecracked, "Now if a kid breaks his racquet or cries on court, they're going to fine him $5,000."

Borg got a service break, thanks to a double fault by Adriano Panatta. But then, unlike the old Borg, who seldom slipped when he was in the lead, he had difficulty clinging to his advantage. Serving sloppily, he gave Panatta several chances to break back, and if the Italian wasn't equal to the opportunity, that had less to do with the Swede's iron will than with Panatta's poor play.

At the press conference, reporters were interested in Panatta only to the extent that he could comment on Borg's shaky form.

Once they had Borg in front of them, they abruptly shifted gears and were less interested in his form than in whether he would play Wimbledon. For British journalists, this was a favorite subject, their singular obsession, and all that spring one could count on them to raise it with every player. Will you play Wimbledon? they asked of men still facing three months of clay-court tennis in Spain, Italy, and France. If the answer was no, the Brits wanted to know why. If the answer was yes, they wanted to know how the man figured to adapt to the unforgiving English grass.

Since Sir Brian Burnett, Chairman of the All England Club, had come to Monte Carlo to arrange a compromise between Borg and the Pro Council, the Brits inquired about the upshot of those negotiations. Then, not content with the Swede's comment that he still hadn't reached a decision, they asked him to post odds on his chances of playing Wimbledon. Was it 50–50? Was it 60–40 in favor? Or 45–55 against?

Although I believed a public press conference was the wrong place to ask whether Borg had rigged an exhibition match with McEnroe, there seemed other questions that should have intrigued journalists more than the odds on his playing Wimbledon. Repeatedly he had recited the short list of Grand Prix tournaments he had deigned to enter in 1982. But I wanted to know how many exhibition matches he would play this year.

As the room turned ominously silent, he fixed upon me what Russell Davies of the London *Sunday Times* has referred to as "those mutely piercing narrow eyes . . . I'm sure the Turin Shroud is one of his old towels." After a significant pause Borg said, "I have no idea. I play the Suntory Cup in Tokyo. After that, I don't know."

"Let's forget the rest of the year. What's your exhibition sched-ule for the next three months?"

"I. Have. No. Idea." The words, spaced for emphasis, fell on that cowed roomful of journalists like icy slabs from a glacier.

"The next month, then?" I persisted.

"I. Have. No. Idea."

As every reporter knew, but few had informed their readers, Borg's tournament schedule consisted exclusively of events where he had endorsement contracts or where his agents at IMG served as promoters. Whether these constituted illegal inducements or not, they obviously provided an added incentive. I assumed, as did most people in tennis, that that was why Borg was willing to qualify for those seven tournaments, but refused to do so at Roland Garros and Wimbledon, where he had no incentive except the same prize money available to everyone else.

Yet when I asked Borg why he played the qualies here and would again in Las Vegas, but not at the Grand Slam events, he muttered that he had to put his foot down somewhere.

Why didn't he put it down in Monte Carlo?

"I decided to give the Pro Council until the French Open to change the rule."

I waited for other journalists to follow up on my questions. I had broken the ice. All they had to do was dive into the cold water with me. But they were less interested in whether his tax deal locked him into the Monte Carlo tournament than in the shakiness of his first serve.

Borg returned to his orange-juice metaphor. He said he was still feeling deconcentrated.

I was feeling a bit that way myself after the press conference when a reporter sidled up and whispered, "Who are you? What are you doing here?"

I told him my name and that I was writing a book about tennis.

"About Borg?"

"He'll be in it. I'm hoping to have a word with him this week."

"Never. He won't even talk to you at press conferences after the questions you asked."

"What's wrong with what I asked?"

"Bjorn hates such subjects. The rest of us know better than to bring them up."

"Does it matter so much what he likes?"

The man laughed. A reporter for a prestigious Swedish newspaper, he told me he had been close to Borg when he first set out on the pro circuit. But the journalist had soon found it impossible to maintain this friendly relationship and, at the same time, preserve his self-respect. Like many top players, Borg demanded absolute loyalty—perhaps obsequiousness is a more accurate term. He refused to speak to journalists who criticized him or asked awkward questions. When he could, he had such reporters kicked out of the room before his press conference.

"That's why reporters are afraid of Bjorn. They don't want to lose a chance to talk to him. They don't like to be treated as an enemy. I know what that's like. I criticized him in the paper for not playing Davis Cup and he didn't talk to me again for years. I don't care so much now, but it hurt me in my job. He is our most famous athlete, yet I couldn't get near him."

As at most Grand Prix events, there was a tournament for the press in Monte Carlo and I had entered, thinking it would be a welcome diversion. Now I wasn't so sure. I had yet to recover from the nerve-racking train ride and the nauseating lunch, and my encounter with Borg had done nothing to improve my digestion. Still, I decided to go ahead with my match.

Upstairs in the clubhouse, in a room reserved for umpires, ball boys, and journalists, I put on my tennis shorts and shoes. It was an elegant, old-fashioned changing room with oak-paneled walls, wooden benches, and lockers. Since all the lockers were filled, I hung my clothes on a hook as I had seen others do.

Then I wondered what to do with my watch and wallet. Surely they would be safe here. After all, this was Monte Carlo, cops were ubiquitous, crime was said to be non-existent, and several officious attendants oversaw the changing room. But finally I dropped my valuables into a racquet cover and carried them onto the court.

Two hours later, having been run ragged by a diminutive Japanese photographer, I returned to the changing room and found my clothes in a damp knot on the floor. My pants pockets had been ripped inside out. My ski parka and equipment bag were gone.

Calling one of the attendants, I pointed to the pile of clothes. "I've been robbed."

He was irate—at me, not the thief. "It's not my fault."

"I didn't say it was. But I thought you'd like to know there are robbers in your locker room."

"I'm not responsible. I can't watch everything."

I lacked the energy to argue. After showering and pulling on my disheveled clothes, I went outside, where the sky was low and dark, with misty clouds clinging to the mountains like carded wool. Shivering, I stood there pondering the revelation that crime wasn't nonexistent in Monte Carlo, just ignored. If one had the temerity to insist he had been robbed, he was held to be a troublemaker.

I stopped by the press room to pick up the transcript of Borg's press conference. Generally, such transcripts give the essence, if not the entirety, of each question and answer. But the transcript of Borg's interview contained neither my questions nor his evasive responses. One more thing swept down the memory hole.

On Thursday, in the quarterfinals, Balazs Taroczy's luck ran out. In the last two weeks he had won half a dozen tight matches. But against Ivan Lendl he got blitzed 6–0/6–1.

Afterward, when asked who he'd like to play in the next round, Noah or Borg, Lendl showed a rare flash of humor. "I'd like to play the one who plays less well, the loser. Unfortunately, I will not have the choice."

Despite Borg's erratic performance thus far, few would have predicted what transpired in the second quarterfinal. It wasn't that the Swede played badly. He barely played at all and appeared not to care how lackadaisical he looked. Once a paragon of patience, he now rushed the net behind punchless approach shots. When serving, he usually stuffs the spare ball into his pocket, but today he kept it in his left hand, which made it impossible for him to hit his two-fisted backhand. Noah had little trouble breaking Borg twice and holding his own serve three times at love.

Yet, even after Borg dropped the first set 6–1, the crowd

expected him to rally. They had seen him come back before; they were convinced he could do it again today. So it was doubly upsetting to watch him shamble through the second set, detached and absent-minded. Once he lost track of the score and started to serve from the wrong side. Another time he hit a short lob and, not bothering to wait for Noah to smash it away, he strolled to his chair and sat down. By the end of the match, if he was anxious about anything, it was only to get off the court.

At the press conference Yannick Noah sounded as incredulous as the crowd had been. "I could hear him whistling to himself during change-overs. I didn't know what to think. Was he trying to win?"

Still, Noah derived great satisfaction from his victory. "I couldn't help thinking that if Borg had won this tournament after a six-month lay-off, it would be bad for us, the other players who are all the time on the circuit, who make a big effort and train every day. I thought it was time to beat him."

In Noah's opinion, Borg stood no chance of regaining his championship form unless he played more. "Maybe if he plays a lot of exhibitions, that might help, but not as much as tournaments would."

When someone asked if he felt he played better with his new mid-size racquet, Noah said he was still adjusting and let it go at that. This was a ticklish subject, since he was under contract to Coq Sportif, which didn't manufacture a mid-size racquet. Not yet, anyway. They were said to be rushing a prototype through production, but meanwhile Noah had to use a mid-size Donnay disguised to resemble a Coq Sportif.

Bjorn Borg arrived looking as impassive and uncaring as he had on court. Witnesses in the locker room claimed that he had shuffled in whistling and dumped his racquets to the floor. Yet he told reporters he didn't remember whistling during the match. He couldn't account for what Noah heard and he didn't want to discuss it.

No, he wasn't disappointed. How could he be disappointed, he asked, when "I felt all the time I was outside the match? And when you're not in a match, you try to do something different. You rush, but you don't realize you rush. I must be more patient."

Still, he said, he was satisfied to reach the quarterfinals after such a long lay-off. Perhaps it was to demonstrate his satisfaction that he left the press conference whistling.

Outside on the patio Pablo Arraya, a cocky quarterfinalist from Peru, asked, "Did you see Borg? I didn't. I saw a blond guy with a headband . . . but I sure didn't see Borg."

That night, however, a lot of people saw Borg. In the past it was rare for him to celebrate publicly even after a triumph. So it was nothing short of astounding when he showed up at Jimmy'Z after his calamitous loss to Noah.

In the purple, throbbing prose of *Society*, a flak magazine published by the Société des Bains de Mer, Jimmy'Z is a discothèque "presided over by the 'Queen of the Night' . . . Régine herself." It's a place "where crazy celebrities can dance until dawn just like the princesses in the fairy tale. . . . Jimmy'Z is young and fearless, and open to the stars, and all are free to laugh and dance and mix with the rich, the beautiful and the bizarre, who may be loaded down with precious jewels or covered in magnificent evening gowns, it doesn't matter, the moonlight performs a strange magic and all the world is young again and we are suddenly and quite inexplicably bewitched."

Without a doubt, Borg acted bewitched, whether by the disco beat or some basic change in body chemistry, it would be impossible to say. While José Luis Clerc chatted up Princess Stephanie—the Princess appeared to have a crush on Argentinians; earlier in the week she had been observed doing cartwheels beside Vilas' practice court—Borg preferred to dance with Nastase's bodyguard, Bambino, who had appropriated a tablecloth and bath towel to dress himself in drag. Then at two a.m. he left with Jody Scheckter, a Formula One race driver, and moved over to the lobby of the Loew's Hotel, apparently still on the prowl for a good time.

Next day Pascal Zimmer told me, "Watch Bjorn every time he plays because it may be his last."

It was said that Borg had no desire to go on with the game. He would play out his current contracts, then quit. If this was no more than one rumor among many, it must be remarked that rumor in Monte Carlo had acquired its own twisted legitimacy and journalists received news releases with opening lines like, "The following is the true account of the rumor that Bjorn Borg, Ivan Lendl and John McEnroe would play an exhibition in Australia during the same time as Wimbledon 1982."

Meanwhile, Thomas Exler, a German photographer, was strong-armed off the grounds of the Country Club and dragged to jail. His crime: offending a member of the royal family.

On a side court Exler, who works for *Tennis Magazine*, the game's journal of record in Germany, spotted Princess Stephanie in an umpire's chair, officiating a doubles match among aging members of the local gentry. Careful to bother nobody, Exler eased himself into position and snapped a few pictures.

Immediately, Princess Stephanie bustled down from the chair ordered him to stop. "You're not allowed to take my photograph."

Exler showed her his press badge. But she snapped, "You're in Monaco and you must obey our rules."

"What rules? The Country Club approved my credentials. They didn't tell me these rules."

"The rule that says you can't take my picture."

With that, she summoned a security guard, who ushered Exler to the main gate and, after attempting to seize his film, transferred him to a plainclothes detective. The detective drove him to headquarters, where the police booked Exler, snapped his mug shot, and put him through the third degree for defying the Princess. No one accused him of threatening or harming her. It was enough that he had talked back.

Since Exler had left his passport at the hotel, things looked bleak and he feared he would be held in jail. But when the police obtained the information they needed from the press office at the Country Club, they released him with a warning not to molest the Princess again.

"Such a thing has never happened to me anywhere in the world," Exler said. "I was nowhere near her. I was just taking pictures. I've taken pictures of everybody, even Henry Kissinger, and never had such trouble."

·   ·   ·

When the remaining quarterfinal matches proved to be lop-sided affairs—Clerc beat Orantes 6–0/6–3 and Vilas brushed aside Arraya 6–1/6–1—I went to the parking lot to interview Lucien Noguès, the racquet-stringer on the Grand Prix circuit. A thirty-three-year-old Frenchman from Toulouse, Noguès is employed by VS Gut, the official string of the tour, and he drives a modified Dodge Sportsman van from tournament to tournament throughout Europe. Since he covers twenty-five thousand miles a year, the van must do double duty, and Noguès calls it his *"atelier* and *salon."* With three stringing machines, he can work inside or, weather permitting, outside under a canvas tent flap.

Furnished in front with swivel chairs for the driver and one passenger, the Dodge has leather banquettes in back, and its floor, walls, and ceiling are carpeted. There is a full kitchen, a cassette recorder, and a color TV set which can be used as a closed-circuit video system, permitting Noguès to follow the action on the courts nearby.

I presumed most tennis players were demanding about their equipment. But Lucien said no. "It astounds me. They're profes-sionals, but they're no better than amateurs about the tools of their trade. Only the players with coaches seem to be well looked after when it comes to equipment."

A curly-haired, compact, affable man, Noguès reminded me of Steve Parker, the WCT trainer who had surprised me with his opinion that many tennis players weren't in good shape. Now Noguès claimed they weren't any better with equipment than with conditioning. Slaves of fashion or of finance, they switched from conventional racquets to large ones, then to mid-size ones without regard for their games or physiques.

"It's as if they're wearing blinders," he said. "They know how to hit a ball. They know the basic strokes. They resist everything else. Maybe they're too nervous. Half of them act as if they're perpetually on the brink of a mental breakdown. Perhaps they feel they just can't absorb any more information. I respect their silence and solitude," he assured me, as though he were dis-cussing a pride of neurasthenic *artistes,* "but learning about equipment and learning about their bodies would bring better results and help prolong their careers."

I asked about Borg's racquets, which were reputed to be strung at a tension of eighty pounds, a detail which journalists marvel over in almost every article about the Swede.

"A fantasy," Noguès said. "That's an invention of journalists. I string Borg's racquets and I can tell you the tension is seventy-four or seventy-five pounds, absolute maximum. It's difficult to achieve even that tension because he uses rather fine gut and it breaks under pressure. But eighty pounds, no, it's impossible."

L'Equipe, the French sports journal, and an equipment firm known by the abbreviation of TBS presented annual prizes to players who did well in French tournaments. For their performances in 1981, Bjorn Borg and Yannick Noah shared the top prize, a cash bonus of $10,000. Friday evening there was a cocktail party in the clubhouse to honor the award winners, and I went, still hopeful of having a private word with Borg.

But the Swede skipped the ceremony. Some said he didn't care to share the spotlight with Noah, whom he resented for accusing him of whistling during their match. So I wound up with several other journalists talking to Yannick Noah about tomorrow's semifinal against Lendl.

Son of a black man and a white woman, Noah had been born in France, but as a child moved to Cameroon, his father's native land. They settled in Yaoundé, where his relatives were prominent members of the Ewondo tribe. Noah's grandfather had been mayor of Yaoundé and his great-grandfather had been a tribal chieftain with seventy wives. Yannick's father, Zac, a soccer star, had been recruited to play in France, but after an injury he took up tennis and taught his son.

It's unlikely Yannick would have gained international recognition if Arthur Ashe had not come to Cameroon on a goodwill tour and spotted the gifted twelve-year-old boy. Although both Ashe and Noah have downplayed the significance of the American's role in Noah's career, it is true that Ashe telephoned the French Tennis Federation and urged them to bring Yannick to France for intensive coaching.

The rest is a matter of record. Noah became the French junior champion and, four years after turning pro, was ranked among the dozen best players in the world. Many believed he had the ability to climb higher, but, like so many French players, he was said to have grown a bit complacent. He owns three cars, including a Porsche, an apartment in Paris, a place in Nice where his mother and sisters live, and a sports complex which he and his father are developing in Yaoundé.

Still only twenty-two, he seemed to be fighting an ongoing battle between the French public's expectations of him and his own desire to do well, yet enjoy himself. Tall and handsome, with widely spaced front teeth—supposedly a sign of good luck in France—he has a reputation as a ladies' man and admits to playing better when in love. He claims he once had sex in the locker room, then went right out and played *un match fantastique.*

A British journalist was asking about Noah's first name. What was its derivation? What did it mean? Perhaps the man believed it was a tribal sobriquet. But Noah explained it was a common name in Brittany. "Yannick is the diminutive of John," he said, "like Johnny."

It interested me what it must be like to live in two worlds, black and white, Cameroon and France, Yaoundé and Paris, the world of his father, the world of his mother. Did he feel divided?

Noah insisted it was different to be black in France. It didn't matter so much here as in America. He didn't suffer from racism.

"To me it doesn't matter if Chip Hooper, for example, is black. If he's a good guy," Yannick said, "that's what matters to me. Or if he's an asshole, I want to know it. But I think he's a great guy."

About tomorrow's match, he said it was all a question of whether he served well and could take the net. He couldn't let Lendl find his rhythm and fall into long baseline rallies. This winter in Palm Springs he had ended the Czech's forty-four-match winning streak by pressuring him.

"Lendl said that was the worst match he's played in five years," a reporter reminded him.

Noah smiled, showing the lucky space between his teeth. "Ivan doesn't lose very often. But when he does, he's a bad loser."

On Saturday, in the first set, it appeared that Lendl would have no occasion to be a bad loser again. He won it 6–1 before most of the crowd had settled into their seats. In the second set, however, Noah exposed the chinks in Lendl's armor as delicately as the diners at the lunch tables above the court laid open their trout *meunière* and lifted out a lattice of bones.

The Czech wanted to pound every shot. He didn't only want to win. He wanted to punish the other player. Since Lendl liked a ball with a lot of pace on it, Noah began chipping to his backhand, hitting low, sliced balls with no speed at all on them. Lendl tried to smack them for winners, but he had to hit up, which gave Noah the chance to hit down. In professional tennis that's a critical difference. The man at the net hitting down almost always wins.

When Lendl realized what was happening, he played touch shots, saving his power until he created an opening. But this reduced the match to a duel of speed and anticipation, and Noah was superior at running, jumping, and stretching. Toward the end of the set he even threw in a few tantalizing dropshots that sent the infuriated Czech skidding across the red clay.

But once he had tied the match at a set apiece, Noah appeared to lose confidence in this slow ball game, which was more like chess than tennis. Afterward he said he had expected Lendl to make adjustments in the third set and thought he could beat him to the punch if he changed the pace first. This violated an elementary rule: stay with a winning game. As soon as Noah put more speed on his shots, Lendl slugged his forehand, leaving the court pockmarked with craters like the surface of the moon after a meteor shower. The Czech won by the seesaw score of 6–1/1–6/6–1.

· · ·

The second semifinal was something of a grudge match. Although both Vilas and Clerc had professed their willingness to fight for Argentina in the Falklands, Clerc had refused to play Davis Cup with Vilas, and, as a result, Argentina had been beaten by France.

Clerc had begged off with the excuse that he was tired and needed a rest. But everybody assumed the real reason was that he resented Vilas' status as a national demigod—a status which Vilas didn't accept with divine detachment, but rather exploited for personal gain. He was said to dominate the Argentinian tennis federation and to demand a disproportionate share of its funds. Clerc, in turn, felt he had proved his worth—he had played better than Vilas all during 1981—and believed he deserved an equal slice of the Davis Cup loot. When he didn't get it, he stayed home.

Now, having declined to play *with* Vilas, he was playing against him and was eager for the opportunity. "I think if I play good," he said, "I have a lot of chance."

Despite a leonine mane of curly hair and the kind of sharply defined musculature seen in anatomy textbooks, Clerc has a curiously high-pitched voice. But if it's strange to have a man his size sound a note from a flute when one expects the sonority of a bass saxophone, it's more unsettling to see him play tennis wearing an elegant gold Cartier watch. It's part of a contract, of course.

While Clerc, with his gold watch glinting, wielded his racquet like a rapier, Vilas swung his like a broadsword and at every stroke he exelled a hoarse breath—not the false intimidation of Jimmy Connors' growl, but a laborer's honest groan of exertion. Before long he had broken the strings on four of his mid-size Slazengers and fought off seven set points in Clerc's favor.

After taking the first set in a tie-break, Vilas bludgeoned his way to a lead in the second. The difference between the two men seemed less that of talent or technique than of personality. While Vilas aspires to be a poet, there was nothing showy about his style. Clerc, however, displayed a comic flair and arched his eyebrows like Groucho Marx, waved a towel at a linesman, teased Vilas for protesting a call, and took a bite at a ball that ticked the net and dropped on his side for a point.

Then as Clerc was serving, a commotion broke out in the crowd. A spectator had collapsed, and people around him called for a doctor, their cries so loud that play had to be suspended. While Vilas went to the sidelines for a strategy conference with Tiriac, then sat and seemed to meditate, Clerc stayed on court and put on a soccer exhibition, bouncing the ball off his feet, his knees, and his forehead, and finally kicking it into the stands.

When the game resumed, Clerc, the good-natured clown, was promptly broken, and Vilas went on to win. Much as Clerc's antics amused the crowd, one had to wonder whether they cost him the match.

On Easter Sunday the casinos in Monte Carlo were full, but the press box at the Country Club was half empty. Now that Borg had lost, many reporters had packed up and left, and some of those who remained expressed less interest in the Vilas-Lendl final than in where the Swede had gone. Geneva? Why? Would he register for the French Open by midnight Monday? Would he play Wimbledon? Was he with Mariana? Someone else? I didn't hear a single comment about today's match, which everyone assumed Lendl would win easily. He had beaten Vilas eight times in a row, seven of them without yielding a set.

On the patio a late lunch was being served and the clatter of plates, silverware, and glasses could be heard down on the court. Far out at sea, sailboats tilted in the breeze, and hundreds of feet above, a few hang gliders described lazy patterns, like scraps of bright paper dancing in the air.

The match looked as lazy as the hang gliders. Like Noah in the second set of the semifinals, Vilas took everything off the ball except its yellow fuzz and pushed it back at Lendl so slowly the Czech could read the Dunlop label. But while he could read the label, Lendl had trouble making out the speed, angle, and spin, and often had to lunge for short balls that bounced no higher than his ankles. Although Lendl tried to be patient, tried to play the percentages, he was by temperament a slugger, not a counter-puncher, and it was clear that he would have problems, psychological as well as tactical, with anybody steady enough to move him around from the baseline.

After dropping his serve in the first game of the first set, Vilas reeled off six games straight and, in the second set, continued to hit a serve that resembled a dropshot. It landed short and stayed low, skittering across the clay like a flat stone skimming a pond. Invariably, Lendl poked it into the net.

While Vilas was putting in a high percentage of his soft first serves, the Czech, in sheer exasperation, was going for aces and coming up empty. He hit three aces in three sets, each canceled by a double fault.

With his serve and return of serve neutralized, Lendl had to depend entirely on his forehand. All winter it had been an intimidating weapon, especially when he hit it inside-out to his opponent's backhand. But since Vilas is a southpaw, that shot came to his forehand, his own best weapon, and he could whip the ball crosscourt or down the line, forcing Lendl into the unaccustomed role of retriever.

When the Argentinian took the second set in a tie-break, the waiters on the terrace began clearing tables and stacking chairs. Lendl looked back at them and shouted some obscure Czechoslovakian curse. But he was a beaten man. The waiters knew it and ignored him.

After he had lost the third set 6–4, Lendl insisted the entire problem had been his serve. "Usually against Vilas I hit a couple of aces a game. Today I was lucky to get two serves in."

Questions about shot selection and strategy he dismissed the way he once dismissed opponents. He had no time and no inclination for tactics. When I asked whether he expected a lot of players would start to slow-ball him, just as they had Jimmy Connors after Arthur Ashe had exposed Jimbo's vulnerability to junk, Ivan Lendl let out a laugh that sounded like a Doberman's bark. "I hope so."

ITALIAN OPEN

AFTER Monte Carlo much of my time went into acquiring press credentials for the rest of the spring and summer. Whereas during the winter, tournaments were grateful for any coverage they got, the major events could afford to pick and choose among journalists, and they did so in a peremptory manner which would have sparked envy in any oligarch.

For public consumption, these important tournaments wring their collective hands and claim they receive so many applications they have to be highly selective in granting press credentials. Like most explanations from tennis authorities, this one contained a nodule of truth buried in a gelatinous mass of obfuscation. Undoubtedly they did receive a lot of applications. But since the journalists they rejected were given misleading excuses, and since the ones they accepted were the same interlocking directorate of hacks, agents, flack men, and apprentice entrepreneurs who showed up at every tournament, one had reason to suspect that press credentials were part of a patronage system which rewarded those who supported it, punished those who criticized it, and regarded everyone else with distrust.

At most large tournaments the task of reviewing applications and granting credentials is delegated to a committee of tennis writers. Although this might suggest that the goal is to assemble an independent press corps, the result is just the opposite. By allowing journalists to judge each other, tournament directors accomplish with one clever stroke several interrelated purposes.

First, they ensure that prominent members of the tennis press are part of the tournament. They're not just *behind* the tournament, they're *in* it. True, such journalists will take an occasional nip at the knuckles of those with whom they are working hand in glove. They may criticize an event for having a weak field or for being poorly organized. But they seldom, if ever, put directors or players on the spot by writing about appearance money, tanking, drugs, corrupt umpires, prize-money splitting, set-splitting, betting, or other subjects which, judging by my experience, would be very difficult for reporters *not* to know about.

Besides serving as part of the tournament's promotional apparatus, the press committee dispenses valuable largesse. It doesn't just decide who receives credentials. It determines who gets which *kinds* of credentials, and this in turn determines who will receive discount or free drinks, meals, transportation, and hotel rooms, who will be invited to official cocktail parties, dinners, gala receptions, and balls, and who will be given the free tennis clothes and equipment, luggage, pens, carrying cases, photo albums, ties, perfume, towels, cologne, cigarettes, wine, and liquor donated by sponsors. Anybody who doubts that these items are highly prized by the press deserves to get caught once in a stampede of reporters rushing to claim their souvenir French Open zipper bags.

Although a press committee may work without pay, its members realize they'll be richly compensated. If they're generous to their colleagues, this generosity will be reciprocated in an orgy of mutual back-scratching. *You make sure I receive first-class treatment at your tournament and I'll look after you at mine.*

As one well-placed Volvo Grand Prix official confided to me, most journalists on the circuit have been co-opted. They can't very well campaign against appearance money and preferential treatment for star players since so many of them demand the same privileges themselves. "For the press to clamor about conflict of interest is the ultimate hyprocrisy," he said. "Whenever there's a freebie, they swarm like flies on shit. Nobody does anything in this business without an ulterior motive."

·　　·　　·

After deciding to skip the French Open, Bjorn Borg won the Suntory Cup, in Tokyo, beating Vince Van Patten and Guillermo Vilas. But when he flew to Las Vegas for the tournament that had been reorganized expressly to suit his schedule, he was knocked out of the qualies by Dick Stockton, an ailing veteran who could no longer make it straight into the draw. The defeat seemed to demoralize Borg, and afterward he announced that he was withdrawing from Grand Prix events for the rest of the year.

Still struggling for a face-saving formula that would satisfy the Swede, the All England Club proposed to let him into Wimbledon without qualifying if he would play seven tournaments in 1982 and three more during the first three months of 1983. Borg rejected the compromise.

Instead, he kept playing exhibitions and special events. He played them in Europe, in Africa, in America, in Asia. He played them throughout the summer and fall, explaining that they were part of his training program for a comeback in 1983. Then after New Year's, when he announced that he was retiring permanently from tournament tennis, he played still more exhibitions, explaining that they were a farewell to his fans. After his much-publicized retirement in April of 1983, he continued playing exhibitions, which he no longer attempted to explain.

By then, he had become what might be the first of a new breed. Just as players in the fifties and sixties had quit the shamateur game as soon as they won a major title that would enhance their income as professionals, Borg had quit the competitive game once it no longer served a purpose. For several years tournament tennis had been a minor aspect of his program, just a form of advertising that kept his price high for endorsements and exhibitions. Now at the age of twenty-six, he had decided to devote himself full time to the most lucrative divisions of the sport/business—marketing and entertainment.

When I obtained the September 1980 issue of the French magazine *Rock & Folk* and read the interview with Yannick Noah, I concluded that the most remarkable thing about it was not that it had caused a stir in France, but that it had not prompted international controversy. In America, when mentioned at all, it had been viewed as no more than a minor nuisance, an instance of press harassment which Noah had had to surmount as he climbed in the rankings. There had been no debate about the truth or falsity of his statements and, in fact, very few of them had been quoted.

Interviewed by two men, Thierry Ardisson and Jean-Luc Maître, Noah had been subjected to a parody of a cross-examination. But while the tone is puckish, the questions and answers convey a specificity of detail that has the ring of truth. Noah revealed he has a false tooth, very dry hair, a scar on his arm, and a heart murmur. He discussed his family's history in Cameroon, his financial support of his mother and sisters in Nice and his father in Yaoundé, the particulars of his endorsement contracts, his loss of religious faith, and his sex life.

The apparent candor of the discussion continued—at least, the tone didn't change—when the talk turned to more ticklish subjects. Thierry Ardisson told Noah that he had been told that Noah smoked hashish as well as cigarettes, and wondered how the drug affected him. "I make love crazily," Noah replied, and, laughing, told about a time when his trainer had accused him of tiring himself out with sex when in fact he was high on hashish. But Noah swore that he would never smoke before an important match. The journalists asked him whether he would, before a big match, use something else, like cocaine. "No," said Noah. Not only would he not take cocaine before a match, he had never tried it at any time. "But some people do it. In tennis, there are never any tests. And when there has been one, everybody knew about it two weeks in advance!"

Ardisson and Maître continued to question Noah about drug use on the tour, trying to find out what he knew about other players' practices. Noah said that he found it was easy to spot a player who was on drugs, easy to spot in the flesh and even when watching a match broadcast on television, just by observing the way the players behaved on court. In every tournament, Noah told them, there were players using drugs, and the problem was getting worse and worse all the time. He didn't like it; indeed, the use of drugs made him angry, Noah told Ardisson and Maître, "because you're not being beaten with the same weapons."

When the two journalists pressed Noah to be specific about which drugs he saw being used by the players, Noah pointed particularly to cocaine and amphetamines. "You take the hit during the tournament and you crash afterwards. You have guys who have played super during one tournament and who you've never seen again. . . . Never heard anybody talk about again . . ."

It was clear to Noah that the drug situation in professional tennis had grown to such proportions that it was out of control— to the point where it was possible that a player would have to become an abuser of cocaine or amphetamines if he hoped to be the best. The problem needed to be brought into the open, to be discussed, to be deplored. Otherwise, there would be deaths.

The interview then shifted to a topic that was just as interesting to me.

J–L.M.: Exhibition matches are fixed, aren't they?
Y.N.: Ah . . . in general, the players reach an agreement to play three sets: one apiece and then an honest third. That, that happens.

It was what the Umpire in Antibes had told me about the Borg-McEnroe exhibition match. It was what Butch Buchholz had sworn he found hard to believe.

Since Noah had entered the Italian Open, I drove out to the Foro Italico a few hours early the first day of the tournament, hoping to talk to him.

In a saner age the Italian Open signaled the start of the summer season, to be followed by the French Open, Wimbledon, then clay-court tournaments on the Continent and in the United States, and finally the U.S. Open. But now that the tennis season has no beginning and no end, and the schedule resembles a snake devouring its own tail, the Italian Open is just one more way-station on the Volvo Grand Prix circuit, which, in addition to prize money, distributes three million dollars a year in bonuses among the top thirty-two singles and sixteen doubles players. For 1982 the bonus for the leading player in singles was $600,000.

All this money had been pumped into the tour in the expectation that top players would sign up for a minimum of ten, and ideally many more, Grand Prix tournaments. Similar hopes had persuaded the WCT to funnel proportionately even more into its circuit. The results had been dismal. The megabucks which were supposed to induce the stars to play more had, as Frew McMillan pointed out in Strasbourg, allowed them to play less.

Ironically, the less they played, the more important they became. They had acquired the shimmering aura of rock and film stars whose quirky habits and sheer unreasonableness were marketable hallmarks of their image. They set down their own rules and, surrounded by agents, lawyers, PR men, accountants, and media consultants, these players served notice that they had computed their value down to the last dime. They assumed they dwarfed every stage they strode upon, and for them a tournament, any tournament, was just another payday.

When Bjorn Borg decided he could do without Wimbledon, that seemed to convince others that they didn't need it either. Because of the continued hostilities in the Falklands, Vilas and Clerc announced they might skip Wimbledon. Lendl allowed as how he was still making up his mind. But Eliot Teltscher was definite: he wouldn't play there. And Vitas Gerulaitis, John McEnroe, and Jimmy Connors had begun to carp about a possible boycott of the All England Club.

If a tournament of Wimbledon's stature couldn't count on the loyalty of the stars, the Italian Open stood no chance. When I arrived at the Foro Italico, there was an air of gloom and bitter disappointment wholly at odds with the brilliant spring sunshine. Of the fifty-one players who had agreed to play in Rome, nine had withdrawn. This included the top two seeds, John McEnroe, still troubled by a sore ankle, and Guillermo Vilas, who preferred to prepare for the French Open. Ivan Lendl gave the same excuse: he wanted to get ready for Roland Garros. But he did so by flying to Tokyo for an exhibition match. Since Victor

Pecci was injured, this meant that of last year's semifinalists in Rome, only José Luis Clerc would compete this year. One Italian paper ran a headline that set a somber tone for the week: BEAUTIFUL FORO, UGLY TOURNAMENT.

Since Cino Marchese had spent months negotiating with McEnroe, I expected the handsome, silver-haired promoter to be enraged by the news that his top seed had absconded. But, looking dapper in a beige linen suit, he put a brave face on things.

This was a new beginning for the Italian Open, he said. In the past it had been run by small-minded people. Now, with IMG behind it, the tournament could build an image that would guarantee its success regardless of whether the best players showed up. As Cino saw it, once the tournament's image improved, then the top players would inevitably follow.

"First, the successful image," he said, flourishing his index finger. "Then the players who are successful."

But how was he going to attract top players? I asked. Would he have to spend every winter negotiating contracts like the one between McEnroe and Lipton Tea?

Cino didn't address that question. "Who loves tennis," he said, "for him there are a lot of possibility to see players among the hundred best in the world. For those who are only curious to see the special wild beast, we won't get them. But there will be good tennis."

Constructed in 1935 under Mussolini's regime, the Foro Italico displays all the signatures of high fascist style. The buildings, the statues, and the obelisk which still bears Il Duce's name all once aspired to monumental grandeur. Now they seem no more than laughable examples of bad taste, and their broad surfaces serve as billboards for graffiti.

Bordered by Viale delle Olimpiadi and Viale dei Gladiatori, the tennis courts are in amphitheaters below the street level, and the warm air that gathers in these hollows is thick with pollen and dust and the smell of grilled meat from the players' restaurant. Surrounding the show court, or Campo Centrale, temporary bleachers now all but obscure the ranks of massive white marble statues of athletes, which have the appearance of curiously inverted Peeping Toms. The statues are nude and seem to be standing on tiptoe, gazing through the iron underpinnings of the bleachers into a stadium full of clothed people.

On the gravel terrace between the Campo Centrale and the field courts, tables and chairs are set up in clusters, some as a café, others, under a canopy, as a restaurant. Waiters wearing white jackets already wilting in the heat move in slow motion, shouting, *"Momento"* and *"Subito."*

Beyond a snack bar, the field courts lie at the bottom of a great oblong cavity styled on the lines of Rome's ancient chariot-race course, the Circo Massimo. Screened off from one another by tall cypress hedges, the red clay courts are surrounded by tiers of bleachers surfaced with marble slabs that have sprouted wild flowers and tufts of moss.

I circled the courts and seemed to pass from one season to another as I advanced from the shadow of one Umbrian pine to the next. In the shade it was a mild spring morning. But in the sunny spaces between trees it was a scorching summer afternoon. Down on the courts the players were slathered with sweat, and I could hear their hoarse breathing and the solid, methodical *thwock* of Pirelli balls against stretched catgut, and the twittering of birds on the verdant heights of Monte Mario, and, closer than that, the clopping of hooves as mounted police patrolled the parking lot.

Somnolent and measured as it was, the clip-clopping of the horses sounded the lone discordant note and alerted anybody who was of a mind to notice such facts that the place was aswarm with police, *carabinieri*, and armed troops in flak jackets. By one of those grotesque coincidences which seem to abound on the pro circuit, this tournament could claim no better than second billing at the Foro Italico. At the end of Viale delle Olimpiadi, in a converted gymnasium barricaded by sandbags, bulletproof shields, and armored personnel carriers, the Italian murder trial of the century was taking place. Several members of the Red Brigades, a gang of left-wing terrorists, had broken four years of silence and were testifying about their roles in the kidnapping and assassination of Aldo Moro, the nation's leading political figure until his death in 1978.

It was as if John Hinckley, President Reagan's attempted assassin, had stood trial during the U.S. Open in a locker room at Flushing Meadows. Or as if the murderers of Lord Mountbatten had been forced to testify in a candy-striped tent at the All England Club during the Wimbledon fortnight. Yet no one at the Italian Open appeared to find this strange. Even when police helicopters clattered overhead or when a team of Army sky-divers jumped from a plane and sailed to earth dangling from bright silk parachutes, they got no more attention than did a droll Code Violation Record thumbtacked to a bulletin board outside the referee's office.

Marzio Miloro, a qualifier, had been fined $200 for violating "Grand Prix Code Section III O (twice) in that: (1) Player told opponent to 'Fuck off' and called him 'Piece of shit' after he lost the match. When leaving court he bumped opponent with shoulder. (2) Then got into a shouting match with spectator, jumped over the fence into the stands and chased spectator up nine rows, shouting at him. They got into 'face to face' argument. Player returned to court, continued shouting at spectator. (It turned out spectator was father.)"

O. Henry couldn't have crafted a better parenthetical climax to a short story of family melodrama.

On a side court made treacherous by the sweeping shadows of pine trees, I watched Alejandro Pierola, a Chilean qualifier who gained my unstinting loyalty for no better reason than that he looked older than I am. Although he admits to being thirty-five, other South American players, who call Pierola "the Indian," claim he's close to fifty. His teeth are discolored and carious, his face is as seamed as an ancient saddle, his skin has the consistency of dry bark, and his arms and legs look as knotted as oak limbs. The only sure method to determine Alejandro Pierola's age would be to saw him in half and count the rings.

His opponent, Andres Gomez, appeared to be attempting to perform that operation with his scythe-like, southpaw forehand.

But Pierola kept dancing out of danger, making Gomez hit dozens of groundstrokes. For an instant in the third set, when the Indian got a service break, it looked like he might upset a man who was eight inches taller, fifty pounds heavier, 140 rungs higher on the computer, and perhaps twenty-five years younger. But gradually, as the torrid afternoon ground on and on, all those years and inches and pounds and computer points came crashing down on Alejandro Pierola like rent long overdue, and he lost the deciding set 7–5.

Completing another circuit of the courts, I sat beside John Alexander, a handsome Australian with a world-class tan and Prince Valiant bangs. At the age of seventeen, J.A. had been the youngest man ever to play a Davis Cup challenge round, and he was hailed as the heir apparent to the long line of Aussie champions that stretched back for decades. However, his career hadn't worked out as he had wished. Briefly, he broke into the top ten, but never won a major title and eventually settled into the mid-20's—his own and the computer's. Now he was thirty-one years old and he had had to overcome a back injury, then struggle through the qualies to recover from a two-year slide that had carried him as low as No. 210.

When he didn't train steadily, J.A. had a tendency to put on weight. Tall and big-boned, he had the frame to carry a few extra pounds and still look good. But he didn't feel good, and with every inch he added to his waistline he lost a step. So, he told me, the qualies had been beneficial in the end. They had forced him to play himself back into shape, making him match-tough much sooner than if he had stepped right into the main draw after his injury.

"Lots of good players in the top twenty wouldn't qualify if they had to do it every week," Alexander said. "Many times you have to play twice a day, and conditions can be bad." It wasn't just a question of poor lighting and unswept courts and matches scheduled at ungodly hours. "There may be only one official, and if you're playing a guy you can't trust, then that puts on extra pressure, extra anxiety. Many young players are unscrupulous," he added, echoing an accusation I heard frequently from veterans on the circuit.

For Borg's refusal to play the qualies Alexander felt complete disdain. "I don't know whether his ego got in the way, but a rule is a rule. If he made his choice, he should have stuck to it and not bitched about it. Can't he put himself out just a little bit for the privileges and rewards he's received from the game?"

Just then Eliot Teltscher passed us and loudly parroted the question that would be flung at him for the next few weeks. "Are you playing Wimbledon?"

"Yes," Alexander called out, "and I'm disgusted that you're not."

I remarked that the debate about Borg appeared to have split the tennis community in two, with older players maintaining the Swede should abide by the rules, while younger fellows felt that there should be exceptions for a great champion.

"They're probably the kind who don't see anything wrong with guarantees," Alexander said of the young players.

What did *he* see wrong with them?

For the next few minutes words tumbled out of him in an angry torrent. "They're illegal. They violate the law. It's deceptive, it deceives the public. It's false advertising. There are cases where the loser in a tournament makes more than a winner. I think it's actually illegal what they're doing. If the Justice Department in the United States viewed it as they should, they'd put players in jail."

This final salvo was one I would hear fired off with rhythmic frequency by players from wildly divergent backgrounds. The American Congress or Justice Department or Federal Communication Commission should step in and straighten out professional tennis, they asserted. At first I regarded this as flattering, if naïve, confidence in my country's legal system, and I pitied the poor fellows who couldn't count on their own countries to do the right thing. But I soon recognized that I was the naïve one and they were the hard-nosed realists.

The fact is, while tennis likes to boast of its international dimensions, the sport is dominated by America and Americans. Of the top ten players at any given time, more than half are likely to be from the U.S. The percentage is about the same as one dips down a hundred rungs on the computer. The Association of Tennis Professionals has eight executives, six of them American. The Men's International Professional Tennis Council has ten members, four of them American, including M. Marshall Happer III, who holds the title of Administrator and is responsible for investigating offenses such as appearance money. The Volvo Grand Prix has its headquarters in New York City. World Championship Tennis works out of Lamar Hunt's home base in Dallas. What's more, two American agencies, IMG and Pro Serv—Lamar Hunt's Pro Man is trying to make it a troika—represent the overwhelming majority of the players, and just as important, they promote tournaments, stage exhibitions, and handle special accounts. For all its vaunted independence, Wimbledon, for example, delegated to Mark McCormack's IMG the job of selling its worldwide television rights and merchandising its name and logo.

Basically it's the infusion of television money which changed the character, the uniforms, and even the scoring system in professional tennis—brightly colored clothes and tie-breaks were dictated by the exigencies of TV—and once more America dominates. To cite Wimbledon again as the most dramatic example, the All England Club collects $2,250,000 in annual broadcasting and television fees, more than half of which are paid by NBC and Home Box Office, the largest pay-TV station in the U.S. The importance of American television can only increase now that NBC has renewed its contract to cover Wimbledon in 1983 and 1984 for $6,500,000 a year.

For better or worse, pro tennis is largely an American product. Much as it may insist on flying various flags of convenience and protesting that it can't control its foreign branches, ports of call, and tax havens, it hasn't fooled the players. Like John Alexander, they realize there's no chance the sport will be reformed unless Americans lead the way, and since there's been so little to suggest that this is liable to happen, some men regard the FCC and Justice Department's inaction as tacit approval of what is going on in the game.

Alexander found this hard to stomach, for he still had vivid memories of the kind of men who once ruled tennis. "Nobody loved a buck more than Ken Rosewall," he told me. "He was indispensable to a lot of tournaments, but he never insisted on guarantees. In fact, Rosewall changed the prize breakdown and insisted on a more equitable division of money. He took money out of his own pocket and gave it to the rest of us."

When I asked if he had heard of prize-money splitting, he admitted he had—not in Grand Prix events, but in exhibition matches. Still, he didn't make a Jesuitical distinction, as some did, between tournaments and special events. As far as he was concerned, it was all tennis, and a man should play honestly for the prize money that had been advertised. Anything else was, in his opinion, fraudulent and illegal.

I had mixed feelings about what I might see in the Adriano Panatta-Bruce Manson match. To be sure, there would be action. How much of it would consist of tennis was another question, for Panatta's career has been pockmarked with incidents on Campo Centrale which ended just short of mayhem and bloodshed.

Correction! There has been bloodshed. While cheering on his Davis Cup teammates in a typically tumultuous match in the Foro Italico, John Alexander had had his forehead laid open by a spectator who heaved a metal object from the stands.

Several players have retreated from the court rather than suffer the outrages which the Italian officials and crowd feel compelled to commit in support of their idol. In 1976 Harold Solomon defaulted in the semifinals against Panatta when he got what he believed were several flagrantly bad calls.

Two years later, again in a semifinal, José Higueras, a Spaniard with a reputation for impeccable fair play, did the same thing when he thought the crowd and the referee had conspired against him. The added peculiarity on that occasion was that the umpire, a sixty-nine-year-old Englishman named Bertie Bowron, walked off before Higueras did.

All day Bowron had been fighting a losing battle, attempting to keep the crowd quiet while Higueras served. When the spectators weren't hurling loud insults at the Spaniard, they pelted him with coins. So the umpire began letting him take two serves whenever the Italians interrupted him. But the tournament referee stepped in and overruled Bowron. This was a blatant violation of the Code of Conduct, which allows a referee to intervene only at the request of the umpire. In protest, Bowron abandoned the Campo Centrale, and Higueras followed.

The day after the Higueras imbroglio, when Panatta played Borg in the final, the Swede held one unassailable advantage. He was blasé about people throwing money at him. Promoters and advertisers had been doing it for years. When Italian fans started flinging coins, he coolly scooped up the cash and beat Panatta in five sets.

While Bruce Manson lacked Borg's experience at coping with such currency transfers, he was not a gladiator who had been thrust into the arena unarmed. A quick, tenacious lefthander with a serve that broke like a pitcher's curve ball, he was six years younger than Panatta and several light-years more mobile. Yet he knew the key to victory was mental.

"Everybody told me to remember I was playing Panatta, not the crowd," Manson later said. "I kept reminding myself not to let the crowd bother me. But then I realized that telling myself this all the time, telling myself not to let them bother me, *that* was bothering me."

One would never have known it in the uneventful first set, which Manson won 6–2. But then in the second, with the chant of "*Adriano! Ad-ree-ano!*" reverberating throughout the sunken marble amphitheater, Panatta embarked on the kind of comeback which generally demoralizes his opponents and galvanizes his fans into xenophobic excesses. When Manson dropped that set and was broken at the start of the third, it seemed the same cruel scenario would hold true for another year. With a close call here and a cacophonous assist from the crowd there, Panatta would slink away with the match.

But Manson knotted the score at three games apiece, then held service, as did Panatta. When it was the American's turn to serve again, the mob shouted encouragement to Adriano and screamed, "Fool!" and "Buffoon!" at Manson. Three times he tossed up the ball. Three times he was interrupted by catcalls and obscenities. Three times he struggled to retain his composure as he fell behind 0–40.

Now Manson teetered on the brink, a single point away from a fatal break. Any ball he hit near a line was certain to be called out. Yet it was Adriano who appeared more agitated. He lifted his arms, a suppliant begging for quiet. He let his hands slap to his sides when he didn't get what he asked for. His people believed they were helping him. Convinced they had brought him this far, they kept yelling, and soon Manson had saved two break points.

At 30–40 the American refused to put the ball into play until the umpire had silenced the crowd. Then he served, rushed Panatta's short return, and volleyed. The ball smacked the tape, wavered on edge, and dribbled down the other side. Point for Manson. Deuce.

Panatta seemed unstrung. He had lost three points straight. Then it was five straight, and he fell behind 4–5, all because of his own fans. Now he had to hold serve to stay in the match— an easy enough order, it appeared, when he went up 40–0. But in what must have seemed to him a living nightmare in which past mistakes are ritualistically repeated, he once again let the lead slip away, and when Manson scrambled to deuce, Panatta jerked his arm back as if to heave his racquet. A ball boy, cringing in terror, ducked for cover.

Although it wasn't what Adriano wanted or needed, his fans were still behind him, chanting his name, screaming encouragement, utterly destroying his equilibrium. Solomon and Borg, Higueras and Bertie Bowron should have been there to witness the moment of recognition, to watch Panatta's face twist in agony as he fell apart under this onslaught of frenzied noise which no one, not even he, the crowd's idol, could control. Like a tragic hero, perhaps he realized then that he had created a monster which was tearing him apart.

Manson won the game, set, and match, and after only one round of play the tournament had a lone Italian left in the draw—pudgy Paolo Bertolucci. What was worse from the promoters' point of view, second-seeded Johan Kriek had been clobbered 6–1/6–2 by Pablo Arraya, and Brian Gottfried, seeded seventh, had fallen to Pedro Rebolledo. In the second round Thierry Tulasne thumped last year's champion, José Luis Clerc, and Balazs Taroczy was beaten by Henri Leconte. After the next round, when Vitas Gerulaitis lost, attendance plummeted and the Foro Italico took on the appearance of just another Roman ruin, with sparse crowds ambling around, looking on distract-edly, chatting companionably. Lovers squeezed into shady corners to kiss, and pretty girls stretched out on warm marble slabs to work on their tans.

In the press room, reporters confessed horror at the notion of watching the Solomon-Higueras match. It was a sultry day and the match figured to last for hours. It didn't make sense, they said, to show up much before the third set. In fact, they thought it might be wise to start the match at 4–4 in the third set. Better yet, in a tie-break.

But, having arranged to interview Solomon afterward, I felt obliged to watch. I would have done so in any case since I enjoy battles between gritty baseliners who have to have the stamina of marathoners, the sense of spatial relations of chess masters, and the broad-gauge imagination of mural painters. To see a man overpower his opponent has, I admit, its exhilarating appeal, perhaps because we all long to believe that our own victories in life will be dramatic and decisive. But to watch one player out-maneuver and out-think another is, to my mind, infinitely more satisfying, for it suggests the subtle stratagems by which most of us survive.

The press-room cynics were right about one thing, though. Higueras and Solomon split the first two sets. But then Solomon snapped. Although he shouted at himself, "Get the lead out of your butt," he didn't have anything left. Maybe it was a question of not having the right replenishment. A tiny man of five feet six and 130 pounds, he once drank twenty-two bottles of mineral water during a long match, yet still lost thirteen pounds. Today between games in the third set he dug into the cooler beside the court, searching in vain for a Coke. He found only cans of the fizzy new Lipton Tea drink, Topspin. Solomon sent a ball boy to fetch a Coke from the bar, but the fellow loped back, shaking his head, shame-faced. He wasn't permitted to bring any drinks on court that weren't part of the promotional package.

Solomon lost the third set 6–0 and, irritated, exhausted, and dehydrated, had, understandably, little desire to sit for an interview. He said he'd meet me tomorrow.

Ever since I had read Harold Solomon's broadside in *World Tennis* against guarantees and appearance money, I had been anxious to talk with him. The ATP Media Guide characterizes him as "an activist in an age of cynicism. . . . With the retirement of Arthur Ashe [Solomon] has assumed the mantle of the 'thinking man's tennis player.' " What's more, he appeared willing to make immense personal sacrifices for his beliefs. Ranked No. 5 in the world as recently as 1980, he had now plummeted to No. 91, primarily, tennis writers implied, because of the demands of serving as ATP President and working for the World Hunger Project, an organization dedicated to eliminating starvation by the end of the century.

Ironically, it was Solomon's involvement with the Hunger Project which alerted me to the possibility that our conversation might not be altogether fruitful. I had read Shiva Naipaul's book *Black & White*, which contained a marvelously funny scene describing his encounter in California with the World Hunger Project, which is a spin-off of est (Erhard Seminar Training), the consciousness-raising group that transformed self-help psychology into a cornucopia of cash.

Next morning we met in the bleachers on the shady side of the field courts. Dressed in shorts, sandals, and a Hunger Project tee shirt, Solomon was a perfect miniature, a doll-like creature covered on the arms, legs, and chest with a mist of fine black hair. A gold neckchain spelled out his nickname, SOLLIE. When he answered my questions in complete sentences that sounded a bit too polished and succinct, I put that down to the fact that he had probably run through all these topics many times before.

To spare him the trouble of slogging through them again, I asked what should be done about guarantees.

"If you have to hide them," he said, "it can't be good for the game. I'd like to see the legal authorities in the States investigate."

Why pass the buck to them? I asked. The Pro Council Administrator had the authority to demand the financial records of any player suspected of accepting a guarantee, and if the player failed to provide them, he could suspend him until he complied. He had the same prerogative of demanding that tournaments open their financial accounts to his scrutiny.

Solomon replied that there was one investigation in progress. Marshall Happer was reviewing the tournament in Stuttgart, which was reputed to give Mercedes automobiles as guarantees. But these things weren't easy to prove, Solomon said. A lot of deals sounded like illegal inducements to him. But he wasn't the judge.

I remarked that guarantees seemed to pose dangers which even an article as unequivocal as his own had not acknowledged. Sure, they misled the public, undercut the incentive of top players, and reduced the prize money for everybody else. But what about their far more pernicious effects? Once a tournament had secretly paid a star $100,000, the last thing it wanted was for him to be beaten or defaulted in an early round. If people were violating one rule, wasn't it logical to conclude they might violate others to protect their investment?

Solomon said he didn't follow my line of reasoning.

I took pains to spell it out for him, repeating what the Umpire in Antibes had told me.

Solomon didn't believe it. He admitted there were problems with the officiating on the tour, but insisted these could be solved. "We need better-trained umpires. They just have to have the guts to impose the rules."

How could he expect men who were poorly paid and absolutely dependent upon tournament directors to risk disqualifying a star or making a close call that might cost them their jobs?

Solomon continued to maintain it was just a matter of umpires getting more training and experience.

"Guarantees are the major problem," he said, as if they existed in that splendid contemporary limbo, the context of no context.

I mentioned an article Arthur Ashe had written for *International Tennis Weekly* in which the former Wimbledon champion stated that one danger of appearance money was that people might suspect the stars were splitting their guarantees with their opponents.

Screwing his face into an expression of total bafflement, Solomon blurted, "Why would anyone split his guarantee? Are you sure Arthur wasn't talking about prize money?"

"No. He referred to guarantees. But you bring up an interesting point about prize-money splitting."

"Well, you know, in certain events, especially when there's a big difference between winning and losing—on the WCT it can be a $68,000 difference—well, it could happen."

"I've been told it *is* happening."

"I have no knowledge of that." His voice assumed the formal cadences of an official speaking for the record. "I have no knowledge of any individual doing that."

"But you've heard of it?"

"No, I've never heard of it."

"If you've never heard of prize-money splitting, why did you bring it up?"

"*You* brought it up," he snapped.

"No. I brought up Ashe's article. He spoke of splitting guarantees. You brought up prize-money splitting."

"It was just hypothetical. I said it *could* happen. It could happen in any sport."

Seeing we were getting nowhere on this subject, I asked about the World Hunger Project. But before long the discussion spiraled off into the same vertiginous pattern as our previous conversation.

Solomon explained that the World Hunger Project had been founded in 1977 by three men, Werner Erhard of est, the pop singer John Denver, and Dr. Roy Prosterman, a professor at . . . There was some confusion here. Was it Harvard or the University of Michigan? Solomon wasn't sure, but it was "one of those or the other." The point was, the Hunger Project had as its goal the conquest of starvation by 1997. Although there was now no direct association with est, Erhard was still on the board of the Hunger Project, and over two million people had been "enrolled." Solomon himself had organized an annual benefit tennis tournament and last year it had raised $50,000 for the cause.

When I asked what, precisely, the cause was, Solomon reiterated the project's slogan—"The end of hunger is an idea whose time has come"—and when I inquired what the World Hunger Project did with its money and its millions of signatures, Solomon said, "Basically, it's a communication and education program. It allows people to look into their hearts to see what they can do about the problem. It attacks the apathy which prevents people from doing something. We have the food and technology to end starvation."

He didn't mean the Hunger Project had the food and technology. "It doesn't treat the symptoms," he emphasized. "It's creating a context within which starvation can be ended."

I urged him to describe that context and what specific steps had been taken to achieve it.

"We bring hunger organizations together and show them how they can work together. We held thirty-seven conferences last year in the United States."

And what had they accomplished? Had any areas of starvation been eradicated? Any individuals been fed?

Again I was missing the point, he said. The purpose of the Hunger Project wasn't to deal with starving people. It was to convince well-fed people that hunger could be wiped out.

"Forty million people will constitute a critical mass," he assured me, "and it'll just happen. The end of hunger will become an idea whose time has come. It used to be *if* hunger will end. Now it's *when* it will end."

Suddenly a critical mass seemed to well up in my own mind and several things became clearer. The World Hunger Project was to starvation what the Grand Prix's Code of Conduct was to rule infractions.

Woozy from the interview with Harold Solomon, I almost walked past the man I had been searching for all week. Yannick

Noah stood alone outside the press room. Although this wasn't the ideal spot to speak to him about dope, I feared I might not get a better opportunity. Introducing myself, I reminded him of our conversation in Monte Carlo the evening before his semi-final match with Lendl. Then, since there was no good way to broach the subject, I bluntly asked about the interview in *Rock & Folk*. Had he ever sued the people who conducted it or accused them of misquoting him?

"No."

"What happened about that article?"

"Just disappeared."

"Was it meant to be a joke?"

I wanted to allow him every chance to explain. From French reporters I had heard rumors that Noah hadn't known he was being taped or that he thought his remarks about drugs were off the record. But with me he made no such claims. He simply shrugged and said, "Yes, a joke."

The shrug unsettled me. "You meant for people to read the interview and take it as a joke?"

"People could take it any way they want," he said flatly.

Before I could ask another question, an Italian photographer bustled over, flourishing a collection of his snapshots.

"I've got a good picture of you here, Yannick." He opened the book to the last page. A chimpanzee was brandishing a tennis racquet and pursing his fleshy lips.

Noah's face flashed with anger. "Fuck you," he said and drew back his fist as if to bash the photographer. But then, in an instant, he turned it into a joke, smothering his rage and tapping the man lightly on the shoulder.

A moment later he left, whether to escape the obtuse photographer or me, I can't say. That afternoon Yannick Noah was upset by Andres Gomez and returned to Paris.

Buster Mottram came off court snarling at the British journalists waiting for him. "I don't need this aggravation, I don't need this shit." But he was smiling, he was happy. He had won in three sets. True, his opponent had been a seventeen-year-old

American qualifier, but it was one more triumph in a season that had been surprisingly successful. Mottram, now ranked in the mid-20's, figured to be seeded next month at Wimbledon.

The British press wanted to talk to him about this. But Buster had no interest at all in talking tennis. When they urged him toward the interview room, he pulled back. "Oh, God, no, not in there with the Italians."

Instead, they lingered at the entrance to the players' dressing room. Buster toweled off his long, rope-muscled arms and told the reporters about a song he had written. It was called "The Average Man." It had been set to a disco beat and would appear next month on an album . . .

The British press was palpably uninterested. Would he play the French Open? they asked.

"I'd rather have a bullet in the head than go to France." Buster sniffed at his wispy mustache, disgusted by the very thought. "I loathe France, I hate the people. They're so rude. The aggro, the people in the hotels—I hate everything there."

He liked the song he had written, however, and believed the reporters would, too. It was recorded on an album called *Half the Day's Gone and I Haven't Got Any Dough*. There were tunes by Paul McCartney and Eric Clapton on the same album and . . .

Not a single reporter, except me, was copying down a word Mottram said. They stood with pens poised on notepads, waiting to ask about Wimbledon.

Buster didn't give them a chance. "What's the difference between the average man in Naples and the average man in Nigeria?"

Someone groaned. Someone else said, "About being seeded at Wimbledon . . ."

"Neither man has much upstairs," Buster solved his own riddle. "But the average man in Nigeria has a lot more below the belt."

"About Wimbledon, how great an advantage is it to be seeded?"

Mottram sighed. It was hopeless. He told them what they wanted to hear. "Obviously, it's a huge advantage."

In a frenzy, they scribbled this hot copy, then dashed for the long-distance telephones.

. . .

In the quarterfinals Wojtek Fibak met Pablo Arraya, an ebullient, long-haired Peruvian, born in Argentina and seasoned by a semester's education at the University of Arkansas. Although there were no more than thirty people watching the match, Arraya acted as if this were the final at Wimbledon or his *alternativa* at the Fiesta of San Fermin.

Fibak ran away with the first set, jerking the Peruvian to the net with dropshots, then passing him down the line. But Arraya caught on to that trick and, in the second set, beat Fibak to the punch—and when he smacked a passing shot for a winner, he waggled his hips and hollered "Olé" like a matador applauding his own artistry and taunting the bull at the same time. Fibak complained to the umpire about Arraya's antics, and the next time he broke into a hula and hollered "Olé," Arraya received a warning for visible obscenity.

"Why?" he demanded. "What's wrong with dancing?"

The umpire ordered him to play on.

When Fibak muttered something, Arraya responded—first with words, then with a crueler taunt. Rather than end points quickly, he punished the Pole, drawing him forward with dropshots, driving him back with lobs, then sucking him in again. The tactic might well have backfired; most pros have little trouble putting away overheads. When they do, it's usually a sign of fatigue, and Fibak was plainly very tired. His narrow shoulders drooped, his pale legs looked rubbery. Between points he retreated to the back fence, to a band of shade no better than six inches wide. If Arraya was a matador, then Fibak was a wounded bull searching for an illusion of security, for the *querencia* where he would lie down and die.

After winning the second set 6–3, Arraya rushed to a 5–2 lead in the third and started dancing again while awaiting serve. There was no hip-waggling now. It resembled a sprightly disco step. Fibak was too exhausted to object. The sun that shone brightly on Arraya fell as molten lead on the Pole, who lost the match and stumbled toward the shade again.

Afterward, in a stunning reversal, Arraya said to me of Fibak, "He's a bit cocky." This was like Muhammad Ali accusing some punch-drunk of being flamboyant. "He told me I should be disqualified for complaining about the officiating. I told him to shut up. He was trying to get to my head."

But the umpire had done worse than get to his head. He had gotten to Pablo's wallet, recommending a fine for "visible obscenity." "They really favor the top players. I've been fined for things Jimmy Connors does all the time."

Still, he was happy to have reached the semifinals, where he would meet the winner of the Teltscher-Dibbs match. "If I play Dibbs, I think maybe I have some chance. He's older, and a lot of times when he gets down a set, he goes lax."

Unfortunately for Arraya, Dibbs went lax one round too early and Teltscher made short work of him, 6–2/6–2. Fast Eddie, bow-legged, built like a fireplug, came off court caked with red clay and flopped on a bench outside the locker room, postponing a cool shower. If that seemed a curious move, it was nothing compared to what followed.

For reasons known best to himself, a British journalist rushed over to Dibbs and asked if he knew how to spell slivovitz.

For an instant Dibbs was speechless. It was the wrong time for a joke. But maybe it was right for a test question. Maybe in England when someone is near to fainting from exhaustion, you run up and check whether he has regained his faculties by asking him to spell slivovitz, just the way an American might spread his hand and ask, "How many fingers am I holding up?"

But Dibbs was having none of it. "Are you kidding? I can't even spell my name."

If Arraya's victory over Fibak was surprising, the whipping Mats Wilander laid on Tomas Smid was nothing short of flabbergasting. Less than two months ago in Milan, Smid had slipped past the seventeen-year-old Swede in a three-set match, but today Wilander wasted the Czech Davis Cup veteran 6–1/6–1.

The upset seemed to leave most journalists mute, and Wilander did little to fill in the silences. A polite, soft-spoken adolescent, he answered questions with monosyllables and remained placidly quiet during the long, awkward pauses. Although he volunteered that this had been "my best win ever," his tone suggested a dusty recording that announces the arrival and departure of trains.

Several reporters observed that Wilander was blond, laconic, patient, and he hit a two-fisted backhand. Did he see any resemblance between himself and Bjorn Borg?

No, he didn't.

When the Brits began trying to pep things up by asking about Wimbledon, there were the first, faint rumblings of discontent among other journalists. Next week, at Roland Garros, the rumblings would reach a crescendo, and when the same question was asked of every man who won or lost a match in Paris, a French reporter exploded, speaking for everybody who was weary of listening to the British press blow a one-note tune on their red-white-and-blue kazoos. "Who gives a shit about Wimbledon?"

Eliot Teltscher certainly didn't, and after defeating Pablo Arraya in the semifinals, he repeated his reasons for not playing at the All England Club. He didn't like the people who ran the place, he didn't like the snobbish English attitude, he didn't like the grass courts, he didn't like the weather.

Just when his press conference was starting to sound like a propaganda campaign paid for by the Argentinian *junta*, some intrepid Italian interrupted to ask Teltscher about this tournament. What was his reaction to being in the final of the Italian Open?

"I don't like the idea of a tournament being two out of three sets, then switching to three out of five for the final. I think it should be consistent throughout."

But tomorrow was the most important match of his career, wasn't it?

"No, I consider the semifinals at the Masters more important."

The next day *Paese Sera* ran a retaliatory article entitled "Mickey Mouse American" which described Eliot Teltscher as a small man with teeth like a rat and a face which wouldn't earn him a single *lira*. With publicity like this, it was little wonder the tournament had had troubles.

If it wasn't bad enough having a rodent contending for the title, his opponent was Andres Gomez, the most famous man in Ecuador, according to his coach. But Gomez' following in Rome was somewhat less avid than in Guayaquil, and although he had won an exciting, if erratic, match against Wilander in the semis, the press predicted the final at the Foro Italico would be full of yawns and empty seats.

That evening I did something that requires an explanation. I interviewed another journalist. Actually, I did more than interview him. I spilled into his lap virtually everything I had learned about the circuit—the illegal guarantees, the prize-money splitting, the betting, the accusations of drug abuse, the preferential treatment of star players, the tanked matches, the dubious business deals between tournament directors and the umpires. Had he been less honorable, he could have taken the material and written it up himself. I realized this, but felt an obsessive need to confide in someone of unimpeachable reputation who had long been associated with pro tennis.

I went to Bud Collins, a sports writer for the *Boston Globe* who is best known as a tennis commentator for NBC, as well as for the Public Broadcasting System. Witty and iconoclastic, full of quips and puns and nicknames for real and apocryphal people, Collins has a resolutely buoyant style, and he seemed the sort, if anybody was, to dismiss what I had to say as a negative minority report from a neophyte who had seized upon a few isolated, sensational stories that didn't do justice to the game.

Instead, Bud Collins sat with me in the bleachers overlooking the practice courts, and listened closely to everything I said. He denied none of it and expressed no doubts at all about what I told him. In fact, far from defending tennis, he confirmed many of the charges against it and recounted a number of anecdotes that amplified what I had discovered.

The appearance of evil was rampant, he agreed, and without

any prompting he cited the example of a WCT tournament six weeks ago in Zurich in which Bill Scanlon had played Vitas Gerulaitis for the title. Since Gerulaitis was already committed to the Alan King Classic, a Grand Prix tournament in Las Vegas, he faced a difficult dilemma if he won his match with Scanlon. Champions of WCT events are contractually obligated to play the WCT finals in Dallas the same week as the Alan King Classic in Las Vegas. So Gerulaitis went on court in Zurich aware that the price of victory would be a fine, a long suspension, or perhaps a lawsuit from the WCT or the Grand Prix, depending upon which commitment he violated. But then the dilemma disappeared. Gerulaitis lost to Scanlon in five sets.

"The Gerulaitis-versus-Scanlon situation looks very suspicious," Collins said. "Even if you give Vitas the benefit of the doubt and say he played his guts out and lost, it still looks bad."

As to the general question of tanking, he conceded that it happened often in doubles. He knew all the rationalizations. But he pointed out that the players were pros, and there was always prize money at stake. Why shouldn't they be expected to make an honest effort?

By way of answering, he remarked that professional tennis was "a civilization all to itself. The rules of the outside world do not apply here."

Collins added, "The game is a scandal. But it doesn't get the public attention and scrutiny you'd expect. It's still played under the rug. In the papers and on TV it's rah-rah for tennis. . . . But a lot of hanky-panky goes on that no one knows about or cares about."

I asked why he hadn't spoken out on these matters.

He maintained he had. "I'm the one who first said those winner-take-all events in Las Vegas [in 1974] were fake." He had also risked his neck in his hometown at his own club when he revealed that Jimmy Connors had received $50,000 in appearance money to play a tournament at the Longwood Cricket Club. But Collins doubted this had accomplished much. Tennis seemed impervious to criticism, and the public ignored accusations that would have caused major scandals and prompted investigations in other sports.

"I used to say, 'This is going to blow up.' But it blows up in one sense, but not in another. It's hydra-headed. It's chaos."

Collins absent-mindedly twisted a copper bracelet on his wrist. Formerly the team coach at Brandeis University, and still an avid player, he clearly loved tennis and regretted that many of his fellow sports writers regarded it as a sideshow akin to professional wrestling.

"There are only two tournaments people know and care about—Wimbledon and the U.S. Open. Other than that, most people look at tennis as a funny little game that goes its own way. The players really take advantage of the public. I used to blame the agents. But the players know the difference between right and wrong. I think the situation is dangerous."

Finally, as Collins viewed it, "Tennis was born in dishonesty and has never grown out of it. Historically, the game has always been a bit of a swindle" in the way it attempted "to uphold the bogus traditions of British amateurism."

This struck me as strong stuff coming from the jolly, bald-headed man Americans are used to seeing on TV praising the traditions of Wimbledon or puncturing the self-serving pomposity of his friend and fellow commentator, Donald Dell. Although he could see me taking notes as we talked, I felt compelled to remind him I was writing a book.

"You can quote me on any of this," said Bud Collins.

Before the final I spoke to Andres Gomez' coach, Colon Nunez, and his good friend Pablo Arraya. Nunez was wearing three wristwatches—his own and Gomez' and one he was holding for Arraya—and he resembled the sort of tout you see in a Mexican border town, his arms encircled up to the elbows with counterfeit Rolexes and Omegas with $10 price tags. When I asked what to look for today, he said Gomez was very nervous and he didn't expect a well-played first set.

Arraya said the key to beating Teltscher was to keep the ball deep and slow, and to hit with backspin. Teltscher couldn't hurt you unless you let him feed off your speed. This didn't bode well for Gomez, who gave almost every ball a thunderous wallop with pronounced topspin.

Neither Nunez' nor Arraya's analysis proved accurate. But then, this week very little had gone according to form. Only one thing seemed predictable: the Foro Italico was less than half full.

From the opening game Gomez performed with the kind of consistency that has been rare in his career. He broke Teltscher three times in the first set and rushed the net at every chance, clearing a path with deep forehand approaches. Even when he stayed at the baseline and rallied, his groundstrokes had too much sting for the American, who made the mistake of trying to match Gomez' power. He might have been wiser to take something off the ball, settle into a slower game, and hope for a few mistakes. But it's difficult to concentrate on tactics when tennis balls are screaming at you as if shot out of a bazooka.

After winning the title 6–2/6–3/6–2, Gomez summed matters up succinctly. "There was only one player on the court today. I never let him get into the match."

Cino Marchese, impeccably attired in gray slacks and a blue blazer, orchestrated the awards ceremony with suave self-assurance. After presenting Gomez with a trophy, he uncorked a magnum of Moët et Chandon champagne, poured the champion a glass, and proposed a toast.

But Gomez preferred to drink out of the bottle. After knocking back a long slug, he suddenly shook the champagne to a froth and squirted it on Cino, who ducked away, then whirled and flung his glass of bubbly on a group of photographers. Gomez giggled, Cino chuckled, the crowd roared, even the drenched photographers laughed.

Standing alone, his hands clasped behind his back, Eliot Teltscher stayed clear of the champagne and the merriment and made no pretense at being a sporting loser. Afterward he disappeared into the locker room and there was some doubt whether he would emerge for a press conference. A representative from Silvy Tricot, the outfit that clothed Andres Gomez, said he had just come from the locker room and Teltscher was very upset and too angry to talk to reporters.

I asked the man if he knew Gomez' coach. He said he did. Colon Nunez had once been a player. "But then he got a body ache and had to quit."

A body ache?

"He hurt himself," the fellow from Silvy said. Then, leaning close, he proudly confided that he had watched the match on television. "I was in the RAI-TV van telling them to put the camera on our label. We have taken care of everything we could control."

Abruptly, Eliot Teltscher entered the press room, radiating hostility. He so obviously resented journalists for insisting on this interview, most of them were cowed into silence. But Bud Collins asked for Teltscher's general reaction to the match.

"I don't have any general reaction. He played better and won more games. That's all there is to it."

Having heard enough, Collins wisely departed.

An Italian, speaking fractured English, asked what Teltscher thought of Gomez' remark that he had never been in the match.

"That's his opinion."

Since there was no translator, I tried to interpret as best I could. At one point I explained to Teltscher that the questions weren't as rude as they sounded. It was just that some of these reporters didn't have a sure grasp of English.

"Then they wouldn't understand my answers," he snapped.

Had Gomez surprised him?

"I wasn't expecting anything. I was just playing."

Inevitably, a British journalist brought up Wimbledon, but Teltscher broke in before he could finish the question. "I'm not discussing that anymore."

Was this the worst he had ever played?

"No, I'm sure I could play a lot worse."

"Are you disappointed?" asked one obtuse soul.

"No. It's not the end of the world."

Fortunately, it *was* the end of the interview. Grumbling and aggrieved, we marched up to the IMG pavilion, where Silvy Tricot was hosting a reception for Andres Gomez. Left alone for a moment with the champion, I mentioned his amusing trick with the champagne. "Cino told you to spray him, didn't he?" I asked. "You two set it up."

Gomez grinned sheepishly. "Yes."

As I left the reception, Cino Marchese was gazing out at the field courts, deserted now, the evening light casting the crooked shadows of pine trees over the marble slabs and down onto the red clay. "The players, they come and go." He intoned his words like a solemn benediction. "But the Italian Open remains. We are building a new tradition."

FRENCH OPEN

CONCEDED to be the most demanding tournament in the world, the French Open, the first leg of the Grand Slam, is played on slow red clay, and from the first round the matches are three out of five grueling sets. There is no evidence that the French author Chateaubriand followed tennis, but he might well have been describing the progress of games at Stade Roland Garros when he wrote that although crimes are not always punished, mistakes are.

Above all else, players in Paris must strike a precarious balance between their endurance and their patience as they maneuver their opponents into morale-killing mistakes. While reckless net-rushers are apt to get passed, or to have their necks wrenched out of sockets as they swivel around to watch topspin lobs sail over them for winners, baseliners run the risk of exhausting themselves. To win a single point sometimes requires an exchange of fifty or sixty strokes, and matches routinely last more than four hours. It is not uncommon to see men faint from fatigue, or cramp up and have to be carried off court looking like gigged frogs.

The nightmare of players who grow up serving and volleying on fast surfaces is the crafty South American or European who learned the game on pulverized brick dust and prefers to die on it than lose. Pavel Hutka, a low-ranked Czech, used to arrive in Paris each spring confident of upsetting anyone who had never seen him play. Thoroughly ambidextrous, Hutka served with his right hand, then transferred the racquet and hit groundstrokes with his left. Or was it the other way around? It sometimes seemed he switched his routine at critical junctures. I once watched an American crumble into ragged bits and pieces and scream at his coach, "You told me to hit to his backhand. How the hell can I do that? He doesn't *have* a backhand."

Although Hutka had stayed home this year, there was no dearth of surprises for the top seeds. José Luis Clerc, a semi-finalist in 1981, found himself thrown up against a short, curly-haired French junior called Loïc Courteau, who hit with two hands off both sides. His shots didn't appear to have much pace, but he cleverly disguised their direction and astonished Clerc and everybody else by sweeping the first set 6–1.

Courteau served for the second at 5–4, only to have the Argentine rally to win 7–5. When Courteau broke to a lead again in the third set, I was curious to see whether Clerc could extricate himself from the web this clever kid was weaving around him. But more than a month ago in Monte Carlo I had agreed to rendezvous with Butch Buchholz at Roland Garros and discuss whether he could confirm what I had learned about prize-money splitting and related matters. Bucking the current of the crowd, I left the Court Centrale and searched for the Executive Director of the ATP.

When I first covered the French Open in the mid-'70s, crowds during the early rounds were small and the tournament had an air of spacious informality. Players relaxed in the shade of chestnut trees with their families and friends, picnicking beside fans who had come to watch them. On the field courts one might find himself sitting with Tom Okker, Fred Stolle, or Jan Kodes and there was no sense that these were numinous creatures set apart from the rest of humanity. You could actually discuss tennis with them, and share the pleasant sense that everybody was here for the same purpose—to celebrate their love of a game that seemed to have limited appeal for the mass public.

Since then attendance had tripled, prize money had made exponential leaps, and the players and their entourages had retreated to preserves which were off-bounds to everybody, including the press. This was just a reflection of the increase of interest in tennis throughout France. Within a decade the number of clubs had jumped by five hundred percent, the number of courts had tripled, and the number of players had quintupled.

While these statistics were impressive and could be viewed as positive indicators, as a financial analyst might put it, they had not made Roland Garros a more enjoyable place to watch tennis. Although the French Open had expanded its facilities, this had created rather than solved problems, bringing in still more spectators, sponsors, and promoters. Now there were no sylvan glades for picnickers. Every spare inch of ground had been covered with food stalls, clothing and equipment booths, and tents leased by advertisers and corporations. The tournament had taken on the flatulent atmosphere of a trade fair.

I passed boutiques that were hustling jewelry, perfume, boots, designer-name luggage, and high-fashion apparel. The New Man clothing tent cautioned that LIFE IS TOO SHORT TO DRESS SADLY, and it wasn't alone in exhorting buyers to seize the day. There were booths full of real-estate dealers hawking condos at the shore or chalets in the mountains; there were Atari video games for sale; there was even an outlet for stamp collectors.

Since it was a school holiday, thousands of kids scurried along the main concourse, kicking soft-drink cans, gobbling Sorbet Roland Garros, and tossing trash into the fountain. Sorbet Roland Garros consisted of a few ounces of sherbet packed into a plastic tennis ball. Just lift the lid and eat. The taste, however, was ruined by the container, which smelled powerfully of uric acid. Once several thousand plastic tennis balls had been splintered underfoot, the place reeked like a *pissoir*.

I found Butch Buchholz watching Harold Solomon struggle against Peter McNamara. Ahead two sets to zero, Solomon had twice reached match ball in the third, only to let the Australian squirm off the hook in a tie-break. Although he couldn't win, he would punish McNamara—or was he punishing himself?— by dragging out the fourth and fifth sets like the deathbed scene in an opera.

When Buchholz had seen enough, we waded through the clogged aisles to the Adidas Players' Lounge, where he managed to persuade the doorman to let me in. Then, summarizing his course of action since our conversation in Monte Carlo, Buchholz said he had mentioned prize-money splitting with a number of players, agents, and ATP officials, all of whom had denied any knowledge of it. He had also brought it up for discussion at the ATP meeting in Las Vegas. Nobody had confessed. Unless I named names, he didn't see what more he could do.

I asked if any ATP officials had missed the meeting in Las Vegas.

He said a few had remained in Europe, Vittorio Selmi among them.

I suggested that he review the matter with the men who hadn't made it to Las Vegas. At first I had been reluctant to mention Selmi for fear of jeopardizing his position. Now I was more interested to see how far Buchholz would push an investigation into a practice which he claimed struck at the heart of the integrity of the game. Repeating that an ATP official had told me splits were commonplace, I emphasized that it wasn't happening just on the WCT. I had spoken to a player who had admitted splitting in a tournament that awarded ATP points.

He acknowledged there might be some truth to this. Paul Svehlik in the Paris office had "heard rumblings about it." But what could he do unless I named names?

I told him I didn't feel it was my place to police the sport. He and his fellow members of the Pro Council had broad powers to conduct an investigation—if they cared to.

This prompted a general disquisition on the problems confronting professional tennis. Players had changed since his day, Buchholz observed. He had to deal with very young men—and, in many cases, utterly uneducated ones—who were making millions of dollars. This, he said in a classic piece of understatement, caused difficulties and would continue to cause them unless drastic measures were taken—not so much disciplinary steps as remedial education and guidance.

Buchholz pointed out that, contrary to the popular stereotype, professional tennis players were, increasingly, products of families who *don't* belong to country clubs, *aren't* especially affluent, *don't* expect their sons to become doctors and lawyers, and *don't* know how to advise their sons once they set out on the circuit. Of course, among the Americans there was a tendency to spend several years at some university polishing their game—not that that guaranteed they received instruction in other subjects—but more and more fellows, Buchholz said, were dropping out of high school and going on the tour, locking into a profession that didn't prepare them for anything else in life. In Europe and South America some of these players were the sort who might formerly have become boxers or bullfighters. They were poor functional-illiterates desperate to rise in a world they knew nothing about.

Recalling Noah's remarks about dope, I strung Buchholz the same line of bait I had dangled in front of Sandy Mayer. At least players were involved in a healthy sport. You didn't see them dying in bed of drug overdoses.

Buchholz took no solace from this. "Not so far. But wait. Since the big money came into tennis, we haven't seen a guy start to slide downhill. They're all too young still. But when their tennis careers end and the cheering stops and they lose a lot of people they thought were friends, then what happens? You remember that pro football player, the guy who used to play for the Kansas City Chiefs [Jim Tyrer], the one who put a bullet in his brain? Well, I look for a lot more of that to happen."

To guard against this, the ATP was attempting to establish a program to prepare players for the circuit, then train them for retirement. Although it struck me as implausible to expect wealthy, famous high-school drop-outs to sit still for alternate education, I wished him well.

Then I returned to Center Court, where Loïc Courteau, age seventeen, had a crowd of fourteen thousand Frenchmen at his feet. José Luis Clerc also appeared to be supine in front of the precocious junior, who led two sets to one and 5–3. Serving to stay alive, Clerc fell behind 0–40, giving the boy three match points.

A club player in this situation might pat a cautious shot and pray for a miracle. But Clerc demonstrated a critical difference between professionals and amateurs. With his back to the wall, he attacked. His Cartier watch glinted in the sun as he served, rushed the net, and saved one match point.

On the next exchange Clerc hit a short ball. Courteau closed on it, slapping it deep into the corner. Clerc could do no more than spoon the ball back. It came at Courteau chest high, slow and fat as a yellow balloon. Virtually any shot would have won the match. Virtually. But the boy tried a drop volley, which Clerc covered and put away. 30–40.

After the Argentine blasted an ace to reach deuce, Courteau got a fourth match point when Clerc fumbled a backhand into the net. But again José fell back on his serve to weasel out of trouble. Although the score went to deuce twice more, he held to 4–5.

Courteau still had a chokehold on the match. He served for it, flinging himself around the court, once tumbling headlong in a somersault that left a streak of clay, like a tire track, down his spine. But Clerc was no longer chasing him from side to side, offering him angles to exploit. Instead, he jerked Courteau to the net and forced him to volley. With his two-fisted strokes, the French boy had limited range and began lunging at low balls one-handed. He lost his serve to 5–5, scrabbled into a tie-break, took the lead 5–2, but didn't have the power or the experience to end the match. When Clerc knotted the score at two sets apiece, Loïc Courteau's day on center stage was essentially over.

The story is the same every year at every Grand Slam event. A young, unknown player with nothing to lose seems undaunted by a top seed and races to an apparently insurmountable lead. But then, just when the match is within his grasp, he suffers a lapse not so much of technique as of imagination. He cannot conceive of beating the star. Subconsciously, the very notion may threaten him more than does the idea of defeat. Players are often asked how they cope with loss. A more intriguing question is whether they can cope with victory, whether they can stare down the man they're about to beat.

As José Luis Clerc said after winning 6–2 in the fifth set, "In the tie-break I saw that he was really nervous, nervous about winning. As soon as I saw that, I played better."

. . .

Later that evening, in the lobby of the Sofitel, I met a clothing rep sitting by himself, looking morose.

"What are you up to?" I asked the fellow, who was usually a gregarious fount of gossip.

"I'm waiting for my girl."

"Where is she?"

"Upstairs, fucking ———." He named one of the most celebrated players on the circuit.

I assumed he was joking. "You'd better let me buy you a drink. She'll be busy for hours."

"I've already had too much to drink. I have any more, I'm liable to . . . to do something."

"You're serious?"

"Yes. She told me she'd like to fuck him. I thought she was kidding. But then he came back from the court with us and asked her to go upstairs and she went."

"Why didn't you say something?"

"What's to say?"

"Well, why the hell wait around here?"

He explained that he had an appointment with the player. They were supposed to go out to dinner.

"Forget that," I said.

"I can't. He's under contract to us. He's our hottest client."

"Jesus, man, what about your girl?"

"She's finished. I'm dropping her."

"I'd drop *him*."

"Impossible. I suppose I shouldn't blame him, I've fixed him up with chicks before. I just never thought he'd take mine." He shrugged, trying to be brave. "Oh, well, they're all shits anyway."

"Players?" I said.

"Women," he said.

Next day, as usual, I checked the bulletin board at the press office to see which players had withdrawn. Victor Pecci, the piratical giant from Paraguay with the explosive serve and flashing diamond earring, won his opening match, then pulled out with a back injury which had sidelined him off and on all spring. I inquired about this ailment and was informed by a laughing Grand Prix official that Pecci had not wrenched a muscle going for an ace. After a Davis Cup triumph over Canada, he and his Paraguayan teammates had repaired to a discothèque. "When Victor's at a disco, he just goes crazy," the official said. He liked to dance and he liked to pick people up. No, not women. He picked up a man—literally—and slipped, landing smack on his coccyx. The pain had been excruciating, both then and in following weeks. According to the Grand Prix official, Victor Pecci was the circuit's first recorded victim of "a slipped disco."

Two other players—Chris Lewis of New Zealand and Jiri Granat of Hungary—had also withdrawn. They complained of severe intestinal disorders. This news seemed inconsequential at the time.

On Center Court, Thierry Tulasne, another French teenager, took on Ivan Lendl, whom most tennis writers picked to inherit Bjorn Borg's crown at Roland Garros. Although the Czech had lost twice to Guillermo Vilas this spring, no one expected that to happen here, and although he was seeded behind Jimmy Connors, no one gave Jimbo much chance of capturing a Grand Slam event on clay.

Jumping several weeks ahead of themselves, some journalists had started writing about *when*, not *if*, Ivan Lendl won the French Open, and they speculated that he might then play Wimbledon. He had already beaten McEnroe four times in a row, most recently on an indoor hard court at the WCT finals in Dallas, and without Borg to block his path, there was no reason he shouldn't capture the Wimbledon and U.S. Open titles as well.

Since it was a foregone conclusion that he would whip Tulasne, the press section was half empty and many reporters who remained for the match appeared more interested in luxuriating in the unseasonably warm sun. At 7:30 in the evening the air was still balmy and redolent of flowers. Two French journalists lit a joint and passed it back and forth with the same mesmerizing rhythm as Tulasne and Lendl exchanged groundstrokes.

Although Lendl himself seldom ventured far from the base-line, he seemed to resent Tulasne for adhering to the same dull tactic. Peeved, he dug a hand into his pocket for sawdust and kicked the clay with his Superga shoes. He had stuffed so much sawdust into his right pocket, he resembled those matadors who pad the crotches of their pants with handkerchiefs, impressing spectators, if not the bull.

Tulasne's basic strategy was to whack high topspin forehands to Lendl's backhand and hope for errors. With a looping wind-up, like a man lashing a whip, he cracked a ball that spurted off the court and drove Lendl progressively deeper toward the windscreen. If he had had the audacity to rush the net and volley, the tactic might have been worth the effort. But it made little sense to waste so much energy forcing Lendl to retreat unless he intended to advance, or to cross up the Czech with a dropshot.

While some matches sound like an artillery barrage, this one had all the acoustical excitement of a leaky faucet. *Plop-plop! Plop-plop! Plop-plop!* Tulasne managed to keep the scores close—7–6/7–5/7–6—but the outcome was never in doubt.

What was in doubt was the public's interest in a style of play which bore the same relationship to classical tennis as trench warfare did to the blitzkrieg. Many clay-court events had turned into battles of attrition in which the spectators were likely to lose patience before the players did. In Paris several men broke the vow of *omertà* which generally prevents players from criticizing one another and spoke out against a trend which they thought might diminish tennis' popularity. Jimmy Connors remarked that Lendl was just "lumbering around the back court" and that Mats Wilander looked like he "was on No-Doz or something."

Peter McNamara opined that people liked to watch him be-cause "I play a different game from Lendl or Vilas. I make more mistakes, mistakes I shouldn't make, but I don't hit the ball fifteen feet over the net every time. I have the old-style game of tennis. I play classical tennis"—by which he meant he went for flat, hard winners and occasionally took the net.

After explaining his own popularity in much the same terms, Vitas Gerulaitis warned, "In five years tennis is going to be very boring and we'll have a draw with a hundred and twenty-eight Borgs."

This prospect of future tournaments dominated by clones of Bjorn Borg provokes fervent debate, especially among veteran and retired players, who, while conceding admiration for Borg's accomplishments, point out that he had the great good fortune to come along during a period when there were few first-rate serve-and-volleyers. As soon as McEnroe reached his maturity, the era of Borg's dominance abruptly ended. According to this theory, the Swede's tumble from the No. 1 rung had less to do with fatigue, boredom, or superstar burn-out than with McEnroe's game; a good offense beat a good defense.

Of course, if the explanation were really that simple, many players would turn to an attacking game instead of cautiously clubbing their strokes with topspin. But there are more complicated factors at work. While McEnroe's style is ideal for the grass at Wimbledon or the Deco-turf at Flushing Meadows, he has yet to prove he can win a major title on clay—and more and more events are played on this slow surface.

Old-timers complained, however, that the pervasiveness of the baseline game wasn't entirely due to the increase in clay-court tournaments. They also blamed money and the ATP computer. Some players, it was said, no longer played tennis. They played the computer, carefully choosing tournaments and a conservative style which ensured good results—not necessarily titles, but a consistent pattern that preserved their ranking. If designated to play on an inhospitable surface in a difficult draw, they would pull out. Theoretically, a man could win the $600,000 annual Grand Prix bonus pool without capturing a single important title, while another man might win the Grand Slam and earn less than half as much in prize money.

In the old days when there was less money, or none, at stake, there was, said the old-timers, also less reason to avoid risks. Why not play exciting points, hit for the lines, and swarm the net? For one thing, this prevented matches from dragging on to marathon length, and back when players barnstormed more than forty weeks a year, that was a crucial consideration. Now, when some players limited themselves to less than fifteen weeks of

tournament competition, they could afford to camp on the baseline, exhaust themselves, their opponents, and the crowd, so
long as that meant winning a few rounds and squirreling away
precious ATP points.

This outspokenness about the ennuis of the clay-court game
was muted, however, by comparison to the increasing complaints about Wimbledon. Vitas Gerulaitis declared the French
Open "is the greatest tournament in the world, for the players
and the spectators. The worst is Wimbledon. Here they try to
improve conditions for the players every year. To get a ticket
for your mother, you don't have to go outside and pay $250 on
the street [to a scalper]. I hope the French Federation makes a
lot of money—they try to put some of it back into the tournament
for our benefit. After all, the players make the event."

"Why do you play Wimbledon?" some logical soul inquired.

"My contracts. If there were a boycott of Wimbledon, I'd be
with the players one hundred percent."

Jimmy Connors eagerly joined the chorus. "I'm not on Wimbledon's all-time favorite list. Wimbledon is tradition, and things
have been the same for a hundred years. Wimbledon's attitude
is they're bigger than the players. But the players make the
tournament. Without sponsors, the players would be nothing,
and without the players, Wimbledon would be nothing. But
Wimbledon doesn't feel that way. They wouldn't mind seeing
my wife play the finals against Peter McNamara's wife. There
are problems—the cars, getting [onto the grounds], the weather,
just everything that helps the players play their best. The Committee [at the All England Club] doesn't facilitate things."

"Vitas said yesterday if it weren't for his contracts, he'd skip
Wimbledon, and if there were a boycott, he'd be the first to join
it. How do you feel about this?"

"First of all, it's not in my contracts to play Wimbledon, the
French or the U.S. Open. But I'd boycott Wimbledon if there
were a good reason, and if *everybody* boycotted the tournament."

. . . .

Next day Paris changed from the warm City of Light into a cold City of Light Rain. The chestnut trees were whipped to green froth by a gusty wind, and I was chilled to the bone and felt faint stirrings of the intestinal virus that had now afflicted a dozen players.

Ilie Nastase appeared to be suffering from the ailment, or something more serious. In the second round he had drawn a tough French junior, a tall, skinny boy named Guy Forget (pronounced For-zhay), who put surprising torque on his lefthanded serve. The fellow also had a habit which annoyed Nastase no end. He held both balls in his right hand while serving, and whenever he got his first serve in, he tossed aside the second ball during play.

Nastase complained that Forget should be penalized for distracting him. While the umpire did give the seventeen-year-old boy a warning, he could not very well penalize him unless he was willing to do the same to Nastase, who mercilessly needled Forget throughout the match. "Did you come without your mother?" he shouted. Then later, when Forget muffed an easy shot, "Little boy, you shouldn't shut your eyes when you hit."

Although the crowd laughed, it would be wrong to suppose that their affection for Nastase was unalloyed. France is a nation well versed in ambivalence, and last year fans at Roland Garros gave vent to a full measure of that trait when they voted two awards for the Rumanian—one for his good humor, the other for being the worst sport in the tournament.

Remarkably, after losing 9–7 in the fifth set, Nastase exuded charm at a press conference which he conducted jointly with Guy Forget. "You shouldn't come to Roland Garros and beat me," he chided the pale, knobby-kneed boy. "You should finish school."

When asked whether he acted up on court to amuse spectators or to upset his opponent, Nastase said, "I do it for me, for myself. If the public enjoys it, so much the better."

Was Nastase aware that a woman had fainted in the stands?

He shook back his oily black hair. "It was probably one of my old girlfriends."

Journalists began lobbing him lines like straight men in a vaudeville act.

"How will you prepare for Wimbledon?"

"I think I prepare with my girlfriend. But I don't think I tell you how."

Another leering, goonish eruption ended the conference.

When it comes to Ilie Nastase, I confess I am more ambivalent than the French. If, as many people maintain, he has frittered away most of his talent and won as few tournaments as possible for a player of his potential, I feel that tennis authorities are partly to blame for having been too faint-hearted to curb his behavior. A few long suspensions—six months, let's say, not three weeks—and judicious fines—substantial sums, not pocket money—might have convinced him to concentrate on his game instead of his sideshow. Even if they failed to achieve that purpose, they would have served notice that the sport has certain minimal standards.

Instead, Nastase had been permitted to fossilize into a perverse institution. Still a drawing card, still beyond the law, he was not so much forgiven for his obscene gestures, for spitting in opponents' faces and calling people kikes and niggers. He was exempted from serious judgment, regardless of how repulsive his behavior became.

Just this past spring at a tournament in Bournemouth he got what he believed was a bad call and spun away from the umpire to a ball girl no older than eleven.

"The umpire is a fag," he told her. "Do you know what that means? It means he fucks other men."

When the little girl didn't respond, he repeated himself, just as all during his career he has repeated every offensive remark and outrageous gesture, perhaps daring anybody to stop him, or maybe waiting like a child, now thirty-seven, for someone to set limits.

By late afternoon I was shivering uncontrollably, my belly quaked, and I staggered through the grounds of Roland Garros bearing my throbbing head on my shoulders as if it were a porcelain jug whose contents I was afraid of spilling. I couldn't conceive of anyone playing tennis in this condition; I no longer had the strength to watch it.

Reluctant to risk a jolting Métro trip, I hobbled to the courtesy cars and begged a driver for a lift to my hotel. I wasn't staying at the Sofitel. I was at a cheaper place on the Left Bank. He wasn't obliged to help me, but he did, I assumed, because he realized how sick I was. It turned out he just wanted to tell me about his job.

He and the other chauffeurs worked more than twelve hours a day, checking in early each morning and knocking off around midnight. Although most players were *bons types*, he said, even good guys sometimes didn't understand how unreasonable it was to ask drivers to deviate from their route and take them to clubs and restaurants, or to pick up their families and friends at the airport.

Citroën had provided thirty-two limousines, and each one was driven three hundred kilometers a day. I could figure out for myself, he said, the enormous distance they would cover during the two-week tournament.

I couldn't figure it out. I could barely hold my head upright and keep from vomiting. But he encouraged me to take a stab at it. Just multiply thirty-two limousines times three hundred kilometers times fourteen days. It was simple, he swore.

"I'm sorry. I'm very sick."

"One hundred thirty-four thousand and four hundred kilometers," he proudly announced.

"Pardon me?" I groaned.

"That's how many kilometers we'll cover. And guess how much gasoline we'll consume?"

"*Je regrette. Mais je suis très malade.*"

"I estimate we'll burn twenty thousand liters."

"Let me off anywhere along here." I was willing to walk a few blocks to escape the man's chatter.

Outside the Café des Deux Magots I saw the same tribe of ragged blacks I had ridden the train with every morning from Cannes to Monte Carlo. I thought I must be delirious, hallucinating. But no, the men were real. They were not, however, selling fly whisks and crude mahogany carvings. They danced to cadences pounded out on a conga drum. One man stripped to the waist and strolled around with a bicycle wheel spinning on its axle, balanced on his shaved skull. Even in my foggy state I recognized that that was something you didn't see every day. I dropped a few *francs* into his hand and hurried to the hotel.

Having fallen into bed with no great conviction that I would ever revive, I woke the next morning feeling better, if not completely recovered. Still weak and unsteady, I returned to Roland Garros. It was to be a strange day. I realized that the moment I spotted Yannick Noah outside the Adidas Lounge standing with a beautiful girl almost as big as he. While her size and pulchritude were impressive, I was struck more by her creamy white Stetson, fringed leather dress, and red hand-stitched boots.

I reached my seat on Center Court during a match between Vitas Gerulaitis and Heinz Gunthardt, the slim Swiss who as a junior had swept the Italian, French, and Wimbledon titles, but since then has never finished a year higher than No. 27. Some say his game is too fragile, his nerves too easily frayed. Once at a tournament in Vancouver, just before he was scheduled to take the court, Gunthardt ran into Peter McNamara in the locker room and lamented that he had lost his tennis shoes. How could he play without shoes?

"I looked at his feet," McNamara tells the story, "and so does Heinz. And he suddenly sees his shoes are right there, on his feet."

Fragile game and frayed nerves notwithstanding, Gunthardt gave Gerulaitis all he could handle for four sets and two hours and forty minutes. Vitas won, but afterward at a press conference he appeared ready to unravel. His close-set eyes were narrowed to slits, his blond, wavy hair stood up like hackles, and he surprised everybody by asking us questions.

"You tell me what you think I did wrong today on court to deserve a $2,500 fine. What do you consider bad behavior?"

A journalist suggested Vitas might have been fined for ridiculing a linesman who had called a foot fault.

"I guess that wasn't very nice, but I was just kidding around.

I was fined for twirling my racquet on my third finger—$750 for each time I did it. And then another fine for walking back to my chair with a ball stuck between my legs. I guess that could be considered pretty bad, but I did it for fun, to make people laugh. My fines might go over the $5,000 limit and for this I might not be able to play Wimbledon."

Given all his griping about the All England Club, I would have guessed he'd have welcomed a suspension during Wimbledon. But no, Gerulaitis was furious.

"Have you had other fines recently?" a reporter asked.

"In Florence I was fined $1,500 for saying two nasty words when I whacked the net. The guy in the chair didn't even hear it, only the Supervisor with big ears up in the stands. When I got to the locker room, I saw this big sign saying 'Fine for audible obscenity.' This is why I don't join the ATP. They don't do anything for you in cases like this."

Vitas would appeal his fines. But since the Pro Council was reputed to be cracking down hard on "audible" and "visible" obscenity, the press sent out stories speculating that one more superstar might miss Wimbledon.

There were over 150 men competing at Roland Garros and almost as many women. There were juniors, there were celebrity matches, there were doubles and mixed doubles events. But I focused on men's singles and, more precisely, on those fellows whom I had gotten to know on the short circuit which I had plotted for myself within the endless cycle of tennis. Thus I continued to keep an eye on Mel Purcell, the friendly, tow-headed, gap-toothed boy from Murray, Kentucky, whom I had watched skate onto the professional scene with all the jittery speed of a waterbug at Indianapolis in 1980, and whom I had interviewed in Milan this past March.

At the French Open he pulled through the first three rounds without dropping a set, but after an easy win over Anders Jarryd, a poker-faced Swede, Mel admitted he felt awful. He was suffering from the same virus I had had yesterday, an ailment which had now laid low more than three dozen players, plus Bill Norris, the ATP trainer.

Purcell clenched his belly and winced while we talked. "I feel proud of myself for toughing it out today. I wasn't feeling seventy percent. Confident-wise, I feel like I can hang in there now against anybody."

He always tried to play Roland Garros with special intensity, he told me. For one thing, he had a French girlfriend. For another, he had a French clothing contract with Trevois. "Is the tournament going to be on TV in the States this weekend?" He was scheduled to meet Vitas Gerulaitis in the next round and he thought that might make an attractive match-up. But I told him only the finals would be broadcast in America.

"Too bad," he said. "There goes my bonus money. Well, Paris, here I come." He limped away, cradling his belly.

Later that evening I saw Mel Purcell with his girl. They hadn't made it into Paris; they hadn't gotten away from Roland Garros. A honey blonde in a baby-blue hostess uniform, she sat cross-legged on a bench while Mel lay on his back in the grass, staring up at the spring moon, one hand still on his queasy stomach, waiting to gain the strength to walk to the courtesy cars.

John Lloyd is now known almost exclusively as the husband of Chris Evert. It was not always thus. A handsome fellow with the fluffy blond locks of a Malibu beach boy—actually, he's from Leigh-on-Sea, England—Lloyd used to be known as "Legs" and he used to be ranked No. 33 in the world. Going into the qualifying rounds at Roland Garros, he was No. 220, but he managed to battle his way into the main draw and advance to the third round, where he ran into Yannick Noah. He gave a good account of himself for a set. Then, sadly, the match slipped away 7–5/6–0/6–3.

Afterward Lloyd murmured, "The key was the first set. The French are great for their players when they're winning. But as soon as they start losing, they get down on them. I thought if I got ahead of him, I had a chance."

Someone suggested he must have been tired. Including the qualies, this was his sixth match in eight days. But Lloyd said the qualies rarely hurt a player physically. Mentally? That was a different matter. "I'm coming on court respecting my opponent too much. I'm a little too negative against players with big names. You've got to play the shots, not the name."

Still, he wasn't the only one on court today who had had the jitters. "Noah was nervous," Lloyd said. "With a crowd like this, I'd be nervous, too."

During his interview Noah seemed pensive, reserved, perhaps remembering the catcalls and whistles which the Center Court crowd had unleashed when he had been broken in the first set. He smiled sadly, showing the lucky space between his teeth. "They want me to play like Borg. I'm not Borg."

Later that day the French learned that Guy Forget isn't Borg either. Fresh from his upset of Ilie Nastase, the gangly adolescent played Jimmy Connors and he teed off on every ball as if he expected to overwhelm a man who, more than any other, feeds on pace. Connors can be out-thought, out-maneuvered, and occasionally outpsyched. But he can seldom be out-slugged. By the time Forget assimilated this fact, he was down two sets to love. In the third, relying on placement more than power, he had better luck, raced to a 5–1 lead, squandered that, and rebounded in a tie-break which he won.

In years past, after the third set, players took a ten-minute break and a cool shower. Now only the court gets a shower. A team of grounds-keepers uncoiled a hose, wet down the clay, and swept the lines. In 1976, during a torrid spring in Paris, they also wet down the bleachers to prevent people from fainting. It wasn't quite that hot this year, but it was getting there, and since the Center Court seemed to gather heat to itself, stewing everybody as if in a great cauldron, I escaped in search of shade.

On a field court an upset appeared imminent—not that many people noticed or cared. José Higueras, the bearded Spaniard who could pose for holy cards of Christ in agony on the cross, had dropped the first two sets to Damian Keretic, an unknown

West German. Lately, Higueras had made a habit of depositing himself deep in a hole and spending the better part of a day digging out. Earlier this month in Hamburg he had played the longest match in Grand Prix history, a five-hour-and-twenty-minute final in which he had outlasted Peter McNamara.

Today he had to contend not just with Keretic but with Court Ten, which was always lethal terrain in late afternoon when the lacy shadows of chestnut trees spread over one end, leaving it dappled with pools of light and dark. At the other end there was a constant din from Center Court and from passers-by on the concourse. And a swirling wind, dry and hot as a sirocco, raked the clay into tiny dunes which erupted with a powdery explosion whenever a ball struck them.

If all this weren't bad enough, three demure ladies in olive-green skirts, their bare shins spackled with dust, sat cross-legged at the sunny end of the court, calling the lines—or, rather, failing to call them. Heat and dust seemed to have mummified the women.

Higueras didn't complain. Perhaps he would be better known if he did spout off from time to time. But he continued to do what he does best—swat groundstrokes. He went about it with the dour, unswerving dedication of an Andalusian peasant plowing acre after acre of baked earth.

Higueras doesn't give away points; he makes the other man win them. In this case Keretic couldn't keep it up. He cracked late in the third set and staggered through the rest of the match like a lost explorer in the Sahara, sun-dazzled, demented, his dreams of victory rattling in the dry pan of his brain like pebbles in a gourd.

Back on Center Court, Connors righted himself in the fourth set and polished off Forget 6–1. At the press conference he was grudging with praise; what he granted the seventeen-year-old boy with one hand he snatched back with the other. "He's got a good first serve. Of course, he doesn't get many firsts in."

Someone asked an innocuous question about Connors' racquet, the Wilson T-2000. Sensitive on this subject, Jimbo, who some of the French seemed to think is nicknamed Jumbo, pounced on it like a starving dog on a bone. He made the racquet, he pugnaciously declared. The racquet didn't make him. "People who see me hit a winner and say it's because of my racquet are full of crap."

For a moment nobody said anything at all. Then he was asked his opinion of Gerulaitis' fines.

"I hope he'll be able to play Wimbledon," Jumbo-Jimbo said. "You need the top guys. With Borg and Lendl not playing, I hope I don't fall down and have to withdraw, and that McEnroe doesn't get defaulted for farting on court. Because without us guys it's"—his voice altered to a high-pitched flute—"*exhibition time!*"

This was a curious remark. Without the best players Wimbledon would be a poorer tournament, yes, a pale shadow of itself, agreed. But an exhibition? Perhaps what Connors meant was that if the top ranked men didn't play Wimbledon, they'd all go off and earn a fortune on exhibitions.

Just as he had in Milan, Chip Hooper caused an earthquake of curiosity in Paris, and *L'Equipe* ran an article translating the gargantuan black's statistics into terms which its readers could better comprehend. Hooper was 198 centimeters tall and weighed ninety-six kilos. His first serve traveled at 209 kilometers an hour and had the damaging impact of a mortar. He could cross the court in two strides, he could volley with lethal authority, he could hit flat or with topspin. He could do everything except leap tall buildings at a single bound.

Ravenous for details, the French took note of his every peculiarity—of how heavily Hooper perspired, how often he changed his soaking shirt, how he swilled down tennis-ball cans full of ice water, how often he spat, how he sometimes paused before serving and, like a baby, burped.

Hooper had another peculiarity. After five months on the circuit, he still didn't have a clothing contract. Every day he sported a different brand name and sometimes showed up in mismatched outfits, as if he had pulled on whatever he found lying close to hand in the locker room. Once he loped out in Adidas jogging shorts and an Ellesse shirt. But then, in a third-round match, he burst onto Center Court dressed in a red Sergio Tacchini warm-up, looking like Conan the Barbarian.

Across the net, Jimmy Arias, an American who stands five feet eight and weighs 138 pounds, seemed pallid by comparison. But he was a good-humored David to Hooper's Goliath. Early in the first set when Arias tried to lob, Hooper bounded high into the air for what he calls his "slam-dunk" smash. The ball metamorphosed into an oblong yellow blur, ricocheted off the clay, and bounced twenty rows into the bleachers. Abruptly, Arias crouched before Hooper, bowing his head and arms in a parody of abasement.

The teenager was far from defenseless, however. He took a vicious swing with extreme topspin and generated more consistent power on his groundstrokes than Hooper did. But even on clay Chip could serve and volley. He won the first set 6–3 and the second 6–4, and Arias clapped a hand over his eyes and cried out, "This is unbelievable."

After that, Arias switched gears and stopped going for winners. He kept the ball in play and made the big man move. It was early evening by now, and a gusting wind bothered Hooper as much as Arias' tactics, blowing dust into his eyes and tinting his hair orange. He might have passed as a kwashiorkor victim— if he hadn't weighed 210 pounds, that is.

He lost the third set 7–6, and as he struggled to reach another tie-break in the fourth, the wind began to comb around Center Court, sweeping soft-drink cans down the steps, creating all the distracting racket of a charivari. Still Hooper clung to his serving power, and that carried him to victory. He dashed off court, slapping the French umpire a high-five handshake that utterly befuddled the man.

Jimmy Arias arrived in the press room first, anxious to get the ordeal over with. He rubbed his sore right elbow. At the age of seventeen he had already developed a painful case of tendinitis.

"How disappointed are you?" an American journalist asked.

The kid looked like he might cry, and I realized, as I did

periodically, just how young these fellows are and how much poise they are expected to have in the face of reporters who can be contemptibly obtuse.

"I'm really disappointed," Arias said in a shaky voice. "I thought I could beat Chip on this surface. And if I beat him, I'd have played Connors next, which would be like a dream come true. But Chip served too well."

Hooper made an entrance in his new Tacchini outfit. "From now on, just call me Sergio Hooper."

Although some journalists expressed surprise that his net-rushing game had worked so well at Roland Garros, Chip dismissed the notion that there was anything unique about clay. "Hey, man, it's still a tennis court. Same size, same shape."

The only thing that had bothered him was the dust. He had had two operations for pterygium; Hooper spelled and pronounced it several times for reporters. A condition common among sailors and sportsmen who spend long hours outdoors, pterygium causes the eyes to film over, and eventually an elastic tissue starts to cover the whites of the eyes, then the corneas. The film has to be peeled off surgically. Hooper had had his second operation less than eight months ago.

Had Arthur Ashe offered any advice this week? someone called out.

The question rankled Hooper. No doubt it would have annoyed Ashe as well. There was something absurd about the assumption that all black players, past and present, must be fast friends. "I'm a big boy," Hooper said. "I can make it without advice."

"But what does it mean to you to be the best black American tennis player since Ashe?"

Chip said it meant nothing. "If you said I was the best player since Borg, now that would mean something."

Had he conjured up any special strategy for his match against Connors?

Chip smiled. "I'm just going to rush the net, hog up the

whole court, and make him hit those babies on the line. If he can do that, he deserves to win."

Next morning I suffered a severe relapse of intestinal virus and feared if I wasn't well by noon I would miss the Lendl-Wilander match. Then by noon, after vomiting half a dozen times, I feared if the convulsions didn't stop I would have to call a doctor. But by that afternoon, as I continued to vomit, I feared I couldn't make it to a doctor. I barely had strength to call a taxi. By the time I reached the American Hospital in Neuilly, my belly had gone into spasms again and the doctor in the emergency room had to shoot me full of muscle relaxants. Just as Mats Wilander was finishing off Ivan Lendl in the biggest upset of the tournament, the biggest of the season, I fell unconscious.

For two days I lay flat on my back with no alternative except to follow the French Open on television. Images of Chip Hooper losing in straight sets to Jimmy Connors, and of Yannick Noah rebounding from a two-set deficit to defeat Wojtek Fibak, reached me through a mist of medication. Although I yearned for more details of the Lendl-Wilander match, I had to content myself with newspaper reports and with a transcript of Lendl's press conference.

Taking his usual tough line, the Czech told journalists, "If you want some sensation, maybe I'll go and hang myself, but I don't think you'll get it."

"Before this match you were said to be No. 1 on clay. How do you feel about that after losing to Wilander?"

"I never answered that question before, and I'm not going to today."

Accusing Lendl of hubris, L'Equipe believed that he had been brought low by overweening self-confidence in the face of the seventeen-year-old Swede. Patrice Hagelauer, a coach of the French National Team, said Lendl had lost sight of the two primary virtues of all great champions—patience and humility.

Obliged to relearn those virtues myself, I botched the job as badly as Ivan Lendl and could not muster the patience to remain in bed or the humility to submit myself to the regimen prescribed by the doctor. The day of the quarterfinals I checked out of the hospital and returned to Roland Garros ten pounds lighter, famished for real food, not bland institutional gruel, and for real tennis, not the neat, miniaturized version captured on a cathode-ray tube. Perhaps due to my depleted physical condition, I found the tournament a changed place, its tone somber, even morbid.

After saving five match balls and laboring for twelve hours and thirty-seven minutes in the first four rounds, Peter Mc-Namara snapped in the quarterfinals and got blitzed by José Luis Clerc 6–2/6–2/6–2. Yet Clerc scarcely sounded euphoric.

"How would you describe your relationship with Vilas?" someone asked him.

"He's not like my girlfriend. But he's another professional player and I say hello to him."

Urged to forecast the semifinals, Clerc delivered himself of a dose of fatalism worthy of Manolete. "I don't know what'll happen in a few days. Maybe I death. Maybe I win the tournament."

After Eliot Teltscher lost to José Higueras, he showed even less inclination than Clerc to gaze into the future. Asked whether he thought Higueras was playing well enough to win the tournament, Teltscher, ever the good sport, said, "I really don't care."

This condition of indifference seemed as contagious as the virus that had landed me in the hospital. After Mats Wilander chloroformed him in the quarterfinals, Vitas Gerulaitis was asked whether the Swede stood a chance of capturing the title. Gerulaitis stopped chewing the dead skin around his fingernails long enough to growl, "That's a silly question. He's in the semifinals. Everybody has a chance in the semifinals. Somebody could fall down and die."

By official count, Wilander had committed just four errors in the first two sets against Gerulaitis, which was as much a reflection of his refusal to take the slightest risk as it was of his inexorable steadiness. So if anybody fell down and died, it was apt to be his opponent or the spectators. Hazarding his own prediction for the semifinals, Wilander said, "Clerc plays a bit the way Lendl plays, so maybe I'll have to play him the same way." He chuckled, "A boring match."

Fastened like a barnacle to Court One are the offices of FIT, pronounced Feet, the acronym for Fédération Internationale de Tennis. There I found M. Marshall Happer III, Administrator of the Pro Council. Understandably, given his manifold responsibilities, Happer appears to be chronically fatigued and has dark smudges under his deep-set eyes. Yet he retains the level, attentive gaze of a smalltown Southern sheriff. Big, rumpled, and quiet, he speaks with a North Carolina drawl, a deceptively versatile instrument for conveying subtle variations of mood. Without raising his voice, he can alter its timbre to imply agreement, impatience, interest, indifference, anger, or good humor. But what he actually thinks behind his haggard countenance, which bears an uncanny resemblance to a bloodhound's, remains strictly his own business.

Concerning Vitas Gerulaitis' fines and possible suspension, he told me he was still pondering the issues, but expected to reach a decision before the French Open ended.

While I explained that I had followed the circuit for a few months and was distressed by much of what I had learned, he waited patiently and impassively for me to make my point. What about appearance money? I finally asked.

Yes, what about it? he said.

Well, there had been frequent allegations and recently the *Washington Post* had printed them, naming names and prices. In a copyrighted article Happer was quoted as saying he was investigating a tournament.

Yes, he acknowledged an ongoing investigation into a Grand Prix event in Stuttgart. It was interesting, he observed, that last year's final for a rather paltry jackpot of $15,000 had been between Borg and Lendl. The problem was . . .

My eyes glazed over as he launched into a semantic discussion of illegal inducements. Most people, Happer contended, had no idea what constituted appearance money or a guarantee.

For a few minutes, like a good charades player, I went along with the game. How many syllables? Was it bigger than a bread-box? Actually, I asked, "What about Gerulaitis? All week he's been claiming he plays Wimbledon only because of his con-tracts. Are they an illegal inducement?"

No, if they were existing long-term contracts that obligated him incidentally to play certain tournaments, or contained clauses offer ing bonuses or threatening penalties, then they didn't violate the rules.

I threw Happer a curve ball. What about the deal Borg and several other players had in Monte Carlo, where they received tax-free residency in return for participating in the tournament there? Wasn't that an inducement limited to a single event, not part of a long-term endorsement contract?

No, Happer didn't consider it illegal.

I gave up. What did violate the rule, which on paper sounded clear, concise, and all-encompassing? "No player shall accept money or anything of value that is given, directly or indirectly, to influence or guarantee his appearance in any Volvo Grand Prix tournament."

As Happer described it, timing was a decisive factor. If a player committed to a tournament, then told his agent to arrange for contracts during or around the dates of the event, that was fine. But if a player entered into new contracts for endorsements or promotions related to a tournament, and only afterward com-mitted to the tournament, that might suggest evidence of an illegal inducement.

Although his every sentence was thick with subjunctive clauses and qualifying phrases, he decried the fact that journalists weren't straightforward and out front. He was tired of allegations and rumors, he said. He was tired of reporters, like those from the *Washington Post*, who demanded what he intended to do, yet refused to reveal their sources and divulge all the information they had gathered. How could he take action unless they told him what they knew?

I didn't understand why it was so difficult for him to track down violators when he had Draconian subpoena powers to help make his case. But I decided to play the game according to the guidelines he laid down. If he wanted names and dates, I'd provide them, then record what use he made of them. Several players had admitted to me that they accepted appearance money, and one of the most successful coaches on the circuit had told me he urged his players to take guarantees since everyone else did. But these were small fry, easy targets whom, I feared, tennis authorities might punish in some melodramatic attempt to prove how rigorous and self-righteous they were. I wanted to find out how eager they were to tangle with the biggest fish in the pond.

I asked when John McEnroe had committed to play the Italian Open.

After a pause Happer said he didn't have the date at hand, but he recalled that Mr. McEnroe, Sr., had requested sometime in April for John to be designated to play Rome in May.

I said it might be worth looking into the contract between McEnroe and Lipton Tea. As far back as January, Cino Marchese had described for me his negotiations to close the deal. Didn't the very existence of negotiations between a tournament official and a player suggest something wrong? Weren't players supposed to select tournaments on basis of prize money, ATP points, and their schedules?

Happer acknowledged that tournaments shouldn't have to negotiate with players.

Apparently these negotiations had gone on through February, I said. Then in March, Marchese had hosted a reception in Milan to announce that McEnroe had signed a contract with Lipton and would play the Italian Open. Wasn't it peculiar that Marchese would know McEnroe's spring schedule when, from what Happer had just told me, Mr. McEnroe had not requested that John be designated to Rome until April? According to Happer's own definition, didn't this constitute an illegal inducement?

Indeed it might. He took notes on what I told him and swore he would look into it.

When would he do that? I asked.

Just as soon as he had time. But he was busy and it might be weeks before he could turn his attention to the matter.

I said I'd check back with him at Wimbledon. Then I brought up prize-money splitting.

Happer caught me off guard by granting that he had heard of it. What's more, he named two players who were rumored to have split at a WCT tournament during the winter. Interestingly, less than a week ago Butch Buchholz, Happer's colleague on the Pro Council, had denied that his investigations had stirred up anything more than vague rumblings about prize-money splitting.

I asked if Happer considered this a more serious offense than accepting a guarantee.

"Damn right, prize-money splitting is more serious." But how was he supposed to prove it? All he had to go on was hearsay.

Why didn't he demand the financial records of the players who were rumored to have split?

He wasn't certain of his jurisdiction in offenses that had taken place on the other circuit. "We let WCT copy our rule book," he said. "It's my understanding that WCT has never collected a fine. Two of our players under suspension went and played WCT."

It struck me that "splits" might constitute behavior detrimental to the sport, regardless of where they happened. But again Happer was uncertain about imposing the Code of Conduct on a player who had committed an offense on the WCT.

When he inquired what else troubled me about the tour, I shot the works, I told him an umpire swore that he had overheard Borg and McEnroe arranging to split sets in a special event. If I thought this would ruffle his bloodhound's face, I was right. But the reaction was not what I had expected. He smiled.

"I think all exhibitions are fixed." There was no code of conduct for these matches, Happer explained. No promoter would permit a player to be defaulted.

Then he related the story of a rigged event which he knew from firsthand experience. It involved players whom he characterized as two of the straightest, most upright gentlemen in the game. "I umpired a Stan Smith-Arthur Ashe match down in North Carolina. It was announced as $6,500, winner take all. That prize'll show you how long ago it was. They were playing before a basketball game. The basketball game was scheduled to start at ten of nine. At twenty-five of nine Arthur and Stan had split sets. By quarter of nine they had wrapped up a third set 7–6 and rolled up the court."

I thought I had lost the capacity to be appalled by anything on the circuit. But I was mistaken. Here I was listening to the Administrator of the Pro Council concede that matches were fixed and/or arranged, yet claim that nothing could be done since these were "special events." Every sport has its exhibitions and special events. Baseball, football, and basketball have pre-season games. Soccer has non-league competition and boxers fight non-title matches. But if it became known that these events were rigged to fit a schedule or to enhance their television pop-ularity, this would prompt legal action and might result in jail sentences or suspensions for the players, and the loss of license for TV stations.

There was still another fact that dumbfounded me. In Monte Carlo, when I mentioned set-splitting to Butch Buchholz, he said, "I find that hard to believe. If this were going on, I definitely would have heard of it." Yet Buchholz's Pro Council colleague Marshall Happer admitted it was commonplace.

I moved on to what the Umpire in Antibes had told me about the suspicious relations between tournament directors and um-pires. Was the Administrator aware that some umpires were accepting substantial inducements, including discounts on lux-ury automobiles, to officiate at Grand Prix matches?

"I can't see anything wrong with an ump getting anything he can in the way of an inducement to work a tournament," Happer said.

But wasn't it possible, I asked, that these business deals, which went beyond salaries and expenses, might compromise an um-pire's integrity? Even if it was unconscious, an umpire might let a friendship or a financial agreement with a tournament director influence his calls. The players already claimed the stars were protected, always got the close calls, and were never de-faulted for conduct violations. Since umpires were discouraged from fraternizing with players, wasn't it judicious for them to remain aloof from tournament directors, too?

Happer believed there were adequate checks and balances. A Supervisor at every tournament graded the performance of umpires. "Any umpire who doesn't default a guy who should be defaulted gets a zero ranking, and we'll get rid of him."

He acknowledged there were instances when an umpire saw or heard something that had escaped the Supervisor. And sometimes a Supervisor assessed a fine for an offense which hadn't even provoked a warning from the umpire. He viewed these as problems which could be solved by better coordination. But as for umpires being reluctant to enforce the rules for fear of losing their jobs . . . no, Happer maintained that they were more likely to lose their jobs by letting the players violate the code. The Supervisors saw to that. The Supervisors stood behind the umpires, Happer said, and the Pro Council and Grand Prix stood behind their Supervisors.

Next day M. Marshall Happer III announced his decision on the penalties Vitas Gerulaitis had received in Florence and at the French Open. For "audible obscenity within the precincts of a tournament site" Gerulaitis had been fined $1,500, and Happer affirmed the assessment of the Supervisor in Florence.

But as for the alleged obscene gestures Vitas had made during his match with Gunthardt, these were, in the Administrator's opinion, an altogether different matter. While "the Supervisor interpreted three [3] acts by Gerulaitis as being obscene gestures and therefore in violation of the Code," Happer had had an opportunity, he wrote in his three-page decision, to review "extensively the video tape records of the incidents and was able to obtain the testimony of Gerulaitis and other witnesses.

The gestures in question are not the type of acts that are obscene *per se*. However, such gestures are *similar* [italics in original] to gestures used to communicate obscene messages and such gestures are a violation of the Code if an obscene message was intended or reasonably perceived.

Gerulaitis testified that he intended no message by such gestures and his testimony is substantiated by the video tape record which indicates that he was unattentative [sic] to his actions and possibly did not realize the similarity of his actions to obscene gestures. Neither the on-court officials or the spectators perceived any obscenity as a result of such gestures.

Under these circumstances there was no clear violation of the Code and therefore the interpretation of the Supervisor must be reversed.

So Vitas Gerulaitis was free to play Wimbledon—the world's worst tournament, in his estimation.

When they learned I was doing a book, several photographers asked if I needed pictures. They all had the standard action shots, but one American informed me he had an exotic specialty, bathtub shots.

"Bathtub shots?"

"Yeah, I try to humanize the stars. I tell them to strip and climb into a bathtub. Then I put their kids in with them and get pictures of them playing together."

"What do they play with if they don't have kids?"

"I'll maybe show them in bed and have their wife or girlfriend bring them breakfast on a tray. Some of them object at first on taste grounds. They say it invades their privacy. But they always wind up loving the pictures."

Since Yannick Noah was the last Frenchman left in the tournament, a large vocal crowd was expected for his quarterfinal against Guillermo Vilas. But as the match started, the Center Court stands were less than a third full. The explanation was simplicity itself. Much as the French love tennis, it was noon and they love lunch even more.

By the time people pushed away from the table, polished off their cognac, and arrived at Roland Garros, they had missed the best part of the match, the first-set tie-break. After Vilas won that, he proceeded to hammer Noah into submission with all the subtlety of a pile-driver. A spectator shouted, "Tiriac, stop your signals!" but Vilas needed no tactical messages from his coach. He took the next two sets 6–3/6–4.

Husbanding their stamina for a Vilas-Connors semifinal, many reporters dismissed the Connors-Higueras quarterfinal as a formality and headed for a cool spot near the soft-drink dispenser. In the press box that left a few mad Spaniards, their pants legs hiked up to their knees, and the redoubtable English in funny paper hats with the VS Gut logo on the bill.

"Didn't Higueras have viral hepatitis?" one Limey languidly inquired.

"Yes. Knocked the stuffings out of him. He lost ten pounds."

"Wonder where he caught it."

"My good fellow, he's from Spain. He probably drank the water in his own house."

"Higueras lives in Palm Springs." Curry Kirkpatrick of *Sports Illustrated* ruined their fun.

Then José Higueras ruined Connors' fun and the high hopes of the tournament promoters.

"Guys have to beat me," Higueras has said. "I don't lose." Jimmy Connors' credo is just the reverse. He relishes beating people. But he has only one way of doing that—hitting bullets. When this doesn't work, he has little to fall back on, and today was one of those times when his style fit tongue and groove with his opponent's. His best shot, his two-fisted crosscourt backhand, came right to Higueras' strong forehand, and Jimbo's spotty forehand floated to the Spaniard's formidable backhand, which he can hit flat or with topspin. In the third set Connors screamed, "I'm missing by a pubic hair every time." But the match was never that close. He folded 6–2/6–2/6–2.

For all his on-court ferocity, Jimbo is a buzzing hive of contradictions, and as I had observed in Milan, a defeat sometimes leaves him placid. Today it transformed him into a comedian.

While Higueras, black beard dripping sweat, explained to reporters that he was playing as well as he had before the attack of hepatitis, Jimbo poked his head into the press room and jokingly shouted, "Get a move on in there."

When it was his turn to be interviewed, his reply to the first question—"What happened today?"—eliminated the need for further discussion. "I got my ass kicked." (The French newspapers translated this as "I was well beaten.")

Now Connors would cross the channel to England and begin preparing for the grass-court season. On the basis of his performance in Paris, particularly his ineffectual serving, few people gave him any chance of winning Wimbledon.

In the lavatory a pride of Spanish reporters, jubilant at Higueras' victory, clustered around the sinks, getting slickered up for a night on the town. Hermès Eau de Cologne had donated several boxes of scented facial tissues, which the Spaniards used to swab their ears, arms, and necks. One fellow stood back to admire the results in the mirror. "*Vengo, chicas appasionadas.* Here I come, passionate girls," he cried out.

"Maybe you'll win the prize," said his friend.

But the prize, awarded by Hermès, was for players. Journalists had been asked to vote for the man and woman at Roland Garros "who showed the greatest qualities of moral behavior as well as sportsmanship and wearing the smartest clothes."

Italians have a saying that marriage is the tomb of love. To listen to tennis players talk, however, the circuit is a cemetery of marriages and love affairs. Having heard many single men hold forth on the subject, I arranged to interview a couple who agreed to speak from experience if I would preserve their anonymity.

We met in the new players' lounge, a bright, airy space with blond wood fixtures and foam-rubber furniture. A few children crawled on the carpet. Younger players crowded around the Atari video games, creating a racket of metallic *pings!* and *ack-acks!* At the table beside us sat Renée Richards and Martina Navratilova, plotting strategy for Navratilova's next match. Richards sounded calm and reassuring, but Martina, full of nervous energy and tensile strength, couldn't sit still. She stood up, stretched, then performed a set of isometric contractions, pushing against the wall until the corded muscles of her shoulders and calves shuddered.

The player, an American, had been married before. Now he traveled with a European woman who worked as a translator or secretary at every tournament her boyfriend entered. It wasn't a question of financial necessity. The fellow made plenty of money. But the temporary jobs helped her ward off the corrosive boredom which ruins the circuit for many wives and girlfriends.

When I asked what their biggest problem was, I expected them to say, "Coping with defeat." But the fellow had come to terms with that. After a loss he just needed half an hour alone to get his head straight.

The most difficult thing, they said, was waiting—for planes, for practice courts, for room service, for tables at restaurants, for a washing machine at a laundromat.

The player gave an example of the sort of foul-up that happened all the time. "You arrive in a city after an all-night flight. You want to get out and practice and try to adjust to local conditions. So you reserve a court and go there and find there's no net or the lights aren't on in the arena or the door's locked. That used to drive me nuts. It could ruin my mood, ruin my game."

"You have to be adaptable," the woman said. "Anybody who's rigid is going to have trouble."

The fellow confessed he had been inflexible when he first set out on the tour and that had wrecked his marriage. "Now I try to be more philosophical. I don't set unrealistic goals for myself like winning Wimbledon or becoming the best in the world. I'm in the game, first, because I enjoy it and, secondly, because it lets me make a good living. But it's hard work. It's big business. It's the entertainment business and people who pay to watch us expect a great performance every game."

The woman added that the pressures naturally carried over into their private life. "If you're having problems in a relationship, traveling on the tour magnifies them. Successful players tend to be selfish and single-minded, and not many women can stand that. It's like any field where the men are workaholics. And there's another thing. You learn very quickly that the man you're living with doesn't just have a relationship with you. The top players are public people and the crowd demands part of them."

The player claimed that personal problems would be easier to cope with if it weren't for the frustrations of the game—"not on court," he emphasized, "off court. The political hassles. The way the tour runs." He especially resented the favoritism and duplicity. "Everybody in tennis wants to have it both ways. Players holler to enforce the rules. But they don't like it when it comes down on them. Umps bitch that there has to be a stricter Code of Conduct. But they've never enforced the one they've got. Tournament directors complain that players are driving away the public with their antics and obscenity. But they'd scream like hell if a top player was defaulted."

When I asked if it would be better if pro tennis had a central power which imposed order on the game, the player grinned. Outsiders, he said, always believed the circuit—now the con-flicting circuits—was senseless and chaotic. But there was order within the disorder. In fact, the disorder was ordained and pro-mulgated by the men in charge. He swore, "The reason the game's the way it is today is that's how the top players and the people who run tennis want it."

You could talk about guarantees, prize-money splitting, tank-ing, rigged matches, and corrupt umpires and try to make a case that they couldn't be policed. But the point was, he said, "If the top players wanted the Conduct Code to be strictly enforced, they could change things overnight. They dominate the game and everybody has to follow their lead. The reason they don't change things is they want to get the best results and the most money in the shortest time possible."

Reform, he said, might be great in the long run. But in the short run anything that was good for the game, good for the greatest number of players, would be bad for the stars, their agents, and a lot of tennis officials. He could not emphasize this enough—reasonable reforms posed a devastating threat to the most powerful people in tennis. That's why the game never changed.

. . .

Mats Wilander had forecast a boring semifinal against José Luis Clerc and indeed it had its moments—in fact, long minutes at a stretch—of metronomical tedium. Clerc repeatedly clobbered the ball, only to have Wilander send it floating back like fluff from a dandelion. Still, I was fascinated by the curly-haired Swede's deceptive style. Although he didn't appear to be particularly fast, he prepared for his strokes early and had an unerring sense of anticipation that saved him a few steps. He seemed to be playing defensively, but I noticed he could shorten his backswing and take the ball on the rise whenever Clerc rushed the net. Time after time he passed the Argentine with backhands down the line, and when he got a short ball, he had the power to put away a winner.

Wilander began by breaking Clerc in the first game and winning the set in a forty-eight-stroke rally which a man behind me counted out loud. In the second set the same pattern applied: the Swede got an early break, and the tall Argentine failed to catch up. In the third set Clerc dropped serve again in the first game, but then blitzed the teenager six games in a row by belting the ball wide to Wilander's forehand and finishing points by hitting inside-out to his backhand.

In the fourth set Wilander raced to a 5–1 lead and reached match point on his serve. But Clerc clawed his way to deuce, then broke him to 2–5, held service himself, broke Wilander a second time, and held service to 5–5. From match ball in the Swede's favor Clerc had gone on a rip. Winning fourteen of sixteen points, ten of them in a row, he looked to have Wilander on the ropes.

But the boy scrambled to 6–5 and shifted the pressure to Clerc, who had managed to put in only forty-five percent of his first serves all day. Once more he had trouble and slipped to 0–15, then 15–30, then 30–40 to give Wilander his second match point.

Clerc played aggressively. Opening the court with a shot wide to Wilander's forehand, he jumped on a short return and smacked it to the Swede's backhand. The ball landed close to the line. But the linesman signaled out. Jacques Dorfmann, the *Juge-*

Arbitre or referee of the French Open, was serving as umpire. He called, "Game, set, and match to Wilander" and climbed down from his chair.

Wilander hadn't moved. He remained in the deuce court as if expecting Clerc to serve. Clerc was at the net, protesting the call, imploring the linesman and the umpire to check the clay for a mark. Both men refused. As far as they were concerned, the match was finished. But then Wilander came over, had a word with Dorfmann, and the umpire clambered back up into his chair and announced that at Wilander's request the point would be replayed.

The crowd was struck dumb for a moment, then burst into applause. Clerc appeared shellshocked, uncertain of himself, and promptly pushed a backhand into the net. Mats Wilander won the match for the second time.

The press room was a pandemonium of intersecting monologues, of loud, argumentative rule-interpretations and baroque theories. Some reporters felt that we had witnessed a historic, heart-warming moment in sport, an epiphany in which a star had been born under the most extraordinary circumstances. Others were just as insistent that the umpire—the tournament referee, Jacques Dorfmann, of all people!—should never have permitted the point to be replayed. Either the ball was in or it was out. If it was out, the match was over. If it was in, Clerc had won the point. This wasn't a club match between two hackers. You didn't let players call the lines or keep score. It was unimaginable that this could happen in any other professional sport. Why have an umpire unless he intended to enforce the rules?

A Grand Prix official informed the clamoring journalists that José Luis Clerc had refused an interview and left Roland Garros. Although normally a humorous, easy-going fellow, Clerc could be stubborn to the point of spiting himself as well as a stadium full of spectators. Last month in Houston he had defaulted in the fourth set of the finals of a WCT tournament rather than allow the match to be moved to a lighted court. That fit of pique had cost him $68,000. So it wasn't surprising that he would cough up $1,000 to skip a press conference.

Reporters asked to speak to Jacques Dorfmann.

"He probably left the stadium, too," a French writer wise-cracked.

But no, Dorfmann appeared and answered all questions with great aplomb. He had seen Clerc's shot out, he said, and so had the linesman. Wilander, however, had persuaded him to let Clerc have two more serves. "The situation," Dorfmann conceded, "was paradoxical." While his decision hadn't respected the letter of the law, he believed it had lived up to the spirit of the law.

"What spirit?" someone shouted.

Dorfmann drew himself up straight in his chair with a *hauteur* that would have daunted General de Gaulle. The spirit of sportsmanship, he intoned magisterially. He had never in all his career witnessed such a gesture of fair play, not on match point in a tournament of this magnitude.

But didn't the magnitude of the tournament make it all the more important that the umpire control the match and abide by the rules?

Dorfmann stuck to his line that while he had violated a rule, no harm had been done and a frightful beauty had been born.

When Mats Wilander arrived, sniffling from a head cold, he wasn't nearly so grandiloquent. Phlegmatic and friendly, he explained that Clerc had "hit a winner and I didn't have a chance. I said, 'I can't win like this' because the ball was good."

Had he ever given away a match point before?

As a matter of fact, he had, just last year in the European Junior Championships against a Yugoslavian named Slobodan Zivojinovic. He had won that match, too, he recalled with a faint smile.

But if Clerc's shot was good, someone demanded, why replay the point?

Wilander admitted, "The rule is if you hit a winner, you win.

But it is difficult for me to give him the point and go to deuce. I could have taken the match, you know."

Had he felt more pressure after that?

"I don't feel any pressure. I just play. I won't get disappointed if I lose."

How did he rate his chances in the final?

"I feel if I play Vilas, I can't really beat him. But I suppose anything can happen. Maybe he'll be nervous."

Afterward Bud Collins marveled about the match point. "It was the wrong decision, and yet everyone went away happy."

Not everyone. Some continued to grumble. You couldn't have Wilander giving away match points, they said. What if he had lost after the umpire had called, "Game, set, and match" in his favor? Controversy would have raged for decades, and there would have been rumors, accusations, and innuendos. It was a professional sport; big money was on the line; rules were rules; players had to play the calls; and officials had to stick to their decisions. Most important, they contended, a nice boy like Wilander had to be protected against his own better nature before somebody took advantage of him.

The second semifinal was an anticlimax. While Higueras was steady, his shots just didn't have enough weight on them. Vilas chased down every ball, cracked it back, and won in straight sets.

For a man who exhibits Job-like patience during baseline rallies, Guillermo Vilas loathes wasting time once he has finished a match. Unlike other players who insist on a shower and a massage before a press conference, the burly Argentine charged into the press room with sweat purling down his arms and dripping off his chin. Caked with moist clay, his muscular legs looked as if they had been batter-fried.

Because both Higueras and he spoke Spanish, a Grand Prix official suggested it might be appropriate to let Hispanic reporters ask the first questions.

"Oh, no, that'll take two hours," Vilas protested. "I'll talk to them later. Let's talk English now. Let's start."

"Are you playing the best tennis of your life?"

"To do a judgment like that, you have to stop to think, and I haven't done the comparison."

He had reached the finals of the French Open without dropping a set. How did he account for that?

"When you're younger, you have a lot of energy, but it's hard to have judgment. Now even when I make a mistake, I know what to do."

He also knew what to do when other people made mistakes. He didn't care for the interpreter's rendering of his answer into French, and he lashed out at her, "We translate exactly what I say or we stop this right now."

Several times, in several ways, reporters tried to persuade him to compare Mats Wilander with Bjorn Borg. But Guillermo gave a garbled, implied comparison to prove all comparisons were odious to him.

"What matters," he declared, "is who does it first. How many people transatlantic every day? But what everybody remembers is Columbus going to America in 1492."

"How's that again?" someone called out.

Vilas didn't care to elucidate. He suffered the Hispanic press to gather close around him and ask questions.

In a corner nearby, Ion Tiriac slouched like a truculent chow dog. But he was more than willing to speak to reporters. Of Wilander he said, "He's a nice human being. He's very correct. And I won money on him today."

How had he won money? I asked.

Tiriac admitted he had been betting on the Swede. Although I presumed this violated the Grand Prix rule against wagering, nobody in the press room made anything of it. Journalists were more interested in asking why the strings on Guillermo's racquet kept popping.

Then Pat Summerall and Tony Trabert, sunburnt and freshly combed, arrived to ask Vilas for a few minutes of his time. CBS was broadcasting the final tomorrow in America and they wanted a comment from him to use as a lead-in. Vilas refused. He wasn't doing any TV, not for the French, not for the Americans, not for anybody. As Trabert and Summerall tried to explain they needed just a couple of quotes, Vilas and Tiriac pushed past them and into the locker room.

Most journalists didn't hang around to talk to José Higueras, who, despite his somber appearance, said he was happy. He loved tennis and enjoyed watching Vilas play the game so well, even though it was against him. He said this was the high point of his career. He had won tournaments in the past, but to reach the semifinals in a Grand Slam event was a thrill for a man who had dropped out of school at nine and got a job at the Real Club de Tennis in Barcelona.

To show what sort of club it was, José passed a finger beneath his nostrils and tweaked the tip of his nose. Very snob, the Real Club. The son of a construction worker, Higueras had started as a ball boy, then discovered he could play the sport better than the rich people who employed him. As a joke, they let him compete for the club team against a rival team which they had no hope of beating. But José had won his match and decided then that tennis might be his ticket to a better life for his family and himself. Now here he was in the semifinals of the French Open. *"La vida es extraña."*

In the press room a thin, personable man with a bright check shirt and an invincible smile asked who I was and who I worked for. After introducing myself and explaining that I was writing a book, I asked who he was and who he worked for. The turnabout appeared to catch him by surprise. Staring at me through glinting spectacles, he chuckled in embarrassment—at my ignorance, no doubt—and said he was Gerald Williams of BBC. He did a TV commentary every evening during Wimbledon.

Taking pains to be polite, yet clearly angling for information, he asked if my book was under contract and whether I had received an advance adequate to cover my expenses. He, too, was doing a book about tennis, but although he said there were publishers interested in it, he had delayed signing a contract. Gerald Williams was recording his experiences as a Christian on the circuit.

"You know, there are a lot of Christians in tennis," he told me, his narrow face beaming.

"So I've noticed."

"Are you a Christian?" he asked.

"Yes, I'm Catholic."

Still smiling, trying to show that he intended no offense, he said, "That doesn't necessarily mean you're a Christian."

I said I thought it did.

"No, it depends upon whether you accept Christ."

"You mean, believe in Him?"

"I mean, accept Him."

"I believe in Him. I don't think He cares whether I accept Him."

Gerald Williams couldn't have disagreed more, but he was too polite, too much a gentleman, to argue doctrine. He urged me to read *Born Again*, by Charles Colson, the Watergate hatchet man famous for saying he'd run over his own mother if she got in the way of his job. Later, serving seven months in the slammer for obstruction of justice, Colson, an ex-Marine whose nickname is Chuckles, underwent a conversion and rode out of prison on a Bible, imbued with religious zeal. Ever since, he has been working the evangelical circuit, which in America is no less complex and profitable than the tennis circuit. *Bjorn Again* . . . I mean *Born Again* would, in Gerald Williams' opinion, teach me what it was to be a Christian.

The day of the final, the temperature on court was 97° F. and the air was heavy with humidity—the worst weather imaginable for a prolonged war of attrition. But both Wilander and Vilas started off determined to prove they could not be beaten from the baseline. The first game lasted seven minutes and it took 154 strokes to play four points. When after sixteen minutes Vilas bottled to the net and knocked off a volley some wag in the press section shouted, "Let's give two points for winning volleys." By the time Vilas had broken to a 4–0 lead, he had soaked through his shirt and the black mat of hair on his chest began to emerge behind the white cotton, like an image on a developing photograph coming into sharper focus.

Serving to reach five-love, Guillermo had to labor like a stevedore. Five times the game went to deuce, four times Wilander gained the advantage only to have Vilas recoup it. On the fifth deuce Vilas glanced into the stands at Tiriac, then served and rushed the net. He won an easy volley, but appeared to learn nothing from it. He seldom put pressure on the Swede again, and it took him fifty-nine minutes to close out the set 6–1.

By now Guillermo was not the only one slathered with perspiration. Spectators seemed to be dissolving into puddles. It wouldn't have been so bad if the match had been exciting or if the action had ever been brisk enough to divert attention from the slow, agonizing incineration of the afternoon. But even the sound of the shots suggested a clock. *Tick tock, tick tock,* Vilas and Wilander patted the ball back and forth.

In the second set, although there were six service breaks in a row, people on Center Court appeared more interested in catching up on their reading. Some scanned the program. Others unfurled newspapers and studied the reports about Israel's invasion of Lebanon.

After two hours and four minutes Vilas hit the first dropshot of the match. It seemed as significant as the invention of the wheel, but he never tried that novel tactic again. He did, however, serve and volley once more, which provided a diversion for conscious spectators. And there were a few dark clouds to entertain those who like to search for the shapes of dogs and sheep. Then there came a clap of thunder, to which the crowd replied, "*Shhh!*" That was fun, too.

Then it was back to work. Guillermo walloped the ball and Wilander punched it back. They reached a tie-break and Vilas got a set point. Emboldened by this advantage, the Argentine took Wilander's second serve early, smacked an approach shot, and rushed the net. The approach was long, alas, and that dissuaded Guillermo from coming in again behind his return of serve.

After Wilander won the tie-break, Vilas slumped in his chair and quaffed half a bottle of mineral water. He held the bottle out to a ball boy and when the fellow was slow in taking it, Guillermo tossed it at him. Would that he had saved this aggressiveness for the third set, which the Swede ran away with 6–0.

With nothing much to engage their attention on court, most journalists began getting their notes in order and whispering back and forth. Wilander had taken the junior title here last year. If he won the main event this year, he would be the first man since Ken Rosewall to accomplish that feat. He would also be the first unseeded French Open champion in over thirty years. What's more—and this one really sent ripples through the press section—he would be the youngest Grand Slam champion in history. Borg had won the French Open at the age of seventeen, but he had been forty-eight days older than Wilander.

I felt forty-eight days older than I had been this morning, and a sizable contingent of the crowd seemed to share my sentiments. During one eighty-stroke exchange of moonballs they started hissing and whistling. Vilas finally got the message. Between games he dipped into a bucket and splashed a cup of ice water over his head. Unfortunately, it didn't wake him up. Wilander broke to 5–4, then served out the set and match, releasing everybody from four hours and forty-two minutes of torture.

Still Guillermo Vilas had the strength to gallop straight into the press room and settle behind the bank of microphones before most reporters had taken a seat.

"Are you ready?" asked the translator.

"I don't give a fuck if they're ready," he told her. "Let's start."

Then he changed his tone and spoke to the press in a quiet, thoughtful manner. "I didn't play strong enough. He was very tough, even when I put pressure on him. I think physically he was stronger than me. His ball is very slow. It took a long time to come down, and that gave him a chance to regain his position. I didn't know how to deal with it."

When asked why he had hit just one dropshot, had only once rushed the net behind Wilander's second serve, and had served and volleyed no more than half a dozen times, he acted surprised and could offer no explanation.

"You fight for a title," he said. "Sometimes you win, sometimes you don't. I don't have any complaints."

Still sniffling with a head cold, Mats Wilander said, "After the first set I thought I didn't have a chance. But in the end I think he was too tired to put pressure on me."

"What does it mean to be the youngest winner here?"

"It really doesn't mean anything to me. Winning is what matters."

"What are you going to do tonight to celebrate?"

"I don't know."

"What went through your mind at the moment of victory and what did Vilas say to you at the end of the match?"

"I didn't hear him say anything and I didn't think anything."

"How do you relax when you're not playing tennis?"

"I rest. I go into my room, I lock my door, and creep down on the bed."

"With whom?" shouted a French reporter. The interpreter refused to translate this to English.

An American journalist said, "Since a lot of us don't know you, please tell us something about yourself."

"I think you know me now."

Leaving Stade Roland Garros, I ran into a frazzled-looking Volvo Grand Prix official. "That was awful," he said of the final. "If they show that piece of shit on American TV, it'll set tennis back ten years."

WIMBLEDON

A LOFTY fortress of tradition, the All England Lawn Tennis and Croquet Club changes at glacial speed. But the public's perception of it changes slower still, since most journalists, like those generals who are always fighting the previous war, persist in filing reports which have little to do with the realities of Wimbledon and even less with the way contemporary players regard the place. Instead, year after year they churn out stories based upon earlier stories, strumming the same dreamy, euphonious tunes, harking back to a halcyon age which reached its highest literary expression in a 1971 piece by John McPhee entitled "Centre Court."

Strawberries in Devonshire cream, the steeple of St. Mary's Church, royalty, fulsome praise—"This is the greatest tournament in the world"—and the obligatory reference to the fragment from Kipling inscribed over the arch leading to Centre Court—"If you can meet with triumph and disaster and treat those two imposters the same"—McPhee's article contains every building block of the basic Wimbledon story. Less gifted authors have had no compunctions about cannibalizing it for a few sentences, and those utterly lacking professional integrity have ripped off whole paragraphs, reshuffled the elements, and published them as their own.

The All England Club is "ordered within ten acres," McPhee wrote, "and all paths eventually lead to the high front façade of the Centre Court, the name of which, like the name Wimbledon itself, is synecdochic. 'Centre Court' refers not only to the *ne plus ultra* tennis lawn but also to the entire stadium that surrounds it. A three-story dodecagon with a roof that shelters most of its seats, it resembles an Elizabethan theater. Its exterior walls are alive with ivy, and in planter boxes on a balcony above its principal doorway are rows of pink and blue hydrangeas. . . . In their pastel efflorescence the hydrangeas appear to be geraniums that have escalated socially."

If run as an account of the 1982 Wimbledon, McPhee's piece would probably strike most readers as essentially accurate. While the names of the players might be wrong, the tone is right, is timeless. A few details might sound anachronistic, but then a large measure of Wimbledon's presumed charm is its antiquated atmosphere.

"Wimbledon is uniquely considerate toward players," McPhee maintained, "going to great lengths to treat them as if they were plenipotentiaries from their respective nations and not gifted gibbons, which is at times their status elsewhere." He praised the Players' Tea Room: "Hot meals are served there, to players only—a consideration absent in all other places where they play." And he extolled the lavishness of the locker room: "The gentlemen's dressing room is *sui generis* in the sportive world, with five trainer-masseurs in full-time attendance."

For tennis writers and fans the world over, not to mention for the 375 members of the All England Club, these lines possess the resonance of the Talmud. They are true, they are eternal, and any contradiction or doubt amounts to heresy. But in fact Wimbledon is no longer unique and, compared to almost any tournament on the Grand Prix or WCT circuit, it is neither particularly considerate nor opulent.

From Hong Kong to Houston, from Monte Carlo to Mexico City, players receive royal treatment in the form of free limousines, free meals and discounted accommodations, free babysitters, abundant free tickets to the tournament, plenty of practice courts, elaborate programs of entertainment for their wives and girlfriends, around-the-clock trainers, masseurs, and doctors, and attentive tournament directors, hostesses, and gofers who dote on the stars and provide whatever they ask for. In some cases this means supplying dope and girls, and in almost every instance it entails the payment of illegal guarantees.

But Wimbledon doesn't need to pay appearance money, and it is less likely to arrange sex or score dope for players than it is to pave Centre Court and use it as a parking lot. This partially explains the crescendo of complaints that plagued the All England Club in the past year. Pampered, paid under the table, and protected by compliant umpires, the top players have lost patience with Wimbledon, which prides itself on treating all outsiders with uniform disdain.

It is this uniform disdain which accounts for the rest of the criticism. In matters petty and profound, the All England Club has, until recently, refused to acknowledge that the players had any legitimate gripes. Instead, Wimbledon chose to establish itself, with the abject cooperation of much of the press, as a theme park, something along the lines of Disneyland, in which crowds gather annually to worship the real and imagined virtues of the nation's past.

In that past, things were reputed to be simpler and people knew their place. If, as McPhee wrote, Centre Court resembles an Elizabethan theater, it is important to note, as he does not, that the crowd is segregated according to the Elizabethan concept of the Great Chain of Being, which bears no resemblance at all to the ATP's computerized ranking. At the top looms God, followed by the sovereign members of the royal family, the lords and ladies, the knights, the foot soldiers and yeomen, the good burghers, and finally the groundlings and stinkards who cluster in the standing-room enclosures. There's none of this democratic nonsense about all men being created equal, nor is there any suggestion that talent or financial success will necessarily allow a man to clamber hand over hand up the Great Chain. It's impossible to buy membership in the All England Club, impossible to buy into the Royal Box, and frequently impossible to buy a ticket without the help of a scalper.

Even having bought a ticket, a man gets no guarantee that he will see any tennis. In a compound designed to accommodate twenty-five thousand spectators, there are frequently in excess of thirty-five thousand souls jostling for space and teetering on tiptoes to catch a glimpse of a court, any court, and many go home having watched little more than the shaggy backs of other people's heads. Those with a ticket to Centre Court are usually better off, but the stadium roof is supported by iron pillars, and the pillars and overhanging eaves ruin the view from an annoying number of seats.

If it should rain and the day's schedule should be curtailed or canceled, that's just another example of the Divinity moving in mysterious ways to test one's mettle. Don't bother asking for a rain-check. Wimbledon, like God, doesn't provide rain-checks or explanations.

To comprehend Wimbledon, one must keep in mind that it is the single Grand Slam event which not only takes place at an exclusive private club, but also covers that club's annual expenses. Essentially, the tournament is a successful fund-raiser— think of it as an alternative to a raffle or bingo—which allows the Club to hold yearly dues down to $17, to serve members subsidized drinks and meals, and to generate over two million dollars in profits. When this became common knowledge after an exposé by the *Observer* in 1981—naturally, the article wasn't written by a tennis reporter—officers of the All England Club tried to laugh it off, remarking that the meals were really quite bad. But this was small solace to the fan who had to fork over more for one ticket than a Club member had to pay in yearly dues, and it offered no compensation to the kid with a grounds pass who had to shell out almost as much for a hotdog as a member paid for a three-course meal.

The advantages of membership, however, are not limited to the "ridiculously low" dues, as Club Chairman Sir Brian Burnett describes them, nor to subsidized drinks and meals. The most valuable fringe benefit is access to tickets. Each member receives one free Centre Court seat every day of the tournament and has the right to buy two more at a bargain-basement discount. According to the *Observer*, members pay £2 apiece for extra Centre Court tickets,

which is roughly a quarter of their face value. The benefit to the member, however, is much greater than the difference between the ticket price and subsidized price. A glance at the personal columns of *The Times* any day will produce offers of tickets at £100 or more. Club members are not supposed to sell them, but it is not unusual for some of their tickets to end up by a circuitous route in the hands of touts. . . .

No wonder membership of the Club is prized. Each year, at the cost of £5o, members can distribute patronage to friends, relations or business acquaintances worth £2,500. . . . The Wimbledon membership is a self-perpetuating oligarchy; its benefits are roughly the equivalent of inheriting a fortune of £100,000.

These shady practices reveal not only the tendrils of hypocrisy which flourish at Wimbledon along with the ivy and the hydrangeas, they explain why Great Britain has such poor tennis facilities, so few indoor courts, and just one player in the top hundred. The All England Club, along with the Lawn Tennis Association, is supposed to nurture a national training program. But, said the *Observer*, "It is hard to avoid the conclusion that the superb record [of Wimbledon] has been built up over the years on a selfish, overlavish use of resources, some of which could have—and most ordinary players would argue, *should* have—been put to use in improving the woeful standards of British tennis generally."

Despite evidence of its peccability, the All England Club has steadfastly refused to allow international tennis authorities much, if any, influence over the tournament. Nominally part of the Volvo Grand Prix, Wimbledon doesn't consider itself bound by the Code of Conduct.

The Club draws up its own list of seeded players, then, still clinging to the Great Chain of Being, it assigns men to two different dressing rooms. Dressing Room Number One, close to Centre Court, is reserved for players with established reputations. Dressing Room Number Two, located behind the field courts, is left to "qualifiers and what-have-you," in the words of Leo Turner, the major domo of the dressing rooms. "There's nothing wrong with Number Two, but the players all want to come in here [Number One]. They don't have a locker [in Number Two] so they put their bags under the seat and then they come to me for a towel and I catch them and send them back."

Megawatts of energy are expended each year catching culprits who have failed to stay in their places and chasing them back where they belong. It's as if the Club views its mission as one of behavior modification and feels it has failed unless players, the press, and spectators slip docilely into the slots assigned to them.

For players, this assignment starts with the dressing room and ends with a court, and a man can calibrate precisely how important he is by where he is forced to play. Since 1977 Bjorn Borg hasn't performed anyplace except Centre Court and Court One. Lower-ranked players are relegated to distant, bumpy cow pastures where the crowd presses in on all sides and sets off a din which makes the Italian Open seem reverentially silent.

It isn't just the surface which is superior on the show courts. So is the officiating. Centre Court and Court One receive a full complement of thirteen officials—twelve linesmen and an umpire—and they employ electronic devices for monitoring the service lines. The remaining sixteen courts make do with six linesmen and an umpire—no netcord judge—and these officials are serving an apprenticeship. If they perform well, they may qualify for minor show courts Two, Three, Thirteen, and Fourteen, and after five years they may graduate to Centre Court or Court One.

It would be wrong, however, to conclude that the arrogance of Wimbledon amounts to total intransigence. There were changes in 1982. Prize money increased by eighty-four percent—it is now nearly a million dollars—and the Club was induced by an American television contract to pitch more than a hundred years of tradition out the window and play the men's final on Sunday.

Tradition isn't all it pitched out the window. Jack Yardley, a groundsman for thirty-two years and just two years shy of retirement, was dismissed because of complaints about the grass.

While Yardley was let go after a long tenure, Teddy Tinling was invited back after more than two decades of banishment. Appointed as liaison between the players and the Club, Tinling assumed much the same position he first held fifty years ago and continued to hold until he put a pair of lace-ruffled panties on Gussie Moran.

The Club also announced that ATP trainers could now work at Wimbledon, just as they did at all other Grand Prix tournaments. And seeded players would receive extra tickets, extra time on the practice courts, and the privilege of bringing a coach or friend into the locker room.

Whether these changes would improve the players' obstreperous moods remained to be seen. But John McEnroe promptly expressed an opinion about Teddy Tinling: he "doesn't know his ass from his elbow."

One thing that had not changed for Wimbledon '82 was John McEnroe. Or, rather, there had been no change in England's alternating fascination and fury with last year's champion, the first in history not to have been made an honorary member of the Club.

To traditionalists, his behavior after the tournament had been as appalling as his on-court insolence. He had not just refused to repent, he had slithered out from under all the penalties imposed on him.

Originally fined $10,000 by referee Fred Hoyles, he appealed and had this axed in half by Marshall Happer. Then McEnroe appealed Happer's $5,000 fine and demanded a three-man board of arbitration to which he had the right to appoint one member. He chose Harry Hopman, the former Australian Davis Cup coach, who had once trained McEnroe. The vote went against him, 2–1, with Hopman the loyal dissenter. But since it took an unanimous verdict to convict, McEnroe paid no fine and served no suspension for a performance which he readily conceded deserved to be punished. It would be hard to say who emerged from this imbroglio looking worse—McEnroe or the tennis officials who once again proved they cannot or will not enforce the rules.

For all the bad press he gets, John McEnroe has his defenders in Great Britain. In fact, he has admirers who view him as a scourge of the Establishment. To the country's punks, he has acquired the status of a Stormtrooper whose belligerence serves as shock therapy in the enclaves of the enemy. He could scarcely be more effective if he waxed his hair into spiky points and dyed it mauve and green, Wimbledon's colors.

A London-based rock group, the Pretenders, dedicated a song, "Pack It Up," to McEnroe and immortalized one of the master's lines, which may someday be chiseled above the quote from Kipling. "You guys are the pits of the world." Thus spake McEnroe during his first-round match last year. The umpire was insulted, as he was meant to be, but he added injury to insult by mistakenly transcribing the salvo as "You guys are the piss of the world."

Punks are not alone in regarding him as an angry, misunderstood young man. Russell Davies remarked in the *Sunday Times*—on the book page, naturally, not the sports page—Wimbledon has limited use for common people: that is, "limited to two weeks in which we supply their revenue. Oh, and one other use: supplying the players. The players are common people, too, and some have become a good deal too common for Wimbledon's liking. But what makes McEnroe's outbursts pathetic as well as objectionable is that they prove he hasn't understood the Ways of the Club; he's up against a whole tradition of English blank-faced absolutism whose self-righteousness exceeds his own. I feel a pang of sympathy for the Brat whenever I hear that the umpire whose ear he's chewing off happens to be a Wing Commander as well."

This year McEnroe started chewing off ears early at a party at Barbarella I, in Fulham, where he came to promote his biography by Richard Evans.

According to *What's On in London*, a young lady introduced herself and said she was from BBC Radio 2.

"They're a bunch of creeps," said the genial young man, "so I'll tell you right now, I'm not having anything to do with them. I've been burned too many times. I've had it up to here."

The young lady stood there embarrassed by this uncalled-for tirade. McEnroe peered at her.

"Are you shameful to be working for BBC?" he asked. The wording was so peculiar that the girl asked him to repeat it, which he did, again saying "shameful" for "ashamed."

Later, Brian Rostron, who works on the *Mirror Diary* and is the son of the veteran tennis writer Frank Rostron, spoke to McEnroe, first telling him who he was. McEnroe turned away abruptly. "I don't have to talk to media schmucks like you."

Buster Mottram also made headlines, but where McEnroe threw down the gauntlet to the press, Mottram hurled it smack in the face of the tennis Establishment. In an article for *News of the World*, Britain's No. 1 player charged that the game's "greed, corruption and hypocrisy make me sick." Fed up with the way the tour was run, Mottram wrote,

In some Grand Prix tournaments, excluding Wimbledon, Paris, the U.S. Open, and the Australian Open, I know that up to 100,000 dollars per player—£55,000—is on offer every *week* to the top few men in the world.

Over the year they can make 1½ million dollars each—just for walking on court.

They are paid through their agents by some of the most influential and respected names in tennis—even some members of the Men's International Pro Tennis Council, who may also be tournament directors.

They draw up the rules we are expected to live by. Yet some bend those same rules on their own account.

A former MIPTC member once told me: "I have to offer appearance money to the stars. If I don't they won't come."

These accusations seemed the sort to stir Marshall Happer into action. All the Administrator had to do was question Mottram, then use his testimony to confront other players, agents, and members of the Pro Council.

What's more, Mottram maintained that appearance money destroyed any chance of strict enforcement of the Code of Conduct.

> Corruption has made discipline in the game a sick joke. It's no coincidence that bad behavior on the court has escalated so much that it's now probably worse than in any other sport.
>
> Players know that the few people who sit in judgment on them are likely to have a vested interest in making sure they are not suspended.

As if paraphrasing the accusations of the Umpire in Antibes, or summarizing my report of those accusations to Buchholz and Happer, Buster added,

> Only a brave, or perhaps foolhardy, referee will disqualify the player. For he is in the pocket of the tournament director, who'd lose a fortune if the star were given his marching orders.
>
> Tough referees would very soon become unemployed referees. Now we even have the absurd situation of players' agents promoting tournaments.
>
> Does anyone believe an agent would stand for his client being thrown out of the tournament he is promoting?
>
> To my mind the biggest hypocrites in tennis are the MIPTC.

Since I assumed these allegations would provoke a reaction from the Pro Council, I sailed into the Wimbledon fortnight convinced I would no longer have to chase after officials asking awkward questions. I had only to wait for the inevitable outcry, then an inquiry and the first steps toward reform.

. . .

Meanwhile I went out to the qualifying rounds at the Bank of England Club in Roehampton. Monday morning preceding the main tournament, several hundred players, teenage striplings as well as gnarled graybeards, gather to see whether they have qualified for the qualies. Since players have to check in by 9:30 a.m. and the first matches don't begin until 12:30, that means three hours of agonized waiting for the lucky ones. For the unlucky, there can be a nine-hour delay before they go on court, and during that dead time, as they drift through the day, it is difficult not to lose their competitive edge. This year, with the clubhouse closed for renovation, players were shunted onto an indoor basketball court where folding tables and chairs gave the cavernous gymnasium the look of a high-school lunchroom, a singularly joyless place inhabited by men and women wound tighter than cheap clocks.

Generally, qualifying rounds are played on the same courts and under much the same conditions as in the main draw. But Roehampton is the roughest approximation of Wimbledon, and a player's morale is eroded by countless reminders that he doesn't rate first-class treatment. While the courts near the clubhouse are in decent shape when dry, those at the far end of the cricket pitch undulate over warped terrain and the chalk lines waver as if laid out by an inebriate. There are only three officials per court—an umpire and two roving linesmen—and players have to chase their own balls. Sometimes there aren't chairs to sit on during change-overs, and instead of bottles of the famous Robinson's Lemon Barley Water, players make do with pitchers of tapwater. Also, the Bank of England Club lies under the landing pattern of Heathrow Airport, and the frequent low-flying planes would unnerve even Bjorn Borg, that epitome of Nordic cool.

But, of course, Borg wasn't here. Borg had refused to qualify. Even if he had agreed to subject himself to this harrowing ordeal, it wouldn't have been at Rochampton. The All England Club had promised that special private accommodations would be arranged if he deigned to play the qualies.

Vijay Amritraj had, however, come to Roehampton, just as he had said he would. A quarterfinalist at last year's Wimbledon, still ranked among the top thirty in the world, he won his first matches with ease, then overcame a two-set deficit in the third round to qualify.

David Schneider, the South African with the lopsided grin, had also fought his way to the final round. But by the time I reached his court, he had blown a two-set lead to a hard-serving American college boy. Part of Schneider's problem was that last week he had played a Davis Cup match for Israel against Belgium on clay and hadn't had time to acclimate himself to grass. Now in the fifth set his game was freighted with tentative gestures and nervous tics. After every point he touched his racquet to the net, scribbled an X on the service line, then dragged the racquet across the baseline. When forced to hike back to the windscreen to pick up balls, he ran his racquet along the green plastic mesh. The sound was like fingernails scraped across a window screen.

Schneider searched the crowd for encouragement. There weren't twenty people watching him, and most were as impassive as commuters queuing for a bus. Then he spotted me and continued to glance beseechingly in my direction after every point. I was with my wife, and we applauded his winning serves and volleys. It made a hollow sound in all that empty space, and the other spectators, frozen in attitudes of indifference, regarded us quizzically. But Schneider seemed to appreciate the support. He got a service break and made it stand up to win the match.

I moved down to the fence around the court, and Schneider put two fingers through the wire to shake my hand. He admitted he didn't remember my name, but he remembered my face and that we had met in Genoa.

"I was looking around," he said, "and you were the only one I knew. It means a lot to have somebody behind you."

Although exhilarated to have made it into Wimbledon, he took time to ask what I had been doing since February. He was still the only player on the circuit to ask me a personal question.

To give Club members plenty of time to digest their subsidized lunches, play at Wimbledon starts at two p.m. and continues, weather permitting, as late as 8:30 or nine p.m. The trouble is that the weather often doesn't permit much of anything except a luxuriant growth of vegetation. The first Monday of the tournament dawned brooding and dark, and by early afternoon a fine mist fell on a landscape of uniform green. Grass, windscreens, hedges, trees, ivy, scoreboards, tents, and linesmen's jackets, everything at the All England Club was green except for one incongruous splash of orange—the new bleachers on Court Thirteen.

The crowd was sparse, but that had less to do with the drizzle than with a tube strike that had prevented people from traveling out from London. Attendance was off by eight thousand from last year's first day, and there was easy access to the field courts via the grid of walkways which are usually so clotted that journalists prefer to remain in the bar, sipping lager and following matches on TV.

Spectators were not the only ones conspicuous by their absence. With the excuse of injury, allergy to grass, aversion to English snobbery, or personal pique at the Grand Prix, more than half the top players skipped Wimbledon. Borg, Lendl, Vilas, Clerc, Teltscher, Noah, Taroczy, Higueras, Ramirez, Dibbs, and Fibak all decided to spend the fortnight in dryer, warmer climes. As a result, the All England Club had its weakest field since 1973, when the ATP boycotted the event.

Play was soon suspended as the drizzle turned into a deluge, and I took shelter in Marshall Happer's office. The Administrator appeared no less fatigued than when I had met him three weeks ago in Paris.

I asked if he had determined whether McEnroe's contract with Lipton Tea constituted an illegal inducement to play the Italian Open.

No, he hadn't had time to look into the matter. That would have to wait until he returned to New York.

International Tennis Weekly had announced that Happer had closed his investigation of the tournament in Stuttgart without imposing any penalties. But Happer told me he was about to reopen the case and thought it prudent not to discuss it.

When I said I had just spoken to Ron Bookman, the ATP Director of Communications, who corroborated Happer's view that many special events were orchestrated entertainments, not honest competitions, Happer stressed, "It's important for people to understand the difference between exhibitions and legitimate tournaments."

Curious as to how categorical he had meant to be when he remarked, "I think all exhibitions are fixed," I inquired about the Volvo Masters. An eight-man round-robin with no ATP points, it had all the earmarks of a special event. Did the Code of Conduct apply to it?

Happer didn't give me a direct answer. He granted there had been tanking incidents in the past, but he felt the format had encouraged them. Now the format had changed. When I asked what he would do if the tanking continued, he said it was difficult to prove a player wasn't putting forth his best effort.

After Fibak's bet in Strasbourg, various ATP and Pro Council officials assured me that, while they had no jurisdiction on the WCT, they would regard wagering at a Grand Prix tournament as a serious offense. Had Happer read in the *Herald Tribune* that Ion Tiriac admitted betting on Mats Wilander during the French Open? And had he heard that *L'Equipe* had run an article which suggested Lendl, too, had been betting?

This was news to him. He asked me to bring him copies of the clippings.

What about Buster Mottram's article in *News of the World*? I asked. It contained allegations about appearance money which implicated members of the Pro Council. It also charged that umpires couldn't enforce the Code of Conduct without jeopardizing their jobs, especially since agents were serving as tournament promoters.

Reiterating his position that Supervisors kept umpires honest, Happer nevertheless said he would like a copy of Mottram's article, too.

To set up something of a controlled experiment, I brought him the articles about betting, but not Mottram's piece. I wanted to see whether the Administrator, or anyone in his office, would bother to track it down.

·   ·   ·

Like players and spectators, the press is stratified by a system that is rigidly hierarchical. The Wimbledon Media Guide lists six separate journalist badges and passes, each with its distinctive color and perks. At a distance of twenty paces, one can decipher a reporter's pedigree and compute how many privileges he has which have been denied to others. Predictably, for an institution which values tradition above all else, Wimbledon has a vibrant old-boy network, and amiable hacks who have had press credentials for decades will continue receiving them as long as they don't foul their nest.

Presiding over the press, Roy McKelvie, during the rest of the year a tennis writer for the *Sunday Express*, displays all the crusty acumen of an alderman. When I first covered Wimbledon in 1978, I met McKelvie in a characteristic pose, seated at his desk, silver hair gleaming, a carnation in his buttonhole, his fist wrapped around a wineglass. ("Wimbledon must be the only major stadium in the world that has two large and well-equipped bars solely for the media," Sir Brian Burnett boasts.)

As I approached, McKelvie extended his free hand. Foolishly, I thought he meant to introduce himself with a handshake. But he brushed my hand aside and, with a lordly snap of his fingers, demanded my identification. Then, with no wasted pleasantries, he gave me the lowest possible accreditation, a Rover's Badge, which entitled me to enter the grounds, but not to sit in the press box or anywhere else. By definition, a Rover must rove. He cannot, however, rove onto Centre Court or Court One. To cover many of the most important matches, I had to watch television.

In 1982 I wrote McKelvie five months in advance, reminding him that I had covered "the Championships" before and mentioning that I was now doing a book about the circuit which would be published in England. The day I arrived to collect my credentials, I knew better than to expect a handshake, but I trusted he would improve on the Rover's Badge I had had in '78.

When I identified myself, McKelvie beamed. "Oh, yes, the *author*."

"We're all authors, aren't we?" I asked.

"Not like you. You're writing a book. I think we'd better give you a Rover's Badge."

As I protested that this would put whole areas of the Club off-limits, McKelvie encouraged me to make ample use of the Video Room.

Having enshrined its code of condescending treatment, Wimbledon has spent decades discoveting and refining new indignities to visit upon novices. During a long rain break I once asked if I could eat lunch in the Press Buffet with a low-ranked player I was interviewing. I was huffily informed that only journalists could dine in the Press Buffet. When I indicated to the uniformed doorman that soccer star Kevin Keegan, cricket entrepreneur Kerry Packer, and Lamar Hunt and his wife were inside, he smiled a wintry smile and reminded me how easily I could lose my own access to the facilities.

After an hour-and-a-half interruption, play resumed and several one-sided matches finished before the leaden sky unleashed another downpour. John McEnroe had brushed aside Van Winitsky, dropping just five games in three sets. But he came to his press conference as testy and disconsolate as a loser. He scratched his head, he gnawed his fingernails, he stared at the microphone, he stared at the ceiling. Congenitally incapable of looking anybody in the eye, McEnroe is one of those men who, because they are ill at ease, put everyone around them on edge. Displaying a curiously inverted stage presence, he makes himself the natural focus of attention by refusing to court anyone's approval. Even in repose, his pale, freckled body exudes impatience and his scowling face conveys little except degrees of contempt. Viewing every question as a veiled criticism, he responds to the most solicitous comments with the adenoidal whine of an adolescent tired of being bugged about leaving his dirty clothes on the living-room floor.

To be fair, last year's champion had some cause to whine. Although he had won handily today, he wasn't playing well. Just last week he had lost to Connors in the finals at Queens, a traditional tune-up for Wimbledon. He had had no rhythm, no discernible strategy, and on top of the twisted ankle that had plagued him all spring, he had suffered a groin pull. Most tennis experts believed that these nagging injuries, like the lapses in his concentration, resulted from McEnroe's poor practice habits. He wasn't working hard enough to retain his No. 1 ranking. A great natural athlete with superb timing and coordination, McEnroe usually didn't have to be in top shape to win. But now that there were so many more demands on his time and so many bizarre characters vying for his attention, he desperately needed to reassess his program. Most people in tennis doubted he had the self-discipline to get a grip on himself and his game.

A reporter opened the interview in a cheery, avuncular fashion. "The umpire said things went well today and you once gave him a big smile."

There was no smile now. McEnroe gave the man a smirk that would have enraged Mother Teresa. "Wonderful!"

Undeterred, another fellow chirped up, "How did the discussions between Teddy Tinling and your father go?"

"Why don't you ask him?" McEnroe shot back.

"I have. Tinling didn't want to say."

"I don't know how it went. I suppose it went okay."

He said he wanted to concentrate on tennis this year and forget last year. He said people at Wimbledon appeared to be making an effort to improve the situation. But then, refusing to end on a grace note, he added, "I'm not saying it's great or anything, but it seems to be getting better. Hopefully, I'll get the trophies I won last year." His adenoids were throbbing now. "You'd think twelve months would be enough time to get them to me."

Jimmy Connors had also waltzed through his first-round match but, unlike McEnroe, he was pleased with his performance, particularly with his serving.

Finally, the man who had so ferociously resisted changing his game had made an adjustment of the kind a club player could have advised him to try years ago. Instead of spinning in a punchless first serve, Connors now tossed the ball well out in front of him and swung all his weight into it. He had even taken to following his serve to the net, a tactic his previous service motion had prevented. As he explained, "It's difficult to go to the net when you're retreating sideways."

Now he wasn't retreating at all. He was charging the ball. For those who had watched him lose matches last winter at five tournaments in a row, the transformation could not have been more amazing had Connors served righthanded.

Somebody asked if he ever thought about the 1981 semifinal in which he had Borg by the neck, two sets to love, but then had run out of fuel, out of imagination, and out of the match. It was the kind of question likely to spark a temper tantrum from McEnroe, and it might have brought a churlish put-down from the old Jimmy Connors. But today he smiled and shook his head, tossing his damp bangs. "I laugh about it. But I don't think about it."

Asked whether Wimbledon was more important to him now than when he had won in 1974, Jimbo wasn't coy. He confessed he was hungry. He yearned to be champion again, and soon. "My time is running out," he said, as though he were older than A. W. Gore, who had captured the title in 1909 at the age of forty-one.

As quickly as that, after two interviews which lasted less than fifteen minutes, the theme of the 1982 tournament was set, and most reporters embraced it as though it had been chiseled in stone. Two Americans, two lefthanders, both of Irish extraction, both fiery competitors battling it out for a second Wimbledon crown. It had all the elements of classic confrontation, they claimed, forgetting that most McEnroe-Connors matches had been ragged affairs. It was youth against age, the impetuous newcomer versus the wily veteran, they wrote, conveniently ignoring the fact that Connors was only twenty-nine. Then, once they remembered this, they pretended that twenty-nine was close to tap city for a tennis player.

It was the hotheaded brat against . . . well, actually, against another hotheaded brat. But for journalistic convenience, Connors had to be portrayed as a reformed knave, if not an absolute gentleman. Where McEnroe sported a quasi-punk haircut and frequented rock concerts, Connors, they emphasized, was a married man, a father, a homebody with responsibilities, a guy who had got his priorities straight now that he sensed the approach of the Grim Reaper. Reading some articles and listening to the BBC commentators, one had to wonder whether they were speaking about the same Jimmy Connors who had a cute habit of grabbing his genitalia after bad calls or stroking his racquet handle as if masturbating at the umpire. And when his wife, Patti, was praised as a stabilizing influence, it called to mind some dreary dame in a dirndl and granny glasses. But when the camera flashed up into the stands, it focused on a gorgeous former Playboy Bunny in cowboy boots and huge sunglasses with gleaming red frames.

A hard rain fell Tuesday afternoon, washing out most matches on the field courts and delaying the women, who traditionally start the second day. There were sixty men who hadn't finished their first-round matches and dozens of others still waiting to begin. If this continued, play would have to commence at noon—a sensible solution, one would have thought. But Wimbledon does not rush into anything, not even into rational decisions.

Of more immediate concern to the Club was the drastically diminished attendance. In the past, people had slogged through monsoons and stood for hours in ankle-deep puddles. In 1978 twenty-seven thousand fans congregated in a cloudburst and stayed until nightfall. Then, passive as cattle, they herded themselves home without seeing a single ball struck.

But this year, by the end of the week, attendance was off by fifty thousand—which, figuring the average ticket price at $10, amounted to a half-million-dollar loss. The deficit didn't end there, though, since Wimbledon counts on raking in enormous profits from its concessions. A double-scoop ice-cream cone cost $1.40, a single glass of champagne over $4, a plastic cup of six strawberries in cream, $1.75. An off-brand bottle of wine which sold for $3 in London ran $9 at the All England Club, and the public was charged $5 to park in a muddy field. Some heretics suggested it was these larcenous prices as much as the transport strike and the weather which had kept the crowds away.

Chip Hooper had been seeded at the French Open and reached the fourth round. He had been seeded at Queens and, in his first professional tournament on grass, had advanced to the quarterfinals before losing to McEnroe. But the seeding commitee at Wimbledon remained unimpressed. Hooper's name went into the hat and he drew Peter McNamara in the first round.

It was a bad draw for both men. McNamara had grown up on grass in Australia, had reached the quarterfinals here last year, was seeded eighth this year, and had demonstrated his mastery of the surface by winning the Wimbledon doubles title. Still, he knew better than to expect an easy match with Hooper, particularly on Court One, the fastest lawn on the grounds.

Because of rain, play was postponed until early evening, when the clouds cleared and the entire English summer seemed condensed into a few bright hours. While shafts of sunlight set the grass aglow, they lacked the warmth to dry it altogether, and as Hooper and McNamara knocked up, the footing was, as the English say, "greasy."

The court was in almost virginal condition, but this was no cause for joy for either man. Although the courts look better the first week, they give an inconsistent bounce, and players don't feel comfortable until the second week, when the grass is worn down and broken in.

With the help of an English journalist, I got into the press box on Court One, despite my lowly Rover's Badge. Ironically, for all Wimbledon's protests that it cannot accommodate more reporters, the press box was half empty. It was this way every day, I discovered, and Centre Court was no different. Except for the finals, there were always plenty of seats.

Standing six feet six, Chip Hooper tossed the ball high, and when he swung through at full extension, walloping the ball at its apogee, it accelerated and struck the court with such force it might have been a cannonball dropped from a tower. On grass his first serve skidded, rising no more than knee-high. His second serve kicked shoulder-high and twisted away from the receiver. McNamara managed to keep the score close, but Hooper's serve made the difference as he took the first set in a tie-break.

After an exchange of breaks in the second set, McNamara began to read Hooper's serve and chip it back low, forcing the big man to bend and hit up. Hooper touched one knee to the ground, genuflecting like an acolyte as he stretched for half-volleys. Then on an important point in the seventh game he made a rookie's mistake. McNamara hit a lob and Hooper let it bounce. Only it didn't bounce. It took a feeble little hop, like a toad in the grass. Chip swiped at it with his Graphite Prince, but poked it long, giving McNamara another service break. The Aussie swept the second set 6–3.

Hooper opened the third by breaking McNamara and easily holding his own serve with the help of several lets which, inexplicably, were not called. Muttering and grinning like a crocodile, McNamara seemed to lose heart and his touch as Hooper started mixing his heavy strokes with drop volleys and lobs. "I can't move this racquet through," McNamara roared and took a couple of angry practice swings after Hooper won 6–2.

By the fourth set the court lay in shadows, and as a damp chill closed over it like a lid, the crowd starting leaving. This was an exciting match, one of the few that would finish today, but it was unbearable to sit and let the cold steal into your bones. Between games Hooper bundled up in a jacket, then removed it as he came back on court.

He was serving into McNamara's body now, and once knocked the Aussie off his feet. Genuflecting, he hit a half-volley for a winner. Then he clobbered an overhead that left a divot in the lawn. He got two break points and on a second serve questioned the linesman's call. When the umpire overruled, giving Hooper the point, the game, and a 4–1 lead, McNamara shouted, "I know he's big, but he's not *that* big."

"The ball was long," the umpire said.

"Just because *he* says it's long." McNamara pointed at Hooper.

"I saw the ball long. Play on," said the ump.

Irked by the overrule and by Hooper's frequent questioning of calls, McNamara stormed back to knot the score. But then Hooper broke him with a delicate lob lofted just over the Aussie's head. Serving for the match, Chip lumbered to the net like a long freight train that keeps coming, car after car. He finished McNamara with a monstrous overhead which caromed off the court like a misshapen egg.

When McNamara refused to be interviewed, Hooper provided enough lively copy for both of them. "I still haven't accepted the fact that I'm playing Wimbledon," he said. "Maybe after a few beers it'll sink in. But right now it's like I'm watching a big picture screen. It's on a different planet."

Had he felt any special pressure on Court One?

He admitted he had, but it was difficult to describe. Mostly, it was psychological. "I don't know how many calories you expend mentally when you have to concentrate all through a match, but it's a lot."

Shrugging off compliments about his power, he showed a big man's pride in his finesse. "I had more luck serving like a baseball pitcher, nipping the corners, jamming him, and changing speeds."

There were rumors that Arthur Ashe might select him for the Davis Cup match against Sweden in mid-July. Hooper couldn't conceal his delight, and it was infectious. After so many taciturn and surly players, it was refreshing to be around one who derived such joy from his success and was eager to share it. Still, he had a peculiar way of expressing pleasure at the prospect of playing on the Davis Cup squad. "If I make it this year, I'm just going to commit suicide."

"What's your real name?" someone shouted.

"Hey, man, where you been? It's Lawrence Barnett Hooper the Third. L.B.H., One Two Three."

The evening of Chip Hooper's triumph, he spotted me and offered a lift in his car. Exuberant, he couldn't stop talking. He liked England, he told me. He liked Wimbledon. He liked playing on grass. He liked London better than Paris. "I'm not into that jet-set scene. People here are friendlier. I went to dinner a few places in Paris. I'd be out just having a good time and I'd start laughing—I've got a big laugh—and people would start looking like I did something wrong."

Much as he was surprised by the suddenness of his success, he was amazed even more by its ease. "Some of these guys, I can't believe their serves. They just hit it flat and hard and it bounces up waist-high and I just smack the crap out of it. That's all I do, just smack the crap out of it."

When I asked about the Davis Cup team, he said if Connors and Gerulaitis refused to play, he deserved the honor. He was playing as well as any other American. Still, he doubted Ashe would pick him. Since both of them were black, people might accuse Ashe of bias, favoring Chip over the white boys. Neither of them needed that hassle.

He did an exaggerated double-take as we passed a blind man standing at the curb with a seeing-eye dog.

"Did you see that?" he asked, gasping with glee. "That's one very well-dressed blind man. How do you explain that? I mean, how can he know what he's wearing? He can't see, but he's dressed perfect. That's what I like about England. Even the blind men dress up."

In the annual Wimbledon liturgy it has become one more predictable trope to remark that British commentators are infinitely superior to those American windbags who feel compelled to fill up every minute of air time with inane chatter and laborious explanations of pictures which speak for themselves. Credit where it's due, the BBC crew is knowledgeable and well seasoned—one might say, marinated—in the lore of "the Championships." Dan Maskell has been a fixture there for over fifty years. Mark Cox is the British former No. 1 and a Davis Cup veteran. John Barrett is a correspondent for the *Financial Times* and a full-time director for Slazenger racquets. And Richard Evans is a regular contributor to the *Guardian* and *Tennis Week*.

Personally, I start off every year impressed by the BBC announcers, who, if nothing else, sound so much more articulate than the run-of-the-mill mike-jockey who doesn't know a dangling participle from a passing shot, and who regards his job less as analyzing the action than as hyping a program which must compete for viewers with "Mork and Mindy" and "Charlie's Angels." But after a few days I grow weary of their unctuous solemnity, which suggests they are covering a state funeral instead of a tennis tournament.

Then, too, the phrases which seem so fresh, so quintessentially British, soon become every bit as annoying as the clichés of American commentators. Time after time Dan Maskell burbles, "Oh, I say, he hit that one smartly," or "Oh, I say, that was a glorious forehand," or when his powers are flagging, "Oh, I say!" But what he says all too frequently is something terminally soporific: "A bit too much ambition on that forehand approach produced that rather unnecessary error."

These turgid patches are enlivened only by unintentional howlers, such as Maskell's analysis of a service toss which made McEnroe sound like a victim of intestinal virus. "John's throw-up has been very bad all day." Last year the depth of Bjorn Borg's groundstrokes seemed to prompt an anatomical report: "Borg has astonished the crowd on Centre Court with a display of his enormous length."

During the telecast of the Buster Mottram-Anders Jarryd match I was curious what the BBC commentators would make of Mottram's article in *News of the World*. It's not every day a nation's No. 1 player accuses the sport and the Pro Council of greed, hypocrisy, and corruption, and I expected to hear an official reaction or at least the opinion of the announcers. But BBC made no mention of Buster's charges.

After Mottram beat Jarryd, I hurried to the press-conference room, a tiny cubbyhole at the bottom of a stairwell as steep as a coal chute. The smallest one I saw on the circuit, it could accommodate no more than two dozen reporters. The rest had to watch on closed-circuit television—which was fine unless you had a question you doubted anybody else would ask.

The room was full of lugubrious Swedes who appeared to be rehearsing a scene for an Ingmar Bergman film. Anders Jarryd seemed to be in the same movie. Studious-looking and somber, he wears steel-rimmed glasses, and his shock of reddish-brown hair is the most colorful thing about him.

A Swedish reporter spoke up in English. (Why they didn't use their native tongue, then provide a translation, I don't know.) "If you could play this match again," the journalist asked, "would you play it a different way?"

Jarryd considered the question at some length. "I don't think so," he said.

"When do you play doubles?"

This, too, gave him a long moment's pause. "I don't know when the doubles start."

The Swedish journalists nodded gravely. Life was like that. Love, death, doubles, you just never knew.

When the moderator announced that Mottram would be here in a minute, he broke the hush as if it were a pane of glass. Buster arrived in high spirits, even though the palm of his racquet hand had an open sore that resembled the stigmata. A blister had formed during the match and a layer of skin had peeled away to expose the bloody pink meat beneath it.

A reporter asked if he felt more pressure today because he was the lone British player with a chance of lasting until the later rounds.

"Oh, yes," Mottram laughed. "I was shivering with fear."

There had been many criticisms of Wimbledon during the last few months, an American observed. Did Buster believe they were justified? And had they brought about changes?

"In the past I've been very critical of the All England Club. But this year things are much better. The criticisms have been partially answered." He mentioned Teddy Tinling's appointment as liaison and a new directory of information as concrete improvements.

When no one else alluded to his article, I asked if he had received any reaction from players, officials, or Pro Council members.

Buster said he hadn't gotten any response at all—which didn't surprise him. "Everyone knows this. It's not a secret."

Although he has the jutting jaw and erect bearing of a Marine Corps drill instructor, there is nothing rigid about Jeff Borowiak.

A native of Berkeley, California, an accomplished musician with a preference for modern jazz, a health-food enthusiast who has sometimes shocked *maître d's* at restaurants by bringing jars of his own food to the table, Borowiak has been described as a man who marches to a different drummer. But he doesn't march. He rides a bicycle, and before his match with Vijay Amritraj, I saw him wheel into the All England Club with his racquets slung over his shoulder.

Vijay is inclined toward more glamorous means of conveyance. Last week on Fulham Road he had pulled to the curb, buzzed down the power window of a chauffeur-driven Mercedes limousine, and shouted at me, "Hey, AP." Beside him sat Al G. Hill, Jr., President of WCT.

I wouldn't be surprised to see him next in a rocket sled. The day of his first-round match he showed up wearing a windbreaker with an 007 patch on the chest. Vijay told me he was negotiating to portray an Indian intelligence agent in a new James Bond film, *Octopussy*.

Regardless of their divergent personal idiosyncrasies, Amritraj and Borowiak get along well on court. Perhaps this has something to do with the influence of Eastern mysticism. One reporter characterized their match as the meeting of a Hindu and a Zen Buddhist, and, indeed, both men did appear to be involved less in competition than in some harmonious effort to achieve a higher plane of being. Although they hit flat, hard strokes and played an aggressive game, they smiled, they applauded each other's shots, they stood and joked at the net after a point-blank duel of reflex volleys.

During a first-set tie-break the linesman called one of Vijay's serves long. But Borowiak insisted he had seen it in and told Vijay to play two balls. The tall Indian came to attention and saluted him for his sportsmanship.

Borowiak won the tie-break and the second set as well. But there was no screaming, no complaining from Amritraj, and no crowing, no baleful glares from the American, not even when Vijay came back to tie the score. Borowiak moaned, "I need a blood transfusion," but that was all. After Amritraj ran out the match, winning three sets in a row, the two men walked off with their arms around one another.

Then, instead of rushing to the dressing room to sulk, Borowiak climbed into the bleachers to speak to some friends. He wasn't annoyed when an aging gentleman scampered over and said, "You've got a good game, son. But you need to learn how to lob. That's the key. Practice your lob."

Nor did he snap at me when I asked for his reaction to the notion that his match had been the meeting of a Hindu and a Zen Buddhist.

"Which one was I?" he said.

"The Zen Buddhist, I suppose."

He shook his head. "I don't know what that is." Then he offered his own assessment of his game. "All the pieces are there. I just haven't put them together."

Since Jeff Borowiak is nearly thirty-three, the pieces of his game, in all probability, never will coalesce. But he will remain the kind of player capable of pulling off an occasional upset and, more important, capable of carrying spectators back through the decades, away from the current messiness and ethical ambiguity of men's tennis, "to that happier time," as Herbert Warren Wind of the *New Yorker* has written, "when so many of us were attracted to sports because the people involved in them made the world seem a finer, fairer, and more enjoyable place. They endowed sports with an elevating spirit that we needed to know existed, and even with a touch of poetry."

All during the first week and well into the second the weather was wretched, and players skidded over the grass, sending up rooster tails of spray, taking pratfalls, sprawling flat on their faces. By Saturday, the halfway mark, only the first round of men's singles had been completed and the doubles had barely begun. To catch up, the Club finally decided to start play at noon and to reduce the first two rounds in doubles to two out of three sets instead of three out of five. Some felt that matches should also be scheduled for Sunday, but the Club insisted on keeping one free day. This was a decision much lamented when that middle Sunday turned out to be clear and warm and the following Monday's program was disrupted by torrential rain.

Now that it looked as though the tournament wouldn't end on time, there were rumors that an indemnity clause in the American TV contract would cost the Club a sizable chunk of money if the finals had to be carried over an extra day. Officials refused to discuss the matter even when the rumor grew more detailed and it was said that the indemnity was for half a million dollars.

He idled away so many hours in the Press Buffet sitting for interviews, Teddy Tinling seemed less a liaison between the Club and the players than one of those gents whose job is to chat up journalists, giving them the cozy feeling that they have gotten an inside story, not necessarily about Wimbledon or even about tennis, but always about personalities, his own included. Still, a lot of reporters swore Tinling was a treasure trove of hard information, knew where all the skeletons were buried, and was daringly frank.

One rainy afternoon while he spooned strawberries and cream out of a plastic dish, I took a seat beside him. He didn't appear to be the sort to serve in any formal capacity at Wimbledon. Bald as a honeydew melon, tall and awkward as an ostrich, Tinling is six feet seven inches of unalloyed flamboyance. A septuagenarian whose lone concession to age is a cane, he eschews the Establishment uniform of pinstripes and a school tie in favor of purple shirts and plaid jackets. Gold, silver, and turquoise gleam on his wrists and fingers and a one-and-a-half-carat diamond dazzles in his fleshy left earlobe.

When I asked how things had been improved this year for players, he, like everyone else, mentioned the information pamphlet and the information booth that had been set up in the Competitors' Lounge.

Critics of Wimbledon had never complained about a lack of information, I said. Rather, they had complained about the dearth of complimentary tickets, the difficulty of finding practice courts, the inefficiency of the courtesy cars, and the haughty attitude of the Club. What had been accomplished by offering information to everybody, but more privileges only to the top seeds?

Tinling smiled. "We're all equal, of course. But some of us are more equal than others. In the entertainment world there has to be some acknowledgment of the star system."

Did he regard professional tennis primarily as entertainment?

Indeed he did, and he boasted that he had held this view long before most people caught on to the trend. Tinling's entire career, as he presented it, was a series of public-relations coups and "firsts." He had designed the first permanently pleated tennis dresses, the first nylon ones, the first ones made of Orlon, the first made of polyester, the first commercially marketable paper dresses. And in 1949 he had put Gussie Moran in lace panties because "people were bored. They wanted some kind of change after the war. They were ready for sex."

They were also ready for press conferences. Tinling said he had organized the first tennis press conference in 1953. "Maureen Connolly talked about lifestyles and her thoughts about love and food."

Persuaded that tennis players are show-biz personalities, he insisted McEnroe had to be more image-conscious. "John has not understood that the public should have access to more facts than those that deal with his performances."

How far was he willing to push that line of reasoning? I asked.

"A lot of players get overexposed," he admitted, "and can't sustain the public's interest."

That wasn't what I meant. Once a player marketed his personal life, could he object that his privacy had been violated when the media scavenged for still juicier tid-bits? Last year at Wimbledon, McEnroe had erupted when a reporter asked if he had broken up with his girlfriend, Stacy Margolin. Refusing to answer any questions that didn't deal with tennis, he had waged a two-week war against journalists who he claimed were exploiting his private affairs. Yet this year he appeared to be exploiting them himself. He had cooperated with Richard Evans in his biography, A Rage for Perfection, which was filled with revelations about his relationship with Stacy Margolin, among other intimate details. Wasn't this the same sort of inconsistency, I asked Tinling, which led the press to repeat lurid stories about lesbianism on the women's tour, yet never write a word about homosexuality among the men?

Tinling fixed me with his pale blue eyes. "I don't see any evidence of homosexuality among the men. Maybe it's in re-action against the Tilden era, which was impregnated with it. Tennis has become a very macho, young-lion situation. They growl and they bark. It's a fine breed of guys, very fine."

But, in his opinion, this fine breed of growling, barking guys had made a tactical error. "If they had wanted to follow through logically and develop tennis as entertainment, the players should have built their own arenas. Now the principal stages for their events are held by the Establishment. I think when Lamar Hunt envisioned his break away, he underestimated how important the Establishment was."

On the horizon loomed another issue which Tinling believed was of paramount importance. "The great next step is the debate about eligibility for the Olympic games in tennis. This will produce two targets for players. Winning the Olympic gold medal may be more marketable than climbing the ATP computer. The Olympic champion might wind up richer than the professional champion."

Determined to pry from him at least one opinion that didn't reduce itself to merchandising and image-mongering, I started to explain what I had learned about compromised umpires. But Tinling cut me off. "Human umpiring is a total anachronism and should have been done away with thirty years ago. I think the players want to complain. I think complaining gives them an emotional release. That's why they haven't insisted that um-pires be done away with."

What did he suggest in their place?

"If you're talking about visual umpiring," he said, "you're already talking about an anachronism. There's no sense dis-cussing a rotten situation. Umpires should simply be replaced by machines. If you can go to the moon, you can certainly work out a proper machine. It's not for me to say how. I blame the players. I blame the Establishment, too. But the players should have stood up and said this isn't good enough."

Apart from machines in place of umpires, what did the future hold for tennis?

He returned to his favorite subject. "I cannot see anything that doesn't relate to the Olympic situation. A lot of the best young juniors are waiting to see what happens. There's not enough room at the top. But having two tops will offer more opportunities."

I asked if there was anything else he cared to tell me about tennis or Wimbledon or himself.

"You won't put a 'g' in the middle of my name, will you? Everybody does."

I promised I wouldn't.

Since that afternoon in Paris when Marshall Happer told me he had umpired a winner-take-all event between Stan Smith and Arthur Ashe which appeared to have been fixed, I had tried to reach both Smith and Ashe. I called their hotels and also left messages at the Competitors' Lounge. Finally, one bleak, drizzly morning Stan Smith called and explained that, although he couldn't meet me in person, he would be happy to answer questions over the phone.

The ATP Media Guide describes Smith's career as "one of Homeric proportions. One of the game's all-time greats—a former World No. 1, the winner at Wimbledon in 1972 and the U.S. Open in 1971—he continues to set the standard for conduct and professionalism in the sport. Smith, a devoutly religious man, is not what one would call a political activist, but rather he is just a fellow who always does the right thing, and has thereby become an off-court leader by example."

Tall, blond, and regally slim, he is the sort of player Wimbledon loves. He has the stiff upper lip and proud carriage of a Grenadier Guard, never complaining, never responding to success or adversity with much more than a bemused smile.

He decried guarantees on ethical grounds. "Tennis has been almost beyond reproach," he told me. "The credibility of the game is quite high. But guarantees might hurt a player's incentive and hurt the public's perception of tennis. One possibility is to make guarantees legal so everything is out in the open. But I feel the money should go into prizes."

As for tanking, he made an interesting observation. Tournament tennis was an unusual sport in that two competitions took place simultaneously—singles and doubles. If major-league baseball consisted of hardball and softball, with some players committed to both, imagine the abuses this would produce, especially if softball offered prizes that were ludicrous compared to those in hardball.

When I pointed out that players also tanked in singles, Smith didn't deny it. But he felt, "Tanking is less a problem now because of computer rankings. You don't see guys giving half-effort—or you don't see it as often—because now, even if you've got a guarantee, a player wants the computer points to maintain or advance his ranking.

"Another problem," he went on, "is the proliferation of exhibitions. Players may not make a 'best effort' in exhibitions."

Wasn't this fraud? I asked. After all, these matches were often televised and touted as legitimate competitions.

"We"—I took it that Smith meant the ATP, in which he holds a seat on the Board of Directors—"have no control over televised special events. Some viewers don't understand this and get a bad impression of tennis." Not that he blamed people for being confused. There was, he admitted, a lot of misleading advertising, since "it's not to a sponsor's best interest to emphasize that a special event is not like a tournament, with a Code of Conduct and so forth."

When I repeated what Marshall Happer had told me about his winner-take-all match with Ashe which had conveniently concluded just in time to make way for a basketball game, Smith not only didn't dispute that it had been fiddled, he confessed it hadn't been winner-take-all either. "You won't get players playing winner-take-all events. They want to know they're going to get something."

Attempting to obtain Arthur Ashe's reaction, I hiked to the trailer belonging to Home Box Office, the cable network for which he worked as a commentator. A production assistant directed me to the Competitors' Lounge, where on the terrace overlooking the field courts HBO had stationed a camera.

In theory, the Competitors' Lounge is the sacrosanct preserve of players and their guests. It is off-limits to the press, who, even as guests, are forbidden to conduct business there. Yet, as always at Wimbledon, the discrepancy between theory and practice creates a parallax of dizzying proportions. Arthur Ashe, for example, was a member of the press. But, of course, he was also an ex-Wimbledon champion and an employee of a company that had paid the Club a handsome fee.

When I entered the ground floor of the lounge, I was stopped by a gentleman in a blue blazer. He had a smile plastered on his wind-burned face and he wore his coppery hair in a style suitable to a character from *I, Claudius*—combed straight forward and cut in bangs across his forehead. As I was telling him I wanted to leave a message for Ashe, the Praetorian guard let Gene Scott, editor of *Tennis Week*, breeze past without a word. I had just seen Scott in the press room distributing complimentary copies of his magazine. He had had journalist's credentials prominently displayed on his coat lapel. Now he wasn't wearing any badge at all.

When the Praetorian guard left and I was scribbling a note to Ashe, the hostess at the reception desk said, "Why don't you just go up and talk to him?"

I gestured to my yellow Rover's Badge. "They won't let me in."

"Sure they will. Everybody does it."

So I climbed the stairs, discovering at every level that the Competitors' Lounge was aswarm with racquet dealers, clothing reps, assorted campfollowers, and journalists, none of them wearing his press badge. Out on the terrace Bambino, Nastase's bodyguard, waddled the length of the balustrade, whacking people on the buttocks and making as if to heave them over the railing onto the asphalt three stories below.

Suddenly someone grabbed my arm. I feared it was Bambino. But it was the Praetorian guard. He wasn't smiling now. "May I see you a moment?" he said in a voice as firm as his grip.

"Certainly."

He steered me onto the hall landing. His face hardened. "You're not permitted here."

"The hostess said I could come up."

"She had no right. We can't have the press interviewing players here."

"I wasn't interviewing anyone. I told you, I'm trying to *arrange* an interview with Arthur Ashe."

"No journalists are allowed here."

I pointed to Gene Scott and half a dozen others.

"Mr. Scott is a player," he insisted.

"No, he's not. He hasn't played here in years."

"Then he must be here as a tournament director."

"Are tournament directors permitted in the Competitors' Lounge?"

"Only with a special pass."

"He's not wearing any pass. Neither are the others."

He sighed. "It's ridiculous, I know. But it's your Rover's Badge that gives you away. You could have taken it off and come up here and talked to the players and I'd have never known you're with the press. A lot of reporters do that. But since you're wearing a badge, I'll have to put you out."

"But not the others?"

"No, they're not wearing press badges."

"Even though you know they're journalists?"

He sighed again and led me downstairs to the reception desk, where I left a note for Ashe.

No one suffered from the foul weather more than Brian Gottfried, the quiet, curly-haired American best known for his Herculean practice habits and unswerving honesty. He has confessed, "If all players behaved like me, nobody would come to watch tennis."

His second-round match against Nick Saviano started on a Thursday afternoon, and by the time that darkness and measurable quantities of moisture were falling, Gottfried had eked through two sets 7–6/7–6 and led 5–2 in the third. When he reached double match point, he seemed a sure winner. But somehow Saviano salvaged both of them and clawed his way back to win the third set 7–5 just as play was suspended for the night.

Next day it rained and the match was delayed, thwarting Gottfried's attempts to end it. Saturday, although it still rained off and on, they managed to finish the fourth set, which Saviano won to tie the score at two sets apiece. Since Sunday was a free day, the match didn't resume until late Monday evening, and in the fifth set Gottfried, his concentration destroyed by repeated interruptions, lost his grip. Saviano polished him off 6–1, having captured seventeen of the last twenty-two games scattered over five days of intermittent rain.

Although Drew Gitlin, a boisterous qualifier, was buried deep in the memory bank of the ATP computer, he had little trouble tearing apart Thierry Tulasne, the French teenager whose clay-court game left him looking on grass like a beached canoeist frantically paddling. When the American won the third set 6–2, there were loud whoops of joy from his family, which, along with a contingent of French journalists muttering about *l'herbe* and *la pélouse maudite*, constituted a crowd of about a dozen people.

Far from disheartened to have achieved his triumph on an almost abandoned field court, Gitlin was ecstatic. He was now into the third round, where he figured to play Jimmy Connors on a show court. "Hey, man," he told me, "like I really don't think they're going to make Connors play in a potato patch."

They played on Court One, a spot with which Jimbo is quite familiar, but which at first left the qualifier short of breath, his feet fumbling to gain a purchase on the slick grass. In the warm-up Gitlin kept glancing into the steeply banked grandstands as if he feared they might avalanche over him. But after squandering the first set 6–2, he settled down and cleverly mixed his shots, taking a strong rip at his serve and return of serve, then punching off-speed groundstrokes that forced Connors to stretch.

A muscular, bandy-legged Californian with a mop of light-brown curls, Gilin broke to a 5–2 lead, executing several drop volleys to devastating effect. At 5–3 he got a set point, only to have Connors save it and charge back to break him, then hold serve to 5–5.

Still Gitlin stayed with his strategy of going for winners on his serve and coaxing errors from Connors with slow, short balls to the forehand. In a tie-break he got a second set point, then a third, and groaned along with the crowd as Connors saved them both. But Jimbo couldn't save another, and the Gitlin family led the applause.

By the middle of the third set on this clear evening—the Rolex clock on the scoreboard read 8:10 p.m.—the temperature had plummeted into the low fifties and spectators breathed out frosty plumes. Behind the press box, in a section reserved for umpires and linesmen, a woman of a certain age sat cradling a bottle of Jim Beam between her sensible brogans. Every few minutes she nipped at the bourbon to ward off the chill. Luckily, she wouldn't work as an official again today. By the time Connors squeezed through the set 7–5, it was nearly nine o'clock.

I expected, I prayed, that play would be suspended. My knuckles were blue, I couldn't stop shivering, and I had a headache from squinting in the gloom. On the field courts, matches had been called for the night, but Connors wanted to continue and Gitlin agreed. It surprised me that he didn't insist on prolonging his shot at the number-two seed for another day. But perhaps he feared that when he woke up tomorrow, Jimmy Connors would still be Jimmy Connors while Drew Gitlin had been cast back into obscurity.

Gitlin lost the fourth and deciding set 7–5, but emerged from the match a winner. I ran into him the next afternoon in the corridor beside Court One. Shoals of schoolgirls in knee socks and straw hats eddied around him, begging for his autograph. Passers-by stopped to shake his hand and say, "We were rooting for you," or "Great match. You'll get him next time." And Gitlin was convinced there would be a next time.

"I came out of the match thinking I can play with anybody.

It gives me a lot of encouragement for the future. I'm doing now what I've always wanted to do. I'm just going to try and take it from here."

One place Drew Gitlin took it was to Cap d'Adge in the South of France, where, at a WCT tournament held next to a nudist colony, he reached the semifinals in singles and won the doubles. In one week he earned over $20,000, more prize money than he had made in a year.

When I met Jim McManus, who is responsible for ATP tournament and player services, it occurred to me that it might be wise to relate to an ATP official the same information I had passed on to Marshall Happer.

A former U.S. Davis Cup team member, McManus sat with me in the Press Buffet, talking amid the clash of plates and cutlery. Because he bears some resemblance to Rod Laver— both men are short, redheaded, freckle-faced, and lefthanded— players preparing for matches with Laver used to like to practice with McManus, and as they chased the American around the court, they could, for a moment, imagine they had the Australian great on the run.

After I synopsized the articles in the *International Herald Tribune* and *L'Equipe* which suggested Ion Tiriac and Ivan Lendl had been betting on matches, McManus' immediate reaction was "Deplorable!" The rule against wagering, he declared, was "of the utmost importance to the integrity of the game."

I remarked that whereas Marshall Happer expressed doubts about WCT's eagerness to enforce its rules, I wondered how serious the people at the Grand Prix were about their Code of Conduct.

"I'd say they're very serious. Tell you the truth, this is the first I've heard of it [the betting]. I'm not opposed to bringing it up to Marshall. I'm sure he'll follow through and question the players." When I said I had learned some players were splitting prize money, he insisted, "I've never heard that in relation to a Grand Prix tournament." But he had heard about a split at a WCT tournament, which he named.

"Where did you hear this?" I asked.

"It may have been from Butch. I don't know if you told Butch."

"No, I didn't." In fact, I had refused to name names for Buchholz and he claimed he knew none. But I told McManus, just as I had told Buchholz, that a player admitted he had split prize money in an ATP-sanctioned tournament. I found it strange that ATP and Pro Council officials granted that prize-money splitting was going on in WCT events, yet seemed to dismiss the possibility that the same players were doing the same thing in Grand Prix events.

"I've never heard of any of that." McManus chuckled. "Guys don't usually come up and confess to us."

McManus readily conceded the relationships between tournament directors and umpires were troubling. He believed this might be a hold-over from the amateur era, when tournaments were social occasions during which players, officials, umpires, and fans mixed on a friendly basis. Once the game went professional, some things had changed radically, but certain anachronistic practices had persisted. Umpires, for example, were still essentially amateurs, and they, like many others involved in running tennis, worked either out of love of the sport or out of a desire to assert their self-importance and profit by personal relationships.

McManus said there had been recent cases in which umpires had become involved in recruiting players. Some went so far as to provide wild cards, or special exemptions, to men who might not otherwise qualify for tournaments. Naturally, this destroyed an umpire's neutrality and, just as naturally, it seemed to give some players an unfair advantage, since it was logical to infer that an umpire who recruited a player might tend to protect him. At the very least, there was an awful appearance of evil.

When I inquired about drugs on the circuit, McManus said that at present the ATP didn't have a program to educate players about the dangers of narcotics or to help those who were addicted. He saw no need for such a program; he didn't know anyone on the tour who took dope. When I expressed surprise, he recalled an article about Vitas Gerulaitis dabbling with drugs.

Had that article prompted an inquiry?

"No," McManus admitted.

Had Yannick Noah's interview in *Rock & Folk* prompted an investigation into his charges that players used amphetamines to pep them up for matches?

McManus said he was unaware of any investigation. But again he promised he'd speak to Marshall Happer about the matters we had discussed.

In the fourth round John McEnroe met Hank Pfister, and as Pfister was about to serve, a couple of reporters came into the press box. McEnroe, eagle-eyed and rabbit-eared, whirled around, scowling. "You people know there's a match going on?"

The two journalists scowled right back.

"Oh, you're mad at me?" McEnroe shouted.

"Just get on with it," said one of the offenders, settling into his seat.

"You're a hundred percent wrong and you're mad at me?"

"Play on, Mr. McEnroe," the umpire finally asserted himself.

Seen through the quirky lens that tennis holds up to itself, McEnroe was right in this instance. Spectators are supposed to be no more than furniture. Repeatedly they are warned not to move, not to talk, not to take pictures with flashbulb cameras, and not to applaud a player's mistakes. When they ignore these warnings, retribution is swift. At the 1981 U.S. Open two men were arrested, fined $250, and banned from the tournament for five years for heckling Chris Evert and Martina Navratilova. For heckling? Yes, for doing precisely what crowds at other athletic events do as a matter of course.

Yet while players demand that paying customers comport themselves like genteel ladies and gentlemen who have swallowed a near-lethal dose of Librium, they refuse to abide by what they see as an outmoded standard of behavior. McEnroe in particular has insisted that players should be allowed to yell and argue, fling racquets and vent their frustrations, just like other professional athletes.

If McEnroe or Pfister had ever suppressed any frustration, physical or otherwise, it wasn't apparent today. After he whacked a wild return of serve, McEnroe screamed, "Oh, that's a nice gust of wind." Pfister, too, had metamorphosed into a meteorologist. Flapping his long arms in the air, he hollered, "There must be a fifty-mile-an-hour wind." Then after a double fault he fumed, "Good serve, faggot!"

"Faggot" is a term of all-purpose opprobrium which players use to condemn poor officiating, devious opponents, and their own mistakes. Whether that is what they call homosexuals, however, is anyone's guess. Every time I asked about homosexuality on the circuit, conversations stopped and the room cleared.

The petulant, long-playing sound track continued as McEnroe muffed an easy shot, took a savage swipe at the grass with his racquet, and roared, "God bless America!"

Less patriotic, but equally vehement, Pfister snarled at a linesman, "That ball hit chalk. Wake up!" Then he kicked a ball and got a warning from the umpire. Pfister—sometimes called Feister by his fellow players—clapped and sarcastically thanked the ump.

Meanwhile the match went entirely McEnroe's way. He won the first two sets 6–4/6–4, and was on serve in the third when suddenly he shouted, "That was a clear netcord." Despite his complaints, neither the umpire nor the netcord judge would change the call.

At the far end of the court, Pfister smiled, taunting McEnroe. "I heard it, John."

"Wanna play two?" McEnroe asked.

Pfister's smile broadened. "No."

After running out the match with another 6–4 set, McEnroe repaired to the press room, which was his cue to scratch his head and gnaw his cuticles. When asked why he had argued so passionately about a let in a match he had never looked in the slightest danger of losing, he said, "You never know, looking back, that could have been the turning point."

Was he having trouble concentrating this year?

"Sometimes I go off into space for minutes at a time. After you win a few big tournaments, you don't have the same intensity to play every point, every game."

What about Billie Jean King? someone suggested.

What about her? McEnroe asked pugnaciously.

Well, she had won dozens of titles, yet seemed more intense, focused, and competitive than ever.

"I'd be far away from a tennis court if I was her age," McEnroe declared, sounding fatigued by the very idea of being thirty-nine.

When was he planning to retire?

At this he grew touchier. "I wanna do what I want. If I wanna still play when I'm—I'm—" he plucked an age out of the air— "when I'm twenty-eight, so what? There's nothing wrong with that."

Nothing at all, the reporters agreed as one. What the hell, play until you're thirty. Play as long as you like, John.

The sun reappeared in the second week and players emerged from the locker room, pale as slugs, blinking in the bright, blinding light. Although it still refused to confirm whether there was an indemnity clause in its TV contract with NBC, the Club rescheduled rain-delayed matches with a briskness which suggested it was under some compulsion to stage the men's final by Sunday and at an hour which allowed a live broadcast in the States. This meant downplaying such traditional events as the junior and veterans' competitions and the mixed doubles, in which matches were haphazardly clustered in whatever free space came available. The eventual champions in mixed doubles, Anne Smith and Kevin Curren, were forced to play four matches on the last day of the tournament to take the title.

While no one in singles faced that kind of suicidal schedule, there were men who complained bitterly about being shut off of Centre Court and Court One, where the grass and the officiating were better and the matches were likely to be televised, thus earning players bonus money from their contracts. The Club explained that the logjam of matches left them no choice except to relegate some players to minor show courts. That didn't satisfy Mark Edmondson, who, even after upsetting Vitas Gerulaitis to advance to the semifinals, declared, "Court Two is terrible and it was a disgrace to put the match there. For the last nine years it's been just about the worst court at Wimbledon and a lot of seeded players have been beaten there. The balls bounce all over the place."

Johan Kriek, the stumpy, contumacious South African, played his quarterfinal against McEnroe on Centre Court, but after winning the first set, he appeared to be lost at sea. Slipping and flopping on his belly, he lay flailing his arms as though swimming toward an unseen shore. By the fourth set he hit the beach and agitated his racquet in his hands like a shipwrecked sailor trying to start a fire by friction.

After losing three sets in a row, Kriek stomped into his press conference in a foul temper and laid into the All England Club, the umpires, and the double standard which he claimed protected the stars. No paragon of good conduct himself, he said McEnroe should have been penalized for verbal abuse and for slashing at the net. "But they cater to him."

It also infuriated him that he hadn't had a chance to prepare properly for today's match. "Thanks to the scheduling committee, I've been playing on outside courts ever since I came to Wimbledon in 1978. Yesterday I bought a ticket to get into Centre Court to see what the place is like. It's totally unlike the other courts. It seems twice the size of the others."

Hoping to end the interview on a note of human interest, someone asked Kriek if he had any superstitions.

"I don't wear the same jockstrap four matches in a row, if that's what you mean."

The story of the '82 Wimbledon was, even more than the ravages of the weather, the reclamation of Jimmy Connors. A self-described "kid from the wrong side of the tracks who'll ride high until he dies," he had enraged the All England Club in 1977 by skipping the Centenary Parade of former champions, a snub which the British press played as if it were only slightly less calamitous than the abdication of Edward VIII. Now, five years later, Connors was the sentimental favorite, since, in Borg's absence, he seemed the one man capable of beating McEnroe.

I was less interested in Connors' rejuvenated image than in the progress of Tim Mayotte, the rangy fellow from Springfield, Massachusetts, whose politeness and civility were said to have prevented him from fulfilling his potential. Since reaching the finals in Strasbourg in March, he had had spotty results, getting knocked out early in several tournaments. But his powerful serve-and-volley game was suited to grass, and last year, his first on the tour, he had reached the quarterfinals here. This year he had faced Sandy Mayer in the third round, had been down two sets to love, but had bounced back to win.

After his fourth-round victory over Buster Mottram, Mayotte's satisfaction was mixed. "It's easy to be nice when you're winning, but it's sometimes difficult for me to control myself. I never realized how tough you have to be to play this game at the top level. You have to be so intensely involved, anything that disturbs you can make you explode. I want to be tough, but still control my emotions."

A former National Collegiate champion at Stanford, Mayotte was the only unseeded player to advance to the quarterfinals. He battled Brian Teacher on even terms for four sets and had no more than a small breathing space in the fifth when, at deuce on his serve, Mayotte hit a let audible to everybody on Court One—audible to everybody except the officials, that is.

So sure was he that the ball had been a let, Teacher didn't bother swinging at it. But there was no call. Although Teacher protested, it got him nowhere. For an instant Mayotte hesitated, as though he might offer to take two. But he held his silence, accepted the point, and clobbered Teacher 6–1 for the match.

After a shave, a shower, and a shampoo, Mayotte came to the press conference with his long brown hair still wet, his face shiny with youth. He said the good thing about making it to the semifinals was getting "a shot at somebody of McEnroe's caliber."

How did he rate his chances?

There were no rash predictions. He recognized the limits of his own game and the inventiveness of McEnroe's. "Mac is a natural player. Everyone knows he's not the hardest worker on the tour. I'm much more a drilled player. My game can be too patterned."

"About the serve in the fifth set," someone said, "the let that went for an ace, did you hear it?"

Mayotte hesitated, just as he had on court. Then he blurted, "No comment," and looked a bit embarrassed. It was as though in that one instant he had become a complete professional. He played the calls and didn't look back.

Brian Teacher, who had already been around the track a few times, didn't waste his breath griping about what couldn't be changed. But he insisted, "No question it was a let."

"Did Mayotte know it?" a reporter asked.

"Yeah, he knew it."

"Should he have said something?"

He paused. "No. It's not his place to say anything."

Dialing his hotel room early one morning, I finally reached Arthur Ashe. He was leaving for the All England Club and told me to meet him on the terrace of the Competitors' Lounge. I arrived before the Praetorian guard went on duty and climbed the stairs through the nearly deserted building. Although it was raining, Ashe was outside, taping lead-ins for today's matches along with Barry Thompkins of Home Box Office and John Barrett of BBC. As the rain pelted down harder, an HBO gofer broke out color-coordinated umbrellas for the men on camera. But I was getting soaked and stepped back inside the building.

When he was finished, I went over and introduced myself, and we settled in a corner, where I told him I was disturbed by what I had discovered during my months on the circuit. I mentioned appearance money, and he took it from there, punctuating his points by jabbing a finger at my knee.

Like everyone else, he said that guarantees misled the public and decreased a player's incentive. But then, proving himself a pragmatist, he added, "Appearance money is a response to the laws of supply and demand. Tournaments know the top players are worth more than the prize money they're offered."

When I mentioned Stan Smith's remark about legalizing the practice and getting it out in the open, Ashe too was adamantly against it. "I'd never vote to legalize guarantees. That's the day I'd resign. The situation is twice as bad as last year. The top thirty players could get guarantees, depending on the tournament. It used to be only fifteen."

Next year, who knew how bad it would be? In his opinion, appearance money had become so rampant, offenders were protected by sheer weight of numbers. The Pro Council was faced with the prospect of disciplining nobody or suspending virtually every well-known player in the game. This, I concluded, was why so little action had been taken.

I asked about his article in *International Tennis Weekly*, which had raised the possibility that players might split their guarantees. But Ashe declared that he had meant they might split prize money. There had been a recent example of this, he said, citing the same WCT tournament which several ATP and Pro Council officials had already mentioned.

When I told him what I knew of the deals between tournament directors and umpires he added to the list of their delinquencies and left no doubt that the appearance of evil had become an ugly reality. "Under pressure, umpires sometimes do the wrong thing. Top players are treated with kid gloves. They definitely get better treatment, unequal treatment. It was that way in my day. It's worse now. The stars are protected, and all the players know it. There's collusion between some tournament directors and some umps. Umps are ordered not to discipline stars."

When I repeated what Jim McManus had said about umpires who helped recruit players and sometimes wild-carded them into tournaments, Ashe confirmed that this happened, but then mentioned a more egregious practice. "We have a situation now where some players not only demand guarantees. They demand that certain umps work their matches."

Finally, I brought up his exhibition match with Smith, and Ashe acknowledged that it hadn't been played under anything remotely approaching tournament conditions. Still, he insisted that "the result wasn't fixed." True, they had faced a deadline and had had to wrap up the final set and get off the court in time for the basketball game. This had required a bit of orchestration. But Ashe preferred to describe the match as "arranged" rather than "fixed."

When I asked whether he was bothered by all the arranging and fiddling that went on in tennis, not only in exhibitions but in tournaments, too, he said yes, very much so. Yet he believed there was little he could do on his own. He just had to stay within the system and keep chipping away at the problem.

Having survived a massive heart attack, then open-heart surgery, and having recently been knocked off his bicycle by a New York City cab, Ashe joked that he had used up two of his nine lives. It seemed to me he would need all seven that remained if he hoped to reform professional tennis from within, for arrayed against him was an army in which the indifferent were allied with the devious. But then, perhaps Arthur Ashe believed that his candor with me was one way of carrying the battle to a wider front.

The interview with Arthur Ashe was the culmination of several months during which my misgivings and suspicions had gradually hardened into the painful certainty that professional tennis was so tainted it was no longer possible to regard it with anything like my old enthusiasm and affection. Not that Wimbledon was rigged or corrupt. From what I gathered, it and the other Grand Slam events were legitimate, gave no guarantees, and cut no crooked deals with umpires. Seen through rose-tinted lenses— the only kind popular among tennis authorities—Grand Slam events are the high points of the season, serene islands in a polluted sea full of sharks. But, observed in a more realistic light, they are less isolated examples of purity, I think, than launching pads from which players catapult to the level where they can demand more appearance money, more preferential treatment, more protection from umpires, and, finally, an almost total exemption from the Code of Conduct at tournaments during the rest of the year.

. . .

After Connors clobbered Mark Edmondson in straight sets in one semifinal and McEnroe did the same to Tim Mayotte in the other, I returned to the Club for the final, although I would have to watch it in the Video Room. Surprisingly, quite a few fully accredited journalists chose to follow the action on TV. Some claimed it provided a better view. Others complained that it was too cold on Centre Court. Still others offered no reason for staying indoors; they clung to their silence with the same tenacity as they clung to the snifters of whiskey they brought in from the bar.

Going through the familiar motions, I scribbled down trivia I had cadged off other journalists and which still others copied from me. It was as if we were all school kids preparing for a quiz. Somehow it was reassuring to record that this was the first time two lefthanders had played for "the Championships" since Tony Roche met Rod Laver in 1968. Only six lefthanders in history had won the men's title. It had been eight years since Connors had captured the crown in 1974. Only one man had come back to take the title after a longer hiatus. Bill Tilden, after nine years.

"And there's Elizabeth Taylor," a BBC commentator advised us.

Swathed in yards of yellow fabric, she looked like a piece of overstuffed Victorian furniture rolled along on casters. James Mason kissed her powdered cheeks, then led her to a seat on Centre Court.

"My God, that's unspeakable," an Englishman moaned.

I thought he was being rude about Elizabeth Taylor. But he was pointing to the video screen for Court Fourteen, where no matches were scheduled today. Two schoolgirls had dashed onto the lawn and, thinking themselves unobserved, galloped around doing somersaults and handstands on the hallowed grass. One girl leaped the net. Her friend tried it, tripped, and tumbled, showing her bright white knickers. A few Australians in the room roared with laughter, but the British were not amused. This was as bad as catching a demented intruder in the Queen's bedchamber. They didn't rest easy until a bobby charged out and chased the girls away.

At first the final had some of the same Keystone Kops quality as the schoolgirls gamboling on the grass. Both Connors and McEnroe played erratically, and McEnroe shouted "Disgraceful," then "Disgusting," as Connors broke to a 2–0 lead and looked likely to make it 3–0. But Mac held serve, broke back, and eased ahead 4–3. Then he had Connors down to 0–40, only to let him scramble to deuce. At which point McEnroe screamed, "Fuck it," and the umpire went diplomatically deaf. It took McEnroe three more break points, but he reached 5–3 and served out the set.

In the second Connors again broke to a 2–0 lead and this time made it stand up, winning 6–3, with a crosscourt drive which Dan Maskell called "a rasping forehand." One of the irreverent Australians boomed, "Rasping? What's that mean? It has a sore throat?"

In the third set McEnroe started off like a victim of repetition compulsion, a poor creature doomed to re-enact all his past mistakes. Once more he slipped behind 0–2, and Connors nursed that single break to a 5–4 advantage. But, serving for the set, he double-faulted twice to let McEnroe knot the score 5–5. In a tie-break Connors' serve continued to fly wild and he looked badly rattled.

Winning the third set 7–6, McEnroe stayed even in the fourth by virtue of what Dan Maskell called "some rather cheeky and impertinent tennis." While nobody in the Video Room understood what that meant, Connors apparently got the message and decided to send one in return. When he butchered one of McEnroe's serves, he grabbed his genitals and gave them a good, firm shake to show what he thought of that shot. But McEnroe didn't take offense—not at Connors, at any rate. Instead, he screamed at a linesman who had a receding hairline, "Baldy! Bald eagle!"

Still R. P. "Bob" Jenkins remained mute, and a moment later he proved himself as blind as he was deaf and dumb. When Connors shot a linesman the *cornuto* sign, index and little fingers extended, it didn't produce so much as a mild rebuke from the umpire.

Perhaps this was what prompted McEnroe to increase the obscenity stakes. Having lost the fourth set in a tie-break, he dropped his serve early in the fifth and flew into a rage at the umpire, who refused to overrule a linesman's call. He started by screaming, "That's unfair," and ended by muttering, "Fucking bastard!" If the insult wasn't audible to Jenkins, it was visible to TV viewers—not that one would have known anything from the BBC commentators, who were busy talking about Jimmy Connors' wife, Patti, who, Mark Cox remarked, must have been "on tender hooks."

Apparently the Wimbledon committee also hung from tender hooks. Or else their hides had grown so thick they had lost the capacity to be offended by anything Connors and McEnroe did. After Jimbo won the match 6–4 in the fifth set, it was announced that McEnroe had been made an honorary member of the All England Club, and Connors had been awarded the 100th-anniversary medal which had been withheld from him in 1977 when he failed to attend the Centenary Parade of Champions.

Because McEnroe had to play the doubles final, his press conference was delayed. I decided to hang around, and it proved to be a short wait. The final was scheduled to be three out of five sets, but, according to a witness in the locker room, McEnroe came off court after losing his singles title and threatened to default in doubles unless it was reduced to two out of three. Peter McNamara and Paul McNamee dispatched McEnroe and Fleming in forty-nine minutes, 6–3/6–2.

Afterward the Aussies were sheepish at having won so easily and said they would have felt better had it been a three-out-of-five match. Usually the doubles final was played the day before the singles final, but this year the rain had wreaked havoc with the schedule. McNamee pointed out, however, that if the singles final had started at noon, there would have been plenty of time to let McEnroe rest before he played a full three-out-of-five doubles final. "But the decision to start the singles at two p.m.

was dictated by other considerations"—which was a euphemistic way of saying that the American TV contract had dictated that the McEnroe-Connors match go out live on NBC's popular "Breakfast at Wimbledon" broadcast. A noon start would have put the match on much too early—seven p.m. on the East Coast—to earn it a decent rating.

The All England Club continued to maintain its silence on this and all other financial matters. Not until four months later would it release the news that although there had been forty-two thousand fewer spectators in 1982, the tournament had made a profit of $2,601,990, a forty-three-percent increase over 1981. Higher ticket prices and an extra day's play had more than compensated for the lower attendance.

As reporters waited for McEnroe, there were rumors that his ragged play in singles and doubles was due to a locker-room altercation he had had last night with the burly Texan, Steve Denton. Denton had complained during a semifinal doubles match that McEnroe was wasting time and purposely upsetting him and his partner, Kevin Curren, by questioning so many calls. Denton thought McEnroe should have been penalized for not playing on. After the match Denton chased McEnroe into the dressing room, slammed the door behind him, and lunged at the No. 1 seed. Although people quickly separated them, Teddy Tinling, who was outside, heard the shouting and reported, "We all expected to see blood seeping out from under the door."

McEnroe entered the press room wearing a faded denim jacket and a bored, blown-away expression.

Someone asked for his general reaction to the singles match.

"What do you think it is?"

"To what extent did your argument with Denton affect your play?"

"It had zero percent to do with today," he snarled. "Zero percent, at most."

When the reporter attempted to follow up the question, the schoolmarmish moderator interrupted, "Mr. McEnroe won't answer any more questions on this subject."

"You wait and see," McEnroe said, "this guy'll write about my argument with Denton instead of my match with Connors."

Quickly another reporter passed on to more urgent matters, such as how much better things had been this year at Wimbledon.

"Things are generally all right here," McEnroe said grudgingly. "So I can't complain."

Waiting for the mini-van to carry me back into the city one last time, I met a couple of friends from Texas who had splurged on tickets to the final at £150 apiece. They had felt a bit miffed, however, when their seats turned out to be in a section reserved for linesmen and umpires. Unknowingly, they had bought complimentary tickets which some official had laid off on a tout.

Just then I spotted Jason Smith and shouted to the black, bespectacled umpire that I had something to show him. It was an item in the June 24 issue of *Pro Tennis*, the official newspaper of WCT. "Beginning in January, 1983, the WCT-Fila white and red warmups for chair umpires and line officials will be replaced by the permanent issuance of a dress shirt, tie and tennis shoes. Gray trousers will be worn and will be furnished by the official."

Jason couldn't suppress a laugh. "I hope my gesture had something to do with the change." His "gesture" had cost him considerable grief and nearly half his income. But he wasn't complaining. "It would be nice to think that something I did was right."

U.S. OPEN (CLOSED)

AT Wimbledon, Ed Fabricius, Communications Director of the United States Tennis Association, tacked up a notice in the press room instructing journalists who wished to cover the U.S. Open to sign up and identify their newspaper or magazine. I did so, then scrawled a note to Fabricius, explaining that I was writing a book, had been on the circuit since February, and regarded the U.S. Open as the natural culmination of the tennis calendar. Although I had an assignment from a British journal— the *New Statesman*—I stressed that I am an American and provided the name of my publisher in the States in case he cared to contact him. To be on the safe side, I wrote a longer, more formal application to William Talbert, Vice Chairman of the USTA and director of the U.S. Open.

When by the first week in August I had not heard from Fabricius or Talbert, I telephoned the USTA offices in New York City. Fabricius was too busy to talk to me, but his assistant, Joanne Collins, pulled my file and informed me, "You've been denied credentials."

Since I had an assignment from a reputable magazine, had filed stories on tennis for Associated Press, and had applied two months in advance, what possible reason was there to turn me down?

She couldn't say; that wasn't her department.

I stayed on the long-distance line, dialing tennis officials who might help. Dewey Blanton, the Media Director of the Volvo

Grand Prix, agreed to speak on my behalf, proposing a compromise. Since the U.S. Open, like Wimbledon, has various classifications for journalists, Blanton asked Ed Fabricius to give me the "B" credentials or to provide a special pass with access to some of the facilities at Flushing Meadows. But Fabricius remained adamant, rejected any compromise, and refused to speak to me so that I could make my case in person.

"This is ridiculous," Blanton said, and since Volvo was the principal sponsor of all Grand Prix events, it cost him some embarrassment to admit his powerlessness. People in tennis wanted "the game to grow," he groused, "but they don't seem to want the press corps covering the game to grow. They want to keep it all to themselves."

Still confident something could be arranged, Blanton introduced me to a man who had close, long-standing connections with the USTA. Like Dewey Blanton, the man didn't understand why I had been denied credentials and he told me he would intervene with Ed Fabricius, who was his friend and former business associate. There was no need for me to make any more long-distance calls. He'd take care of things. He told me to go to the press trailer the first day of the tournament. He couldn't guarantee I would be on the "A" list, but I would get a badge of some sort.

From the Parker Meridien Hotel in midtown Manhattan a chartered bus transported players, reporters, agents, and assorted hangers-on across the 59th Street Bridge to Queens, then up the long, bleak strip of Northern Boulevard to the USTA National Tennis Center and the Louis Armstrong Stadium. It was difficult to accept that this blighted area was part of the same circuit which ran through Paris, Rome, Monte Carlo, and Wimbledon. Here the halt and the lame, the drunk, the drugged, the demented, and the dispossessed staggered along the sidewalks, past the stripped-down hulks of abandoned cars and the bricked-up windows of abandoned buildings.

Inside the bus, some players hooked themselves onto their Walkman headsets and dozed off. Others leafed through newspapers, but nobody mentioned the story that had recently made headlines. Vitas Gerulaitis had been named during the trial of a dope dealer, Richard Purvis, who had pleaded guilty, then turned government witness and testified that Tony Goble, charged with conspiracy to possess and distribute cocaine, had said that Gerulaitis offered to pay $20,000 to buy a share in a $144,000 cocaine deal. Federal agents had had Purvis telephone Gerulaitis in January to get him to discuss his part in the deal. But Vitas had been asleep when Purvis called.

Since no charges had been filed, the Pro Council did not plan to conduct an investigation or to question Vitas. Instead, most tennis authorities simply repeated that there was no drug problem on the tour.

Only Arthur Ashe had taken the more enlightened position that where there was smoke there might be hashish, where there were young men making millions of dollars there might be cocaine. In a syndicated column which had appeared before Gerulaitis' trouble, Ashe advocated that tennis players should undergo regular urinalysis to determine whether they were competing on dope. It was much the same suggestion Noah had made two years ago, to no avail.

At Flushing Meadows, on the grounds of the 1963 World's Fair, I went to the press trailer and encountered the usual cast of characters—French, Italians, Swedes, British, and Japanese, some of them reputable writers for legitimate journals, many of them equipment reps, agents, PR men, and tournament promoters flying under false colors.

I introduced myself to Joanne Collins at the credentials desk, and she informed me nothing had changed. There was no press pass for me.

What about the man who was supposed to have spoken with Fabricius? I had been assured I would receive some sort of badge; I had come a considerable distance on that assurance.

She claimed to know nothing about that.

"I'd like to speak to Mr. Fabricius," I said.

"He's not here."

"Where can I reach him?"

"Just wait outside until he comes back."

I went for a brisk walk, fighting to overcome my disappointment. Then I returned to the trailer, where Joanne Collins said she had talked to Fabricius. "You were denied credentials and that's it."

"Is he here? I'd like to discuss this with him."

"Why?"

"I'm doing a book. I want to learn everything about the circuit. I've interviewed accountants, trainers, racquet-stringers, clothing reps. I'd like to interview a press officer and get an idea how he operates."

Ms. Collins said the USTA Communications Director had no time to communicate with me. For more than two weeks, during and after the tournament, I tried to reach Ed Fabricius, but he refused to grant an interview or to speak on the telephone.

During my time on the tour I had been stood up, I had been stiffed on bills, I had been robbed, and I had been hospitalized. But this was the worst. I could not help recalling my conversation with the Umpire in Antibes, who had warned me that anybody who asked the wrong questions or complained about the shoddy practices in pro tennis would find himself out of the game.

That first day I paid my way into the USTA National Tennis Center, and given my foul humor, I was not in the best condition to be a dispassionate observer, especially since I had read dozens of articles which had primed me to expect the worst of Flushing Meadows.

Louis Armstrong Stadium was said to be a stark, inhuman structure where the Deco-turf shimmered like a griddle, hot enough to fry eggs during the day, and where, at night, players groped blindly, trying to follow the trajectory of the ball while thousands of yawping, drunken fans flung insults and beer cans. One thousand seven hundred jets a day took off from nearby La Guardia Airport and most of them appeared in danger of crash-landing on the Stadium court. A peculiar odor permeated the place and insinuated itself into the weave of a spectator's clothing. On a fiercely hot day in late August, when the temperature and humidity hovered in the nineties, one could be forgiven for thinking the smell was of broiling human flesh. Usually it was just sizzling hamburgers. But in 1981 a garbage dump caught fire and play had to be suspended until the smoky stench cleared.

Unhinged by heat, confused by flora and fauna never glimpsed at other tournaments, and suffering acrophobia in the press box, which is perched on the uppermost rim of the Stadium, journalists at the U.S. Open are prone to send back reports which resemble those dispatched by Mungo Park during his explorations of Africa. Even before the tournament switched from Forest Hills to Flushing Meadows, bizarre tales about it had become part of the folklore of the circuit. In 1977 someone shot a fan in the leg during the Dibbs-McEnroe match. The same year, after the final, a crowd dashed onto the court and Connors skipped the awards ceremony, saving his energy for a punch-out with a few spectators. Next year, on a practice court, Connors again got caught up in a love-hate relationship with the crowd, dropped his shorts, and flashed his pale buttocks in their faces. Ilie Nastase topped Jimbo two years later, changing his shorts right on the Grandstand court.

So as I entered the National Tennis Center, irate at having been denied press credentials, I was ready to add a few withering lines of my own to the rabid legends. But I soon found I liked the place.

A perfect example of the architectural principle that form should follow function, Louis Armstrong Stadium and its outlying courts were constructed for a dual purpose. For forty-nine weeks a year they are open to the tennis-playing public. For three weeks, during the qualies and the main draw of the U.S. Open, the emphasis is on tennis-*watching*. Thus in the Stadium and the Grandstand no iron girders or overhanging roofs obstruct the view as they do at Wimbledon. The walkways leading to the field courts are wide and logically laid out so that even on the most crowded days spectators can move from match to match more rapidly and comfortably than at Roland Garros or the All England Club, and everybody who buys a ticket gets a reserved seat in the Stadium.

While social stratifications hold little sway here, it is true that there are corporate tents, clubs, lounges, and private restaurants which are off-limits to the average fan. But, unlike at Wimbledon and Roland Garros, comparable facilities are available to the public, and at prices more reasonable than in London or Paris. I never ate or drank so well at any European tournament.

There was a *boulangerie & patisserie*, there was a stand that sold knockwurst and sauerkraut, a stand with pineapple on a stick, wedges of cantaloupe and watermelon, and strawberries and whipped cream. People who preferred a quick sandwich could grab a hotdog or hamburger, while those with more sophisticated palates could sample Black Forest Ham and Brie on a Croissant, or King Crab Salad on a Croissant, or Curried Tuna on a Brioche. To wash this down, there were imported and domestic beers, imported and domestic wines, mixed drinks, soft drinks, and imported and domestic mineral water.

But of infinitely more significance after my sole-destroying days as a Rover at the All England Club, there was none of this bellying up to a counter, ordering a pork pie or a *sandwich jambon*, and standing in a clogged aisle wolfing down food while someone dripped ice cream down your back. Even families who had brought their own lunch in a basket found free tables and chairs.

This is not to claim that Flushing Meadows is a homey, much less a beautiful, spot. But, like New York City, it is exciting, loud, extroverted, simultaneously iconoclastic and celebrity-obsessed, yet always saved by a sense of self-mocking humor. If genial anarchy distinguishes the Italian Open, if haughtiness and linguistic imperialism are the *cachet* of the French Open, and if implacable class-consciousness and a hierarchical view of the world characterize Wimbledon, then an unrelenting democratic impulse and an unabashed commercialism are the hallmarks of the U.S. Open.

Unfortunately, democracy can sometimes turn demagogic, and the give-and-take of commercialism can be perverted into rapacious hucksterism. All tournaments are out to make a buck, but, of the Grand Slam events, the U.S. Open alone has a split program. At sundown it clears the grounds, then sells separate tickets for a limited schedule of evening matches.

While spectators don't appreciate paying double what they would have to lay out at Wimbledon or the French Open for the same number of matches, players don't like adapting to radically changed conditions. Tennis at night, especially on fast Deco-turf, is an altogether different game, demanding sharper eyesight, swifter reflexes, and unswerving concentration. Even Bjorn Borg has found it impossible to adjust.

Yet if it is difficult for players to cope at night at Flushing Meadows, it is harder still for them to handle the changing conditions in the men's final, which starts in the afternoon and ends long after dark under artificial lights. Although it makes no sense to schedule the final at that hour, it makes money. Reluctant to forgo its profitable telecast of Sunday football games, CBS mandated the late start, and the USTA meekly capitulated.

I had my final meeting with Butch Buchholz, Executive Director of the ATP, in the lobby of the Parker Meridien. A swank hotel now owned by Air France, the place had had layers of Gallic charm grafted onto an old building, and the result was unsettling. At the reception desk all the clerks, even those with Brooklyn accents, greeted guests with a hearty *"Bonjour!"* and called the bellboys *chasseurs*.

There were some real Frenchmen staying there, however. Yves Montand occupied the penthouse, and dozens of his countrymen glided elegantly through the corridors, wearing tight suits and dangling leather purses from their wrists. Their wives and girlfriends lounged in string bikinis around the rooftop pool. By comparison, the tennis players who came to the Parker Meridien for discounted rooms appeared crude and self-conscious as they slunk past the mirrored walls of the lobby in their shorts and shower clogs.

I saw Mats Wilander go by. The seventeen-year-old French Open champ was now tonsured like a monk. He told reporters he had had his long, curly blond locks shorn in the hope of regaining his anonymity.

Buchholz and I sat in a corner under spreading branches of plastic vegetation. He claimed to be pressed for time, but he didn't appear harried or worn down by his duties. Big, tan, and handsome, he composed himself in a chair, his hands clasped in the lap of his olive-green suit.

I mentioned the bets Ion Tiriac and Ivan Lendl were reputed to have made on Grand Prix matches. Buchholz dismissed these as minor incidents, just a matter of wagering a dinner. When I asked whether he had come to that conclusion after questioning the players, he conceded he hadn't. He hadn't spoken to either man. "Tennis players don't have a history of betting," he said. "They'll tell you, 'I'll bet you five bucks a guy breaks serve' or something like that. I don't think it's a serious thing. If you know differently, I'd like to know."

I wouldn't have pursued this subject at all if it hadn't been for the Grand Prix's attitude toward the betting incident in Strasbourg. Although they claimed they couldn't crack down on infractions on the WCT circuit, I had been led to believe that they would react swiftly to admissions of gambling on their own tour.

"Your instinct is that it isn't serious enough to merit your consideration?" I asked.

"No. I think it'd be serious if guys were betting at Wimbledon, you know, or real big things. Tennis players have just never been big gamblers."

Following up on our discussions about prize-money splitting, I reminded him that when we had spoken in Paris he had maintained his inquiries had produced nothing more than vague rumblings.

"Well, you told me about it," Buchholz replied, "and I said to you, 'You give me specific names.' And you weren't ready to do that."

Yes, but after my refusal to give him names, I had talked with a number of ATP and Pro Council officials who gave *me* names. At a time when Buchholz claimed to know nothing, his colleagues cited specific players and events.

Abruptly, Buchholz changed his story. "I shouldn't say I haven't heard something." He mentioned a WCT tournament and two players who were rumored to have split there.

Was any disciplinary action contemplated? I asked.

"We have no jurisdiction over there." He insisted, if it were happening on the Grand Prix, "we'd consider it very serious." Then he took off on a tangent. "Michael, I'm not sure. You know, to say that I was an absolute bulldog terror going after that thing like crazy, I did not." But he promised he had looked into it, and the players reputed to be splitting were denying everything. There was no indication, however, that their financial records had been examined.

Didn't splitting constitute behavior detrimental to the sport? I asked, as I had several times in the past.

"They could say, 'It's an exhibition. I'll do whatever the hell I want.' "

"Well, that brings up a question about exhibition matches," I said.

In April I had told him about a special event in which two top players—now I identified McEnroe and Borg—were said to have agreed to split sets. Buchholz had expressed incredulity in Monte Carlo and he did so again at the Parker Meridien. But his doubt had acquired a hard crust of pragmatism. "I don't know whether you can prove that. I've never heard of anything like that happening before and I don't know why they would split it. But it's an exhibition. So, I mean, they can do whatever they want."

What concerned me, I told Buchholz, was that in checking out the story about Borg and McEnroe, I had talked to Marshall Happer, who stated, "I think all exhibition matches are fixed."

"Michael, I really believe this," Buchholz said. "I think you're heading in the wrong direction, I just don't believe these guys would do that. Maybe I've just got too much tennis player in my blood, but I just don't believe that happens. I'd *love* for you to have Marshall Happer sit *right* there—" he flung his hand at an empty chair—"and say that in front of me."

"I'm supposed to meet Marshall on Monday, September 13," I told him. "Why don't you come?"

Without responding to the invitation, Buchholz plowed on. "I would *love* to sit there and hear him say it. There are no Grand Prix rules for it. You know, to say that a guy's going to throw an exhibition and that he might, you know, ah, tank the doubles or, I mean . . ." He caught himself and repeated, "Tank the doubles?" No one had mentioned doubles. He was too upset to talk straight. "I don't even know what they do in exhibitions. But I can't *imagine* . . ."

For several minutes we trampled on each other's lines, and while we slapped the subject back and forth, like two players at the net exchanging reflex volleys, Ron Bookman, the ATP Director of Communications, stopped at the table for a moment. Soon after Bookman left, I mentioned he had been among those who had told me that exhibitions were just entertainment, not honest competition.

Buchholz wouldn't budge. There had been some reference to Borg's calamitous loss in Monte Carlo, followed by his triumph over Vilas at an exhibition in Tokyo, then his ignominious defeat in the qualifying at Las Vegas. But Buchholz refused to grant that this pattern suggested the exhibition might have been fiddled.

"Did you see the Vegas match?" he demanded. "He [Borg] just went through the motions. He was so pissed off. He was so tired and so pissed off because he had to play the qualifying, he was serving with two balls in his hand and couldn't hit his famous two-fisted backhand."

The logic here eluded me. Anxious to prove players have too much pride to make pre-match arrangements, eager to defend the integrity of exhibitions, adamant that pros always went out to win, he described Borg putting forth less than his best effort at a legitimate Grand Prix event. If with prize money and ATP points at stake the Swede was willing to waltz through a match, how could Buchholz fail to believe that some exhibitions were fixed?

He had toured the United States for ten years, he told me. "We played for a percentage. We used to have promoters coming all the time, saying, 'Hey, I got a big crowd out there and I want you guys to play three sets tonight.' But we'd say, 'Screw you, buddy. There's no way.' Nobody's going to go out there and bag it in front of five thousand people."

He did concede, "I don't think anyone's busting their guts" in exhibitions. "A few years ago didn't Borg and McEnroe or somebody go through Europe and they played ten matches and I don't think Borg won once? Borg has a different mentality playing exhibitions. And also it really hurt the exhibition market in Europe for a while. But I don't think they sit in the locker room and say, 'Okay, John, you're going to win tonight, and, Bjorn, you're going to win another night.' They just don't do that."

I saw no purpose in prolonging the debate. "You have your point of view on this. I'm supposed to meet Marshall the Monday after the tournament. Two o'clock in his office." I said it was fine with me if he came to the interview.

Then I repeated what I had told him in Monte Carlo. Some umpires insisted they couldn't enforce the Code of Conduct because they were under pressure from tournament directors to protect the top players.

"If any Grand Prix tennis umpire's doing that," Buchholz erupted, "I want his ass thrown out."

Despite this vehemence, he didn't believe it was happening. He said low-ranked players always accused top players of getting away with murder, while the stars thought they were held to a standard that wasn't applied to everybody else. Still, if umpires were making accusations, "I'd like to know the tournament director, I'd like to know the tournament, and I'd like to know the umpire. And the umpire who's going around saying that, he has an obligation to tell Marshall Happer. He has an obligation as the umpire of being a fair person to help this sport. And he's also being paid to do a job. And he's being certified by the Grand Prix. If he's doing that—" knuckling under to a tournament director—"he's doing a disservice to his profession, he's doing a disservice to the sport of tennis, and he's doing a disservice to all the players. And he is, he is—" Buchholz groped for a word vile enough to describe such an umpire.

I mentioned that I had heard doubts that an umpire who made accusations against a tournament director would receive the support and protection of tennis authorities.

"You ask Marshall about that?" he said.

I had asked the Administrator, and he agreed with Buchholz. But I had also spoken with Jim McManus, and by the time I finished recounting what he had told me about umpires and tournament directors, Buchholz seemed thunderstruck.

"This . . . this . . . this is mind-boggling. How can an umpire, how in hell can an umpire be out there soliciting players [to enter tournaments]? I mean, that's imposssible."

I assured him I was just relating what I had been told by one of his employees. When I added that McManus claimed umpires were not just recruiting players, but offering wild cards to those who couldn't otherwise qualify, Buchholz insisted, "The only possible thing is that a player might say, 'If *that* umpire's there, I'm not coming there.' "

When I quoted what Arthur Ashe had told me about collusion between umpires and tournament directors and about the fact that some players demanded that certain umpires officiate at their matches, Buchholz admitted, "There are guys who will say, you know, 'I'd rather have Frank Hammond.' Or 'I don't want to have Frank Hammond.' Or 'I'm comfortable with Roy Dance.' Or 'I'm not comfortable with him.' Or 'I like Mike Blanchard.' I mean, that, I'm sure, does happen. But no one is using it to get players, in my opinion, into tournaments. The Supervisor is the one who appoints umpires for the matches." And he swore that even if a player of John McEnroe's caliber expressed a strong preference for a particular official, it wouldn't influence a Supervisor. "What do you think a Supervisor's going to do? He's going to say, 'Too bad!' "

We had reached another impasse and I could do no more than remark that "People who are in the ATP with you or on the Pro Council with you are saying something different to me, apparently, than they're saying to you." Was it possible I was getting caught in the crossfire between opposing camps? I was aware of warring factions within the ATP. Perhaps he wasn't getting accurate reports from his staff. Maybe people jockeying for positions were feeding me information which had been withheld from him.

"I will talk to McManus," he said, then started to muse about the new state of affairs among umpires. "It's a professional breed out there now. Whether that's good or bad for the sport, I don't know. It used to be amateur. Now these guys are pros, and we're getting competitive. I don't know whether it affects the game or not."

"Don't you think it's better if they're professional, autonomous?"

"It's better. But you're going to get situations where Frank Hammond's going to say, 'I want $5,000 to be the referee.' And this guy's going to say, 'I want $6,000.' It's out of control right now. No control!"

"You mean, prohibitively expensive?" I asked.

"It could be expensive. But also, there's no rules to what a guy can ask for. Should we have career umpires? It's a big question." He shook his head. "I don't know."

I wasn't sure I understood the nature of his concern about compensation for umpires. Was he referring to the dubious business deals between tournament directors and umpires?

"Business arrangements in terms of they're going to be paid?" he asked.

"They have other business involvements. I know umpires in Europe are buying cars through tournament directors."

"Umpires . . . buying cars through . . ." He spoke slowly, gravely, weighing each word until his voice died. "I'm not so sure that's bad." Another long pause. "Other than the fact that someone could say, well, he owns that umpire." Voice full of emotion, he declared, "You've got a situation where there's an integrity there, and you cannot in any way, shape, or form have that screwed around with. You can't screw around with it."

As I summarized a hypothetical case in which an umpire might buy an expensive car at a discount of thousands of dollars, Butch Buchholz began nodding his head. "You agree with me, then?" I asked, meaning that this was a dangerous practice.

"Absolutely. It can't be done. That's the problem, Michael. We don't have rules for that right now." Then he said, "Maybe I've had my head in the sand. I just think we have so many other problems in the game, no one's thinking about the officials."

"What's a more important problem?"

"Well, I think the guarantee situation. Is it bad for the game? Good for the game?"

"Don't you think all these things are linked?" I asked. "What I'm told is that the guarantee situation is the locomotive that's dragging along these other problems in its wake. If you give a guy $100,000, which already violates the rules, then some unprincipled people could be tempted to take the next step. If you've got that kind of investment in a guy—"

"The next step, the next investment, is the umpire to protect that player," he finished my sentence for me. "This is just mind-boggling to me. I can't believe it's happening."

He fell silent for a few seconds, then took off on another tangent, telling me what I really ought to examine was what constitutes a guarantee. For minutes on end he unspooled his ideas about the elements that had to exist before a pay-off could be deemed an illegal inducement, and as I sat listening, I realized this amounted to a kind of Inquisition in reverse. Tennis authorities didn't break you down with questions. They did it with lengthy, impenetrable, casuistical explanations. Small wonder so few journalists had chosen to investigate the seamy underside of the sport. When you did, you were confronted with people who deflected your attention from scams involving hundreds of thousands of dollars by demanding that you submit yourself to their semiotics.

The day of the semifinals, I settled in front of the TV in my hotel room. Although it couldn't compare with live action and my surroundings fell short of the intense meridional colors of Monte Carlo or the dense golden light of Rome or the scented spring air in Paris, this view had its advantages. With the camera tightly focused on the Stadium court, I could concentrate on the game, and marveling at Vilas' muscularity or the ballet of Connors' footwork, I could forget for a while everything that was seamy off court, behind the scenes.

Perhaps if I had turned down the volume, I could have continued to enjoy myself. But the CBS team of commentators— Pat Summerall, Tony Trabert, John Newcombe, Brent Mussberger, and John Tesh—kept up a grating chatter. Before the day was over, I would have many occasions to repent that I had ever found fault with BBC's announcers.

"Just look at this tremendous crowd," Summerall chortled, as if he had a percentage of the gate. "And look at this tremendous tennis facility. There are a lot of groceries at stake today."

Indeed there were, said Tony Trabert, whom Summerall calls Trabs and Newcombe calls Tony. "This is the richest tournament in the world."

Summerall asked how much Trabs had made when he won the U.S. Open in '53 and '55.

"Nothing," chirped Trabs. It was an amateur event in those days.

Big Newk said he had received only $500 for expenses when he won the title in 1967. But when he recaptured the crown in 1973, five years after tennis turned professional, he got "about $12,000, I guess."

Trabs corrected Big Newk. In 1973 the first-place prize was $25,000. Now it was $90,000.

In the first set Jimmy Connors blew Guillermo Vilas off the Deco-turf, 6–1. But then Vilas began breaking down Connors' forehand, hitting heavy topspin off his own forehand and slicing his backhand. It was primarily these sliced strokes that suckered mistakes from Jimbo and won the set for Vilas, 6–3.

At the start of the third, as Connors continued to be dogged by unforced errors, Summerall informed viewers that this was the first time since 1968 that the top four seeds had advanced to the semifinals. Big Newk politely interjected that it was the first time since 1969.

John Newcombe is generally the most astute member of the CBS team, but commenting is a sideline for him, just another means of maintaining high visibility and enhancing his multifarious interests, which run the gamut from clothing contracts to syndicated columns to tennis camps on four continents. An attractive Australian and an amiable, indefatigable self-promoter, he has succeeded in marketing his own handsome, mustachioed face so widely that he is known behind his back as Big Cute.

When Summerall remarked that lefthanders had won the U.S. Open for the last eight years, Newcombe coyly said, "Here's a test question for the fans. Who was the last righthanded champion?"

The others more than matched Newcombe's oleaginous charm.

Summerall: "Is he an Australian?"

Trabert: "Does he have facial hair?"

Newcombe, in an unconvincing show of modesty: "Is he ugly?"

Summerall: "It must be Big Newk!"

A moment later Newcombe redeemed himself, pointing out that Connors had changed tactics. He was now hitting to Vilas' forehand, working to the Argentinian's strength. He did so, Newcombe explained, to neutralize Vilas' ability to switch the pace and spin. While off his backhand Guillermo could hit either topspin or slice, he used an exaggerated Western grip on his forehand which prevented him from hitting anything except topspin off that wing. This allowed Jimmy to groove his swing and rip the high-bouncing balls back at Vilas. He quickly killed the next two sets and the match, after which he strutted about, shaking his fists in the air.

In a courtside interview with John Tesh, Connors still fizzed with energy. "I enjoy playing in New York City. The people here are crazy. They enjoy seeing two guys going at each other, spilling blood. That's the kind of guy I am."

And that's the theme that had been established at the U.S. Open. No longer portrayed as the Ancient Mariner, a decrepit thirty-year-old desperate for another title, Jimbo was New York's adopted child, a cocky, street-wise scrapper who asked no quarter and gave none.

By the time Lendl and McEnroe entered the Stadium, the shadow of the enormous scoreboard had cast half the court into gloom. Both men seemed to appreciate the shade; the temperature was in the nineties.

Tall and pale, with hollow cheeks and long canines and incisors, Ivan Lendl looked like he had spent the summer in a root cellar. With his high Irish complexion, McEnroe had a bit more color. His arms were freckled, and as he warmed up, his face became pink as a baby's bottom.

Although McEnroe had captured the U.S. Open title three times in a row and was the top seed, it was foolish to rate him the favorite today. Since July 1981, when the Czech had drubbed him on this same court in a Davis Cup match, he had lost to Lendl five times straight, indoors and out, on hard courts and clay. Lendl had won sixteen of seventeen sets and had dropped his serve only twice in their last three matches.

As he demonstrated in the first set, Lendl had come to dominate McEnroe with stark power, particularly off his forehand. Sometimes he followed through with a wrist snap that sent the ball screaming crosscourt. Other times he took the ball closer to his body and rifled it inside out, stroking deep, acutely angled shots into the ad court. When McEnroe attempted to rush the net, Lendl hit straight at him. Perhaps mindful of the WCT finals in April when the Czech had zapped him four times with pulverizing shots to the body, Mac flinched and his volleys fell short.

Lendl's service was almost as intimidating as his forehand. Putting in fifty-seven first serves, he won forty-seven of those points. Even on his second serve he often forced shallow returns, which he ripped for winners.

Afterward McEnroe whined, "He forces me to do things I don't like to do. I get disorganized"—which was certainly an accurate description of his game today.

There had been stories that he was indeed very disorganized and was running around with rock stars and the *glitterati*, including the crowd at Andy Warhol's *Interview* magazine, which had recently featured him in a cover story. All winter I had listened to umpires and players offer opinions about McEnroe's irascibility and erratic behavior. By the time I reached New York City in August, these theories had spread far beyond the circuit, and I heard essentially the same rumors from theatrical agents and movie people, some of whom claimed to have witnessed McEnroe's unorthodox training habits.

It struck me, though, that there was a more prosaic explanation of his petulance, his rudeness, and his deteriorating performance. Although he had been criticized for his behavior, it had helped carry him to the top of the ATP computer and made him a multimillionaire. McEnroe himself admitted he should have been defaulted at times and that that might have curbed his antics. But why should he change when there was no inducement, no tangible advantage? Why should a man of his wealth be deterred by a few tax-deductible fines of $1,000? Why should he quit interrupting matches and screaming at umpires when he had defenders who viewed this as a shot of adrenaline to pep up the game and give it mass appeal?

Predictably, considering the shortsightedness of tennis people, no one seems to have expected McEnroe's conduct to affect his game. But it had, and, like a tinhorn potentate, he now wanted to impose his will on everyone. Not content to play his opponent, he insisted on calling the lines, lecturing umpires, chastising spectators, vilifying journalists, and choreographing courtside cameramen and photographers. So convinced was he of his own righteousness, he no longer even bothered swinging at balls which he believed were out.

Early in the first set against Lendl he started carping about bad calls and, during one change-over, walked past the umpire holding his nose. Then when Lendl broke him and was serving for the set at 5–4, McEnroe exploded, insisting a shot from the Czech was long. The video replay showed the ball well inside the line, but there was no doubt in McEnroe's mind that he had been victimized.

"Do something right!" he hollered at the umpire. When the man shook his head, Mac screamed, "What does that mean? You didn't see it?"

After he lost the set 6–4, he once again let a ball land close to the line, not deigning to hit it. When the linesman signaled that it was good, McEnroe cried out and crumbled to the court, kicking his feet.

Losing in straight sets 6–4/6–4/7–6, he seemed as much a victim of his own mouth and megalomania as of Ivan Lendl's terrifying power.

Afterward Lendl clapped a WCT cap on his head and marched over for an interview with John Tesh. This was comparable to a New York Yankee wearing a Los Angeles Dodgers cap at a press conference. Perhaps it was an example of Slavic wit. Then again, it might have been part of a promotional contract, just like the Ben Gay and Orange Crush labels on his shirtsleeves.

Late the next afternoon I stationed myself in front of the television for the season's finale, which, when I had set out on the circuit last February, had figured to pit McEnroe against Borg for the top spot in the world. Now neither man was in the running. Regardless of who captured the U.S. Open, Connors would be No. 1 according to the arcane calculations of the ATP computer and No. 1 in the hearts of the fans. As at Wimbledon, he had become by default the sentimental favorite. As *Sports Illustrated* observed, "Ain't it funny how slime slips away?"

By 4:17 p.m., when the NFL football games ended and the TV signal could be switched to Flushing Meadows, it was 100° F. on court. Ivan Lendl started off hotter than the Deco-turf, breaking Connors in the first game of the first set. But then Jimbo broke right back and it was clear that Lendl wouldn't have an easy match today. His serve streaked back at him faster than he had hit it, and the more pace he put on his forehand, the less time he had to set up for the next stroke. Far from being afraid to hit to the Czech's flamethrower of a forehand, Connors had built his strategy around attacking Lendl's strength, shattering his confidence.

Aware that whenever he missed a first serve Connors would jump on the second, Lendl began pressing and put in only forty-two percent of his first serves. Impatient, he rushed his strokes and tried to out-muscle Connors. He might have been wiser to take the net before Jimmy did, but he came in just a dozen times in four sets.

Although the scores of the first two sets were one-sided— 6–3/6–2 for Connors—it was a gripping match, a bare-knuckled brawl pitting power against raw power. Yet CBS managed to squander some of the drama and most of the continuity by swinging the camera away from the court, searching the stands for celebrities. Then, after filling every long break in the action with paid commercials, it crammed the shorter breaks with shameless self-promotion.

Four times the camera panned Mike Wallace's craggy mug, and the viewer was advised that Wallace was preparing a profile of Martina Navratilova for his show "60 Minutes." William S. Paley, Chairman of CBS, repeatedly loomed onto the screen. As the day wore on, the entire corporate chain of command passed in review, link by link, while the announcers provided cute captions as if for photos in a trade journal.

When Lendl rebounded from a service break and won the third set, Pat Summerall greased the path for his partner by asking, "Who's the last man to win the U.S. Open title twice without dropping a set?"

Trabert: "Is he ugly?"

Summerall: "Is he sitting next to me?"

Newcombe: "Does he have the same early-home-at-night habits as me?"

Summerall: "It's Trabs!"

After trading early service breaks in the fourth set, Connors appeared tired, depleted, and one wondered whether he had burned out in the first two incandescent sets, just as he had at Wimbledon in 1981, when Bjorn Borg rallied to beat him. All afternoon it seemed Jimbo had played right up to the ragged edge of his ability. Now, while he had nowhere to go but down, Lendl had room to raise the level of his game.

At 15–30 on his serve Lendl walloped an ace, his fourteenth of the day. The next point, a long baseline rally, looked sure to exhaust Connors, but abruptly he attacked Lendl's backhand and stabbed a volley into the open court. 30–40. Then he dashed in again behind a blistering approach shot and blocked Lendl's backhand pass for a winner and a service break.

For four games he cleverly protected that advantage with a mixture of cautious shot-making and histrionic aggression. When Lendl smashed an overhead too close to him, Connors waggled his finger in warning, stood at the net, and chewed out the Czech, who backed off. Then as Jimbo held service to 5–3, he stomped and strutted, thrusting out his pelvis like El Cordobés challenging a bull with his manhood. He stiffened his index finger, jabbing at the air and screaming, "One more, one more!" Serving at 5–4, he launched into his fancy strut again, keeping score with his fingers, shouting ferociously, rushing the net twice in a row to capture his fourth U.S. Open title.

I went to Marshall Happer's office half-expecting to find Butch Buchholz waiting for me "to have Marshall Happer sit *right* there and say that in front of me." But Buchholz never showed up.

"Have you had any results in the Stuttgart investigation?" I asked.

"I found them guilty and fined them $20,000," Happer said. Now the tournament had a right to appeal. It was up to the Pro Council to affirm or reverse Happer's verdict. There was no mention of fines or suspensions for any players accepting the appearance money Stuttgart had presumably given. Borg and Lendl had played last year's final for a purse of $15,000.

"Have you had an opportunity to talk to Mr. McEnroe about that Topspin contract?"

"No, I haven't," he said. "I've got your note on it and I've got a huge file of bits and pieces of that kind of stuff. I just haven't dealt with it yet."

Responding to Happer's challenge to be specific, I had described the history of the Topspin contract more than three and a half months ago.

"How about those wagers?" I asked. "Have you had a chance to speak to Tiriac or Lendl?"

"I got that in the . . . you know, on the list. I don't know what I'm going to do with it."

I told him Butch Buchholz had expressed the opinion that these wagers probably weren't serious incidents. Did Happer share that opinion?

"Well, as I recall, you were talking about a minor amount of money."

"No, there was no specification about the amount."

"There was something, you know, that was $100."

"That was Fibak in Strasbourg," I reminded him.

"I can't remember the amounts involved. You know, I guess the worst thing about gambling is that you start defrauding the public and somebody starts fixing matches. You know, that sort of thing."

It seemed to me he guessed right; that was the worst thing about gambling—defrauding the public and fixing matches. But it was difficult to see how tennis authorities could ever find out whether such things were going on, since they showed no interest in looking into admitted incidents of wagering.

"I assume what you're talking about," Happer said, "was included in the French article you sent me—which I just haven't got to."

What about Buster Mottram's article in *News of the World*, the one that accused members of the Pro Council of violating the rule against appearance money and charged that umpires were in the pocket of tournament directors?

"I haven't seen that." In short, he hadn't bothered to look it up, or to speak to Mottram about it, in the two and a half months since Wimbledon.

From what I gathered from our conversation in Paris, "The feeling of the Council is that [exhibition] matches do not fall under the Code of Conduct."

"No, they don't," Happer said.

"Therefore, anything that went on in those matches would not be subject to your penalties, including conduct detrimental to the game."

"Well, if they commit a criminal offense, that's another matter. But . . . uh, there's not really anything we can do about a private promotion."

I reminded him that I first spoke to him about exhibition matches after I had heard that McEnroe and Borg had split sets in a special event. I now understood this was a common occurrence.

"An exhibition is an exhibition," he said. "I mean, it's not a competitive match. You know, what's bad is that the people who buy the tickets to them don't understand that."

"Ron Bookman said knowledgeable people know this."

For the first time a smile touched his thin lips, but not his bloodhound's eyes. "He means *very* knowledgeable people. But if the Junior League somewhere brings in two [players] and has a promotion, they think they're playing for real."

I pointed out that exhibition matches were frequently identified as "Challenges" or "Shoot-outs" and the advertising contained no parenthetical disclaimers that these events were just for entertainment. "Doesn't this pose a potential problem?" I asked.

"That's why we don't like exhibitions."

"As a lawyer, have you expressed your opinion to the ATP?"

"Well, there's not anything I . . . It's not a matter of expressing an opinion. I mean . . . ATP doesn't like them either. Nobody does except . . . There are a couple of good things about exhibitions," Happer started over. "One is—and probably the most important is—that in cities or countries that cannot afford tournaments, this is an opportunity for them to see a top player. But to market those as serious tennis is a bit fraudulent."

"Are you concerned that the Federal Communication Commission or the Justice Department might go after these exhibition matches the way they did those bogus winner-take-all matches?"

"I don't know what they're really saying out there," he claimed.

"Are they saying they're playing for prize money?"

"In some cases there seems to be prize money," I said. "So I guess it would depend on how the Justice Department or the FCC interpreted these exhibition matches—whether there was full disclosure of the nature of the competition."

Happer's drawl remained slow and unemphatic. But after just citing a hypothetical instance of the Junior League promoting an exhibition and being deceived into thinking it was an honest competition, the Administrator reversed fields. "Well, you know, I'm not so sure people come out expecting to see serious tennis. I think it's an opportunity for them to see [players] and, ah, oftentimes it's a social event."

"For the players or for the fans?"

"The fans. The Junior League somewhere will build a social function around an exhibition."

I explained that I had heard about McEnroe and Borg allegedly splitting sets from an umpire who, although upset and disgusted, had not objected to the tournament director. When I asked the man what he would have done if he discovered set-splitting in a Grand Prix event, he admitted he still wouldn't have told the tournament director.

"That's terrible," Happer drawled. "Get rid of him." But he didn't ask the umpire's name or anything else. As with prize-money splitting, there seemed to be an automatic assumption that set-splitting just couldn't happen on the Grand Prix. I never understood this boundless faith that players might be delinquent in WCT or special events, but never in Grand Prix tournaments.

I pointed out that when I had first raised questions about the influence of tournament directors over umpires, Happer had contended that Supervisors kept everybody honest. Yet, since then I had spoken to Jim McManus, who maintained some umpires were now recruiting players for Grand Prix events. "Had you heard about this?" I asked.

This news had left Butch Buchholz dumbstruck, but the Administrator was neither surprised nor perturbed.

"Well," Happer dragged the word out, "there are obviously some referee types, you know, who recruit players. But the bottom-line decision on a default or this sort of thing is [with] the Supervisor, who is employed by us. So we watch that some. This is not to say that there's not a chair umpire who is afraid to rock the boat by enforcing the Code of Conduct because he's afraid the tournament director won't have him back. However, the chair umpire has got a real problem, because if he does that, the Supervisor gives him a zero on his evaluation. If we give him a zero, he's *done*. He's not going to be recertified."

McManus had also maintained that umpires were giving players wild cards.

"There's nothing wrong with that," Happer said. "That's what wild cards are for."

"But isn't it up to a tournament director to give somebody a wild card, not an umpire, not a referee?"

Suddenly he sounded less sure of himself. "I mean, I don't understand."

I explained how a player who entered a tournament via a wild card provided by an umpire might assume he had an advantage with that umpire. "Wouldn't you?" I asked the Administrator.

"The *umpires* are not recruiting players," he insisted. "The *tournaments* are recruiting players."

"Okay, let's say it's the tournament that's recruiting players, but the man who's talking to the players is, in fact, an umpire or a referee."

"Well, then, you know, he's got a problem. But the Supervisor ought to overrule that. There's not anything the umpire who's recruiting players can do with the Supervisor there. He can't fix the draw. There's gotta be an honest draw because the Supervisor's sitting there."

"And if he winds up in the chair in one of these matches—"

"The Supervisor, first of all," Happer said, "is going to decide whether he gets in that chair or not. And if a guy gets up there and is dishonest, he gets him out of there. That's the Supervisor's job. That's one of the vital importances of having a Supervisor there."

When I repeated what Arthur Ashe, Happer's colleague on the Pro Council, had told me about top players being protected, about collusion between umpires and tournament directors, and about players who demanded that certain umpires always officiate at their matches, the Administrator said, "I don't think that's an accurate statement."

"By Arthur?"

"Yeah. I think that, first of all, the top players are not protected from the Code of Conduct. . . . You can't say that we're not picking on the top guys. Who can say we haven't gone after McEnroe? Who can say we haven't gone after Connors? Who can say we haven't gone after Gerulaitis? He paid $20,000 in fines in the last year."

"One thing troubles me," I told the sleepy-looking, sleepy-sounding Administrator. "When I talked to Butch Buchholz about various matters that we've discussed today, he seemed to take a much different line not only than the Pro Council takes, but even people on his own staff take. We discussed this question about exhibitions and Butch said, 'No player would ever agree to split sets. I just don't believe that.' " Was there a communication breakdown? After all, Butch was on the Pro Council, and one would assume these issues had been discussed at meetings.

"I don't know." Happer began to hedge. "I mean, you know, I can only suspect what happens" [in exhibitions].

"Well, you're obviously conversant enough with these matters that you knew about that Stan Smith-Arthur Ashe thing."

"I knew that because I was sitting in the damn chair."

"But it sure didn't surprise you when I said about this Borg-McEnroe set-splitting."

"It doesn't surprise me at all," Happer admitted. "I guess the long and short of it is it doesn't make any difference who wins or loses. It doesn't count and it probably doesn't affect either one of them's earnings. They're playing for a fee or a percentage of the gross or something."

I told the Pro Council Administrator, "I talked to Butch way back in March about exhibition matches and he just said, 'No way. This is not happening.' So I went to him the other day and I said, 'Everybody, including Ron Bookman, McManus, Ashe, Happer, so forth, they tell me these things are going on.' He said, 'Well, I just don't believe that.' So I said, 'Come to the meeting on—' "

"Now, Mike, now, Mike, now," Happer interrupted, "you know, stay with the facts. I don't tell you things are going on. I tell you I'm not surprised when you tell me. You know, I told *you* about one."

"Right, and I confirmed it with Arthur and Stan."

"I mean, don't . . . don't go out and write that I said McEnroe and Borg split sets, because I don't know that. I don't even know what the scores are in those exhibitions. I don't even see them. But I am certainly not surprised at any of this. But it would be a mistake to quote me and say Marshall Happer says that they are all doing this in every one of them, because it may not be. For instance, Connors played Borg in this Michelob Light thing."

"This summer after Wimbledon?" I asked.

"Yeah. Which, incidentally, I never heard anybody announce any prize money. Which would have been honest not to, because they were all being paid to play. But those two guys were playing on national television . . . and, uh, I thought they were almost playing a hundred percent."

Contrary to what the Administrator said, Borg and Connors were playing for prize money—$50,000 to the winner, $25,000 to the loser. At least, that was what was advertised.

"I say *almost* a hundred percent," Happer went on, "because there was some kidding around that is *not* Borg."

"Well, I'm glad we had this opportunity to talk," I said and reminded him that when I had spoken to him in Paris about special events, "Your comment was, 'Oh, hell, that's an exhibition match' and, you know, you just said, 'I think all those things are fixed or rigged or arranged one way or the other.' "

"I would not be surprised," Happer conceded, but then emphasized, "I just want to make it clear I don't follow the exhibition circuit. It's all I can do to follow the tournament circuit."

I strolled from Marshall Happer's office down Park Avenue to the law offices of Paul, Weiss, Rifkind, Wharton, and Garrison, where John McEnroe, Sr., is a partner.

In the lobby a conscientious receptionist registered my name in a log book. Then Mr. McEnroe's secretary overwhelmed me with her friendliness and surprised me by saying, "You once worked here, didn't you?"

She continued smiling as I said, "No, I didn't."

Mr. McEnroe, in a great display of busy-ness, was straightening and stacking a sheaf of papers on his desk. All around the office, other piles of legal briefs, letters, books, and magazines awaited his attention. Behind him, atop a cabinet, lay dozens of copies of his son's biography, A *Rage for Perfection*, and of Andy Warhol's *Interview* magazine with John's picture on the cover. There were photographs of John, some nearly life-size, mounted on cardboard, but not framed or hung. They leaned against the wall and gave one corner of the room the look of a gallery the day after a big show has closed.

I remarked that the U.S. Open must have been a hectic time for the McEnroe family.

"Yeah, it's always busy. Everybody wants a little bit of your time."

I promised him I would take as little of his time as possible.

"Turrr-riffic!" he exclaimed with a brusqueness that made me fear I would soon be back on the street.

But I was mistaken. Despite his protests that he didn't have time to talk, John McEnroe, Sr., was like a self-cleaning oven. Once you flipped the switch, he shimmered with kinetic energy, generating all his own heat and steam until he had exhausted a subject. An hour later, when the cassette on my tape recorder ran out, he was still talking.

Heavy-set and solid, he nevertheless seemed to have the metabolism of a jockey. He jawed on a stick of chewing gum; he fiddled with a pair of nail clippers; he put his feet up on his desk; he swung them down; he scratched his face; he gestured with his hands, his left fist gleaming with a fat gold watch and a ring as big as a walnut; he propped his feet on a telephone stand and pulled up his knee-length socks. After Marshall Happer's lethargic, poker-faced response to every question, Mr. McEnroe was as lively as a leprechaun. But a hard-bitten leprechaun who spoke with a New York accent full of grit and vinegar instead of blarney.

I told him Arthur Ashe said he was the only man in tennis not caught up in conflict of interest. Did he perceive conflict of interest as a potential problem for the sport?

"It's not a potential problem!" he blurted. "It's a real problem." Describing the elaborate procedures his law firm took to avoid the mere suggestion of conflicts, he chuckled. "That's not the way it is in tennis. There are a number of people out there who represent players, who run tournaments, who obtain sponsors, who guide the direction of the tour, who get involved in the media side, who sell space at the tournaments, and, at the same time, are taking pieces of the players' pie. It's far from a potential problem. It's a very real problem."

Mr. McEnroe went on to add, "What has happened is these agencies have evolved into organizations that not only represent players, but, in fact, run tournaments and end up putting their players into their tournaments."

I summarized Buster Mottram's published complaint that when agents served as tournament directors, umpires were doubly reluctant to enforce the Code of Conduct. Then I told him of umpires who admitted to me they would never default a top player for fear they would lose their jobs.

He said he had never given the matter much thought, but didn't feel that officials responded unethically to such pressures. He did volunteer, however, that a sticky dilemma existed in "eight-man round-robins or things like that, special-type events, which are essentially sold for television syndication purposes. If you default a player in the middle of that, you know, it's a very serious problem. Or a match where it's being televised live at the moment, and again you have a situation where there's a problem, where you default a player and there's not another match to follow or there's not something else scheduled. You're left with, what? An hour or two hours of television time with nothing to do. Those are all very difficult circumstances. There's no way to deal with them."

But, for him, these were theoretical dilemmas since "I happen to think the Code of Conduct is generally being enforced. The fact of the matter is, my objection, if anything, is that the Code of Conduct is being selectively enforced against certain players who perhaps have a reputation . . . and an official goes out determined to show that he's not going to take any nonsense, or to make his mark by showing that he's going to be a tough guy. I think there's more problems with that."

From my observation, Mr. McEnroe stood alone in his opinion that umpires trying to act tough posed greater problems than did timid or compromised officials. But he was an energetic advocate of his position. Why, he demanded, were umpires never disciplined for their errors? Why were they allowed to exercise such arbitrary power? Why did they crack down on John when he yelled or vented his anger at himself? Why was John criticized when he was right and officials were wrong?

"People always talk about the player problem thing," he rambled. "They never talk about the other side of the coin and what causes those kind of things that creates the questioning in the players' minds, that makes them lose confidence in a given official or perhaps in officials as a group, if enough of these things happen. I mean, I'm all in favor of there being a Code of Conduct and it being properly enforced, in a reasonable, fair, and even-handed manner. No one can argue about that. There's no room for vulgarity or obscenity on a tennis court any more than there is any other place.

"At the same time—" he brushed aside my attempts to interject questions—"the idea that a player is expected to be a completely silent automaton on the court is a joke. These are athletes! These are not some kind of breed apart. The temperament and the drive and the things that spur [John] are all the same kinds of things that spur other athletes.

"While I admire greatly Bjorn Borg's talent and his temperament, I find his temperament more aberrational than John's. I don't understand how someone can do what he does in the pressure cauldron that these guys are in all the time and be as apparently phlegmatic about it."

He reiterated he had no objections to the Code of Conduct as long as it applied equally to everybody. But there were plenty of explosive, short-tempered players "that nobody ever hears about, or hardly ever hears about, because they're off on the back courts." And such hotheads got away with murder, he said, as did men who unleashed their tirades in foreign languages. "Guys say the most vile things, and everybody laughs. They think it's funny. Nastase can say whatever it is in Rumanian and people think it's funny. And, in fact, he's probably saying some of the most terrible things."

"But you mentioned eight-man exhibition matches." I tried to wrench the discussion back onto the track that interested me.

Well, that was just one example, he cut in before I could complete my question. "I'm thinking of some of the WCT events where they sell, you know, the events on television. They have a package and they program them and they syndicate them themselves. I mean, it's very difficult for them to syndicate an eight-man-event package and have one of them become a thirty-two-minute default."

This time I broke in. "WCT matches aside, in the case of special events or exhibition matches, the Code of Conduct doesn't apply to those at all, does it?"

"No, no, no, of course not." He darted out of the chutes again, explaining, defining, delivering peremptory opinions. "There's nothing magic about the Code of Conduct. It's just something conjured up by the Pro Council."

I said I had heard and read that a lot of exhibitions were "orchestrated or arranged to fit a TV slot or to give the viewer maximum enjoyment."

"I don't know that to be so," he declared, "although I've read about it and heard about it. There's no question that you cannot make in the player's mind an exhibition event in Birdrock, Minnesota, equivalent to the finals of the U.S. Open. . . . You can't get an athlete to bring to bear all those intangibles that he brings to bear in a situation where there's a true championship or something like that at stake. And I'm not suggesting for one minute that the players aren't trying. But something in here—" his fist flashed with gold as he tapped his heart—"is why a McEnroe or a Lendl or a Connors or a Borg or whomever are consistently the ones who are coming through in the major events and winning because they have that little something that they can switch on."

"In an interview with Yannick Noah, I read where he said many of these exhibitions matches involved splitting two sets, then playing an honest third. That doesn't involve an intangible. That involves orchestration or arrangement."

"I don't know of any such occasion," McEnroe asserted. "But I'm willing to believe that if Yannick Noah tells you he's done it, he's done it. I don't know of any such agreements. I'm not suggesting they never happen, because maybe they do. But, clearly, those are the kind of events, those are the kind of events," he floundered, "where if it happens, it happens. That's not happening in a serious forum."

I told him an umpire claimed that John and Bjorn Borg had split sets in an exhibition match. I had since had many people assure me this scenario was common. "But I wanted to run that by you," I said to Mr. McEnroe.

"I know of no such, uh, I'm not saying, as I said before, it never happened. I know of no such . . ." He searched for the word to describe what he hadn't known. Leaning back in the chair, he slipped a hand under the beltless waistband of his trousers, reached down to his crotch, and rearranged himself. Perhaps he had learned this move from Jimmy Connors. "And, uh, I'd be inclined to think that that's probably not too likely in John's case. But, uh, but I'm not trying, again, I'm not trying, I'm not commenting on that with respect to John. I just don't, I don't know that that's so. I would doubt it. Although I don't want to sound naïve. I realize that there are times when that may make a certain amount of sense."

"Why?"

"If they were doing it from an entertainment-value viewpoint, that may make sense at times," he repeated. "I mean, it's something that's labeled an exhibition and is nothing more than exhibition. Uh, that may be, uh, not terrible."

There was no chance to correct him—like many special events, the match in question wasn't labeled an exhibition—for Mr. McEnroe had rushed on with his disclaimer. "As I said, I do not know of it and, uh, in any of the events with which I am associated, which are very few—which are none." He laughed. "I'm not associated with any of them." Yet with respect to all those events with which he wasn't associated, he asserted, "It doesn't go on. It wouldn't go on."

"Would that trouble you legally? I mean, if these matches were broadcast, for example, or televised, [and] if something like that was going on?"

After all his voluble pronunciamentos, Mr. McEnroe subsided into silence. Although he claimed not to be associated with any exhibitions, I assumed that he negotiated the contracts for ones that John played. But he said, "I've never given it a moment's thought, to be perfectly honest with you. I've never given it a moment's thought."

When the discussion turned to guarantees, he wasn't sure he understood the rule, and on both our parts there ensued the customary grunting and heaving, pulling and shoving, as if we were shifting tons of debris in order to uncover a tiny ceramic doll of no great value. After Mr. McEnroe explained at length why he felt it was proper for him to arrange contracts, public appearances, and clinics that corresponded with Grand Prix tournaments, I pointed out that, according to the Pro Council, the crucial question was whether the negotiations and contracts were consummated before a player asked to be designated to a tournament.

"But isn't that absurd!" he burst out. "What they say is if his appearance or failure to agree to appear is conditioned upon getting such an arrangement, then, in their view, it's probably a violation of the rule. But why should it be improper? In this case I feel sorry for the agencies because they have obligations to their players to do the most they can for them. What if IMG has one of its stable of players and they say, 'Look, if you go here and play, I can put this together for you. But if you don't and you go over *here* and play, I can put *this* together for you.' And one package is a much more attractive financial package than the other. Why does Frank Sinatra book New York as opposed to Podunk State Teachers College? Because he, presumably, gets more money here and has a greater potential to make money here. And so I think that these rules are crazy. There are people out there who are concerned, and I think they use this almost *reductio ad absurdum* argument. 'Well, if this was allowed to happen, the public would view professional tennis the way they view professional wrestling.' I mean, you know, that's just utter, complete, pure nonsense."

He objected to the injustice of the rule for the top players. "Without putting names on it—I don't know who they are—but player No. 76 on the computer, whoever that may be, I have no idea who it is, he has no opportunity to do something like this. He doesn't have a commercial value." But, by implication, such players and the Pro Council were attempting to restrict stars like John McEnroe from capitalizing on their celebrity.

"Isn't that unfair to a player," demanded Mr. McEnroe, "when a tournament knows that if they have one of the very, very top players that instead of selling $300,000 worth of tickets they'll sell $450,000 worth of tickets? I mean, John announced to go to the Atlanta tournament two years ago and it was all a very-last-minute thing. It was a front-page story in the newspaper and the overnight sales went through the roof. My point is that just the fact that he was announced for the tournament, the gate and the advance sales skyrocketed. Now, why is not a player who has that kind of clout, why should he not be able to participate in some way? Why is someone not allowed to say to him, 'Well, you know, if you come here, just for, *just* for your coming here, we'd be willing to give you X dollars,' because they know he's going to generate that much more money for them? And I don't understand why that's not acceptable. Now, the reason you've given is that people would start to suspect the tournaments or the results, and they would also suspect whether or not a player was putting forth his best effort. I mean, I just find that a specious argument because, in my judgment, the player *has* to continue to do well, has to continue to be a major factor, because as soon as he stops, he's no longer going to be in the category of those guys I'm willing to pay for."

"Isn't there another possibility?" I asked. Once promoters paid vast sums to guarantee a player's appearance, they might take steps to protect their investment and ensure that the star made it to the later rounds.

"Again, that's nothing I've ever heard," he insisted. The rules were clear on how a draw should be conducted, and they were supervised and open to the public. "So I don't understand how that can happen."

I laid out for him what I had learned both from my own observation and from reliable sources about the dubious relationships between umps and tournament directors, especially their side deals, such as discount car purchases. Then I quoted Arthur Ashe about collusion to protect the top players.

"I guess maybe I'm very naïve," Mr. McEnroe said. "That thought would no more cross my mind that somebody would do that. My assumption is they would follow the rules and have a draw set up."

"You're still talking about a draw," I said. "In this case I'm talking about the umpires in the chair. I'm talking about the guy who—"

"You mean, he's going to call the close ones for the guy who's being protected as opposed to the other guy, or something like that?"

"That's what I'm told."

"Lemme tell you—" he laughed—"lemme tell you, I ain't seen that anyplace, and I can also tell you that John sure hasn't." He burst into laughter again.

"Well, it seems to me this is a thing that is so subjective that—"

Once more Mr. McEnroe plowed on. "I've seen John go through one of his routines as frequently in the first round when he's up five-love, forty-love, as in a semifinal when he's in the teeth of a tough, tough match. If John felt or knew, or any other top players felt or knew, that in a crunch situation, in an early round, they were going to get the benefit of the doubt, there'd be absolutely no reason to go through those kind of situations. So that's all brand new to me. Arthur, first of all, Arthur says things a lot of times that aren't necessarily correct, even though Arthur has a marvelous, marvelous image, and he deserves it. But, that being so, he's still not right all the time."

"Granted," I said, then sat back and let him talk.

"He [Ashe] and I have very serious disagreements about the circuit and the rules. Right now we just put in, we, the top players, in this very recent discussion—I hesitate to call it a 'confrontation'—*discussion* we had with the Grand Prix Council over the rules for 1983, [we] just put forward a proposal that every draw should be composed of only forty-eight players, but on a sixty-four draw basis, with the top sixteen seeds drawing byes."

In effect, the stars demanded to start every tournament a step ahead of the other players. With one win they would vault to the third round, earning more money and more ATP points for less work. They would also get an extra day for travel, for rest, and to acclimate themselves to a time change, a new surface, or different balls. In short, they had proposed to institutionalize the preferential treatment which they were now often getting illegally. Mr. McEnroe insisted this was better for tournaments.

The other players and the Pro Council, Arthur Ashe foremost among them, objected to this proposal.

"I think Arthur believes most of what he says," Mr. McEnroe allowed. "I just think he's not right all the time. He's not God, you know. None of us are susceptible to never making mistakes. I'm sure that he disagrees with me on my position about so-called guarantees or appearance money."

"I know that he absolutely, unequivocally thinks that there should not be these guarantees," I said.

"And there aren't!" Mr. McEnroe proclaimed. "There is a Grand Prix rule against them and we abide by that rule, in spite of the fact that I think the rule is outrageous and improper."

When I inquired about the Topspin contract with Lipton Tea, Italy, Mr. McEnroe claimed it was in no way related to John's commitment to play the Italian Open—a commitment which his twisted ankle had prevented him from fulfilling. He insisted it was a contract which ran for two or three years and was not connected with any tournament.

Point by point, I described the pattern of events—Cino Marchese's mention of "negotiations" as early as January of 1982, the announcement in Milan in March that John would endorse Topspin and would play the Italian Open, and, finally, the fact that apparently Mr. McEnroe hadn't asked that John be designated to the tournament until sometime in April.

"I don't remember when he was designated," said Mr. McEnroe. As for Cino's remarks to me and his comments quoted to the press, as for the announcement in March and John's designation in April, he maintained, "You're telling me things about which I have absolutely no knowledge—I mean, how they did it or why or what Cino Marchese said. There was no relationship whatsoever to me between those things."

Weary though I was with this hair-splitting about what constitutes a guarantee, I wanted to make certain I had the complete picture of McEnroe's contract with Topspin. Or, at least, as complete a picture as any outsider could obtain. Thus, when I returned to Rome, I called Palita, S.P.A., the Italian branch of Lipton Tea, and I spoke to Maurizio Giurleo.

According to Mr. Giurleo, the Topspin endorsement had another year to run and John's appearance, or failure to appear, at the Italian Open was "no constraint" upon the contract. By this, he explained, he meant the contract couldn't be revoked because McEnroe didn't play in Rome. But, he added, there was a bonus clause which provided more money if he played the Italian Open. How much more, Giurleo wouldn't say.

Of far greater significance, Mr. Giurleo acknowledged that Cino Marchese had "initiated" and "negotiated the general terms" of the Topspin contract. Afterward Mr. Giurleo and Mr. McEnroe, Sr., had had only to hammer out a few details.

I asked whether Cino Marchese was an employee of Palita or of Lipton Tea. Mr. Giurleo replied, "Absolutely not. He's a promoter." That is, he and his colleagues controlled the promotional rights to the Italian Open. In short, an endorsement contract between a player and a private corporation had been initiated and negotiated by a third party who had a financial interest in a tournament which the player would receive a bonus for playing.

All this information was available for the asking. Where, I wondered, was the difficulty in determining whether the rule against direct or indirect inducements had been violated?

Implicitly, Mr. McEnroe provided an answer to the question that had puzzled me for months. While insisting that he saw no connection between the Topspin contract and the Italian Open, he didn't understand what would be improper even if there were a connection. "If a guy is rendering value for value, it should not be a violation of anything. And it's been suggested to me that that's the same position taken by the powers-that-be, if you will, even if that's not quite what the written rule suggests."

Although delivered with no special emphasis, this observation of Mr. McEnroe's seemed a perfect paradigm of the way "the powers-that-be" operate in tennis. Although the Code of Conduct may appear to be as clear-cut and straightforward as the lines on a tennis court, its enforcement is as arabesque as the designs on a Persian carpet.

Mr. McEnroe proceeded to tell me John had signed for the 1983 Grand Prix season, which required that he commit himself to twelve tournaments instead of ten. However, he added, some "players did say they wanted some rules revised. . . . I know that the group of players who signed with that *caveat* includes John, Borg, Connors, Lendl, Vilas, Gerulaitis, Clerc, Fibak. I don't know if I left anybody out," Mr. McEnroe mused. "It's essentially the top seven guys in the world, plus Fibak. We do anticipate serious discussions. All of the players had a statement that said, in essence, we reserve the right, after we see what progress has been made, to withdraw our commitment."

"When you say 'all the players,' you mean—"

"All the players I've just mentioned. Not *all* the other players. My suspicion is the great bulk of them did nothing. I mean, did nothing except sign. The rules aren't aimed at anybody but the top five to ten players anyway. In spite of all the talk and all the B.S. that goes on, the rules don't really obtain to anyone except the very top players. That's the only reason the Council goes about devising rules."

"They don't apply to anybody else," I said, "because the other people don't have the options or alternatives that the top players have."

Mr. McEnroe was blunter about it. "The other players essentially have no choice. The other players have to go where— Listen, I don't know, I don't want to analogize exclusively to show business, but it's *like* show business. I mean, the Beatles or the Rolling Stones or the Frank Sinatras of this world, they go and put on a show at Vegas, and they have five opening acts, or whatever the number is, and they have a supporting orchestra and they have stagehands and they have this and that. So that one guy or that one group or those few groups end up supporting hundreds and thousands—I mean, in show business it's thousands, probably—of people because they provide a forum where their services are required. The top ten players in the world provide that forum to the other two hundred players who are out there on the circuit. I mean, I'm not suggesting that they would have *nothing* to do. But I'm suggesting that without that *cadre*—" he pronounced it "cod-ray"—"of people at the top there would be a lot fewer opportunities for the other more journeyman-type players."

"No one likes [it]," he assured me, "when John loses in the first round. There are plenty of guys out there that on a given day can beat a John McEnroe or a Jimmy Connors in the first round. But nobody's happy with that. Except the guy who beat him." Mr. McEnroe chuckled. "I don't mean to suggest he should be forgotten. But I'm just saying it's not necessary to give him that opportunity every tournament, every single night."

To the contrary, I had always operated on the assumption that in tennis the point, and the appeal, of the game *was* to give a qualified challenger a fair shot at the top players at every tournament every night. But Mr. McEnroe was pursuing his own vision of the sport/business. "We're not suggesting the Grand Slam events should be revised or something like that. We're talking about the so-called regular Super Series events [on the Grand Prix]. And it's better for everyone, it's better for the game even, if these guys more or less achieve what they're supposed to.

"The occasional upset's fine, and the occasional youngster who comes out of nowhere. I mean, look at John. John came out of nowhere in '77 and all of a sudden he was a hotshot. Look at Wilander! There's always going to be that kind of thing. And that's great. That adds interest to the game as well. But, nonetheless, it's that select group that really provides the great bulk of things.

"And they're the ones who the Council, by their rules, are trying to control and make it hard for. I think these rules are outrageous and bordering on the illegal. If they are legal, it's only marginally so. But they clearly are not moral in the sense that they're not right, they're not just, they're not fair."

For months I had listened to men fret about improving the game's image, not its substance, about marketing a player's name and his personality, not necessarily his performance. And I had watched players who were judged to lack commercial appeal shunted onto bad courts, into second-class locker rooms, and far into the background where no one, frequently not even tennis officials, cared about them. Now I was told that it was the rules of the game, not their violation, which were outrageous and bordering on the illegal. It was the implementation of those rules, feeble and feckless as it was, which Mr. McEnroe viewed as wrong, unjust, and unfair. Under the circumstances, I felt I had not only come the full sickening circle, I had short-circuited.

• • •

Reluctant to end my research on this note, I arranged to speak with Arthur Ashe again. We met in his offices on Madison Avenue—INTERNATIONAL COMMERCIAL RESOURCES, read the sign on the door—and sat in a large conference room on either side of a long table that was bare except for a telephone console. In one corner of the room several boxes lay scattered on the maroon carpet. The boxes contained women's shoes. In the opposite corner there were three more boxes, these marked MADE IN BRAZIL.

Although pressed for time—Ashe had to leave soon for the Davis Cup semifinals in Australia—he looked sleek and relaxed in photosensitive glasses, a pale green shirt and tie, and polished loafers. Only his linen trousers seemed out of keeping with his fastidious appearance. The trousers were so badly wrinkled, one of Ashe's employees joked that he looked like he had got caught in the rain.

I went straight to the heart of the matters that most troubled me. To his knowledge, had prize-money splitting ever occurred on the Grand Prix?

"It might have," he admitted. "But I don't think we have the disparities in first- and second-prize money that would lead one to succumb to that temptation."

What had prompted him to suggest in his syndicated column that tennis players should be tested for drugs?

"Basically, my editor said, 'Hey, is there any drug abuse in tennis?' I said, 'I don't know.' But he said, 'I want you to do a piece on drugs in tennis.' I said, 'I don't know if there's anything in the air about it. [But] I'll write what I think.' I talked to some of the players, just asking them, 'How do you think the pro tennis group should deal with this?' So some of the players gave me some feedback. Interestingly enough, there were two fathers of two teenage male professionals. One just explicitly told me part of the reason he travels as much as he possibly can with his son is the drug situation. A *father* told me that. He said, 'Look, I know tennis players are in the fast lane and it's glamorous. I'm not from a big city, but it goes on in our local high school, and I know if it goes on there, it's got to be happening here.'"

"Were the players in favor of urinalysis?" I asked.

"It was about fifty-fifty. Some said, 'Hey, no, that's an invasion of privacy.' I said, playing devil's advocate, 'Well, yes, you may say it's an invasion of privacy, *but* . . . but are you going to wait until somebody really gets nailed? Or are you going to take measures now so that we know the chances are greatly reduced that it'll ever crop up?' "

Ashe added, "We should [do something] in light of all the problems that football and basketball have had. In baseball it seems you either chew tobacco or get drunk." He smiled. "Why even let it happen in tennis? Why don't we get out in front of this thing? Which we have, as far as a place where the players can go now. Literally just two weeks ago we established a relationship with this organization called Comp-Care. Comp-Care will, for free, help you deal with your drug problems anonymously, if you want."

After months of listening to stone-faced players and officials deny there was any drug use, much less a drug problem on the tour, it was a relief to hear Arthur Ashe speak openly and for attribution. Obviously, there wasn't just a problem. There was need for a therapy program.

(Months later I called Comp-Care, which referred me to Dr. Robert B. Millman, Director of the Drug and Alcohol Abuse program at the Cornell University Medical College in New York City. A psychiatrist as well as an internist, Dr. Millman said he was treating a variety of professional athletes for drug abuse, among them an unspecified number of tennis players.

(When I asked whether drugs were a problem on the circuit, he answered, "Absolutely." The money and glamour of the game brought players into frequent contact with entertainers and celebrities who tended to be heavy users of cocaine. Many players succumbed to temptation, dabbling in drugs either to imitate their up-scale peers or to cope with the pressures and anxieties of the sport.

(Since Dr. Millman dealt with other professional athletes, I asked whether tennis players abused drugs on the same level as, say, American football and basketball players, many of whom have recently admitted to being addicts or heavy users. It is estimated, for example, that as many as thirty percent of the men in the National Basketball Association take drugs.

(Insisting on a distinction between use and abuse, Dr. Millman expressed the opinion that tennis players are often more sophisticated and from more stable environments, and tended to abuse drugs less than football or basketball players did. The level of use might be much the same, but "tennis players are better able to integrate drugs into their lives." Even so, he emphasized that cocaine had a subtle, yet detrimental effect on their performances and frequently ruined their concentration. I told him I had heard that some tennis players were now taking heroin. Dr. Millman confirmed this and explained that most heroin was snorted, not mainlined. After all, no tennis player wanted to go on court with needle tracks up and down his arms. But, however the heroin was taken, Dr. Millman stressed its devastating effects. Even occasional users and non-addicts were left depressed, physiologically depleted, and inclined to want to get high again to relieve their anxiety.

(Of course, marijuana and alcohol also presented serious problems, which had consequences for a player's mood and performance. But, at least, the men did their drinking and smoking off court. Dr. Millman wasn't so certain that cocaine was confined to recreational use. He had heard of tennis players who took cocaine during matches. Admitting he couldn't prove it, he said he had been told some players dusted their wrist bands with cocaine and took occasional snorts to perk them up on big points.

(For a player who wanted to improve his game, amphetamines had longer and more dramatic effects, Dr. Millman said.

(Recalling the interview in which Yannick Noah had spoken of players who popped pills to prime them for important matches, I mentioned that the French No. 1 claimed he could tell whether an opponent was on speed. Dr. Millman agreed that the signs were readily apparent—dilated pupils, total concentration, and controlled rage.

(Like Noah, the doctor also stressed the drug's appalling down side. It raised a player's blood pressure, made him paranoid, even psychotic, and carried the danger of strokes, heart attacks, and death. Those who managed to get off amphetamines often found they couldn't muster the same motivation, and for a combination of physical and psychological reasons, they rarely played up to the limits of their ability again. "Speed makes you better," Dr. Millman said. "Then it makes you worse."

(The same might be said of the other drugs used by players on the pro circuit.)

Ashe was also willing, even eager, to speak about collusion between umpires and tournament directors. "I'm convinced of it," he said. "I don't mind saying that on the record. . . . If umpires were consistent in the application of the rule, I wouldn't feel that way. But the umpires today, they have more competence, in the sense that they know the rules, but they're still in the process of learning the nuances of how to handle certain situations. By and large, if the player on the court is a top-ten player, they are reluctant to issue that first warning. They stretch the rules, they *really* stretch the rules, for the top players. Yet you have other umpires who'll be very trigger-happy with player No. 70 and, for the same infraction, won't do anything to player No. 6." For evidence of this, he encouraged me to consult the list of fines levied at tournaments.

I asked him to amplify his remarks about players who demanded that certain umpires always officiate at their matches.

"We *know* that there have been examples of players requesting certain people to staff certain administrative positions at a tournament. We know that. We have evidence of it. So that in itself leads me to believe that there is even *more* going on between tournament directors and officials." As for people who rejected the notion that there were improper relationships between tournament directors and referees and umpires, "Across the board, I'm saying, 'That's bullshit!' "

I mentioned that some umpires were buying cars through tournament directors who had access to—

"Saabs, Volvos, Mercedes," Ashe swiftly filled in the blanks.

"It's not proof of any evil," I admitted. "But the appearance is lousy."

"The appearance is . . ." His voice died. Then he wistfully said, "Yeah, but, you see, the entire tennis community is cynical about these things. Everybody is cynical to some degree."

Ashe didn't strike me as cynical and I told him so. Not only was he sensitive about his own potential conflicts of interest, he recognized immediately all the troubling implications of the side deals which umpires cut for themselves. In addition to those buying discounted cars, there were umpires who served as clothing and equipment reps, or who acted in other entrepreneurial capacities that undermined their neutrality. "I don't think that looks good," he said.

When I told him I had had a long talk with John McEnroe, Sr., he said, "He's a fascinating guy. He's a character. He has a lot of things he wants to get off his chest."

One of the things he had gotten off his chest, I said, was his conviction that tennis is essentially entertainment. Several times he had implicitly compared his son with Frank Sinatra.

"He's partially right," Ashe observed. "*But* . . . Frank Sinatra doesn't get to headline Caesars Palace because he is ranked No. 1 in the hit parade of stars." In show biz, personal preference, hype, subjective opinion, and complicated business arrangements dictated who got on stage and who received top billing. In sport, talent was supposed to be the lone criterion—talent as demonstrated by results in honest match play. Ashe stressed, "Our system of placing players in events, *à la* putting X on the stage, is done competitively. And that competition has to be fair, consistent, and publicly known and, as much as possible, adhered to."

"If you have a top player," I pointed out, "it is conceivable to give him preferential treatment to maintain his top standing, and then you have a self-fulfilling prophecy. Liz Taylor and Richard Burton are stars and will always be stars—"

"Because they've always been stars," he said.

"But if you give a top player advantages that help him maintain his star status, then I feel that's unfair."

"So do I," Arthur Ashe agreed.

Because his voice was quiet and calm, the impact of his agreement sank in slowly. Like me, he objected to preferential treatment for stars—treatment that ranged across a spectrum from such petty matters as more practice time and the rescheduling of matches to the payment of illegal guarantees, the corruption of umpires, and a callous indifference to ethical questions. Needless to say, this cynicism has ramifications whose seriousness couldn't be determined by either of us. It couldn't really be judged by anybody short of the Justice Department or the Federal Communication Commission. But, for the moment, it seemed to me sufficient that Arthur Ashe believed that much about professional tennis is unfair—unfair to more than ninety percent of the players on the circuit, unfair to the honorable men and women who have devoted their lives to the game, and, finally, unfair to the sponsors and fans who have a right to expect more than a shabby burlesque.

Of course, if tennis were merely burlesque and no more, it wouldn't be worth saving; it could be allowed to decay and die. But it has the new vitality and the ancient traditions, the attractive personnel, the sheer excitement, and symmetrical beauty to be much more than vaudeville. Its reform would not take years of study and countless hours of committee meetings. Nor would it cost millions of dollars. Professional tennis could be completely changed in a matter of weeks if it had the courage and decency to enforce the rules it has already written for itself.

EPILOGUE

DURING the time since I dropped off the tour, professional tennis has suffered a series of shocks—on court, off court, and, most important, *in* court.

Off court, an intriguing incident transpired in early 1983 on the tiny Caribbean island of Antigua. When Buster Mottram met Van Winitsky, a low-ranked American, in an exhibition match at a resort hotel, people in the stands started to heckle Winitsky. Unable to abide their catcalls, he charged into the crowd and struck a spectator. British free-lance journalist Richard Evans was present, and, on the basis of his report, Marshall Happer, administrator of the Pro Council, launched an investigation of the incident. Although this had occurred at a non–Grand Prix event, the verdict was that Winitsky had violated the Volvo Grand Prix rule against conduct severely detrimental to tennis. He was suspended for thirty-five days—the first penalty ever imposed for misconduct in an exhibition match.

Interestingly, my reports to Marshall Happer of prize money splitting, betting, and set splitting at WCT and/or exhibition matches had prompted no action from the somnolent administrator, who claimed he had no jurisdiction in non–Grand Prix events. It is worth wondering what, if anything, would have befallen Van Winitsky had he been a star instead of one of the faceless men slotted somewhere between 50 and 100 in the rankings.

. . .

On court, John McEnroe reasserted the supremacy that had slipped from his grasp during 1982. After losing to Ivan Lendl in the final of the Volvo Masters in Madison Square Garden, McEnroe turned more aggressive, rushing the net behind every serve and return of serve at the U.S. Indoor Championship in Philadelphia. He beat the Czech in the title match, then did the same thing with the same tactics at the WCT Finals in Dallas.

Unfortunately, McEnroe's performance was marred by repeated complaints about the officiating, as well as repeated foot stamping, screaming, and racquet throwing. Afterward, Lendl objected that McEnroe's antics had upset him and charged that the American was protected by intimidated officials and got preferential treatment. In the future, the Czech vowed, he would fight back—with his fists, if he had to.

In mid-May *Harper's* magazine published a 10,000-word excerpt from *Short Circuit*. Within a week, word of the book spread from the United States to Europe, where I was in Rome, covering the Italian Open for the *Washington Post*.

On Sunday, May 22, shortly before the championship match, I was entering the Campo Centrale when I was summoned by Cino Marchese, the ubiquitous Silver Fox, a big, friendly tennis entrepreneur with whom I had always had amiable dealings. When I went to see what Marchese wanted, he grabbed me by the front of my shirt and flung me against the wall of the tunnel leading to the press box. Tightening his grip, he pressed his other fist against my chin, and jammed my head back against the bricks. "You focker," he shouted. "You focked me. I've read *Harper's*. You put me in the shit. Now I'm going to put you in the shit."

For the next five minutes, in full view of tournament officials, ballboys, linesmen, and impassive journalists, Marchese leaned his ponderous bulk against me and shouted obscenities into my face, punctuating his flavorful command of the vernacular with repeated shoves. Finally, his voice was so loud and his language

so vile that an official named Mauro Petetta trotted off Center
Court and told Marchese to take me elsewhere. Neither Mr.
Petetta nor anyone else suggested that Marchese let me go.
Instead, I was hustled down a side tunnel and into a small room,
where I was held while Marchese continued to brandish his fist
in my face, threaten me with bodily harm, and swear that he
would have me barred from all tennis tournaments.

Cino's primary objection was that I had quoted his remarks
about guarantees and appearance money. When I pointed out
that his comments were not much different from those made at
a public press conference by Paolo Galganni, the president of
the Italian Tennis Federation, who had claimed that the Italian
Open had been ruined because it didn't give guarantees, Marchese
insisted I still should have known not to quote him. Although
he had seen me taking notes during interviews and had never
asked that his remarks be kept off the record, he demanded that
I go with him to see Bob Kain, the head of the tennis division
at International Management Group. Since in one of his many
incarnations Marchese is an IMG agent, he was anxious that
his boss be told that I had lied, that I had misquoted him, that
I hadn't understood his poor English. (In fact, Cino speaks
excellent English.) When I refused to disavow what I had written, he renewed his threats.

Finally, after forty minutes, anxious to escape the room and
Marchese's clammy grasp, I said I'd welcome the chance to
speak to Kain. Cino led me up to the IMG hospitality terrace.
But there was no hospitality for me. He introduced me to Kain
as "the shit who wrote the *Harper's* article." Although he was
icily calm compared with Cino, Kain's behavior was, in its way,
almost as unnerving. When I told him his agent had assaulted
and threatened me, Kain blithely responded that that was between Marchese and me—at which point the Silver Fox seized
my arm and said I was lucky he hadn't broken me in two. Kain
peered off through his spectacles, searching the sky for thunder
clouds.

I suggested that if Marchese and IMG had objections to *Short
Circuit*, they were free to denounce it or to try to produce
evidence to refute it. But to manhandle me and attempt to

prevent me from covering tennis was much more harmful to the game than anything I had written.

While Marchese was growling into my ear, Kain, the perfect picture of preppy coolness, scratched the crocodile on his chest and said my book was no big deal. Tennis was more popular than ever.

In that case, I said, detaching myself from Cino's meaty claw, I trusted no one would object if I went and watched the final.

I dispatched an account of the incident, along with a formal protest, to Marshall Happer. Since the Code of Conduct mandated punishment for players who assaulted other players or spectators, and since there was a rule against conduct severely detrimental to tennis, I was curious to see what the administrator would do about a Volvo Grand Prix tournament director who assaulted a journalist.

Several days later, Happer called from Paris, where he and other members of the Pro Council had gathered during the French Open. He had two questions: Had I reported Marchese to the police? Had Marchese physically prevented me from leaving the room under Center Court? Coming from anyone else, these would have struck me as singularly peculiar inquiries. But from previous dealings with Happer I had learned to expect his poker-faced, lawyerly efforts at damage control.

No, I had not called the police. It seemed more appropriate, not to mention fairer to Marchese, to keep this a tennis matter, not a criminal charge. I also conceded that Cino hadn't tied me up or held a gun to my head. But I pointed out that at six feet seven inches and well over 220 pounds, the Silver Fox was six inches taller and more than fifty pounds heavier than I, and he had positioned his formidable bulk between me and the door and had kept one fat fist in my face.

Now it was Happer's turn to concede. Yes, he said, Marchese had admitted to being furious and "touching" me—but "only to get my attention." Yes, as a lawyer Happer knew that any unwanted touch was an assault and that one could be "held" as effectively by intimidation as by rope. The administrator assured me that the matter would be discussed at the Pro Council meeting and that he would respond to me in writing. But, as so often in the past, he doubted he had jurisdiction in this matter. (In fact, Happer never sent the written report, nor did he bother replying to the protests of the *Washington Post*.)

Didn't he, I asked, feel that my run-in with Marchese substantiated the claims of those umpires who had told me they feared that if they reported serious wrongdoings on the Volvo Grand Prix they would put themselves at personal risk?

Happer vehemently disagreed. But he didn't say how he would or could protect such umpires, nor did he offer any assurance that I would be safe at future tournaments.

During the 1983 French Open, the fabric of professional tennis, after years of fraying, unravelled in long skeins of filthy yarn. The trouble started when Donald Dell sold the American television rights to the Grand Slam event to NBC. This presented ticklish legal difficulties, since CBS had broadcast the tournament for the past three years and had a contractual right to match offers from other networks. CBS sued the French Tennis Federation and NBC, eventually winning a $117,000 settlement out of court. Undaunted, Dell served beside Bjorn Borg in the NBC booth, where he found himself in the position of providing commentary for a final in which one of his clients, Yannick Noah, became the first Frenchman in thirty-seven years to win the title.

Fed up with such blatant conflicts of interest, *Sports Illustrated* called Dell "the octopus of tennis, his tenacles reaching everywhere . . . We're supposed to believe that he can promote a tournament's interests, his player's interests, his own interests and the interests of unwitting viewers all at the same time."

Yet as powerful an octopus as Donald Dell is, he could do nothing to protect Noah, whose celebration after beating Mats Wilander in the final was cut drastically short. Earlier in the month, after performing poorly at the World Team Cup, a round robin event in Dusseldorf, Germany, Noah flew back to Paris, skipping his later matches. The Pro Council found him guilty of misconduct, suspended him for six weeks, and fined him $20,000, sidelining the French No. 1 for the summer and barring him from the Davis Cup matches against Paraguay.

The severity of this penalty paled by comparison with the one doled out to Guillermo Vilas. Found guilty of accepting an illegal guarantee of $60,000 at the tournament in Rotterdam, the Argentinian was fined $20,000 and suspended from the circuit for a year. Since Vilas was nearly thirty-one, some felt the suspension would effectively end his career.

In the imbroglio following the Vilas case, International Tennis Federation President Philippe Chatrier warned the press to expect other explosive revelations. Investigations of several star players were said to be under way, and more suspensions looked imminent at Wimbledon. Ivan Lendl was being pressed hard to explain how he had happened to show up in Milan as a substitute just at the moment when Jimmy Connors dropped out of the tournament.

Since both Lendl and Connors are clients of Donald Dell's agency, ProServ, and since the Milan tournament director, Sergio Palmieri, is the ProServ representative in Italy, the situation had a taint that attracted the attention of the usually drowsy tennis press. AP and UPI both ran articles that claimed the Czech had agreed to enter the tournament after intense financial haggling. UPI charged that Lendl had been "hired" to play, and it quoted a tournament organizer who said this had been the only way to save the event after Connors' defection. Asked whether he believed Lendl had received an illegal guarantee, Italian Tennis Federation President Paolo Galganni replied, "I don't think he was in Milan to see the Duomo."

But after a dramatic build-up suggesting that the Pro Council finally intended to enforce its rules, the opposition regrouped and counterattacked. Twenty players signed a petition defending Vilas. McEnroe, Connors, Lendl, and Gerulaitis went on record against the guarantee rule, and there were persistent rumors that the stars would start their own tour unless Vilas' suspension were reversed.

To close observers, there had from the beginning been reason to doubt that the Vilas case signaled a significant change in pro tennis. Although Marshall Happer happily assumed the mantle of "hardhitting, aggressive administrator," he had had little or nothing to do with uncovering the evidence that convicted Vilas.

The tournament in Rotterdam is a municipal event, and its records are public information. Since tournament officials had not had time to disguise Vilas' guarantee as an endorsement contract, they realized their violation of the rules would be revealed once they filed a financial statement with the city government. So they turned themselves and Vilas in.

Happer had had an open-and-shut case dumped into his lap and had never used the considerable investigatory powers that the Code of Conduct puts at his disposal. After trumpeting, "We are about to see a change. The boat is going to have to be rocked," he sounded a more restrained note later in the summer. "If a player denies [taking guarantees], I can't do much." As for the statute that empowered the administrator to demand all records "relating in any way to such alleged guarantees," Happer said lamely, "I don't think that rule gives me authority to examine players' entire personal records."

During Wimbledon Jimmy Connors sent me a message via an interview with the BBC, during which he said, "I don't think it'd be wise for him to show his face around the locker room again." Perhaps Big Jimbo was so busy watching for me he forgot to keep his eye on the ball. In the fourth round, Kevin Curren aced the defending champion thirty-three times, and Connors, last year's sentimental favorite, reverted to form and left the court in defeat, snarling and sulking, skipping his press conference and speeding off in a rented limo.

With Connors' early exit, attention focused on the Lendl-McEnroe semifinal, their first encounter since Lendl had threatened to retaliate. But once on Centre Court, the Czech showed no stomach for battle. He never raised his fists and didn't do much damage with his racquet either. McEnroe dispatched him in straight sets, then did the same to Chris Lewis, the surprise finalist from New Zealand.

As the dust cleared after Wimbledon, there were none of the explosive revelations promised by Philippe Chatrier. The Lendl investigation ended in a stalemate. Marshall Happer subpoenaed the financial records of the Milan tournament, and when the organizers wouldn't or couldn't provide details of a bank account in Liechtenstein and a contract between Lendl and Achilli Motors, a major sponsor of the event, Happer suspended the tournament from the 1984 calendar. There was no explanation why Lendl couldn't have supplied a copy of the contract, nor why he wasn't suspended along with the tournament. For the second year in a row, the Czech was at the center of serious charges about illegal guarantees; but again, as in the case of Stuttgart, it was the tournament, not the player, who was penalized.

In early July Guillermo Vilas announced that he would appeal his fine and suspension. Pending a final verdict, he was free to continue playing the Volvo Grand Prix circuit. As the summer wore on and he alternated tournament play with an exhibition tour with John McEnroe, it became clear that no decision would be reached for months. What had seemed such a draconian punishment in early June struck some observers as a cosmetic gesture. Once public interest died down, they said, the Vilas case would be dismissed. Or maybe, said the more cynical among them, Vilas would be used as a scapegoat, the lone victim penalized for the crime of getting caught.

As for the more serious consequences of guarantees—the preferential treatment of stars, the corruption of umpires, the violation of tax laws, the unfairness to lower-ranked players, and the deception of the fans—no tennis official, except Arthur Ashe, admitted there was a problem. It appeared that John Alexander, the Australian Davis Cup veteran, had been right. Little would be done to reform the sport/business unless legal authorities stepped in and made tennis clean up what has become a very sleazy act.

During August, the act got sleazier. Ilie Nastase, in yet another of his angry outbursts, kicked a linesman, and the man was injured severely enough to require medical attention. Predictably, Nastase was fined and suspended. Just as predictably, the Rumanian was still free to play the U.S. Open, where, even more predictably, his match against Peter Fleming was showcased for television. If there was any lesson in all this, it was a reiteration of the obvious: the stars were beyond the rules and their misbehavior could be marketed.

In the first round at Flushing Meadow, John McEnroe met Trey Waltke, a sprightly pint-sized fellow who had upset him twice in the past. Known to the other players as "Westwood Willie," a mellow resident of southern California, Waltke remained unperturbed while McEnroe ranted and raved, abusing officials and fans. When a courtside spectator clapped too enthusiastically for Waltke, McEnroe cursed him, challenged him to a fistfight after the match, and flung a handful of sawdust in his face.

Although he managed to squeeze past Waltke in five sets, McEnroe ran into Bill Scanlon in the fourth round and couldn't put in his own serve or return his opponent's. His defeat was lamented by no one—certainly not by Jimmy Connors, who waltzed into the final where Ivan Lendl was waiting to avenge last year's loss. But once again the scowling Czech, so merciless against weaker opponents, proved he lacks the nerve to win a Grand Slam event. Although Connors was in far from top form— he had a sore foot and a case of diarrhea that once sent him scrambling off court to a toilet—Lendl couldn't cope with the pressure. Serving at 5–4 in the third set to take a two-set-to-one lead, Lendl double-faulted away his advantage and stumbled like a zombie through the rest of the match, losing ten games straight and 6–0 in the deciding fourth set.

For Connors, it was his fifth U.S. Open title and hundredth tournament victory. During the match he achieved another milestone. Displaying impressive ambidexterity, he shot a linesman a double phallic salute, raising the middle fingers on his right and left hands. At the age of thirty-one, he shows no signs of losing his small motor coordination. Half a dozen years from now, Jimbo, like his old friend Nastase, should still be quite capable of kicking an official.

. . .

All during the summer of 1983, the Pro Council, the Association of Tennis Professionals, and the International Tennis Federation mounted a low-comic campaign to discredit *Short Circuit*. It started with the industrious Marshall Happer typing out passages from the book and dispatching them to players and officials whom I had interviewed. According to a reliable source at the Volvo Grand Prix office, Happer hoped to find people who would deny having talked to me or who would claim I had misquoted them. But by his own admission, all Happer ever came up with was a "handful" of players who complained that their remarks had been "wisecracks," "semi-serious," or "kidding." Although it struck me as improbable that players would joke by making charges about guarantees, tanking, gambling, prize money splitting, match fixing, and drugs, perhaps they were practicing for careers as comedians after they left the circuit.

The ATP, the players' union, certainly set them an example of slapstick humor and goofball logic. When the Pro Council had little luck finding men who had been quoted in *Short Circuit* and were willing to recant, the ATP decided to quiz players whom I had not interviewed and who had not read the book. These men professed to be troubled by my journalistic methods and my findings. Naturally, since they hadn't read *Short Circuit* and had never met me, they knew nothing about my methods or my findings. Nevertheless, *International Tennis Weekly*, the ATP's official newspaper, ran several columns full of vague harrumphing and ponderous cud-chewing.

One player, Bruce Manson, said he'd like to find out where I had obtained my information about rule infractions. I called the ATP office and said I would be in New York during the U.S. Open and would happily treat any ATP member or official to a dinner and to a thorough explanation of the sources, assumptions, and discoveries in *Short Circuit*. No one accepted the offer.

Instead, the International Tennis Federation took its turn and started doing dizzy pratfalls, *à la* the Marx brothers. Having received an utterly false and misleading letter from an Associated Press editor with whom I had had no personal or professional dealings, the ITF promptly released the news that I had never worked for AP and had never been authorized to use the name of the Associated Press in applying for accreditation. Marshall Happer, who had spent months accusing me of purveying unsubstantiated rumors, unverifiable assertions, and pure hearsay, hurried to Gene Scott, the publisher of *Tennis Week*. Without bothering to check the facts or to contact me for comment, Scott ran a story suggesting that I had researched *Short Circuit* with bogus press credentials.

This prompted a rebuttal from Byron Yake, General Sports Editor of the Associated Press, who stated in writing that *Short Circuit* had accurately represented my professional relationship with AP. Gene Scott had the good grace to run a correction in *Tennis Week*. But the Pro Council and the Volvo Grand Prix were in no mood to be gracious. Three weeks after Byron Yake had set the record straight, Jerry Solomon, tour director of the Volvo Grand Prix, continued to pass around to key media people the error-ridden letter that the Associated Press had disavowed.

Always an optimist, I wanted to offer Marshall Happer every opportunity to make good on his claim that he welcomed "help in policing our sport." When *World Tennis* magazine published an article by Steve Goldsteyn charging that Jimmy Connors had accepted a guarantee at the Grand Prix tournament in Las Vegas, I contacted the administrator by telephone and told him what I had learned. According to my sources, Connors had received the guarantee in cash in front of witnesses. I gave Happer the name of one witness and also informed him that Connors was alleged to have signed a receipt for the money, which was said to have come from "the cage" at Caesars Palace, the window where gamblers cash in their chips.

Happer was quick to recognize the significance of this last detail. If the money had indeed come from the cage, there should, according to Nevada Gaming Commision regulations, be a record of the transaction. Happer had only to demand the tournament's financial records, as well as Connors', then compare these with the records from the cage at Caesars Palace. For additional evidence, he could pursue the receipt signed by Connors and interview the witness. But as of four months after our conversation, Mr. Happer had not announced any new investigation.

When the Milan tournament, which had been dropped from the calendar, was quietly reinserted into the 1984 schedule, I called the Volvo Grand Prix office for an explanation. Dewey Blanton, the media director, said Happer was now satisfied that he had all the information about Ivan Lendl's alleged guarantee. The administrator had decided that no rule had been broken. But Blanton could not say what specific information Happer had obtained nor how it refuted the copyrighted article in UPI that stated that Lendl had been "hired" to play in Milan.

There was a similar shortage of detailed information when the World Championship of Tennis dropped its lawsuit against the Pro Council, the Association of Tennis Professionals, and the International Tennis Federation. Having accused these groups of unfair trade practices and attempting to monopolize pro tennis, Lamar Hunt, WCT's founder, had seemed poised to use the case to force legal authorities to examine the conflicts of interest and dubious deals rampant in the sport. Instead, without explanation, the Grand Prix agreed to let WCT rejoin its circuit for 1984. The past simply disappeared. Irreconcilable differences, substantive disputes, charges by the Grand Prix that the WCT tour was rife with ethical improprieties, allegations by WCT that the Grand Prix had rewritten its rules to kill off competition—everything was swept down the memory hole.

While WCT and the Grand Prix avoided litigation, others saw it as the one way of getting satisfaction. Chris Schneider, the courtside spectator at the U.S. Open who had gotten a faceful of sawdust from John McEnroe, filed suit for $6 million. He argued that McEnroe had assaulted, humiliated, and harassed him.

As if Guillermo Vilas didn't have enough to worry about, the New York *Daily News* reported that he would be named in a "palimony" suit filed by Mikette Von Isenberg, "a California socialite and former Wilhelmina model." Von Isenberg's suit was actually directed at Vilas' coach, Ion Tiriac, with whom she had a child seven years ago. Vilas would be named in the suit, according to Von Isenberg's lawyer, Marvin Mitchelson, because "he and Tiriac share the income of their ventures 50–50."

Half-convinced that Charles Dickens was correct—the law is an ass—I turned my attention from legal matters and contacted one of the most important sources in *Short Circuit*, the anonymous umpire in Antibes, all of whose allegations were later corroborated by people willing to speak for the record. The umpire passed on an intriguing tidbit of information that had begun to perk during Wimbledon and had been quietly brewing ever since. After the publication of *Short Circuit*, a number of Grand Prix umpires took the initiative of writing Marshall Happer to suggest reforms of the way officials are hired and compensated. Like the umpire in Antibes, these men felt they could best maintain their integrity if they were assigned to tournaments on a rotating basis by an autonomous authority and were paid a fair wage that would leave them less tempted by the favors that unprincipled tournament directors dangle in front of them.

Happer's response . . . well, there had been no response. He had never answered. Instead, he continued to assure the press that umpires were adequately protected. Without fear of reprisal, they could tell him when they felt they were being intimidated or compromised by tournament directors. Yet when umpires did approach him through the proper channels, the administrator didn't reply.

Ironically, umpires were forbidden from expressing their opinions to the media. The Code of Conduct contained a rule that stipulated umpires could not hold news conferences or comment about players and matches. And this was one rule Happer enforced.

In early December, news was released that Yannick Noah, the French Open champion, would leave Paris and move to New York City. At first, it sounded like a straightforward career decision. Noah said he wanted to escape the distractions of

France, where he was a leading celebrity, and settle in a place where he could concentrate on tennis. In New York City, he explained, he wouldn't be bothered by the press and autograph hounds, and he could find challenging practice partners. John McEnroe and Vitas Gerulaitis lived there, and if Noah hoped to achieve his goal of becoming No. 1 in the world, he had to work out with the best players.

A few days later, however, it was clear that Noah's motives were far more complex. At a press conference in Paris, the muscular black player, his hair in the distinctive Rastafarian dreadlocks that have become his hallmark, admitted he was "fleeing." Since winning the French Open, "Life in France has been unbearable." Confronted by a room full of reporters, he suddenly raised a hand to his face, his voice faltered, and he broke down and wept.

"I don't sleep at night," he said. "I just wander through the streets crying. Last night I got to the Alma Bridge and looked down at the Seine. I thought, should I jump or not?

"I'm not happy about leaving, but I have no choice. I'm stagnating. I'm floating. I can't practice here because I don't feel good about myself. I'm totally flipped out."

The next day he flew to New York to "find a place to rest my head."

While most of the press seemed surprised by Noah's break-down, I could not help seeing it in the context of what I had witnessed on the circuit—the relentless competition, the deracinating travel, the loneliness, the indifference of the officials who are supposed to oversee the sport, the predatory entrepreneurs and agents, and, above all, the emotional immaturity of the players. I thought of Bjorn Borg retiring from active competition at the age of twenty-six, claiming he was fed up and anxious to enjoy whatever remained of his youth. I recalled a conversation with Vitas Gerulaitis, who had expressed the opinion that before long all the top players might be high school dropouts. Tennis, Vitas said, wasn't such a complicated game. You had to be just smart enough to do it, but dumb enough to believe it mattered.

I also recalled my interview with Butch Buchholz at the 1982

French Open. He felt many young, ill-educated boys on the tour needed guidance and remedial programs. Otherwise, he feared, they would crack under the pressure, perhaps even commit suicide.

But Buchholz had been a faint and ineffectual voice in 1982, and now he was no longer an ATP official. Louder voices had been raised in praise of the junior training programs that had put boys like Wilander, Noah, and Jimmy Arias in the top ten. No one bothered asking whether such programs were good for anything except drilling players in the fine art of the backhand and overhead. No one questioned the wisdom of isolating fellows from the age of ten or eleven, taking them away from their families and boarding them in camps, giving them an unrealistic sense of superiority and an even more unrealistic set of expectations, then sending them out at fifteen or sixteen to follow a circuit that snakes around the globe.

Alone, unsupervised, ignorant of the ways in which they were manipulated, these adolescent millionaires suffered a murderous tunnel vision that left them ill-equipped to make ethical judgments about tanking, prize money splitting, gambling, orchestrating exhibitions, and taking guarantees. It also left them ill-equipped to cope with the demands of success, which, as Yannick Noah had learned, can be as devastating as failure.

For the first time in years, the Australian Open, the final leg of the Grand Slam, managed to attract several top-ten players. It was no easy thing to lure the stars Down Under. The tournament date had had to be shifted from the end of December to the end of November, and the prize money was increased to over one million dollars. Then, too, a number of players were battling for bigger shares of the Volvo Grand Prix bonus pool. Ivan Lendl and Mats Wilander were virtually deadlocked in their struggle for the $600,000 top prize.

Wilander, however, professed to be less swayed by loot than by the chance to gain experience on grass. He and his Swedish teammates would be pitted against Australia in the Davis Cup final on these same courts several weeks later. Whatever his reasons, the nineteen-year-old blond served notice that he was at home on any surface. Rebounding from a shaky first set, Wilander beat John McEnroe in the semifinals, then blitzed Ivan Lendl 6–1/6–4/6–4 in the final, for his second Grand Slam title.

Finally, in mid-December, a three-man committee of Bill Talbert, Forest Hainline, and Vic Seixas began hearing testimony in Guillermo Vilas' appeal of his conviction for accepting a guarantee. What they heard could hardly have been less flattering to the already tarnished image of pro tennis. The director of the Sports Palace in Rotterdam, Mr. Hoekwater, testified that Ion Tiriac had called on July 26, five weeks after the announcement of Vilas' fine and suspension, and offered the tournament director, Piet Bonthuis, $60,000 to change the books, erasing the record of the payment to Vilas. Tiriac called again on July 28 and allegedly offered Bonthuis $300,000 to say that he had pocketed the guarantee paid to Vilas.

When it was Tiriac's turn to testify, he swore that a tournament official in Rotterdam had tried to extort money from him. In return, the man would issue a public denial that any guarantee had been given Vilas.

With that, the committee retired to ponder the facts, figures, and conflicting statements. They estimated they would make no decision for another month.

And so the 1983 Grand Prix circuit ground to an end. Nothing had changed. Despite all the noise, none of the previous summer's promises had been kept. No new rules had been passed to deal with unethical tournament directors and umpires, and no teeth had been put in the old rules that tennis authorities claimed couldn't be enforced as written. Candid players and officials had no reason to believe their protests would prompt reform. Crooked players and officials had little cause to worry. As Bud Collins had summed up the situation eighteen months ago, "Tennis was born in dishonesty and has never grown out of it."